PRAISE FOR
ON DUBLIN STREET

"This book had some funny dialogue, some amazingly hot sex scenes, and emotional drama. Did I mention the amazing sex scenes?"

—Dear Author . . .

"This is a really sexy book and I loved the heroine's journey to find herself and grow strong. Highly recommend this one."

—*USA Today* Happily Ever After

"Young's voice is riveting, and once I opened the book, I wanted to hang a 'do not disturb' sign around my neck until I was finished. This book definitely landed on my 2012 top picks!"—Fiction Vixen Book Reviews

"This book is fun. Sexy. A little dark. While the hero is extremely dominant, he also shows his softer side just when she needs it."

—Smexy Books Romance Reviews

"Every page sizzles when these two get together, but this book is so much more than a hot romp. This book has heart—and lots of it. . . . *If* you want a book that will lure you in, grab you by the scruff of the neck, and never let you go until you finish reading the last page, then *On Dublin Street* is the book for you." —TotallyBooked

"Brilliantly written with just the right amount of hotness, sexiness, and romance and everything else in between." —Once Upon a Twilight

ALSO BY SAMANTHA YOUNG

On Dublin Street

DOWN
LONDON
ROAD

SAMANTHA YOUNG

NEW AMERICAN LIBRARY

New American Library
Published by the Penguin Group
Penguin Group (USA) Inc., 375 Hudson Street,
New York, New York 10014, USA

USA | Canada | UK | Ireland | Australia | New Zealand | India | South Africa | China

Penguin Books Ltd., Registered Offices: 80 Strand, London WC2R 0RL, England
For more information about the Penguin Group, visit penguin.com.

First published by New American Library,
a division of Penguin Group (USA) Inc.

First Printing, May 2013

REGISTERED TRADEMARK—MARCA REGISTRADA

LIBRARY OF CONGRESS CATALOGING-IN-PUBLICATION DATA:
Young, Samantha.
Down London Road/Samantha Young.
p. cm.
ISBN 978-0-451-41971-2
1. Americans—Scotland—Fiction. 2. Bartenders—Fiction. I. Title.
PR6075.O847D69 2013
823'.914—dc23   2013001071

Printed in the United States of America
10 9 8 7 6 5 4 3 2 1

Set in Garamond

PUBLISHER'S NOTE
This is a work of fiction. Names, characters, places, and incidents either are the product of the
author's imagination or are used fictitiously, and any resemblance to actual persons, living or
dead, business establishments, events, or locales is entirely coincidental.

The publisher does not have any control over and does not assume any responsibility for author
or third-party Web sites or their content..

For Robert

—

DOWN LONDON ROAD

CHAPTER I

I looked upon the piece of art and wondered what the heck I was looking at. To me it was just a bunch of lines and squares in different colors with some shading here and there. It looked familiar. In fact, I thought I had a picture Cole had drawn me when he was three years old tucked away somewhere that bore a remarkable resemblance to it. Although I doubted I could expect anyone to pay three hundred and seventy-five pounds for Cole's drawing. I also doubted the sanity of anyone who would pay three hundred and seventy-five pounds for the piece of canvas that looked like it had been sitting next to a railroad at the exact time a train full of paint careened off the rails and crashed.

However, chancing a glance around me, I could see that most of the people in the gallery liked the artwork. Maybe I wasn't smart enough to get it. In an effort to appear more sophisticated for my boyfriend's sake, I adopted a pensive expression and moved on to the next canvas.

"Um, okay, I don't get it," a low, husky voice announced beside me. I would have known that voice anywhere. Its American-accented words were disturbed here and there by a lilt, or the sharper consonants of a brogue, all a consequence of its owner having lived in Scotland for almost six years.

Relief flooded me as I brought my head down to meet the gaze of my best friend, Joss. For the first time that evening, I smiled brightly. Jocelyn Butler was a straight-talking, ballsy American girl who tended bar with me at a pretty swank place called Club 39. It was a basement bar on one of the city center's most famous streets—George Street— and we'd been working together for five years now.

Kitted out in a designer black dress and Louboutins, my vertically challenged friend looked hot. So did her boyfriend, Braden Carmichael. Standing behind Joss, his hand resting possessively on her lower back, Braden exuded confidence. Drool-worthy, he was the kind of boyfriend I'd been searching for, for years, and if I didn't love Joss so much and Braden didn't adore her past all reasoning, I would have trampled over her to get to him. Braden was almost six and a half feet tall, which was ideal for someone of my height. I was a striking five foot ten—that made me more than six feet tall in the right heels. Joss's boyfriend also happened to be sexy, rich, and funny. And he loved Joss to distraction. They'd been together for almost eighteen months. I could feel a proposal brewing.

"You look amazing," I told her, eyeing her curves. Unlike me, Joss had big boobs, along with hips and an ass that wouldn't quit. "Thank you so much for coming. Both of you."

"Well, you owe me," Joss muttered, her eyebrow arching as she glanced around at all the other paintings. "I'm going to have to do some serious lying if the artist asks me what I think."

Braden gave her waist a squeeze and smiled down at her. "Well, if the artist is as pretentious as her art, why lie when you can be brutally honest?"

Joss grinned back at him. "That's true."

"No," I interjected, knowing that if I let her she would do just that. "Becca is Malcolm's ex-girlfriend and they're still friends. You go Robert Hughes on her ass and it's my ass that gets kicked to the curb."

Joss frowned. "Robert Hughes?"

I sighed. "He was a famous art critic."

"I like that." Joss grinned evilly. "You know they say honesty is next to godliness."

"I think that's cleanliness, babe."

"Of course it's cleanliness, but surely honesty is a close second?"

The stubborn glint in Joss's eyes caused my throat to almost close up. Joss was a force to be reckoned with, and if she had an opinion or wanted to say something, there was little you could do to stop her. When I first met her she was an incredibly private person, preferring not to get involved in her friends' personal affairs. Since meeting Braden she'd changed a lot. Our friendship had grown, and Joss was now the only one who really knew the truth about my life. I was thankful for our friendship, but in moments like these I sometimes wished she was the old Joss, the one who kept her thoughts and emotions locked up tight.

I'd been dating Malcolm Hendry for almost three months. He was perfect for me. Kind, laid-back, tall—and wealthy. Malcolm was the oldest of all my "sugar daddies," as Joss jokingly called them. Although at thirty-nine, he was hardly *old*. He was, however, fifteen years my senior. I didn't care. Convinced that he might be *the one*, I didn't want Joss jeopardizing the progress of our relationship by insulting his good friend.

"Jocelyn"—Braden gripped her waist again, eyeing me and my growing panic—"I think it best if you practice the art of artifice tonight after all."

Finally reading my expression, Joss placed a reassuring hand on my arm. "I'm kidding, Jo. I'll be on my best behavior. I promise."

I nodded. "It's just . . . things are going well, you know."

"Malcolm seems like a decent guy," Braden agreed.

Joss made a sound at the back of her throat, but we both ignored it. My friend had made her opinion clear on my choice of boyfriend. She was convinced I was using Malcolm and he was using me. It was true that he was generous and I needed that generosity. However, the bigger truth was I really cared about him. Ever since my "first love," when I was sixteen years old, John, I'd fallen for charming providers and the idea of security for me and Cole. But John had gotten fed up with playing second fiddle to my family, and after six months he'd dumped me.

It had taught me a valuable lesson.

It had also given me a new requirement in a boyfriend—he had to have a good job, be driven, hardworking, and have a good income. No matter how hard I worked, with my nonexistent qualifications and lack of any real talent, I was never going to make enough money to secure a stable future for my family. I was, however, pretty enough to secure a *man* with good qualifications and talent.

A few years after I pieced myself back together from the heartbreak of my failed romance with John, Callum entered my life. Thirty, a well-off solicitor, gorgeous, cultured, sophisticated. Determined to make it last, I became what I imagined was the perfect girlfriend to him. It was a habit, becoming someone else, especially since it seemed to work. Callum thought I *was* perfect for a while. We were together two years—until my secretiveness about my family and my inability to "let him in" drove too deep a wedge between us and he left me.

It took me months to scrape myself back together after Callum . . . and when I did, it was to run into the arms of Tim. Horrible decision. Tim worked for an investment company. He was so mind-numbingly self-absorbed that *I* actually dumped *him*. Then there was Steven. Steven was a sales director for one of these annoying door-to-door sales companies. He put in long hours, which I thought might work in our favor, but it didn't. Joss thought Steven had dumped me because of my inability to be flexible about anything because of my family obligations. The truth was I dumped Steven. Steven made me feel worthless. His comments about my general uselessness brought back too many memories, and although even I thought there was little to recommend me other than my looks, when your boyfriend said the same and ultimately made you feel like a paid escort, it was time to call it quits.

I took a lot of crap from people, but I had my limits, and the older I got, the narrower those limits became.

Malcolm was different, though. He never made me feel terrible about myself, and so far our relationship was moving along nicely.

"Where is Lotto-Man?"

I shot a glance over my shoulder and searched for him, ignoring Joss's sarcasm. "I don't know," I murmured.

With Malcolm I'd literally hit the jackpot, as he was a solicitor-turned-lottery-winner. He'd won the EuroMillions three years ago and given up his job—his career, in fact—to begin enjoying a new life as a millionaire. Used to being busy, he'd decided to try his hand at property development and now had a portfolio of properties he owned as a landlord.

We were standing in an ancient redbrick building with its dirty windows made up of rows of small rectangles that you'd be more likely to see on a warehouse than an art gallery building. Inside was a different matter altogether. Outfitted with hardwood floors, amazing lighting, and partition walls for the art, it was the ideal gallery spot. Malcolm had divorced a year before his win, but of course a good-looking, wealthy man attracted young women like me. He'd soon encountered Becca, a savvy twenty-six-year-old Irish artist. They'd dated for a few months and remained good friends even after they broke it off. Malcolm had invested money in her art, renting a gallery a few blocks away from my old flat in Leith.

I had to admit the gallery and the art show were impressive. Even if I didn't happen to understand what the art was saying to me.

Malcolm had managed to gather a group of private buyers to attend this special opening of Becca's new collection and thankfully the art was speaking to *them*. As soon as we'd arrived, I'd lost my companion for the evening. Becca had come hurrying toward Malcolm and me in metallic leggings and an oversized sweater, her bare feet slapping against the freezing-cold wooden floor. She'd given me a flustered smile, grabbed Malcolm, and demanded that he come introduce her to the people who had shown up. I then proceeded to walk around the gallery wondering whether it was that I had no taste for art or that this art was just atrocious.

"I'd thought about buying something for the flat, but . . ." Braden gave a low whistle as he saw the price tag of the canvas we were standing in front of. "I make it a rule not to overpay when I'm buying shit."

Joss snorted and nodded in absolute agreement. Deciding it best to change the subject before one of them encouraged the other to be openly rude, I asked, "Where's Ellie and Adam?"

Ellie was a sweetheart and could put a positive spin on anything. She also managed to temper the blunt tongues of her best friend and her brother, which was why I'd specifically invited her.

"She and Adam are staying in tonight," Joss replied with a quiet seriousness that concerned me. "Today she got the results from the MRI. Everything's all clear, of course, but it brought it all back for her."

It had been just over a year since Ellie had had brain surgery to remove benign tumors that had been causing physical symptoms and seizures. I didn't really know Ellie at the time, but Joss had crashed at my old place once during Ellie's recovery, and I knew from what she'd told me it had been a pretty hard time for them all. "I'll try and pop round to see her soon," I muttered, wondering if I could squeeze in the time to do that. Between my two jobs, looking after my mum and Cole, and accompanying Malcolm whenever he wanted me somewhere, my life was pretty hectic.

Joss nodded, a crease of concern between her brows. She worried about Ellie worse than anyone. *Okay, maybe not worse than anyone*, I thought, shooting a glance at Braden, whose own brows were knitted together in a troubled expression.

Braden was quite possibly the most overprotective brother I'd ever met, but since I knew all about being overprotective of a younger sibling, I had no room to make fun.

In an attempt to pull them out of their dark thoughts, I joked about the utterly crap day I'd had at work. Tuesday, Thursday, and Friday nights, I worked at Club 39. On Monday, Tuesday, and Wednesday during the day I worked as a personal assistant to Thomas Meikle, an accountant at Meikle & Young's accountancy firm. Mr. Meikle was a moody bastard and since "personal assistant" was really just a posh word for "gofer," I suffered constant whiplash from his colorful temperament. Some days were fine and we got along well enough; other days, like today, "I didn't know my arse from my elbow"—direct quote—and was utterly useless. Apparently my uselessness had hit a new record today: There hadn't been enough sugar in his coffee, the girl at the bakery ignored my instructions to take the tomatoes off his sandwich, and I hadn't mailed out a letter Mr. Meikle had *forgotten* to give me. Thankfully, tomorrow was my day off from Meikle and his vitriolic tongue.

Braden once again tried to persuade me to leave Meikle and come work part-time at his estate agency, but I declined to accept his help, just as I had refused Joss's many offers of help in the past. Although I was grateful for the kindness, I was determined to always make my life work on my own. When you relied on people you cared about, put your trust in them with something huge like that, they inevitably disappointed you. And I really didn't want to be disappointed by Joss and Braden.

Obviously feeling more persistent tonight, Braden was relaying the benefits of working for him. Suddenly I felt the hair on the nape of my neck stand on end. My muscles tensed and I turned my head slightly, Braden's words becoming muffled as I checked out who or what had caught my notice. My eyes flickered across the room and then my breath hitched as my gaze paused on a guy who was staring at me. Our eyes met, and for some absolutely bizarre reason the connection felt physical, like acknowledging each other's presence had actually locked me in place. I felt my heart rate pick up, the blood rushing in my ears.

There was a fair distance between us, so I couldn't make out the color of his eyes, but they were thoughtful and probing, his brow creased as if he was just as confused by the static between us as I was. Why had he caught my attention? He was not the kind of guy I usually responded to. Aye, he was pretty good-looking. Messy dark blond hair and sexy stubble. Tall, but not as tall as Malcolm. This guy was probably six feet tall and no more. I would stand a few inches taller than him in the heels I wore tonight. I could see the muscles in his biceps and the thick veins on his arms because the idiot was wearing a T-shirt in late winter, but he wasn't built like the guys I dated. He wasn't broad and beefy. He was lean and sinewy. Mmm, "sinewy" was a good word for it. And did I mention the tattoos? I couldn't tell what they were, but I could make out the colorful ink on his arm.

I didn't *do* tattoos.

When his eyes lowered under their lashes, I inhaled at the shock-like feeling that jolted through me as his gaze traveled down my body and back up again. I felt like squirming, overwhelmed by his flagrant perusal, though usually, if a guy checked me out like that, I would just smile back flirtatiously. The moment his eyes came back to my face, he offered me one last searing look—a look that I felt like a callused caress down my body—and then dragged his gaze away. Feeling dazed and decidedly turned on, I watched him stride off behind one of the art walls that divided the gallery into sections.

"Who was that?" Joss's voice broke through my fog.

I blinked and turned back to her with what I imagined was a stupefied look on my face. "I have no idea."

Joss smirked. "He was hot."

A throat cleared behind her. "What was that?"

Her eyes twinkled mischievously, but when she turned to face her scowling partner she had schooled her expression into one of innocence. "I meant from a purely aesthetic point of view, of course."

Braden grunted but pulled her tighter into his side. Joss grinned back at me and I couldn't help but smile. Braden Carmichael was this no-nonsense, straight-talking, intimidating businessman, and yet somehow Jocelyn Butler had managed to wrap him around her pinkie.

I think we stood there for about an hour, drinking the free champagne and discussing everything under the sun. Sometimes I felt intimidated when the two of them were together because they were so intelligent and knowledgeable. I rarely felt I had anything profound or interesting to add to the conversation, so I just laughed and enjoyed them teasing the hell out of each other. When I was by myself with Joss, it was different. I knew Joss better than I knew Braden, so I was confident that she would never want me to feel like I had to be anybody other than myself. It was a nice change of pace from the rest of my life.

We chatted with some other guests, trying not to seem confused by their enthusiasm for the art, but after an hour Joss turned to me apologetically. "We have to go, Jo. I'm sorry, but Braden's got a really early meeting tomorrow." I must have shown my disappointment because she shook her head. "You know what? No, I'll stay. Braden can go. I'll stay."

No. Absolutely not. I had seen myself through situations like this before. "Joss, go home with Braden. I'm fine. Bored. But fine."

"You're sure?"

"Positive."

She gave my arm an affectionate squeeze and took Braden's hand. He gave me a nod, and I returned it with a smile and a "Good night," then watched as they walked across the gallery to the clothes rail where all the guests' coats were hanging. Like a true gentleman, Braden held Joss's coat for her and helped her shrug it on. He kissed her hair before he turned to pull on his own coat. With his arm wrapped around her shoulders, he led her out into the cold February night, leaving me inside the gallery with an unfamiliar ache in my chest.

I glanced down at the gold Omega watch Malcolm had bought me for Christmas, and as always when I checked the time, I bemoaned the fact that I couldn't sell it yet. It was possibly the costliest gift I'd ever received, and would do wonders for our savings. There was always the hope, however, that my relationship with Malcolm would turn into something more significant and selling the watch would no longer be an issue. But I never allowed myself to get my hopes too high.

It was nine fifteen. My pulse picked up a little and I riffled through my tiny fake Gucci clutch purse for my phone. No messages. *Dammit, Cole.*

I had just pressed SEND on a text message reminding Cole to call me as soon as he arrived home, when an arm slid around my waist and the woodsy, leathery smell of Malcolm's aftershave filled my nostrils. Not needing to tilt my head back to meet his gaze since I was wearing my five-inch heels, I turned and smiled, covering my worry for Cole as our eyes met. I'd gone for sophisticated in the Dolce & Gabbana red pencil dress that Malcolm had bought for me on our last shopping trip. The dress showed off my trim figure to perfection. I loved it. I would be sad to add it to my eBay pile.

"There you are." Malcolm grinned at me, his brown eyes bright as they crinkled attractively at the corners. He had a head full of lush dark hair with a sexy sprinkling of gray at the sides. He wore suits all the time and tonight was no exception, the Savile Row tailoring exquisite. "I thought your friends were coming tonight or I wouldn't have left you all alone."

I smiled at that and placed my hand on his chest. "Don't worry. I'm fine. They were here, but they had to leave early." I looked at the phone still curled in my hand. Where was Cole? Little gremlins awoke in my stomach to nibble anxiously at my insides.

"I'm buying one of Becca's paintings. Come and pretend with me that it's brilliant."

I chuckled and then immediately felt bad, biting my lip to stall the sound. "I'm so glad I'm not the only one that doesn't get it."

His eyes darted around the room, his lips curled in amusement. "Well, thankfully these people know more about art than we do, so I'll at least get a return on my investment."

He kept his arm around me and guided me through the gallery and behind a couple of walls, where Becca stood under a huge monstrosity of splashed paintwork. I almost tripped over my own feet when I saw whom she appeared to be arguing with.

Tattoo Guy.

Crap.

"You okay?" Malcolm glanced down at me, frowning as he felt the tension in my body.

I smiled brightly. Rule number one: Never let him see you as anything but positive and charming. "I'm great."

Tattoo Guy was grinning at Becca, his hand on her hip, trying to pull her to him, his expression bordering on appeasing. Willfully, I ignored the catch in my breath at the flash of his wicked white smile. Becca still looked a bit put out, but I totally understood when she stepped into his embrace. I thought any woman would have forgiven the bastard anything when he smiled at her like that.

Averting my eyes from Tattoo Guy, I followed Malcolm as he came to a stop and the couple turned to us. Becca's cheeks were flushed pink, and her eyes sparkled with excitement. "Just ignore me and Cam. We're just fighting because he's an eejit."

I didn't look at him, but I heard him chuckle. "No, we're fighting because we have different taste in art."

"Cam hates my artwork," Becca said with a huff. "He can't be like other boyfriends and lie at least. No. Brutally honest, this one. At least Malcolm likes my work. Did Mal tell you he's buying my painting, Jo?"

You'd think I'd be jealous of Malcolm's obvious affection for Becca, and I know it sounds horrible, but until I saw her artwork I *was* a little jealous. I wasn't exceptionally smart. I didn't draw. I didn't dance. I didn't sing. I was just an okay cook . . . Thankfully, I was pretty. Tall with legs that went on forever, I'd been told countless times I had a good body and great skin. Combine those with huge green eyes, long, thick strawberry blond hair, and delicate features and you were left with an attractive package—one that had been turning heads since I was a teenager. Aye, I didn't have much, but what I did have, I used to my family's advantage.

To know that Becca was cute and talented *had* worried me a little. Perhaps Malcolm would get bored of me and go back to her? Actually, though, Malcolm's less-than-enthusiastic response to her artwork made me feel better about his relationship with her. Not that that made any rational kind of sense.

"He did. Good choice." I smiled at him and I could tell he was dying to laugh. His hand slid from my waist down to cup my hip and I moved in closer to him, chancing a glance at my phone. Still nothing from Cole.

"Jo, this is Becca's boyfriend, Cameron," Malcolm suddenly said, and I drew my head up quickly to finally study the man I had been avoiding looking at for the last few seconds. Our eyes met and I felt that frisson of excitement ripple through me again.

His eyes were cobalt blue and seemed to be stripping me back to nothing as they perused me for a second time. I watched his gaze quickly flicker over me, noting Malcolm's hand on my waist. I stiffened as Cameron took us in, drew some kind of conclusion about us, and slammed his expression shut with the hard pressing together of his lips.

"Hi," I managed and he gave me a barely there nod. The blaze in his eyes from earlier had definitely gone out.

Becca started chattering to Malcolm about the painting, so I took the opportunity to check my phone once again. At a disgruntled snort, my head shot up, my eyes clashing with Cameron's. I couldn't understand the distaste in his expression or why I felt the sudden need to tell him to go fuck himself. Faced with animosity or aggression I tended to flinch and not utter a word. In this case, the condemnation and judgment in this tattooed idiot's face made me want to slam my fist into it and break his already imperfect nose. It had a little bump near the bridge that should have marred his good looks, but instead just added to his ruggedness.

I bit my tongue before I did something out of character and let my eyes fall to his tattoos. On his right forearm was beautiful black script—two words I couldn't make out without giving away that I was trying to read them. On his left arm was a colorful and detailed image. It looked like a dragon, but I couldn't be sure, and Becca moved closer to Cameron's side, obscuring it from sight.

For a moment I wondered how Becca could go from dating thirty-something Malcolm in his tailored suits to twentysomething Cameron with his seventies aviator watch and leather bracelets, a Def Leppard T-shirt that had been run through the wash too many times, and ratty Levi's.

"Mal, did you ask Jo about the job?"

Bemused, I looked up at my boyfriend. "Job?"

"Becca, it's fine, really," Cameron insisted, his deep voice sending a shiver of something I didn't want to admit to through my body. My eyes swung to collide with his and I saw him staring back at me, his expression blank.

"Nonsense," Malcolm answered good-naturedly and then eyed me thoughtfully. "You're still looking for another bartender at the club, aren't you?"

We were. My friend and colleague (and my only one-night stand—I'd been a mess after Callum), Craig, had left us for Australia. Tuesday had been his last night and our manager, Su, had been interviewing for a new bartender for a week now. I'd miss Craig. Sometimes his flirting got to be a bit much, and I never had the balls to tell him to shut up (Joss did), but at least he was always in a good mood. "Yeah, why?"

Becca touched my arm and I looked into her pleading face. It suddenly occurred to me that even though she was a few years older than me, she looked and sounded like a little girl, with her wide blue eyes, smooth skin, and high-pitched voice. The two of us couldn't have been any more different. "Cam is a graphic designer. He worked for a graphics company that does all the marketing and branding for household names around the country, but they had budget cuts. Last in, first out sort of thing, and Cam just started with them a year ago."

I shot Cam a wary but sympathetic look. It wasn't easy losing your job.

I didn't know what I or the bartending position had to do with it, though.

"Becca." Cam sounded annoyed now. "I told you I'd deal with this myself."

She flushed a little under his penetrating gaze and I suddenly felt a connection to her. I wasn't the only one he intimidated. Good. "Cam, let me help." She turned back to me. "He's struggling—"

"I'm struggling to find graphic design work." Cam cut her off, his blue eyes burning with frustration. It suddenly occurred to me that his apparent bad mood might have nothing to do with me and everything to do with his situation. "Malcolm said there was a full-time position open at Club 39 and I have experience bartending. I need something to get me through until I can find another job. If you could get me an application form, I'd appreciate it."

Why I decided to be helpful considering I didn't very much like him, or his attitude, remained a mystery as I replied, "I'll do one better. I'll speak to my manager and I'll give her your number."

He stared at me a moment and I couldn't for the life of me work out what was going on behind his eyes. Finally, he nodded slowly. "Okay, thanks. My number is—"

At that moment my phone vibrated in my hands and I lifted it to stare at the screen.

I'm home from Jamie's house. Stop panicking. Cole.

The tension melted from my body and I sighed, quickly texting him back.

"Jo?"

I glanced up and noted Malcolm's raised eyebrows.

Damn. Cam's number. I flushed, realizing I'd completely blanked on him when I got Cole's message. I sent him a sheepish smile of apology, one that ricocheted off his steely countenance. "Sorry. Your number?"

Unamused, he rattled it off for me and I typed it into my phone.

"I'll give this to her tomorrow."

"Yeah, sure," he responded in a bored tone, suggesting he didn't think I had the brain cells to remember to do that.

His attitude toward me pricked, but I decided not to let it bother me, snuggling more happily into Malcolm's side now that I knew Cole was tucked in safe in our flat on London Road.

CHAPTER 2

While Becca no doubt tried to talk Malcolm into extending the lease on the gallery, I wandered off toward the coat rail, my back to the room as I called Cole.

"What?"

I made a face at the way my little brother had taken to answering the phone lately. Apparently, becoming a teenage boy meant that the carefully seeded manners I'd tried to plant in him were no longer applicable. "Cole, you answer the phone like that to me again and I'm selling the PS3 on eBay." I'd dipped into our savings to buy him the video console for Christmas. It had been worth it at the time. Apparently becoming a teenager meant Cole no longer had the ability to show excitement. I tried to make Christmas as thrilling as possible for Cole when he was a kid, and I got all juiced up on how crazy happy he got when Santa was coming. Those days had disappeared somewhere, and I missed them. However, the sight of Cole's shy grin when he opened his PS3 had given me that feeling back for a moment. He'd even patted me on the shoulder and told me I'd done good. *Condescending little shit*, I thought affectionately.

Cole sighed. "Sorry. I told you I was home. I got a lift off Jamie's dad."

I breathed an inward sigh of relief. "Have you done your home-work?"

"I'm trying to do it just now but someone keeps interrupting me with paranoid texts and phone calls."

"Well, if you contact me at the time you say you will, I won't bug you so much."

He just grunted. This was a response I was becoming familiar with.

I nibbled on my lip, feeling my stomach flip unpleasantly. "How's Mum?"

"Out for the count."

"You had dinner?"

"Pizza at Jamie's."

"I left you a PopTart if you're still hungry."

"Cheers."

"You going to bed soon?"

"Yeah."

"Promise?"

Another big sigh. "Promise."

I nodded, trusting him. He had a small group of friends he played video games with and didn't get into trouble with; he was studious, and helpful around the house on occasion. As a little boy he'd been the sweetest thing to ever come into my life. He'd been my shadow. As a teenager things like being openly affectionate with your big sister were uncool. I was learning to adjust to the transition. I refused, however, to ever let a day pass without him knowing how loved he was. Growing up, I'd never had that in my life and I was going to make damn sure that Cole did. No matter how goofy he thought I was. "I love you, baby boy. I'll see you tomorrow."

I hung up before he could grunt at me again and spun around, only to inhale sharply.

Cam stood before me. He looked at me as he pulled Becca's phone out of her coat, which was hanging on the rail. His gaze skimmed down my figure again before coming to rest on the floor as he said, "You don't have to ask about the job for me."

I narrowed my eyes at him, my hackles rising. What was with this guy? What was with my reaction to him? Like I gave a crap what he thought about me. "You need the job, right?"

Those deep blue eyes of his met mine again. I watched the muscle in his jaw flex along with his biceps as he crossed his arms over his chest.

I had a feeling it was just pure muscle underneath his shirt.

He gave me no verbal answer, but with body language like that I didn't need one.

"Then I'll ask."

Without a word of gratitude—not even a nod—Cam turned away and I felt the tension begin to drain out of me. Then, as he stopped and slowly turned back, the tension built up again, as though someone had stuck a plug in my sink.

Although Cam's lips weren't full, the upper lip had a soft, expressive curve to it, giving him this perpetually sexy curl. That expressiveness seemed to vanish whenever he directed dialogue my way. His lips thinned. "Malcolm is a good guy."

My pulse picked up speed, having had enough experience of people's perception of me to know where this was going. I just didn't want it to be going there with this guy. "Aye, he is."

"Does he know you're seeing someone behind his back?"

Okay . . . I hadn't expected it to be going *there*. I found myself mirroring him, my arms crossing over my chest defensively. "Excuse me?"

He smirked, his eyes running the length of me for the fifteenth time. I saw a flicker of interest he couldn't quite hide, but I guessed his disgust for me overruled any masculine appreciation for my body. His eyes were hard when they met mine. "Look, I know your type well. I grew up watching a parade of gorgeous bimbos walk in and out of my uncle's life. They took what they could and then fucked around on him behind his back. He didn't deserve that, and Malcolm doesn't deserve some empty-headed footballer's-wife-wannabe who thinks that texting on her phone during an adult conversation is socially acceptable or that planning to meet up with another man tomorrow while her boyfriend is standing across the room isn't morally and emotionally bankrupt."

I tried to ignore the twist in my gut at his unwarranted assault. For some reason this asshole's words penetrated. However, instead of waking up the shame that only I knew existed within me, his words ignited my outrage. Usually, I swallowed my irritation and anger at people, but for some reason my voice wouldn't listen to my brain. It wanted to spit his words right back at him. I was determined, however, not to approach him in the "empty-headed" manner he expected.

I frowned at him instead. "What happened to your uncle?"

At the darkening of Cam's face, I braced myself for more insult. "Married a version of you. She took him for everything. He's now divorced and in debt up to his eyeballs."

"So that would explain why you think it's okay to judge me? A person you don't even know."

"I don't need to know you, sweetheart. You're a walking cliché."

Feeling the anger boil, I reined it in and turned it down so it simmered carefully, taking a step toward him as I laughed softly, humorlessly. As our bodies closed in on each other, I tried and failed to ignore the crackling of electricity between us. I felt my nipples harden unexpectedly and was glad for the placement of my arms over my chest so he wouldn't see. He inhaled sharply at my closeness, his look searing, and I felt it like pressure between my legs.

Ignoring the absurd sexual attraction between us, I glowered. "Well, I guess that makes us a pair. I'm a brainless, morally corrupt, money-grabbing bimbo and you're a jumped-up, pretentious, artsy-fartsy know-it-all dickhead." Fighting to cover the trembling coursing

through me—a reaction to the adrenaline spiked by my actually standing up for myself for once—I took a step back, satisfied at the flare of
surprise in his eyes. "See, I can judge a book by its cover too."

Not leaving him a chance to make a smart-ass retort, I put a swing
into my hips to overcome the trembling, and sashayed across the gallery
and around the wall until I found my boyfriend. Becca had been mo-
nopolizing Malcolm's time for too long. I sidled up to him, sliding my
hand along his back and dangerously close to his delicious bottom. His
attention was immediately wrenched from Becca as he stared into my
now glittering eyes.

I licked my lips provocatively. "I'm bored, babe. Let's go."

Ignoring Becca's huff of annoyance, Malcolm congratulated her
once more on a great showing, and then ushered me out of there, eager
to receive the promise in my eyes.

Malcolm groaned in my ear, his hips moving against mine in staccato
jerks as he finally came. The muscles in his back relaxed beneath my
hands and he collapsed on me for a second as he tried to catch his
breath. I tenderly kissed his neck and he pulled back, his own affection
for me clear in his eyes. It was nice to see.

"You didn't come," he observed quietly.

No, I hadn't. My brain was too switched on, thoughts of the evening, of Cam and the argument refusing to let me out of their clutches.
"I did."

Malcolm's mouth twitched. "Sweetheart, you don't have to fake it
with me." He kissed me softly and pulled back, grinning. "I'll get you
there." He made to move down my body and my hands tightened on
him, stopping his descent.

"You don't have to." I began to sit up and Malcolm pulled out of me
fully, leaning back on his side to let me move. "You've had a long day.
You should get some sleep."

His large hand came down on my naked hip, stopping me from

getting out of the bed. I glanced back at him and saw concern in his eyes. "Did something happen? Are you okay?"

I decided to lie. "When I called Cole earlier it sounded like Mum was having some trouble. I'm just worried."

Malcolm sat up now, his brows drawn together. "You should have said."

Not wanting to upset him, or our relationship, I leaned over and pressed a firm kiss to his mouth, pulling back to gaze into his eyes so he'd know I was sincere. "I wanted to be with you tonight."

He liked that. He smiled at me and gave me a quick kiss. "Do what you've got to do, sweetheart."

I nodded and threw him a smile before I hurried to clean up so I could leave. I had never once spent the night with Malcolm. I left after we had sex because I guessed that's what he'd want. I guessed that's what would make him happy. And since he'd never asked me to stay, I assumed I'd guessed right.

By the time I was ready to leave, Malcolm had fallen asleep. I stared at his strong, naked body flung across the bed, and I prayed that this was the relationship that was going to make it. I called a taxi and when it rang my phone twice to let me know it had arrived, I left silently, trying to ignore the disquiet that had settled over me.

Almost a year ago I'd moved my family from our large flat on Leith Walk to a smaller flat off the Walk, on London Road, technically on Lower London Road. It doubled my travel from work, meaning I had to get a bus into town most days instead of walking. It was worth it for what we saved on rent, though. My mum had rented our flat on Leith Walk when I was fourteen years old, but before long it had fallen to me to make the payments, just as it was up to me now. This new flat had been in a right sad state of affairs when we took it, but I'd actually managed to persuade our landlord to let me decorate it out of my own pocket. Something I could do on a small budget.

Less than ten minutes after I left Malcolm's, the taxi driver dropped me off at the flat and I let myself into our building, immediately going up on my tiptoes so my heels wouldn't make a noise. As I took the narrow, dark spiral staircase up toward our flat I didn't even see the dank, graffiti-covered concrete stairwell anymore, I was so used to it. Our old stairwell had been like that too. You could hear everything in those spaces and since I knew how annoying it was to be woken up by drunken neighbors in their clattering heels and alcohol-soaked joviality, I took care not to make any noise as I made my way up to the third floor.

I let myself quietly into the dark flat and slipped my heels off, tiptoeing down the hall to Cole's room first. I cracked open his door and from the light spilling in under his curtains I could make out his head buried nearly all the way under his duvet. The worry I always felt for him eased a little now that I could see with my own eyes that he was safe and sound, but that worry never, ever completely disappeared— partly because parents never, ever stopped worrying about their kids and partly because of the woman who slept in the room across the hall from him.

I slipped into my mum's bedroom, only to find her sprawled across her bed, the sheets twisted around her legs, her nightdress rucked up so I could see the pink cotton underneath. I was just thankful she was wearing underwear. Despite everything, I couldn't let her freeze, so I covered her quickly with her duvet and then clocked the empty bottle by her bed. I quietly reached for it and left the room to take it into our small kitchen. I placed it with the others, and noted it was time to take the box of bottles down to the recycle bin.

I stared at them a moment, feeling exhausted, and that exhaustion turned to resentment for the bottle and all the troubles it had caused us. As soon as it had become clear that Mum no longer had an interest in anything, including authority over her own home, I took over from her. These days I paid the rent on our three-bedroom flat on time every month. I'd saved a lot, I worked a lot of hours, and best of all, my mum couldn't get anywhere near my money. That never used to be the case, though. There was a time when money was a worry, when feeding and clothing Cole was a deep worry. I'd promised myself we would never go back to that. So even though there was money in the bank, I knew it was money that would stretch only so far.

I'd tried to erase much of our former life. When I was growing up, my uncle Mick—a painter and decorator—used to take me with him on the jobs he did for friends and family. I worked with him right up until he moved to America. Uncle Mick had taught me everything he knew and I'd loved every minute of it. There was something soothing about transforming a space, something therapeutic in it. So every now and then I'd go bargain hunting and I'd redecorate the flat—just as I had done when we'd moved into the new one. Only a few months ago I'd wallpapered the main wall in the living room in this bold chocolate paper with grand teal flowers on it. I'd painted the other three walls cream and I'd bought teal and chocolate scatter cushions for our old cream leather sofa. Although in the end it wouldn't be us benefiting financially from the change, the first thing I'd done when we moved in was strip the hardwood flooring, restoring the floor to its former glory. That had been the biggest expense, but it had been worth it to feel proud of our home, no matter how temporary. Despite the lack of expense on the rest of the decor, the flat looked modern and clean and well cared-for. It was a home Cole wouldn't be ashamed of bringing friends back to . . . if it weren't for our mum.

Most days I coped with the hand that Cole and I had been dealt. Today I felt emotional. I felt further than ever from the peace and security I strove to find. Perhaps it was the weariness causing my blood to heat.

Deciding it was time to catch some z's, I strolled quietly down to the end of the hall, ignored the drunken snoring from my mum's room, and slipped silently behind my door, closing the world out. I had the smallest room in the flat. Inside it was a single bed, a wardrobe—most of my clothes, including my eBay pile, shared space with Cole's in the wardrobes in his bedroom—and a couple of overflowing bookshelves. My collection ranged from paranormal romances to nonfiction history books. I would read anything. Absolutely anything. I loved being transported somewhere else, even back in time.

I stripped out of the Dolce & Gabbana and put it into my dry-cleaning bag. Only time would tell if I got to keep it or not. The flat was freezing, so I hurried into my warm pajamas and dove under the covers.

After such a long day, I thought I'd fall asleep instantly. But I didn't.

I found myself staring up at the ceiling, playing Cam's words over and over inside my head. I'd thought I was used to people thinking I was worthless, but his attitude for some reason stuck in my side like a knife. And yet there was no one else to blame but myself.

I chose this path.

I turned on my side, pulling the duvet up to my chin. I didn't think I was unhappy.

I didn't know if I was happy, though.

I supposed it didn't matter as long as the end result was that Cole was happy. Our mum was pretty rubbish at being a mom—and fourteen years ago I'd promised myself to watch out for my baby brother. As long as he grew up with self-worth and I had the means to get him whatever he needed to start out right in life, that was all that mattered.

CHAPTER 3

Staring at the electricity bill in frustration, I decided I'd have to look at it again when I wasn't so tired. I'd had a few hours of sleep before I had to get up for Cole in the morning, which I always did because I liked to see him off to school. And then I'd come home and spent the day cleaning the flat, rousing Mum long enough to help her get washed and dressed, and then I'd left her watching some daft talk show while I went off to do the food shopping.

I squinted at the electricity bill. I doubted I'd be able to figure it out. I could never understand how the tariffs worked. However they were calculated, they put me out of pocket. "Assholey scumsuckers," I hissed, throwing the bill on the coffee table and ignoring the startled look from Cole, who was still wearing his school uniform. Ever since he got old enough to start emulating me, I'd watched my language around him. I hated slipping up.

If I pretended I hadn't said it, then maybe he would too.

I flopped back on the couch and closed my eyes against the light in hopes that it would ease the headache behind my eyes.

I heard Cole shuffling around, followed by the sound of a drawer being opened seconds before something small landed on my chest. I peeled my eyes open and glanced down at the tiny missile.

Nicorette Gum.

I felt my mouth quirk up at the corner and looked up at Cole from under my lashes as he stared down at me. "I don't need the gum anymore."

Cole gave me the grunt and shrug that were becoming all too familiar this year. "You swore a lot when you were trying to quit smoking."

I arched an eyebrow. "I quit over three months ago."

He gave me that damn shrug again. "Just saying."

I didn't need a cigarette. I needed sleep. Okay, sometimes I really *wanted* a cigarette. The desperation had finally gone—that jittery rawness inside my body where every nerve ending felt like it was screaming at me for a cigarette. I swear I could have ripped someone's face off for a cigarette during those first few weeks after quitting. I'd like to say that I was motivated to quit smoking because it was the right thing to do. But no. I'd seen some of my friends attempt to quit and had not fancied going through the ordeal of it. I had enough going on in my life without adding squashing an addiction to the list. No, I quit smoking for the one thing in the whole world that meant anything to me, and right now he was folding his tall body back onto the floor, where his own comic book drawings were scattered in front of the television.

Cole had asked me to quit years ago when he first found out that cigarettes "were bad." I hadn't done it then because he'd never really pursued the issue, being that he was seven years old and more interested in *Iron Man* than in my bad habits.

Then a few months ago his health class was shown a pretty disgusting video of the damage smoking did to the lungs and the consequences . . . such as lung cancer. Now, Cole is a smart kid. It's not like he didn't know that smoking killed. Since every cigarette packet had a bold print label over it that said SMOKING KILLS, I'd be pretty worried if he hadn't known.

However, I don't think it had occurred to him until then that smoking could kill *me*. He came home in a belligerent mood and flushed all my cigs. I'd never seen him react so strongly to anything before—his face almost purple with emotion, his eyes blazing. He demanded that I quit. He didn't have to say anything else—it was written all over his face.

I don't want you to die, Jo. I can't lose you.

So I quit.

I got the patches and the gum and went through the horrendous withdrawals. Now that I didn't have to pay for the patches and gum, I was saving money, especially since the price of cigarettes just kept climbing. It seemed to be socially unacceptable to smoke anyway. Joss was absolutely ecstatic when I told her I was quitting, and I had to admit it was nice not having to put up with her wrinkling her nose at me every time I returned from break smelling like cigarette smoke. "I'm fine now," I assured Cole.

He kept sketching a page in the comic book he was creating. The kid was seriously talented. "What's with the swearing, then?"

"Price of electricity has gone up."

Cole snorted. "What hasn't gone up?"

Well, he would know. He'd been watching the news avidly since he was four. "True."

"Should you not be getting ready for work?"

I grunted. "Aye, okay, Dad."

I was awarded another shrug before he bent over his sketch pad again, the signal that he was preparing to tune me out. His strawberry blond hair slid over his forehead and I fought the urge to brush it back. His hair was getting too long, but he wouldn't let me take him to the barber's to get it cut.

"You done your homework?"

"Mmm-hmm."

Stupid question.

I eyed the clock on the mantelpiece of our fireplace. Cole was right.

It was time to get ready for my shift at Club 39. Joss was on shift with me tonight, so it wouldn't be too bad. There were perks to working with your best friend. "You're right. I better—"

Crash! "Aw, fuck!"

The crash and the curse word lit up the apartment and I thanked God that our neighbor downstairs had moved out and that the flat below was empty. I dreaded the day a new tenant moved in. "Jooooo!" she shrieked helplessly. "Johannaaaaa!"

Cole stared at me, defiance burning in his eyes despite the tight pain in his boyish features. "Just leave her, Jo."

I shook my head, my stomach churning. "Let me get her settled so you don't have to worry about her tonight."

"JOOOOOO!"

"I'm coming!" I yelled and threw my shoulders back, bracing myself to deal with her.

I threw open her door, not surprised to find my mum on the floor beside her bed, gripping the sheets as she tried to pull herself up. A bottle of gin had smashed across her bedside table, and pieces of glass had fallen to the floor beside her. I saw her hand drop toward the glass and I rushed at her, jerking her arm roughly. "Don't," I told her softly. "Glass."

"I fell, Jo," she whimpered.

I nodded and leaned down to put my hands under her armpits. Hauling her skinny body onto the bed, I pulled her legs up and slid them under the duvet. "Let me clean this up."

"I need more, Jo."

I sighed and hung my head. My mother, Fiona, was a severe alcoholic. She had always liked a drink. When I was younger it hadn't been as bad as it was now. For the first two years after we moved from Glasgow to Edinburgh, Mum managed to hold on to her job with a large private cleaning company. Her drinking had worsened when Uncle Mick left, but when her back problems started and she was diagnosed with a herniated disk, the drinking became excessive. She quit her job and went on disability allowance. I was fifteen years old. I couldn't get a job until I turned sixteen, so for a year our lives were pretty much shit as we lived off welfare and the little savings that Mum had put away. Mum was supposed to keep active—to at least walk around—because of her bad back. But she only made the pain worse as she became more of a hermit, vacillating between long periods of bed-ridden drinking and short bursts of angry, drunken stupors in front of the television. I dropped out of school at sixteen and got a job as a re-ceptionist in a hair salon. I worked crazy hours to try to make ends meet. On the plus side, I'd never had really close friends at high school but I made some good friends at the salon. After reading some vague article about chronic fatigue syndrome, I began to make excuses for my schedule—always having to be at home to look after Cole—by telling people my mum had chronic fatigue syndrome. Since I knew very little about the complicated condition, I pretended to find it too upsetting to really talk about. It felt, however, much less shameful than the truth.

I looked up from under my lashes, the resentment in my gaze burning through the woman on the bed and not even causing her to flinch. Mum had once been a stunning woman. I got my height, trim figure, and coloring from her. But now, with her thinning hair and bad skin, my forty-one-year-old mum looked closer to sixty.

"You've got no gin left."

Her mouth trembled. "Will you go get me some?"

"No." I never would and I'd forbidden Cole from getting alcohol for her as well. "I have to get ready for work anyway." I braced myself.

Her lip immediately curled up in disgust, her bloodshot green eyes narrowing hatefully. Her accent thickened with her venom. "Cannae even get yer mam a fuckin drink! Yer a lazy wee slut! Don't think I dinnae know what yer up to oot there! Whorin around. Spreadin those fuckin legs fur any man that'll have you! I raised a whore! A goddamn whore!"

Used to my mum's "split personality," I shuffled out of the room, feeling Cole's fuming anger as I passed the door to the sitting room and wandered into the kitchen for a sweeping brush. Her voice rose, her insults coming quick and fast, and I glanced at Cole as I passed, saw his fist crumpling around a piece of paper. I shook my head at him to let him know I was okay, and continued on into our mum's room.

"What are you doin'?" She stopped her tirade long enough to ask me as I bent to clean up the broken bottle.

I ignored her.

"You leave that there!"

"You'll cut yourself if I leave it, Mum."

I heard her whimper again and felt the change. I'd been dealing with her long enough to know which side of her I was about to be subjected to. There were only two choices: the pitiful sweetheart or the acerbic bitch. The pitiful sweetheart was about to make an appearance. "I'm sorry." Her breath hitched and she started to cry quietly. "I didn't mean it. I love ye."

"I know." I stood up. "But I can't get your drink for you, Mum."

She sat up, her eyebrows drawn together, her fingers trembling as she reached for her purse on the nightstand. "Cole will get it. I've got money."

"Mum, Cole's too young. They won't serve him." I'd rather she believe that it didn't have anything to do with him being unwilling to help. I didn't want him having to deal with her bile while I was out at work.

Her arm dropped. "Will you help me up?"

This meant she was going out herself. I bit my tongue to stop myself from arguing with her. I needed to keep her sweet if I was going to be gone. "Let me get rid of the glass and I'll be back to help you."

When I stepped out of her room, Cole was already waiting by the door. He held out his hands. "Give me that." He nodded at the glass. "You help her."

An ache gripped my chest. He was a good kid. "When you're done, take your comic book into your room. Stay out of her way tonight."

He nodded, but I saw the tension in his body as he turned away from me. He was getting older and more frustrated with our situation and his inability to do anything about it. I just needed him to get through the next four years. Then he'd be eighteen and legally I could get him out of here and away from her.

When Joss discovered the truth about my situation, she'd asked me why I didn't just take Cole and leave. Well, I hadn't done that because Mum had already threatened to call the police if I ever did—it was her guarantee that she'd have us around to keep her fed, to keep her company. I couldn't even petition the courts for custody because there was the risk I wouldn't get him, and once the social services found out about our mother, they'd probably put him into care. Moreover, they'd have to contact my dad and I really didn't want him back in our lives.

I spent half an hour getting Mum into a decent enough state to leave the house. I didn't have to worry about her wandering in and out of the pubs or restaurants on our busy street, because she seemed to be just as ashamed of her condition as we were. The need for drink was the only thing that compelled her to go out, and even then she'd taken to buying it online so she didn't have to go out for it too often.

By the time I was washed and dressed for work, Mum was back in the flat with her bottles of gin. She'd sat herself in front of the television, so I was glad I'd told Cole to head into his room. I popped my head around the door of his room and told him, like I always did, to call me at work if he needed me.

I didn't say good-bye to Mum when I left. There would be no point.

Instead, I stepped out of the building and braced myself for the night, compartmentalizing my worry and anger so I could focus on my work. In the mood to walk, I'd left the flat early. I marched briskly down London Road, turning the fifteen-minute stroll into ten, but as soon as I got to the more familiar Leith Walk, I slowed. The wonderful smells coming from the Indian restaurant beneath our old flat along with the crisp, cold night air woke me up a little. I strode up the street, the busy, wide street with its restaurants and shops, passing the Edinburgh Playhouse and the Omni Centre, and wished I was dressed up for a night out at the theater or the movies. I crossed the street near the top of the Walk, turning onto Picardy Place, and as I headed toward George Street, I prayed I could put the scene I'd left back at the flat behind me.

Our manager, Su, worked odd hours. She rarely worked the weekends during opening hours, trusting her long-standing staff members and the security guys to take care of the place. Sometimes she worked Monday through Wednesday at night, forgoing Thursday through Saturday, which happened to be the busiest nights. I didn't mind. It was actually nice not to have a manager breathing down my neck, especially since my boss at my day job was such an irritant.

It didn't occur to me not to give Su Cam's number. He'd been an asshole to me, but I couldn't help but feel for him being out of a job. I guess fate felt the same way, because for the first time in a long time, I caught Su just before she left. We met on George Street, at the top of the steps to the bar, and I literally had to stand in her path to stop her escaping, she was so clearly desperate to be away from the club.

"Jo, what's up?" she asked, almost bouncing on the balls of her feet as she tilted her head back to meet my gaze. At five one, Su was this tiny, curly-haired, energetic fortysomething whose mind always seemed to be on anything but what it was supposed to be on. It amazed me that she managed Club 39, but the owner, some elusive person named Oscar, was one of Su's closest friends.

I smiled down at her brightly. "Are you still looking for a bartender?"

Su sighed heavily, jamming her hands into her coat pockets. "Yeah, I am. I want another guy like Craig, so obviously I get a ton of girls applying and no guys as hot as Craig."

Charming.

It hadn't escaped my notice that the bartending staff at Club 39 were all attractive, but to hear it put so bluntly without any regard to ethics in the workplace made me choke on a snort. I covered it quickly with a rueful smirk. "Well, I may have the answer to your problem." I pulled out my cell phone. "His name is Cam, he has bartending experience, he can start immediately, and he's pretty hot." *A total dick, but a good-looking one.*

Su took his number with a wide, infectious smile. "Sounds promising, Jo. Cheers."

"No problem."

We bade each other good night and I hurried down the basement steps, smiling a bright hello to Brian, the security guy, and Phil, our doorman for the night.

"Evenin', Jo." Brian winked at me as I passed.

"Evening. Did the missus forgive you for forgetting her birthday?" I asked, slowing down as I turned to wait on his answer. Poor Brian had arrived at work on Saturday night in the worst mood. He'd forgotten his wife's birthday, and rather than being angry, Jennifer, his wife of ten years, had been hurt. There had been tears. Brian, who looked like a grizzly bear but was more the cuddly kind, was distraught.

Not so much now, if his grin had anything to do with it. "Aye. I had that movie set up like you said. Worked like a charm."

I chuckled. "I'm glad to hear it." I'd suggested that Brian talk to Sadie, one of the students who worked at the bar and was in the film club at Edinburgh University. I thought she might be able to get permission to use one of the uni's projectors so Brian could take Jennifer to a private screening of her favorite movie—*An Officer and a Gentleman*—on the big screen.

"You still dating that lottery winner, Jo?" Phil asked, his eyes running the length of me. Not that there was anything to see—I was wrapped up in my warm winter coat.

I tilted my head to the side, my smile flirtatious now. Phil was just a few years older than me, single, cute, and perpetually asking me out to no avail. "I am, Philip."

He sighed heavily, his dark eyes glittering under the twinkle lights around the club door. "You let me know when that ends. I've got a big shoulder here for you to cry on."

Brian snorted. "Maybe you'd have a chance with her if you didn't spew shite like that."

Phil huffed and swore at him. As this was almost a ritual now, I laughed and left them to their bickering.

"There she is." Joss grinned at me as I wandered into the empty club. She was leaning against the bar, and her expression changed when she saw my face. "Something happen?"

"I had"—I glanced around to make sure we really were alone—"a difficult time with Mum tonight." I took the steps down to the bar and ducked under it. After I brushed past her, I heard her footsteps following me into the small staff area.

"What happened?" Joss asked quietly as I shoved my bag in my locker.

I turned to her, shrugging off my coat to reveal the same uniform she wore—a white tank top with CLUB 39 scrawled across the right breast and black skinny jeans that made my long legs look even longer.

Joss stood before me in all her attitude. Her thick mane of blond hair was pulled back into a messy ponytail and she gazed at me in concern with her exotic gray feline eyes, her full lips pursed. Joss wasn't a traditional beauty, but she was sexy. I could see why Braden had fallen for her. Her cool smart-assery was so at odds with her unintentional but overt sexuality, any guy would be intrigued.

Yeah. We made a pair. And we got good tips.

"Mum fell out of bed, broke her last bottle of gin, and took her usual tantrum when I said I wouldn't get more for her. Once she calmed down I had to help her get ready so she could leave the flat to get some booze." I snorted bitterly. "Then I had to leave Cole there."

"He'll be fine."

I shook my head. "I'll worry about him all night. You mind if I keep my phone on me?"

Joss's brow puckered in consternation. "Of course not. But you know what the solution to that is, right?"

"A fairy godmother?"

"Yes." Her mouth tilted up on one side. "Except instead of a fairy godmother, he's a suit-wearing fairy caveman."

I didn't get it.

"Braden! He's offered you a job so many times, Jo. Part-time or full-time. Just take it. If you took a full-time position, you'd be working during the day so you wouldn't have to worry about working nights away from Cole."

I tried to feel only gratitude as I strode past her and into the bar and tried very hard to ignore the irritation. "Joss, no."

She followed me and I didn't even have to look at her to know she'd be wearing the mulish expression she used to reserve for when people asked *her* questions she didn't want to answer. "Why tell me these things unless you want a solution?"

"That's not a solution," I replied quietly, tying the short white apron around my waist "That's a handout." I shot her a smile to soften the blow of my words.

My friend clearly wasn't having any of that tonight. "You know, it took me a long time to figure out that we can't do everything on our own."

"I'm not on my own. I have Cole."

"Okay." Joss shook her head and took another step in my direction. I turned toward her slightly, my stomach flipping at the edge in her voice. "I'm just going to say it."

Brace yourself, Jo.

"How can you take Malcolm and all those other guys' help but not a friend's?"

Because it's a totally different thing! "It's different," I told her softly. "It's just part of being in a relationship with a guy who has money. I'm not good at many things, Joss. I'm not a scholar like Ellie or a writer like you. I'm a girlfriend. I'm a good girlfriend and my boyfriend likes to show his appreciation by being generous with his money."

I was surprised by the utter fury that flashed in Joss's eyes, and I automatically stepped back. "One: There's much more to you than that. Two: Do you realize you pretty much described yourself as a glorified whore?"

She might as well have punched me. Hurt cut me deep as I reared back from her words, feeling the sting of tears in my eyes. "Joss . . ."

I saw regret pass over her face, and she ducked her head, shaking it. "There's so much more to you, Jo. How can you be happy to let people think these shitty things about you? Before I knew you, I thought you were a cool girl but a mercenary gold digger. I had you pegged all wrong—and so does everyone else. And you let them think that. Do you know how many times I wanted to kick Craig in the balls for the way he talked about you? No one respects you, Jo, because you don't ask for that respect. I've only known the truth for a year and I'm finding it hard to hack it. I don't know how *you* hack it. I don't even think you do."

Laughter and chatter filtered into the bar from the door and Joss moved away from me in preparation for our first customers. I watched her, feeling shell-shocked and raw . . . like someone had scrubbed off the top layer of my skin and I was exposed and bleeding.

"I respect you," she told me softly. "I do. I know why you do what you do, and I get it. But from one ex-martyr to a current martyr . . . get over your bullshit and ask for help."

The customers entered the club and I turned to serve them with a bright fake smile, pretending my closest friend in the world hadn't just called me out on all the things I feared about myself.

As the night wore on, I was able to push Joss's opinion to the back of my thoughts, and I flirted with good-looking customers, leaning across the bar to whisper in their ears, giggling at their jokes—good or inane—and generally pretending to have the best time in the world.

The tip jar filled up fast.

Two seconds after an attractive thirtysomething guy wearing a Breitling sports watch slipped me his number before he left the bar, Joss was at my side shaking up a cocktail.

Her eyebrow was quirked up in question. "Weren't you just telling me last night how much you like Malcolm?"

Still feeling sore from her earlier flaying, I shrugged nonchalantly. "Just keeping my options open."

She sighed heavily. "I'm sorry if I hurt your feelings back there."

Not acknowledging the apology, not sure I was even ready to, I nodded down the bar. "Your customer is waiting."

For the rest of the night I avoided conversation with her and constantly checked my phone in case Cole tried to contact me. He didn't.

When the club closed and we'd cleaned up, Joss cornered me as I shrugged my coat on.

"You're a huge headache, you know that." She huffed as she pulled on her own coat.

I snorted. "That's the worst apology I've ever heard."

"I'm sorry what I said came out so bluntly. But I'm not sorry for saying it."

Pulling my bag out of my locker, I shot her a weary look. "You used to let people get on with their lives. You never butted in where you weren't wanted. I liked that about you."

It was Joss's turn to snort. "Yeah, I know. I liked that about me too. But Braden's rubbing off on me." Her mouth twisted into a grimace. "He has this thing about sticking his nose into the lives of the people he cares about whether they want his nose there or not."

I felt some of the hurt from our earlier encounter recede, a warm balm spreading gently over it. "You saying you care about me?"

Joss grabbed her own bag and strode over to me. Her defiant gray eyes had softened with a surprising amount of emotion. "You've turned out to be one of the best people I know and I hate that you're in such a shitty situation and you won't let anyone help you. A few months after I met Ellie, she told me she wished I'd trust her more. I finally get how frustrating that must have been for her—to see that I needed someone and I wouldn't let her be that person. I feel that way about you, Jo. I see a good person with all her life ahead of her and she's taking a path to inevitable misery. If I can stop you from making the same mistakes I did . . . well, I will." She grinned cockily. "So be prepared to be corralled. I've learned from the master." Her eyes glittered with anticipation. "And he's waiting outside for me, so I better go."

Joss left before I could respond to her threat. I wasn't entirely sure what she meant, but I knew that when she wanted to be, she was the most determined person on the planet. I did not want to be someone she was determined to save.

It sounded exhausting.

CHAPTER 4

"I'm sorry, Malcolm. I can't." I felt my heart rate speed up as anxiety crawled into my gut to play kickboxer. I hated turning down his generous offer. Once I started throwing the word "no" around, things usually went downhill from there.

"Are you sure?" he asked quietly on the other end of the line. "It's not until April. That gives you plenty of time to find someone to look after your mum and Cole for the weekend."

Malcolm wanted to take me to Paris. I wanted to be taken to Paris. I'd never been out of Scotland, and I imagined I was like most people my age in that I wanted to see a bit of the world outside the one I'd been raised in.

But it wouldn't happen.

"I don't trust anyone else to look after them."

Thankfully, Malcolm's sigh didn't sound exasperated and to my surprise it was followed by, "I understand, baby. Don't worry about it."

Of course I still did. "Are you sure?"

"Stop worrying." Malcolm laughed softly. "It's not the end of the world, Jo. I like how much you care about your family. It's admirable."

A flush of heat, of pleasure, rose from my chest all the way into my cheeks. "Really?"

"Really."

For a moment I didn't know how to respond. I was relieved that he was being so laid-back about my "no," but I was still anxious. Only now I was anxious for a different reason.

My affection for Malcolm was growing deeper by the day. So was my hope.

The past had taught me that hope was far too fragile a thing to cling to.

"Jo?"

Oops. "Sorry. Woolgathering."

"About me, I hope."

I grinned, and let the purr enter my voice. "I can come over after work tonight to make it up to you."

Malcolm's own voice deepened. "I look forward to it."

We hung up and I stared at the phone in my hand. Dammit. I *was* hoping.

Hoping that this time it really was going to work out.

"According to Braden I ambushed you."

I glanced up in surprise as I pushed my bag into the locker. It was Friday night and the bar was already in full swing. I was late for work, so I hadn't had time to really chat with Joss and Alistair, who was covering Craig's shift and was already manning the bar. I'd ducked out during a lull in the crowds to get a drink of juice and some chewing gum from my bag. "Pardon?"

Joss leaned against the doorway to the staff room, the music from the bar beating loud behind her. She had a disgruntled look on her face. "I told Braden what I said to you last night and he said I ambushed you."

I smiled. "Maybe a little."

"He told me I have a lot to learn."

That earned an eyebrow raise. "Apparently so has he."

"Yeah." Joss huffed. "He's sporting a bruise the size of my fist on his upper arm. Condescending asshat." She shrugged. "He also, maybe, was kind of, possibly, a little bit right."

She looked so uncomfortable it was almost funny. "Joss, you were trying to be a good friend."

"Braden says I have to be stealthy. That includes not using the word 'whore' in any capacity."

I flinched. "Aye, that would be good."

Joss took a step toward me, all her self-assurance seeming to have disappeared. "That came out all wrong last night. You know that, right?"

"Does this mean you're keeping your nose out of my business, by any chance?"

She scoffed. "Yeah, okay."

"Joss . . ."

"I'm just going to be better at it. Less ambushing, more corralling."

There was that word again. "You know, I would think if you were trying to be 'stealthy,' you wouldn't tell me about your intentions to veer me from my 'path of misery.'"

Joss crossed her arms over her chest, her eyes narrowed on me. "Don't you air-quote me, woman."

I held up my hands in surrender. "Hey, I'm just saying."

"Ladies!" Alistair's head appeared at the doorway into the bar. "A little help!"

I grabbed my gum and brushed past Joss. I smiled as I guessed at what was really bothering her. "I'm not mad at you, you know." I looked over my shoulder to see her following me.

She nodded, giving a little shrug as if she didn't care when she obviously did. Which was why I wasn't mad at her. "Okay, cool."

We hit the bar to see the customers standing all along it.

"So, you and Cole are still coming to dinner on Sunday?"

I grinned at her, thinking of the Nichols family and Elodie's mouthwatering roast dinner. "Wouldn't miss it."

· · ·

The Nicholses' home was the kind of home I'd wished Cole and I had been brought up in. Not for the fact that it was this gorgeous period flat in Stockbridge—although that certainly would have been nice—but because it was full of warmth and real familial solidarity.

Elodie Nichols was Ellie's mum. When she was younger she'd fallen hard for Braden's dad, Douglas Carmichael, and she'd then fallen pregnant. Douglas had broken things off but offered financial help and a lackadaisical impersonation of a father. Braden had stepped up to the plate, taking his younger half sister under his wing and playing man-child dad/big brother. The two were close—so close, in fact, that Braden was closer to Elodie and her husband, Clark, than he was to his own mother. As for Douglas, he'd died a few years ago, leaving money to Ellie and his businesses to Braden.

Ellie had two adorable half siblings—Hannah, who was a year and a half older than Cole, and Declan, who was eleven. Not surprisingly, the two shy teens didn't spend time with each other when I brought Cole to these dinners. Declan always monopolized Cole's time any-way—Declan had a large collection of video games for them to zombify themselves in front of.

About eight months ago, Joss had taken me on a night out with Ellie. After five minutes I got the distinct feeling I was being taken under their wing. Ellie immediately asked me to her family's Sunday dinner (while Joss smirked happily at someone else getting the "Ellie treatment"), insisting that I bring Cole. After two months of dodging the invitation, I finally got to the point where I felt rude declining. I dragged Cole along and we both enjoyed ourselves so much, we tried to make Sunday dinner at the Nicholses' house whenever we could.

I loved it because it was the only time Cole and I really got to be ourselves. Whatever Joss had said to the Sunday gang, no one ever asked about Mum, and Cole and I could relax for a few hours each week. Plus, Elodie was the epitome of a mother hen, and having never had that, both my brother and I enjoyed being taken care of for once.

Sunday dinner included the Nicholses, Ellie and her boyfriend, Adam, Braden, and Joss.

While we waited for dinner to be ready, I usually hung out with Hannah. Looks-wise, Hannah was a smaller version of her gorgeous big sister. Tall for her age, and if she was going to be following exactly in her sister's footsteps, Hannah had already reached her full height at five foot nine. She was absolutely stunning with short pale blond hair, wide velvet brown eyes that peered out from under a stylish fringe, and delicate features including an adorable pointed chin. She was going to be a little fuller-figured than I ever would be, already sporting a decent cleavage and a nice curve to her hips. At fifteen-going-on-sixteen she could pass for eighteen, and if it hadn't been for her shyness, she'd probably have had boys beating down her door and causing Clark no end of aggravation.

As big a bookworm as I was, Hannah was an even bigger one, hiding behind literature and her schoolwork. I thought it was a shame that she wasn't more outgoing, since she had an amazing personality. She was sharp as a tack, kind, funny, and a little snarkier than her big sister. I'd taken to sitting in her large bedroom, going through her piles of books while she chatted away to me about everything and nothing.

"That was a good one," Hannah observed and I turned around from her bookshelf to see that she was looking up from her laptop. Apparently I'd done something more interesting than her friends on Facebook.

"This?" I waved the teen book at her. I didn't really read young adult books, but Joss had waxed lyrical about them so I decided to give them a try. Hannah saved me a ton of money, acting as my own personal library.

She nodded and smiled, a dimple dipping in her left cheek. She really was adorable. "There's a hot guy in that one."

I raised an eyebrow. "Age?"

"Twenty-four."

Pleasantly surprised, I smiled, flipping through the pages. "Nice. Who knew teen fiction had gotten so risqué?"

"The main character is eighteen. It's not gross or anything."

"Good to know." I stood up from my kneeling position and wandered over to her huge bed to flop down beside her. "I wouldn't want you corrupting my innocence."

Hannah chortled. "I think Malcolm's already done that."

I gave a wee huff of amusement. "What would you know about that stuff? A boy caught your eye yet?"

Of course, I'd expected her to shake her head, frowning like she always did when I asked her this question. To my utter surprise, her pale cheeks flushed red.

Interesting.

I sat up and pushed her laptop off her lap onto the bed so I could have her full attention. "Tell me everything."

She slanted me a look. "You can't tell anyone. Not Ellie or Joss or Mum—"

"I promise," I replied hurriedly, feeling a bubble of excitement for her. First romances were so exhilarating.

Making a face at my obvious anticipation, Hannah shook her head. "It's not like I'm going out with anyone."

I grinned. "Then what is it like?"

She shrugged uncertainly, her eyes suddenly filled with dismay. "He doesn't like me the same way."

"Who doesn't? How do you know?"

"He's older."

Worry stabbed me in the gut. "Older?"

Hannah must have heard the note of reproach in my voice because she waved my concern away quickly. "He's just eighteen. He's in the last year at school."

"So how did you meet?" Although I was willing to be a friend to Hannah, I also wanted the details so I could figure out whether there *was* reason to be concerned or not. Hannah was a young fifteen when it came to boys and I didn't want anyone taking advantage of her.

Relaxing, Hannah turned toward me, getting more comfortable with confiding her boy story to me. "Last year these boys started to make fun of me and my friends. We didn't really bother when we were together. It was just names, and they're just a bunch of idiots who skip school and bully everyone who actually likes school." She rolled her eyes at the stupidity of the young male species. "Anyway, one day last year I missed the bus, so I began walking home. They followed me."

I gripped her duvet cover, my eyes wide. "Di—"

"It's okay." She cut me off, reassuring me. "Marco stopped them."

My lips twitched as I tried to contain my smile at the dreamy way she said his name. "Marco?"

She nodded, her smile more than a little bashful. "His dad is African American but his mum's family is Italian American with family in Scotland. He's from Chicago but he moved here last year to live with his aunt and uncle. He was with a couple of friends and he saw the boys following me and taunting me. He scared the guys off, introduced himself, and then walked me home even though it was in the opposite direction from his place."

So far, so good.

I nodded, encouraging her to continue.

"He told me anytime I missed the bus he would walk me home. He started hanging around with his friends at the end of school and waiting to see if I got on the bus. The couple of times I missed it, he was true to his word and walked me home."

What was this kid after? "So has he asked you out?"

Hannah heaved a dramatic sigh. "That's the thing. He really is just looking out for me, like I'm a wee sister or something."

Okay, maybe he really was just a good kid. "Is it your shyness? Do you not talk to him?"

Hannah laughed, such a grown-up sound of tart amusement I had to remind myself for a second I was talking to a teenager. "That's the thing. I clam up around other boys, and you'd think with how hot he is, I wouldn't be able to talk to him. But he makes it really easy. He's really down-to-earth."

"How do you know he doesn't fancy you?"

Her cheeks flushed a deeper red than before and she bit her lip, her eyes flickering away from mine.

"Hannah?"

"I may have mmmhed imm," she mumbled.

I leaned closer, suspecting I already knew the answer to my next question. "What was that?"

"I may have kissed him," she answered grumpily, her cheeks brightening again.

I grinned teasingly. Little Hannah had her sister's impulsiveness when it came to her crushes. Ellie had told me all about the night she'd thrown herself at Adam. Adam was Braden's best friend, and out of respect to Braden had held Ellie at arm's length for a long time. Ellie had not made it easy on him. "How did that go?"

Hannah's brow puckered as she stared at the ground. "He kissed me back."

"Yay!" I punched the air like a goofy idiot.

"No." Hannah shook her head at me. "He then pushed me away, didn't say a word, and has avoided me for the last month."

Feeling my chest ache at how crestfallen she looked, I slid my arm around her shoulders and hugged her to my side. "Hannah, you are beautiful and funny and smart and there are going to be a ton of boys who won't push you away."

I knew how empty my words were. There were no words that helped ease the pain of teenage unrequited love, but Hannah hugged me back, appreciating my efforts nonetheless.

"What's going on?" Ellie's worried voice brought our heads up. She stood in the doorway, her slender arms crossed over her chest, her eyes creased in concern. Her blond hair was much shorter than it used to be. For weeks after her surgery she'd worn head scarves to cover the patch of hair that had been shaved. As the hair grew in, she'd chopped it all off into a sexy pixie cut that she absolutely hated. It was now chin length and as überchic as Hannah's.

I felt Hannah tense against me, obviously afraid that I would share the news about her secret crush on the elusive Marco. I sympathized with her. He did sound intriguing. It was bad enough moping after a mysterious African American, Italian American, Scottish Italian hottie, without your annoying family knowing all about it. "I was just telling Hannah all about my first love, John, and how he broke my heart. She was giving me a hug to say she was sorry."

Hannah's fingers squeezed my waist in thank-you as Ellie's eyes grew round. "You've never told me about John."

Not wanting to actually get into it, I sat up on the bed, pulling Hannah with me. "Another time. The smell of food is wafting up the stairs, which means it's almost ready."

Ellie looked a little disappointed as she led us out of the room. "I know! We'll have a girls' night in this month and we can talk about our first loves."

"Aren't you and Joss dating yours?"

Her mouth turned down at the corners. "Just yours, then?"

I grimaced. "Sounds like a real good time."

"Every time you hang out with Hannah, you get a little more sarcastic. I'm banning you from her company."

Hannah grinned happily at the thought that she might have influenced me, and I couldn't help but laugh, affection filling my chest with warmth. "Only wild horses, Ellie. Only wild horses."

Once we were seated around the table, Elodie clucked around us, making sure we all had what we needed.

"Are you sure you don't want any more gravy, Jo?" she asked, the gravy boat hovering precariously in the air in her light grasp.

I smiled around a potato and shook my head.

"Cole?"

"No, thank you, Mrs. Nichols."

He made my heart hurt with his beautiful manners, and I nudged him with an elbow, grinning at him. Cole flicked me a look that clearly said, "You're such an idiot" and continued to eat.

"What were you and Hannah talking about in her room for so long?" Elodie asked as she settled back in her seat at the end of the table. Clark sat at the opposite end. Ellie, Adam, Joss, and Braden sat across from me, while I was between Cole and Hannah and Declan was on Cole's other side. I could tell Elodie was pretending she didn't really care what we had been talking about but in truth was dying to know.

"Books," Hannah and I answered in unison, causing Clark to chuckle.

"I'm guessing it wasn't about books." Adam threw Hannah a boyish smile and she blushed. These girls and their susceptibility to a roguish Scotsman . . . I was suddenly thankful Malcolm wasn't the least bit roguish. All that angst and drama? *Does he like me, doesn't he? Is he just flirting?* No, thank you!

"How cannily deduced, Adam." Braden's mouth twitched as he took a sip of coffee.

Joss smiled around her fork.

Adam shot an unimpressed look down the table at his friend. "I think we need to come up with a child-friendly phrase for f-u-c-k off."

"Duck off?" Cole suggested.

"Exactly." Adam gestured with his fork. "Braden, duck off, you sarcastic dastard."

Ellie giggled. "Dastard?"

" 'Bastard' with a 'D,' " Hannah supplied helpfully.

Clark's laugh was cut short by Elodie's huff of outrage. "Hannah Nichols." She sucked in her breath. "Don't you dare say that word again."

Hannah gave a long-suffering sigh. "It's just a word, Mum. It means a person whose parents weren't married when they were born. We only make the word offensive by implying that there is something morally wrong about that. Are you suggesting it's morally wrong to have a child out of wedlock?"

Silence reigned around the table as we all looked at Hannah in mischievous glee.

Elodie made a little spluttering sound, breaking that silence as she turned sharply to skewer Clark to his seat with her blazing gaze. "Say something, Clark."

Clark nodded at his wife and then turned to his daughter. "I think you should have joined the debate team after all, sweetheart."

Braden's deep laugh was a catalyst for the rest of us. We all chuckled and Elodie's grimace melted as our good humor got to her. She sighed wearily. "My fault for raising a clever girl, I suppose."

She was more than clever. Hannah was a superstar and I was glad she was surrounded by people who told her every day how special she was.

Chatter filled the room as we broke off into separate conversations. I was just asking Cole if he'd finished the comic he'd been working on when Joss said my name.

I looked over at her and saw her eyes dancing with mischief. I immediately went on the defensive. "Yeah?"

She smiled saucily. "Guess who was at the bar last night."

I'd always been crap at guessing games. "Who?"

"Hot guy from the shitty art show."

"Hot guy?" Braden turned from his conversation with Clark.

Joss rolled her eyes. "Nothing more than an adjective and a noun put together, I promise."

"What hot guy?" Ellie peered past Adam to look at Joss, completely cutting off whatever her mum had been saying to her.

"There was this hot—" She caught herself. "I mean a guy who may or may not have been marginally attractive. I wouldn't know because I don't notice the hotness of any guy but my wonderful and oh so handsome boyfriend, who fills me with such—"

"Okay, no need to lay it on so thick." Braden bumped her with his shoulder and she fluttered her eyelashes at him in mock innocence before turning back to Ellie.

"There was this guy at the art gallery thing that you missed and he was checking out Jo." Joss's gaze swept over the table to land back on me. "Turns out Cam was in need of a job and Jo got him one at the bar. I was showing him the ropes last night."

Well, that had been fast. I felt my stomach flip at the thought of having to work with Cam, at having to see him again. "He's Becca's boyfriend. She asked it as a favor."

Joss nodded. "He told me. He seems like a really nice guy." No one could miss the enthusiasm in her voice and I knew exactly what she was up to. Was this part of Joss's corralling? Trying to play matchmaker with some random guy just because she saw us checking each other out? I blamed Ellie. This was clearly her influence.

"Should I be worried?" Braden asked the table, and I laughed, some of the tension easing out of me.

Joss waved him off as if his question was idiotic. "I'm just saying that our new colleague was very cool and it will be nice for Jo to have someone new to work with."

Ellie frowned. "Why are you speaking like that?"

"She's trying to set me up with Cam even though I have a boyfriend. And he has a girlfriend. Not to mention that when we talked Cam treated me like I was a piece of dirt." There. I'd said it.

Braden's brows drew together, a dark glint in his eyes that I'm sure I'd see in Adam's too if I took the time to look. "What are you talking about?"

"Yeah." Joss leaned forward on her elbows, her "whose ass do I need to kick?" face on. "What are you talking about?"

I shrugged, suddenly uncomfortable with all the attention. I was especially uncomfortable with how tense Cole had gotten. I could feel his expectant gaze on me. "He just wasn't very nice."

"And yet you got him a job?" Elodie asked, clearly confused.

"He needed it."

"Well, he seemed perfectly nice last night and he said he was grateful to you for giving Su his number."

Now it was my turn to frown. "He did?"

Joss nodded, relaxing back into her chair. "Maybe you misunderstood."

No, I hadn't misunderstood Cam's attitude, but since I now found myself surrounded by two overprotective men, one overprotective wee brother, and an overprotective best friend, I'd decided it was better to go along with that. "Yeah, you're probably right."

Silence fell over the table for a second and then . . .

"He's very interesting," Joss murmured, chewing on a piece of succulent chicken.

"Who?" Ellie asked.

"Cam."

Braden choked on a sip of coffee.

"Joss," I groaned. "Stop. I'm dating Malcolm."

"Oh, is Joss trying to play matchmaker?" Elodie finally caught on. When I nodded, she wrinkled her nose at Jocelyn. "You're not very good at it."

Affronted, Joss sniffed. "Well, give me a break. It's my first time."

Hannah giggled into her water. "That's what she said."

We all froze again in silence and then Adam spluttered, choking on his laughter. Just like that, he set us all off like dominoes around the table. All except Elodie, who sat back in her chair with a totally bemused look on her face. "What? What did I miss?"

CHAPTER 5

By the time my shift came around on Tuesday night, I'd managed to work myself into a bit of a state. As always, it was a rush to get home from my day job, scarf down the macaroni and cheese Cole had made, get washed and changed into my bar uniform, make sure Cole had done his homework and Mum was still alive, and then head off to the bar.

I'd been dreading it the entire day.

Butterflies flurried in my stomach as I gave Brian and our doorman a tight smile. I didn't stop to chat with them, desperate to get the first meeting with Cam over with. I passed through the entrance and braced myself to enter the club. As soon as I did, I stopped, my gaze frozen on the guy behind the bar.

Cam.

He stood, leaning his elbows on the black granite countertop and his head was bent over a napkin he appeared to be sketching on. His messy dark blond hair fell carelessly into his eyes. I watched as he brushed it away and I noticed a masculine Indian silver ring on the ring finger of his right hand as it winked under the lights. He looked just the same as the last time I'd seen him—same unkempt sexiness, same aviator watch and leather bracelets. His T-shirt was the only change. He wore the slim-cut white T-shirt with CLUB 39 scrawled across the chest that all the guys had to wear. It was the chest and shoulders, even when hunched over, that seemed much broader than I remembered.

I took another step and the sound of my boot on the floor brought Cam's head up.

My breath hitched as our eyes collided.

Heat suffused my cheeks at my body's instant reaction to this man's attention. I could feel my breasts swell and my lower belly squeeze, and as we continued to stare at each other in intense silence, my mind and body went to war. My body was panting, *"He's hot. Can we have him?"* while my mind was screaming, *"Oh, dear God, what the hell are you thinking?"*

Everything had blurred around me—the only thing in sharp focus was Cam and all the places where I wanted to feel his touch.

Malcolm's face suddenly floated before my eyes and I flinched, breaking whatever bizarre spell we'd fallen under.

I gave Cam a tight smile and strode toward him, my eyes glued in front of me and very deliberately nowhere near him.

Cam had other plans. As I lifted the counter to join him behind the bar, he stepped in front of the doorway to the staff room, blocking my way. I stared at his black engineer boots for a second and then, realizing I must look like a total idiot, I let my gaze travel north. His arms were crossed over his chest as he leaned against the doorframe and I couldn't work out what his expression meant at all. He was worse than Joss. If Joss didn't want you to know what she was feeling, she'd slam down this blank mask over her face. It seemed Cam had bought his mask from the same store as Joss.

"Hullo." I waved.

I actually waved.

Oh Jesus, let the floor open up and swallow me.

Cam's lips twitched. "Hi."

Why was this so awkward? Usually, I could flirt and charm the pants off any man. I'd suddenly reverted to acting like a reticent seven-year-old. "So you got the job, then?" *No, Jo, he's just here for the banter.* I rolled my eyes inwardly at myself.

If he had an equally sarcastic thought, he was gracious enough not to verbalize it. "I did."

What was with the one-word answers? My mouth twisted as I remembered his wordy assault on me last time we'd met. "You were a lot more loquacious last time we spoke."

Cam raised an eyebrow. "'Loquacious'? Does someone have a Word of the Day calendar?"

So much for gracious. I tried to ignore the wince of hurt at his teasing remark. But that was hard to do when someone's teasing felt a lot more like mocking. I glared at him. "I do." I brushed past him, my elbow hitting him in the arm as I headed into the staff room. "Yesterday's word was 'asshole.'" As I opened my locker I felt a sense of pride at having stood up for myself with him again. My body still trembled, though. I was not good at confrontation and I didn't want to have to be. I resented his presence in my life already.

"Okay, I deserved that."

I shot a look over my shoulder and saw that he'd followed me into the room. In the brighter light, his cobalt blue eyes glittered at me enigmatically. He was sporting stubble. Did the man ever shave? Damn him. I dropped my gaze and turned away from him.

"I actually wanted to thank you for giving Su my number."

I nodded, balancing my bag half in, half out of my locker, pretending to riffle through it for something.

"She said you recommended me."

My bag was exceptionally interesting. *Receipt for Mr. Meikle's sandwich and soup, chewing gum, tampons, pen, a leaflet a street person had given to me about some band . . .*

"She said, and I quote, 'Jo's right—you are hot.'"

I flushed, just barely choking back the groan of embarrassment. I shoved my bag in the locker and slipped my phone into my pocket.

Taking a deep breath, I told myself I could do this. I could work with this annoying asswipe. I spun around and almost lost my footing at the playful grin on his face. It was quite possibly the "nicest" look I'd received from him yet.

I hated him then.

Not once in my life had I ever been physically attracted to a guy who was so utterly horrible to me. I knew, though, that once I spent more time with him, his bad attitude would shave the attraction down to nothing. It was just a matter of patience. For now, I threw back my shoulders, inserting a little flirtation into my smile as I passed him. "I said *pretty* hot.'"

"There's a difference?" he asked, following me into the bar.

It occurred to me that it was Tuesday night. A slow night. That meant it would be just the two of us working together.

Great.

"'Pretty hot' is a few levels lower on the scale than 'hot.'" I didn't look at him as I tied the tiny apron around my waist but I could feel his gaze warm on my face.

"Well, whatever you said, I appreciate it."

I nodded but still wouldn't look at him. Instead I slipped my phone out of my pocket just to double-check that I didn't have a message from Cole. Nothing.

"Are you allowed to have that?"

I glanced over at him now, a furrow of confusion between my eyebrows. "What?"

Cam gestured to my phone.

"I keep it on me. It doesn't seem to bother anybody else."

He smirked and reached for the napkin and pen he'd left on the counter. He tucked the napkin into his jeans pocket before I could see what he'd been drawing, and slid the pen behind his ear. "Oh, of course. Wouldn't want to miss the latest gossip."

I grunted, and grabbed a dish towel to give my hands something to do. Otherwise I was going to wrap them around his bloody neck.

"Or sexting from Malcolm—also known as the cash point."

My blood ignited. I couldn't remember the last time I'd been this mad at anyone. Oh, wait. Yes I could. It had been at Cam only a week before. I spun around to face him, my eyes narrowed as he leaned back against the bar, his expression taunting and arrogant. "Has anyone ever told you, you are the most despicable, judgmental, self-righteous, obnoxious fuckwit that ever existed?" My chest rose and fell with my rage.

Cam's expression darkened, his gaze flickering over my chest before trailing back up to my face. His scrutiny just made me flush even more. "Careful, sweetheart. You'll use up your entire calendar of words in a night if you keep this up."

I closed my eyes, my hands clenched into fists at my sides. I had never been a violent person; in fact I abhorred violence. Since my dad had been too handy with the slaps and punches when I was a kid, I always froze when someone got too aggressive with me. Despite all that, I had never wanted to throw something at someone as much as I wanted to throw something at Cam.

"A heads-up." Cam's deep voice washed over me. "So you're not too disappointed that Disney lied—no matter how much you wish it, I'll still be here when you open your eyes."

"I forgot to say condescending," I muttered unhappily. "Despicable, judgmental, self-righteous, obnoxious, condescending fuckwit."

At the warm sound of his laughter, my eyes popped open. He was smiling again. He must have noted my surprise because he shrugged. "So I might have been wrong about you being stupid."

No, I wasn't stupid. But I wasn't educated. I hadn't finished school or gone to university. And that just made me even more uneasy around him. If he found out, it would be just the ammunition he needed to torment me more. I was saved from having to continue our conversation as voices filtered into the club. The first customers arrived and we were soon too busy serving them to say anything more to each other. I watched Cam out of the corner of my eye to see how he was doing, but he was absolutely fine. An old pro at bartending.

A couple of times our bodies brushed each other and I felt like I'd been hit with a bolt of electricity. I also finally got a good look at his tattoo. It was a fierce black and purple dragon—the body and wings curled around his biceps, the long scaly neck and head inked on the top half of his forearm. The artistry on it was amazing. However, I couldn't make out the script on his other arm without drawing attention to the fact that I was looking. Not that I thought he wasn't aware of my attention. Nor was I unaware of his. The worst moment came when I poured a draft of lager at the taps, and Cam leaned past me for some napkins that sat on the lowest shelf behind the bar. It brought his body up against mine. I inhaled the masculine scent of bay rum and soap as he leaned down, and then I stopped breathing altogether. His face was at eye level with my chest.

My whole body tensed, I was so hyperaware of him.

Prolonging the torturous moment, Cam's fingers missed the napkins and he had to lean back in, his cheek brushing my right boob.

I sucked in a breath and he froze momentarily.

When he straightened, I chanced a glance up at him from under my lashes and the darkly sexual glint in his eyes felt like a physical caress down my stomach toward my sex. My sensitive nipples peaked against my bra. *Uh-oh. Oh, my.*

Cam's jaw clenched and he backed away. I finally came to my senses, only to discover the draft had overflowed over the glass and my fingers, and I had to start again.

After that I tried to avoid any sort of physical contact with him. I'd never felt so intensely attracted to someone before. Usually, it took me a while to get to know a guy before I felt that kind of deep tingling in all my good-for-nothing places. Why did *this* guy have to cause such a visceral reaction in me?

The night plodded on, broken up between bursts of customers and quiet lulls. It was during one of those lulls that I slipped my phone out and checked it again. I had a text from Cole telling me the fuse in the plug for the toaster had blown and we didn't have any in the flat. I texted him back to let him know I'd get one tomorrow. I just hoped I remembered.

"Is it the guy from the other night or Malcolm?"

I shoved my phone back out of sight and when I looked up Cam was sneering at me.

Well, if he wanted to believe the worst in me, let him. "It's the guy. His name is Cole."

The sneer morphed into a glower. "How can you be so brazen?"

"Probably the same way you can be such a prick."

"Whoa, Jo!"

Startled, my head whipped to the side, following the familiar voice. Joss stood on the other side of the bar with Ellie at her back. The two girls stared at me openmouthed, although Joss's lips were beginning to curl up at the corners. She looked at Cam. "You must have really pissed her off. It takes a lot to make Jo insult someone."

Cam grunted. "That's funny. I've lost count of her insults."

Joss looked back at me, her gray eyes glowing with pride. "Johanna Walker, you just hit a new level of awesome."

I chuckled, my cheeks still flushed with embarrassment that I'd been caught swearing at Cam. "Only you would praise me for calling someone a prick."

"Oh, no, I would too," Ellie added, sliding closer to the bar, her eyes more assessing as she looked at Cam. "Especially if the person deserved it."

I almost laughed at Joss's and Ellie's role reversal. Ellie was usually the one who gave everyone the benefit of the doubt, but she looked a little wary of Cam. I could only assume it was because she'd never seen me get riled up at someone before and thought there must be a good reason for it. She'd be right.

Joss's eyes danced as they searched my face and then Cam's. "Els, this is Cameron MacCabe. Just call him Cam. Cam, this is my friend Ellie."

"Your boyfriend's sister?" Cam asked casually, as he stepped toward them.

"Yeah."

He stuck his hand out to Ellie, a friendly, gorgeous smile on his face that made my heart thump. A painful ache pierced my chest. He hadn't smiled at me like that. "Nice to meet you, Ellie."

Apparently, Ellie wasn't immune to his charm—she beamed back at him, all her wariness disappearing. She shook his hand. "Joss says you're a graphic designer?"

A customer came up to the bar, so I served him while Cam spoke with my friends. I managed to listen to the customer with one ear and to Cam with the other.

"Aye, but I'm struggling to find a job here. If I don't get one soon I might have to leave Edinburgh."

"Oh, that would be a shame."

"Yeah."

"Any luck finding an apartment?" Joss asked him, and I suddenly realized that the two of them must have gotten along well enough on Saturday night to manage a real conversation during the busy hours.

"I've seen a few I'm interested in. None as nice as the place I have now, but you have to live where you can afford to, right?"

"What about Becca?" I asked before I could stop myself. I handed my customer his change and waited for Cam's answer.

Cam's brows drew together as he looked at me. "What about Becca?"

I'd been to Becca's flat for a party. It was a huge place in Bruntsfield and she shared it with three other people. Still, I thought there must be room for Cam. "She's got that big old place on Leamington Terrace. Surely there's room for you."

He gave a sharp jerk of his head in rejection to the suggestion. "We've only been dating a month."

"How did you meet?" Ellie asked. I wasn't surprised. Ellie was a hopeless romantic and looked for a love story wherever she could.

My stomach flipped unpleasantly as I thought of Cam and Becca creating a love story together.

What was wrong with me? I was with Malcolm and Cam was a bloody pain in the butt.

"A party a friend hosted."

"You must get on well, what with Becca being an artist too?"

His mouth quirked up at the corner. "We have a difference of opinion on what constitutes art, but aye, we get on well enough."

"Meaning you're just as condescending to your girlfriend as you are to me?" I grumbled and subsequently ignored Joss's little noise of amusement.

Cam flashed me a surprisingly coaxing smile. "You were there, Jo. Don't tell me you didn't think her art was shit."

Joss laughed outright while I just shook my head, trying not to encourage him with an answering grin. "You're supposed to be her boyfriend. You're supposed to support her, not take the piss out of her."

"You've met Becca, right? Like she needs anyone else blowing smoke up her arse. The girl's the most arrogant person I've ever met."

"Wait—" Ellie looked confused. "You don't sound like you like her very much."

"Of course I do," Cam grunted. He shrugged and shot Ellie a roguish smile. "I find her arrogance sexy . . . as well as amusing."

I looked away, pretending interest in the customers out on the small dance floor. I wondered if Malcolm felt that way about Becca. And if he did, how did I fare in comparison? Unexceptional and insecure?

God, I hoped not.

"You okay, Jo?" Joss asked, bringing my gaze back to them. They were all staring at me, including Cam.

I nodded, giving Joss a soft, reassuring smile. "Sure."

Her brow furrowed. "Is Cole okay?"

I flinched inwardly, aware of Cam's body tensing at the mention of Cole's name. I didn't want him to know the truth about Cole. If he was so determined to see what everybody else saw when they looked at me, then I didn't want to change his misconception. "He's fine." I didn't elaborate, hoping she'd drop the subject.

Of course Joss didn't. "He seemed quieter than usual on Sunday. Is everything okay with him?"

Yes, now shut up! "Of course."

Ellie threw me a sympathetic look. "When Hannah hit fourteen she went into classic teen mode. Moody and quiet. It's worse when they're shy like Hannah and Cole because when they're feeling down about something they become so introverted."

Crap.

Cam straightened to his full height so that he stood a few inches taller than me. His eyebrows were raised in question. "Fourteen?"

Thank you, Joss and Ellie.

"Cole," Joss explained to him, seeming way too eager to share information about me with him. I was seriously considering giving both Ellie and Braden a lump of coal for their Christmas present this year as a thank-you for turning Joss into a normal person who annoyed her friends with her terrible matchmaking skills. "Jo's little brother. She takes care of him."

Cam's gaze sliced to me, his eyes sharp as he took me in, in all my new colors.

Yes, Cam, I read and write and I have a pretty good vocabulary. I'm not cheating on my rich boyfriend. I'm being a responsible adult to the teenager under my care. There go all your little preconceived notions. Asshole.

I shrugged at the questions in his eyes.

As for Joss, she could not be stopped. "We all let Jo keep her phone on her in case Cole needs her, so cut her a little slack if you see her checking it obsessively. She's a little overprotective. She's a really good sister."

Would you stop pimping me out! I threw an accusatory look at Ellie, whose eyes grew round with confusion. "I blame you," I told her.

Ellie sighed, the confusion melting from her gaze as understanding dawned. "Would it help if I trained her better?"

"It would help if you hit the RESET button on her."

"Hey," Joss protested.

Ellie shook her head vehemently. "No, I like the new Jocelyn."

"Well, I'm lost." Cam's gaze bounced back and forth between us.

Yeah, if only you'd stay lost. "Never mind." I shook my head and looked at Joss. "What are you doing here tonight anyway?"

Joss smiled wickedly. "Just checking in."

I couldn't help the irritation that settled into my eyes and Ellie choked on her laughter. "I think it's time we checked out." She took hold of a reluctant Joss and tugged on her arm.

"Fine," Joss muttered, her calculating gaze shifting between me and Cam. "Jo, tell Cam about Cole's comic books."

I groaned inwardly. "Good night, Joss. 'Night, Els."

Ellie waved and ushered Joss out of the bar.

Even though the conversation around us was a wordless babble of noise above the music, silence reigned within the bubble containing me and Cam behind the bar. No noise could penetrate the thick tension between us.

Finally Cam took a step toward me. For the first time since I'd met him (and it was weird to realize that I'd met him only twice, since it seemed like we'd known each other a lot longer), Cam looked uncomfortable. "So . . . Cole's your wee brother, then?"

Screw you. I stared at him blankly, trying to decide what I should say. Finally, I came to the conclusion that it would be better if Cam and I remained at a distance. No matter how much Joss wanted him to see me in a different light, I didn't want him to. He'd jumped to his conclusions like everyone else, and frankly I didn't want to be on friendly terms with someone who had taken to tearing me down, and that was before he had gotten to know me. I sighed and strode past him. "I'm going on break."

Cam didn't answer me.

And for the rest of the night he endured my cold-shoulder treatment in tight-lipped silence.

CHAPTER 6

As I had been on every Wednesday that had come before it, I was shattered the next day. My Tuesday shift at Club 39 followed by my Wednesday day shift at Meikle & Young was the worst part of my week. I shared the job as personal assistant to Mr. Meikle with another girl called Lucy. I had never met Lucy, but we left little messages all the time to let each other know what had been done and what still needed to be done, so I felt like I knew her. She always put smiley faces at the end of any request so it didn't come off as a demand. I thought that was nice and often wondered if Mr. Meikle was pleasant to the girl with the smiley faces. I hoped so.

He certainly wasn't pleasant to me.

That morning I'd almost managed to get everything right. With three hours to go in the workday, I had been sitting franking mail that was to go out that night, trying to get Cam's stupid, arrogant voice out of my head, when Mr. Meikle came out of his office and obnoxiously waved a letter in my face.

As I gazed up at him from my seat I wondered for a second if his problem with me had something to do with my height. I was a good three inches taller than he was, and he always looked rather nonplussed when we were standing together, and smug whenever I was sitting and he was standing over me. "Sir?" I asked, my eyes crossing as I tried to make out what the bloody hell he was dangling before me.

"I was about to sign the letter you were sending out to this client, Joanne, when I discovered two errors." His face was red with frustration as he pulled the paper back to shove two fingers in my face. "Two."

I blanched. Damn my lack of sleep. "Sorry, Mr. Meikle. I'll fix that right away."

He harrumphed and slapped the letter on my desk. "It had better be perfect. Lucy can always manage it, for goodness' sake." He strode back to his office and then snapped around, his eyes narrowed behind his glasses. "I thought I had two appointments this afternoon, Joanne?"

I had worked for Mr. Meikle for almost two years now, so it was long past the appropriate time to correct him on my name. He'd called me Joanne instead of Johanna since the beginning, despite the fact that he was the one who handed me my wage slip every month. The wage slip that clearly said "Miss Johanna Walker" on it. Numpty.

"Yes, sir." In fact one of his appointments was with Malcolm. "You have Mr. Hendry in fifteen minutes and a four o'clock appointment with Mrs. Drummond."

Without another word he slammed back inside his office. I stared at his door and then at the letter he'd slapped on my desk. Turning it over, I noted he'd circled the two errors in red pen. I'd missed the apostrophe in "Meikle & Young's" and had missed the colon after "telephone number." "Pedantic twit," I muttered, pushing my chair back to the desk. It took me only seconds to find the file on the computer, fix the errors and print the corrected version off. I left it with him without a word and closed his office door behind me.

The firm rented its space on the first floor of one of the old Georgian buildings on Melville Street. The street was quintessential Edinburgh—picture-perfect period properties with their black wrought-iron fencing and shiny big doors. Mr. Young's office and reception area were in the front of the converted flat, and two other accountants' offices were across the hall from Mr. Meikle's. Meikle's reception area had a large window that looked down over the street. So did his office. It was a pity his personality didn't match the refined elegance of the firm's residence.

When Malcolm walked in, I hurriedly clicked the solitaire game off my screen so he couldn't see I was mucking around, and I beamed at him, pleased to see him. This was where I'd met him.

After breaking up with Steven, I'd dated a few duds. Then several months later, Malcolm had walked into Meikle's office for a consultation. While he waited for Meikle to call him into his office for his appointment, Malcolm charmed the pants off me with his self-deprecating humor and great smile. He'd asked for my number, and the rest, as they say, was history.

"Hi, baby." Malcolm grinned at me, and I watched him with pleasure as he approached my desk. He wore another beautiful gray suit from Savile Row, his face cleanly shaven, his skin tan even in winter. *Such a distinguished, classy man, and he's mine,* I thought appreciatively.

And he came bearing gifts.

He held out a coffee cup and a brown bag. "Latte with chocolate sprinkles and a white chocolate chip cookie." His warm lips brushed mine slowly, gently, seductively. I was disappointed when he pulled back, but he'd brought my favorite coffee and cookie so I wasn't complaining. In fact, my insides melted. "Thought you might need the pick-me-up. You work too hard."

"Thank you." I bestowed my most grateful smile on him. "I really needed this."

"Thank me later." He winked at me and I made a face, unable to stop the laughter bubbling up at his boyish grin.

Shaking my head, I waved him toward the seats. "I better let Mr. Meikle know you're here."

A few seconds later, Meikle came out to greet Malcolm and they disappeared inside his office. I sat back with a contented sigh to enjoy my latte and cookie.

I smiled down at the cup and slid a glance toward the office door. *You've done well for yourself this time, Jo.*

Don't mess it up.

Feeling a little more awake now, I stared at the computer in boredom. I'd done everything that needed to be done today. I glanced at the filing system. It hadn't been looked at it in a while and it always needed reorganizing. I grabbed my coffee and took it over to the filing cabinets, where I slowly began to work my way through the system. Sure enough, there were misfiles. Mine or Lucy's? Probably both.

When Malcolm appeared twenty minutes later, he stepped out of the office alone.

His eyes warmed as they traveled over the length of me. I was wearing a black pencil skirt with a high waist and a pale pink silk blouse tucked into it. I wore black kitten heels so as not to tower over Mr. Meikle. Malcolm sauntered over to me and I turned into him, not caring how unprofessional it was to let him kiss me. My lips tingled as he pulled back, his eyes drowsy with heat now. "We still on for shopping tomorrow?"

"Of course."

"How about Saturday? Are you free? Becca wants to take us out to dinner as a thank-you to me for the gallery showing and to you for getting Cam the job at the bar."

I had to stop myself from tensing against him. "What? The four of us?"

Malcolm nodded, brushing a loose strand of hair behind my ear. "I could pick you up this time?"

I don't think so. My throat almost closed up at the thought. Malcolm had never been to the flat. He'd never met Cole. And for now it would stay that way. "I can meet you there," I insisted.

He trailed his fingers down the thin fabric of my sleeve, as his lips curled in amusement. "I have to meet your family sometime, Jo."

There was a part of me that was really happy that Malcolm was interested enough in me to want to meet my family, but there was this bigger part that wanted to erase all knowledge of London Road from his mind so he'd never be able to find the flat and my mum. Ever.

I feigned an enthusiastic smile. "Hmm. Soon."

I didn't know if he believed me or not, but he pressed a hard kiss to my lips that promised more of the same to come later and left me to the rest of my workday.

Cold latte in hand, I was still standing by the filing cabinets when Mr. Meikle stepped out of his office minutes after Malcolm's departure. I looked over at him warily. He just stared at me. Almost passively. *Where was the glare?*

Still staring.

Okay.

This is officially creepy.

Meikle cleared his throat. "I didn't realize you were in a relationship with Malcolm Hendry."

Oh, balls. Thank you, Malcolm! I cleared my own throat. "Yes, sir."

"For three months now?"

"Yes."

"Well." He shifted, looking decidedly uncomfortable. I couldn't help my eyebrows as they rose to new heights. I'd never seen my boss as anything but self-assured and pompous. "Well, then. I, um, well, I, um, appreciate your professionalism."

Hold the phone.

What?

"Sir?"

He commenced with more throat clearing, his eyes shifting around, unable to meet mine directly. "Mr. Hendry is an important client." As his meaning dawned on me, his gaze finally met mine. "You could have used that to make your position here more comfortable and you didn't. I appreciate your professionalism and discretion."

It was the first time Mr. Meikle had rendered me speechless because of something positive he'd said to me. Usually, I was choking back irritation at his high-handed arrogance and condescension. It was also the first time my boss had ever looked at me without a grimace or preemptive disappointment, as though, no matter what, he knew I would never live up to his exacting standards. I'd grown used to that look, so it was strange to be on the receiving end of a compliment from him.

I eventually found my voice. "I like to keep my personal business just that, Mr. Meikle. Personal."

"Yes, well, good for you." His eyes filled with irritation. "Lucy is always chattering on about that fiancé of hers. As if I have time to listen to such piffle." And with that he disappeared back into his office and I suddenly felt sorry for Lucy. Perhaps it was time to start leaving *her* smiley faces.

Cole had told me he had a presentation for English the next day, so I didn't want to interrupt his work by asking him to make dinner. Instead, I texted him earlier in the day and told him I'd bring him home a bag of fish and chips. I got Mum a haggis supper just in case she felt like eating. I hurried home with the dinner since I'd bought it from a shop on Leith Walk and didn't want it to get cold. As soon as I got in the door, I headed for the kitchen, switching on the kettle and pulling out plates.

Cole appeared in the doorway, his hungry eyes fixated on the fish and chips bag. "Can I help?"

"Tell Mum I got her a haggis supper if she feels like coming out into the living room to eat with us."

His eyes narrowed at my request, but he did as he was told. After that he sat himself down on the floor at the coffee table and waited for his food, switching the television to a comedy show.

I had just put the dinner out on the table, along with a glass of juice for Cole, tea for me, and water for Mum, when she appeared. The dark gray long johns she wore were actually loose on her, and she shuffled toward us as though she was in pain. She probably was.

She sat down on the edge of the couch, the bruised circles under her eyes so prominent I could barely take in anything else. She didn't make a move for her food—she just looked at the plate with the battered haggis and chips on it. I pushed it toward her, chewing on a chip. "Dinner."

At her grunt, I turned away and stared at the telly. My brother and I pretended to be watching the show, but I could tell by the stiffness of Cole's body that he was just as hyperaware of Mum as I was.

Five minutes later the tension had only just begun to slowly drain from us as Mum managed to eat some of her food, even if it was at the pace of a moonwalker, when she ruined it.

Like always.

Focused now on the TV show, Cole had laughed at a joke and turned around to see if I was laughing too. He'd done this since he was a toddler. Anytime he found something funny, he'd look to me to make sure I found it just as amusing. I smiled at him as I always did.

"Pfft."

My muscles immediately grew rigid at the sound, as did Cole's.

A "pfft" from Mum was usually followed by something unpleasant.

"Look at him," she sneered.

I was sitting on the floor like Cole, so I had to look over my shoulder to see what she was bitching about. My blood heated when I saw she was glaring at Cole.

"Mum . . . ," I warned.

Her face scrunched up into a hateful, ugly expression. "Laughs like that fuckin useless bastard of a man."

I shot a look at Cole and a burst of pain exploded in my chest at his downcast expression. He stared at the rug, as if trying to block her words out.

"He'll turn out just like his dad. A piece of shit. Looks just like him. A piece of—"

"Shut up," I snapped, twisting around to face her, my eyes flashing furiously. "You can either sit here and finish your dinner in total silence or go back to your bed and drown yourself in drink. Either way, you keep your nasty, gin-soaked thoughts to yourself."

Mum blustered incoherently and threw the plate onto our table, sending some errant chips flying. As she pushed herself up off the couch, she began muttering under her breath about ungrateful kids and no respect.

As soon as she had disappeared into her room, I let out a sigh of relief. "Cole, ignore her. You're nothing like Dad."

Cole shrugged, refusing to look at me, the color on his cheeks high. "I wonder where he is."

I shuddered at the thought of ever finding out. "I don't care, as long as he's far away from here."

Later that night, after I'd cleaned up the flat, done the dishes, and sprayed the sitting room and kitchen with air freshener to get rid of the fish-and-chips smell, I flopped down beside Cole on the couch. He'd finished his presentation and was now surrounded by pieces of a comic he was working on.

I handed him a mug of hot chocolate as I squeezed onto the other end of the couch, skirting his drawings. I squinted at a piece of paper that was upside down, trying to make out the image. "What's this one about?"

Cole shrugged, his eyebrows drawn together. "Don't know what's happening with this one."

"Why not?"

"Jamie and Alan were helping me with it, but . . ."

Uh-oh, the irritation in his voice did not sound good. "But . . . ?" I frowned. Now that I thought about it, it had been a week since Cole had asked me if he could hang out at Jamie's. "Have you two fallen out?"

"Maybe." At least that's what I thought his mumble translated into.

Oh, boy. Cole was a laid-back guy and a fight with his friends rarely happened, so I didn't even know if I wanted to be made aware of why they were fighting. But it was Cole . . . "What happened?"

The blush on his cheeks made me even warier.

Oh, crap, this better not be teenage-boy gross. "Cole?"

He shrugged at me again.

"That's it. I'm getting you weights to wear on your shoulders so you can't do that to me anymore. I thought I told you shrugging does not equate to an answer. Neither does grunting."

My brother rolled his eyes at me.

"Or that."

"It doesn't matter, all right?" he bit out, flopping back against the couch to sip at the hot chocolate, refusing to meet my eyes.

"It matters to me."

His huge, long-suffering sigh could have filled up a hot-air balloon. "He just said something that pissed me off."

"Oi," I admonished. "Watch the language."

"He annoyed me."

"What did he say?"

The muscle in Cole's jaw flexed and for a moment I could see him older, a man. My God, where had the time gone? "He said something about you."

I winced. "Me?"

"Yeah. Something sexual."

Oh, Christ. I flinched. There were just some words you didn't ever want to hear coming out of your baby brother's mouth. "Sexual" was definitely one of them. "Okay."

Cole looked up at me from under his lashes, his mouth twisted into a frustrated grimace. "All my mates fancy you, but Jamie went too far."

I did not want to know what that meant.

Instead I thought about how close the two of them were. "Did Jamie apologize once he realized he'd gone too far?"

"Yeah, but that's not the point."

"It is the point." I leaned forward so I could catch his gaze, so he could see how much I meant what I was about to say. "Life is too short to hold on to silly grudges. Jamie was man enough to apologize. Be man enough and gracious enough to accept the apology."

For a moment he held my gaze, processing my advice. Finally he nodded. "Okay."

I smiled and sat back. "Good."

Once he'd turned his attention back to the comic, I reached for my latest paperback, readying myself to escape into someone else's world for a while.

"Jo?"

"Mmm-hmm?"

"I googled that guy you're dating. Malcolm Hendry."

My head snapped up from my book, my pulse racing a little faster all of a sudden. "Why?"

Cole shrugged. Again. "You haven't said much about him." He scowled at me. "He's a bit old, do you not think?"

"Not really."

"He's fifteen years older than you."

I really didn't want to be having this conversation with Cole of all people. "I like him a lot. You will too."

Cole snorted. "Yeah, like I'm going to meet him. I met Callum only a handful of times and you dated him for two years."

"I don't want to introduce you to someone who might not stick around. But I have a good feeling about Malcolm."

His next question was asked softly but with a hint of disdain that shot me right in the heart. "Is it because he's loaded?"

"No," I answered tightly. "It's not."

"You date a lot of wankers, Jo, and I know it's because they've got money. You don't have to." His face was starting to color now with frustrated anger. "*She* makes you miserable enough—you don't need to be going out with some tool just so we don't have to worry about money. As soon as I turn sixteen I'm getting a job so I can help."

I think it was the longest Cole had ever spoken in one sitting in about a year. And his declaration felt like a punch in the gut. I sat up straight, my own cheeks blazing hot with annoyance. "Don't use the 'w' word. And to answer your question, I'm dating a guy I really care about, and he just happens to have money. And you are not getting a job at sixteen. You're finishing high school and you're going to uni or art school or whatever the hell it is you want to do. But I'll be damned if you end up in some crap job because you're a bloody high school dropout!" I was breathing hard with fear at the thought of it.

Cole stared at me, his green eyes round with astonishment at my outburst. "Jesus, chill, Jo. It was just an idea."

"It was a bad idea."

"Aye, I'm getting that."

I relaxed at the teasing in his voice and leaned back into the couch, pulling my paperback up to my face. "Just draw, you pain in the ass."

He choked back his laughter and put down his mug to start drawing again.

After a minute, I looked at him over the top of my book. "Just so you know . . . I love you, baby boy."

"Mmm-hmm, lu uu uu."

I deduced that was "Mmm-hmm, love you too" in teenage muttering.

My lips twitched against an answering grin, a warm contentment settling in my chest as I stared down at the pages of my book.

CHAPTER 7

Even though it was the end of February, and March was but a day away, Edinburgh was still freezing. The frigid sea air rushed up toward New Town, blasting those who were unfortunate enough to find themselves walking north toward it, unprotected by the buildings.

Malcolm and I stayed out of the direct lambasting of icy wind as we strolled along George Street, going in and out of dress shops, and then down Frederick Street and onto the cobbled Rose Street, one of my favorite lanes in Edinburgh. It was packed with restaurants and pubs and boutiques, and we had lunch in a pub before carrying on to Harvey Nichols on St. Andrew Square.

"No, no, this is awful," I told Malcolm through the curtain of the changing cubicle. By this point I'd tried on at least fifteen dresses and neither of us could agree on one that we both liked. Becca was treating us to dinner at the Michelin Star restaurant Martin Wishart and Malcolm insisted on buying me something new to wear.

"Why? What's wrong with it?" he asked, his voice coming closer to the curtain.

I couldn't believe he wasn't bored out of his mind yet, but he seemed to be pretty patient with shopping. In fact, I got the distinct impression he enjoyed it. Or at least, he enjoyed spoiling me . . . which was lovely.

Staring at my reflection in the mirror, I wrinkled my nose in distaste. The dress was so sheer you could almost see my nipples through
it. Add the fact that it had a cut-out back and a short hemline and I
might as well pin a piece of paper to my chest that said FOR SALE.

"Let me see."

"No." I moved to hold the curtain closed, but I was too late.

Malcolm's face appeared in the gap he'd created and his dark eyes
glittered mischievously as they ran down the length of me and then
came to rest on my chest. The mischief slowly disappeared and when he
looked back up at me there was heat in his eyes. "If we weren't in a
changing room right now . . ."

I felt a niggle of something in my gut and wondered if it was disappointment. I imagined that if this was Joss and Braden or Adam and
Ellie, it wouldn't have mattered if they were in a changing room. Braden
and Adam would have pounced on their girlfriends with no thought to
the consequences.

I shook myself for those thoughts. So Malcolm and I didn't have an
all-encompassing passionate relationship. It didn't mean what we had
wasn't great.

I forced myself to grin incredulously. "You think this is hot?"

"For the bedroom, yes."

"I don't think that was the intent here." I looked down at it dubiously.

"Try on the green one. It's the same color as those gorgeous eyes of
yours."

I pressed my mouth to his lips for the compliment and let the curtain fall back so I was alone again in the cubicle.

He was right. The green shift dress by Lanvin was stunning.

Malcolm got a cab to a development site he wanted to visit, detour-
ing to drop me off at home. He knew I wouldn't invite him inside. I was
all set for dinner with Becca and Cam on Saturday night. Well, ready in
that I at least had designer armor to wear and Malcolm to act as a buffer.

Tonight at work there would be no designer armor and no Malcolm.

I despised the flurry of butterflies that awoke in my stomach at the thought of working with Cam and all the things he might say to damage my already fragile ego.

It seemed I still needed to grow a thicker skin.

There was a kaleidoscope of butterflies in my belly by the time I got to the bar and when I stepped into the main room and saw Cam and Joss laughing about something as they cleaned glasses, the butterflies swarmed upward to my chest and I couldn't breathe for a moment.

What was that all about?

I took the stairs down to the bar and ducked under the counter, throwing a smile of hello their way before hurrying into the staff room. Two seconds later, Joss was at my back and the music on the stereo system blasted on. I heard Brian yelling at someone to turn it down and the noise muted to a bearable level.

"What's up? You looked like you had swallowed a very sour lemon when you came in just now," Joss observed.

I shrugged out of my jacket, smirking. "Did I? I can't imagine why."

"You're afraid I'm going to try and set you up with Cam."

"Am I? I can't imagine why."

Joss made a face. "Okay, enough with the sarcasm. Look. I'm not going to."

I turned toward her, shoving my phone in my back pocket. "What? The matchmaking is over before it's even really started?"

She clenched her jaw for a second before replying, "Yes. And that's a promise."

"What brought on this change of heart? Not that I'm complaining," I hurried to assure her.

Completely deadpan and traumatized, Joss held my curious gaze. "Ellie made me watch an adaptation of Jane Austen's *Emma* so she could show me the dos and don'ts of matchmaking. This was followed by a redundant showing of the teen movie *Clueless*, which happens to be based on Jane Austen's *Emma*." She let that sit with me, clearly urging me to find it as horrifying as she had.

I tried to stifle my laughter. I really did.

Just not hard enough.

I threw my head back, falling against my locker in a fit of giggles. I couldn't get the image out of my head and I could just imagine how seriously Ellie had taken the whole thing. "Oh, my God," I gasped through my laughter. "That must have been so painful for you."

Renewed excruciation flickered across her face as though she was having a flashback. "Painful does not even cover it. You know what's worse than watching a romantic drama?"

"No."

"Analyzing one."

Well, that set me off again.

"Stop laughing. It's not funny."

"Oh, it's *so* funny. And just what you deserved."

Joss groaned. "Yeah, probably."

After I'd stemmed my laughter, I shook my head, wiping the tears from my eyes. "I still can't understand why someone who rolls her eyes at romance films is writing a romance novel."

She glowered at me. "It's not a romance. It's my parents' story."

"Yeah, your parents who had a flaming, passionate romance."

Joss's eyes narrowed dangerously. "Do you want me to go back to matchmaking?"

I shuddered at the thought. "Definitely not."

"Be quiet, then."

At her belligerent expression, I snorted. Clearly she was mad that her attempts to lead me from my "path of misery" had failed so soon. "You know, if it makes you feel any better, I really do care about Malcolm. And I'm not actually miserable."

Her eyes dimmed a little, any air of teasing between us dying out immediately. "My worry, Jo, is that you're not happy either."

For a moment, I felt breathless again. I stared over her shoulder at the wall where our shift schedule for the week was pinned to a notice board surrounded by staff memos, cocktail recipes, and contact numbers. When I could breathe again, I dragged my gaze back to hers. "I know that Malcolm will make me happy."

She threw me a look that clearly screamed, *Are you serious?* "How lukewarm of you. You've been together for over three months. I think you'd know by now whether or not you're in love with him."

I slammed my locker shut, preparing to go into the bar for opening. I thought about today in the changing room at Harvey Nichols and found myself getting defensive. "Look, not all relationships are like you and Braden, or Ellie and Adam. They aren't all passionate sex and absolute adoration. Sometimes it's slow and secure and warm. That doesn't make it any less meaningful."

Joss passed me, her nose wrinkled with irritation. "Slow, secure, and warm? We're not talking about an old guy in a Zimmer with a lap blanket. We're talking about sex and love."

"Who's talking about sex and love?" Cam's deep, raspy voice tugged at my lower belly.

As I stepped behind the bar, I couldn't look at him.

I had hoped those last few times in his company were a complete anomaly, but it was clear they weren't—my body seemed to vibrate and come to life around him, and I was beginning to feel guilty about my attraction toward him.

"Jo and I were," Joss answered, her voice still gruff with frustration. She leaned back against the bar and stared at me, her expression unreadable in the dim light.

Cam raised an eyebrow, shooting me an equally unfathomable look. "Trouble in paradise?"

Since he hadn't asked me with a sneer in his voice this time, I shook my head and deigned to answer him. "No, we're fine. Joss is just having 'a moment.'"

She grumbled under her breath, but customers started trickling in, and then pouring in, and soon we were too busy to have much of a conversation.

For the first two hours, I somehow miraculously managed to avoid Cam's end of the bar. I worked at the opposite end and Joss worked in the middle. I chatted sporadically with her about nonsense anytime we were close enough to hear each other over the music. Braden, Ellie, and Adam came in and took their usual table directly across from us so that Braden and Joss could screw each other with their eyes. I, on the other hand, did a good job of pretending that my entire body wasn't aware of every single move Cam made, of every wicked smile he flashed at an attractive customer, at the way his jeans cupped his bite-worthy ass every time he bent over for something, or that when he reached up for a new bottle of Jack Daniel's his T-shirt rode up to show a slab of taut abs.

It was just pure muscle under there.

I wondered what it would be like to have him stretched out naked on a bed, his hard body and golden skin laid out for me to savor. I would start with the sexy V cut of his hips, licking along the definition, pressing wet kisses up his sculpted torso, then flick his nipples and feel him harden against me—

"Jo!"

I jolted out of my daydream, spilling the fresh orange juice I'd just taken out of the fridge. I gaped at Joss, my cheeks flushed with embarrassment.

She was gazing at me with a quizzical smile. "You were gone for a minute there. Where did you go?"

The red in my cheeks deepened and I cast a quick look at Cam, who was busy serving a customer. I was thankful for the low lighting that hid my cherry red cheeks, but unfortunately Joss must have caught the embarrassment in my eyes and the quick, not so surreptitious look I'd shot Cam. She glanced down the bar at him and then back at me. "Oh, okay." She grinned.

I groaned inwardly and turned back to serve my customer her Alabama Slammer.

Two minutes later the crowd around the bar started to wane. I was readying myself to be teased mercilessly by Joss when I heard her swear under her breath.

Snapping my eyes over at her, I saw the clench to her jaw and followed her narrow-eyed gaze across the bar. A curvy brunette had taken a seat next to Braden and engaged him in conversation. Braden didn't look like he was being anything but polite, but the brunette was sitting awfully close to him. My eyes met Ellie's and she threw me an "uh-oh" look.

Joss was too classy to get into a bitch fight, especially with someone who was just sitting a little too close to her boyfriend. The girl would have to—

Oh, no. The brunette's hand had landed on Braden's thigh.

"Be back in a second," Joss muttered furiously as she passed me.

She was too busy leaving the bar area with cool eyes and a burning rage to notice that Braden had already removed the woman's hand from his thigh. I leaned against the bar with my elbows, settling in for the show. It was a shame I was too far away to hear Joss. She could flay someone alive with her words and do it with a great deal of self-possession. I was eternally envious of her ability to confront an aggressor without turning into a gibbering chalk-faced idiot.

A customer approached the bar, and I reluctantly drew my gaze away from the scene. As I was pouring the guy his whisky, Cam's familiar and sexy scent infiltrated my olfactory senses and I could swear I swayed a little.

At the feel of his warm breath on my ear, my fingers trembled and I froze as I pulled the bottle away from the glass. I could feel the heat of his body all the way down my left side, as though he was actually pressed tight against me.

"I'm sorry for being a dick," he murmured, his voice deep with sincerity.

The vibration of his words against my skin caused a shimmer of delicious shivers down my spine. It completely turned me on. I only just managed to stifle my surprised gasp.

Feeling off balance, I glanced at him over my shoulder, only to find he was very definitely almost pressed up against me. It took a minute for his apology to register with me.

Cam sighed, his chin dipping so that our noses were close to touching. My eyes tangled with his and I knew that I wouldn't be able to move even if I wanted to. "I don't know you," he continued, his eyes searching my face. "And I shouldn't have presumed to." That searching look of his finally came to rest on my lips, and as his eyes turned molten with sexual awareness another rush of unexpected tingles awoke between my legs. I licked my lips, wondering what his mouth would taste like, and his breath hitched.

He leaned away from me, his eyes wary as they met mine. I saw the consternation in them and my whole body tensed.

Cam was just as attracted to me as I was to him, but he didn't want to be.

Why? Was I "beneath" him?

A sharp pain sliced across my chest and I pulled my gaze away and back to the drink I was making. And because I had just spent the previous evening preaching to my wee brother about being gracious, I nodded. "Apology accepted."

"So why do you have to look after your brother? Where are your parents?"

I turned away, brushing past Cam to slide the drink over to my customer. I took the money for it, hit the till, and then handed back the customer's change. Just as I glanced around to answer Cam, another customer appeared.

The bar got busy again, and Joss skipped down the stairs and under the counter to help us out. I watched, while I served a customer, as Ellie, Adam, and Braden left. I gave Joss a teasing smile. "You kicked him out?"

She shrugged. "If he's going to be attracting hot women who don't care if he has a girlfriend or not, then, yeah, I'm kicking him out."

"What if he goes to another bar? There are more attractive women out there who will come on to him."

"Yeah, but I don't have to see it this way."

"Good point," I murmured, eyeing Cam as he leaned over the bar so a female customer could say something in his ear.

The unexpected explosion of jealousy that ripped through me when he pulled back and smiled at her with blatant sexual cockiness nearly floored me.

What was I doing? What was my body doing?

I was with Malcolm. I was happy with Malcolm.

Deciding it was time to go on break, I gave Joss the heads-up and hid out in the staff room for ten minutes. Berating myself for a good portion of that, I managed to get myself together enough to return to work. When I came back out, the bar had hit another lull of quiet and Joss and Cam were leaning against the bar, talking to each other. I drew a deep breath and decided to be a grown-up.

"What's up?" I asked congenially as I approached them.

Joss gave me a surprisingly uneasy look. "Cam asked about your family. I thought you'd already told him. Sorry."

My heart flipped in my chest, a rush of queasiness making my skin prickle. "Told him—"

Realizing what I thought she meant, she rushed to clarify. "About your mom's *illness* and how you have to take care of her and Cole."

An immediate rush of relief overwhelmed me and I let out a deep breath. "Right."

Unfortunately, I'd given away too much. When I chanced a look at Cam, I saw his suspicious gaze flickering between me and Joss. He had just opened his mouth, presumably to ask another question, when Joss derailed him. "So what about you, Cam? Your family from here?"

Although his eyebrows were still drawn together in curiosity, he nodded. "My parents live just outside Edinburgh. Longniddry."

Nice, I thought. Longniddry was this lovely village situated near the water. It was a beautiful place with rough beaches and old cottages. I wondered what it must have been like to grow up in such a place.

"No overbearing brothers or sisters?" Joss continued her interrogation. "No car crashes or drug addicts or medical problems?"

I tried to contain my snort.

Cam shrugged good-naturedly. "Not that I'm aware of."

Looking nonplussed, Joss eyed him warily. "Are you telling me you're actually a well-adjusted individual?"

He threw her his hot grin and I succumbed to another heated flare of sexual attraction. "I like to think so."

Joss shot me a look that said *Well, at least I've got you* before she shook her head at Cam as though she were disappointed in him. "And here I thought we could be friends."

Cam laughed. "I could invent a tragic past if that helps?"

"Or unearth some deep, dark family secret I can turn into a book."

"I'll get back to you on that." He smiled and then looked at me carefully, his gaze lowering a little under his eyelashes. He had sickeningly long eyelashes for a man. "I made the mistake of telling Becca I had this Saturday off and I hear she's booked a table for four at Martin Wishart."

Yeah, I'm sure the last thing you want to do is sit down for a meal with me. "Malcolm told me."

"So I guess we're having dinner together."

Joss chuckled, and as she turned to serve a customer she rather unhelpfully advised, "Try not to kill each other."

I smirked and shot a look at Cam, then immediately wished I hadn't. He appeared to be trying to work me out, as though I was this mysterious puzzle he was drawn to solving.

My body flushed with pleasure at his attention, but my brain screamed at me to run as far away from him as possible.

CHAPTER 8

As much as Joss acted as a buffer between me and Cam, the tension between us refused to dissipate. Friday night I danced around him like an idiot, desperate not to have a repeat of the previous evening. Joss kept eyeing me as if expecting me to hatch an alien at any moment, I was acting so strangely.

When Malcolm had phoned me during the day I'd felt this whoosh of guilt at the sound of his voice, as though I had cheated on him in a way with my impure thoughts about Cam. I wasn't perfect. It wasn't as though I hadn't been ruthless when going after men. I tried not to think about the girls who had been hurt by their defection, and I tried to rationalize that somehow it was okay to have been party to such a betrayal because Cole needed me to marry someone like Malcolm. There was no truth in that. That somehow suggested there hadn't been a choice for me, but of course there was a choice. I had chosen. And I had chosen selfishly.

I drew the line at physically cheating on someone, though. I particularly drew the line at being the direct betrayer.

Lusting after Cam seemed like one step too close toward that.

Thankfully, as always, Friday was really too busy to make much conversation with my colleagues. Cam cracked a few jokes, made us laugh, and Joss, as always, was her witty self. I, on the other hand, decided to try to diminish my awareness of Cam by focusing on filling up the tips jar.

I flirted my ass off and ignored the way Joss rolled her eyes at my girlish giggling. She'd once told me I had a fake giggle and a real giggle. My real giggle was apparently "adorable," but my fake giggle—the one I used to convince a guy that I thought he was the funniest man I'd ever met—drove her up the wall.

If only she knew that just made me want to do it more.

I was serving drinks to three guys who weren't mind-blowingly attractive but were charming and sexy in their own way, and I was enjoying their attention.

"Seriously, you should just jump over the bar and come spend the rest of the night with us," one of them insisted, flashing me a crooked smile. I could usually read when a guy was being lascivious, but these guys were just having fun.

I leaned my elbow on the bar, handing the shortest guy his change with one hand while resting my chin thoughtfully in the palm of my other. "Hmm, where would you take me?"

"I heard Fire is a pretty good nightclub," the one in the middle suggested, his eyes glinting with hope.

I snorted and gestured around the bar. "Leave one club for another. No, you'll have to do better than that." I smiled slowly and watched the three of them lean in closer, their eyes dipping to my mouth.

"The Voodoo Rooms." The short one nodded at his mates as if it was a great idea.

I shook my head sadly in response. "Expand your horizons, boys."

The one with the crooked and very hot smile leaned on the bar so that our faces were only an inch apart. My eyes smiled into his as he stared at me intensely. I suddenly realized he'd stopped playing and was serious, and my smile wilted a little. His gaze dropped to my lips. "I'll take you anywhere, darling, anywhere in the world, if you'll give me your number."

I heard the clearing of a deep throat before a warm hand pressed against my belly. I jolted in shock and twisted my head around to see Cam leaning into me.

It was *his* large, warm hand pressed to my belly.

He put pressure on me and eased me back off the bar. "Excuse me," he muttered, his expression blank except for the muscle jumping in his jaw. Cam's touch set off sparks in my body, my skin prickling with excited heat, and in my dumbfounded reaction I let him push me back from the bar, his body curling into mine as he reached past me. His hand slid around to my waist, nudging my tank top up so his callused hand gripped my bare skin, holding me in place as he bent down for a bottle of liqueur. When he straightened, our eyes met, and it took everything in me not to reach for him too.

As if it suddenly occurred to him that he was still touching me, he leaned back and nodded at me, then strode down to his end of the bar. I stared after him too long, wondering why he'd felt the need to touch me, to move me rather than just ask me to move. Usually, I would read that as interest, as an invitation, but Cam was sending me a whole bunch of mixed signals. I stared so long that when I turned back to the guys I had been diligently flirting with, they were gone. And so was their prospective tip.

Crap.

Bloody Cam.

The rest of the shift flew by and as I had taken to doing the last few nights, I hurried out of the bar as soon as we'd cleaned up at closing, desperate to get away from Cam.

It was a freezing-cold, brisk walk back to the flat, avoiding drunks who took one look at a single female and decided she'd make great target practice. Joss hated me walking home alone after our shift, but I was used to it, and had a rape alarm on my key ring and a small can of pepper spray in my bag as a precaution.

I hurried quietly up the damp stairwell of my building, and almost melted against our front door with relief and exhaustion. Home at last.

Deciding that a cup of tea would be nice to take with me to my room I headed for the kitchen to switch on the kettle but was stopped dead in the doorway.

A haggard resentment rippled through me at the sight of my drunken mother passed out on the kitchen floor. Thankfully, she was wearing pajamas. There had been times I'd discovered her like this and she'd been naked.

I wondered how long she'd been there and feared that she'd not only gotten a chill from the cold kitchen tiles but hurt her bad back. Shaking my head, biting back the tears of frustrated exhaustion, I shrugged out of my jacket and took a minute as I decided how I was going to carry her back to her room without waking up Cole and without doing any more damage to her back. I supposed I could drag her as carefully as I could manage.

Attempting to move quietly, I did just that. I lifted her under the arms and began to slide her body out of the kitchen. Her foot hit the edge of the door, slamming it back against the wall and I winced, frozen on the spot. I hoped I hadn't woken up Cole.

Unfortunately, I'd just begun to drag her again when I heard his bedroom door open. I twisted around to find him standing in the hallway, staring at me with bleary eyes.

"Sorry, sweetheart. Go back to bed," I whispered.

But Cole just grunted and shook his head, stumbling toward me. "Need a hand?"

"I'm okay."

He grunted at that again and came around to the other end of Mum. With ease he lifted her feet and we began to carry her toward her room. I eyed him as much as I eyed where we were going. Cole was my height and still growing. He was a smart kid, and one who hadn't had it easy in the parent department. It had given him this weary glint in his eyes that made him look more mature than he was. I was saddened that my wee man had had to grow up so fast.

This of course was not the first time he'd helped me carry our mum to her bed.

Once we had her on the bed, I set about tucking her duvet around her, trying to offset any damage she may have caused to herself from lying on the cold floor. Assured that she was warm enough, I slipped out of her bedroom and met Cole in the hallway.

I gave him a smile that trembled with my tiredness, with my sadness.

He saw it and his own sorrow flickered across his expression before he killed it with a smirk. "I've had an idea for a new workout fad. It'll make us loads of money."

My lips twitched. "And what's that?"

"It's called Drunk Mum. It involves heavy lifting and some cardio."

I stared at him a moment, letting his joke sink in, and then I burst into giggles, pulling him to me for a hug. I felt the tears creep into the corner of my eyes as he hugged me back.

He was my saving grace.

I didn't know what I'd do without him.

CHAPTER 9

B y the time I woke up it was midmorning. I lay under my duvet refusing to get out. To save on our heating bill, I had the heat set on a daily timer. It came on for two hours in the morning and then back on at five o'clock in the evening. The air outside my warm cocoon in the bed was freezing and I moaned at the unfairness of having to get up.

Cole had woken me for a second a few hours earlier to remind me he was going to Jamie's and would be staying there all day and night. I remembered grumbling at him to take twenty pounds out of my purse in case of an emergency, before falling back asleep.

My eyes rolled to the side to check the time on my bedside table alarm clock. It was ten thirty. I really needed to get up and get some food shopping done before I had to get ready for my big, horrible night with Becca and Cam.

Euch.

"Okay. One, two, three," I counted. On "three" I threw back my covers and jumped out of bed. It was the only way to get me out of it. I couldn't do that slow, sliding-out-from-under-the-sheets thing or I'd fall asleep in midattempt. Shivering, I gazed longingly down at my mattress.

With a pout, I hurried into the hall to flip the hot water on for my shower. A cup of tea kept me warm while I waited, and I opened Mum's door to check on her.

She was awake.

"Morning."

"Morning," she mumbled, clutching her blankets closer to her. "It's bloody cold."

That's because you passed out on the kitchen floor for God knows how long. "Do you want a cup of tea and some toast?"

"Aye, that would be good, darling." She slipped farther down so she was curled into a ball.

After I'd made her tea and toast, waiting around to make sure she ate it, I left her alone and got ready for the day. Besides getting food, I needed to get a birthday card for Angie, my friend from the salon I worked at years ago. Before Joss, I didn't have close friends because of . . . well . . . my secretiveness, but Angie and Lisa from the salon had been girls I'd hit the town with and the closest thing I'd had to best friends. I hadn't seen either of them in months, although we still exchanged regular text messages.

I shrugged on my wool jacket that cinched in at the waist, wrapped an oversized scarf around me, and pulled my knit Uggs up over my skinny jeans. My freshly washed hair fell around my shoulders and down my back in thick tumbles and I knew I should tie it up, but I shivered at the thought of leaving my ears naked to the cold. I grabbed my gloves and bag and I was all set.

Shouting a good-bye to Mum, I hurried out the door, as always looking forward to being anywhere but stuck in the flat with her. I took the stairs slowly as I began to pull on my gloves and at the sound of male laughter I stilled at the corner of the staircase that would take me down to the floor below us.

The empty flat directly beneath my flat didn't appear to be empty anymore.

The door to it had been thrown open, and I watched wide-eyed as two guys carried a coffee table up the last few steps and onto the landing.

"You hit the leg." The extremely tall, dark-haired guy in a rugby shirt smirked at his companion as they leveled out on the landing.

The other guy was a little shorter, with broad shoulders and messy dark hair squashed under a beanie hat. When he turned to smile cheekily at his friend, I knew I was in the presence of a player. The guy was gorgeous and that smile told me he knew just what to do with it. "He'll never notice."

"There's a bash in the wood."

"Ach, it gives it character."

I took another step down and my movement drew both of their gazes. I felt an uneasy squirm in my stomach as I glanced at the open door to the flat. We had a new neighbor. A new neighbor who would have to endure my mum's wailing drunkenness.

Great.

The beanie hat guy grinned appreciatively at the sight of me, his eyes drinking me in from my boots to my head. I flicked a quick look at his friend and discovered I was under his smiling perusal too. My automatic flirt kicked in and I gave them a half smile back and a wave of my fingers. "Hey."

Beanie Guy adjusted the weight of his side of the coffee table as he asked, "You live here?"

"The flat above you."

He made a huffing sound and shook his head as he stared at his friend. "Cam's always been a lucky fucker."

I instantly tensed at the name.

"What's taking so long?" a deep and very familiar voice asked from inside the flat.

My mouth was already falling open when Cam stepped out of the flat to greet his friends.

"Cam?" I squeaked in disbelief.

Startled, Cam looked up at me, astonishment slackening his features. "Jo?"

"Eh . . ." The tall friend's head turned from me and Cam to Beanie Guy. "The lucky fucker already knows her."

I ignored them, my heart hammering in my chest now as my eyes pinned Cam to the landing. He stood before me in one of his worn T-shirts and jeans, his engineer boots on, his hair a mess and his eyes dark with lack of sleep. Despite his obvious tiredness, he seemed to hum with an energy that sucked me in. When he stepped into a room, you felt his vitality, his strength. There were few people in this world who had that kind of presence about them. Braden Carmichael was one. Cameron MacCabe was definitely another.

And he was moving into the flat beneath mine?

I couldn't get my pulse to slow at the thought of Cam being so close to all my secrets and shame. "You're moving in?"

His eyes flew past me to the floor above us. "You live here?"

The rocks settled heavily in my stomach. "The flat above you."

"Jesus." Cam sighed, seeming as unhappy about the revelation as I was. "Small world."

More like small city. "Very," I murmured. How had this happened? Did fate just hate me? Of all the coincidences in the world, why did I have to be landed with such a huge and very crap one?

"Eh, this is getting heavy," Tall Guy complained, nodding at the coffee table.

I eyed the size of his biceps and doubted he found it at all heavy.

Cam gestured to the flat. "Take it in, guys. Thanks."

"No, no." Beanie Guy shook his head, smirking, his eyes still on me. "First introduce us to Miss Scotland."

I felt my cheeks heat at the compliment, hating that it somehow added substance to Cam's opinion of me.

Cam's body tensed and he crossed his arms over his chest. "Just take it in the flat."

My God, I was so unworthy that he couldn't even introduce me to his friends. Ignoring the hurt that had gripped my chest, I smiled at Beanie Guy. "I'm Jo."

Beanie Guy and Tall Guy's mouths dropped open. "Jo?" they asked in surprised unison . . . as if they'd heard of me.

My brow puckered in confusion as I slid a questioning look at Cam. His whole body was rigid now as he gave his friends the tiniest shake of his head.

His friends didn't take whatever hint Cam was sending them. "Jo from the bar, Jo?"

Cam had spoken about me? I shifted uneasily, not sure in what light I'd been painted. "That's me."

The two of them grinned and Beanie Guy gave me a nod of hello. "I'm Nate and that's Peetie."

I eyed the tall guy incredulously. "Peetie?" Not the kind of name you'd expect for someone of his size.

Peetie had a nice face, friendly and open. "Gregor. My surname's Peterson."

"Ah, I see."

"Cam's told us all about you, Jo," Nate continued, avoiding Cam's glower.

Feeling a little shaken that Cam had spoken about me to his friends and far too curious about *how* he'd spoken about me, I decided it was time to move along so I could wrap my head around the fact that Cam was my new neighbor.

Come to think of it, he had been speaking to Joss about finding a cheaper flat.

Again . . . of all places, why did it have to be in my building?

I decided to pretend like I didn't care what Cam had said. "Well, don't believe a word of it." I ignored Cam as I passed him, and smiled at his friends. "Cam has the unfortunate habit of forming an opinion before he really gets to know someone."

Nate nodded. "Yeah, he told us what a remarkable dick he was to you."

That stopped me in midstride, and I twisted around to stare at Cam.

He shrugged at me, his expression still deadpan. "I told you I was sorry."

My eyes swung to his grinning friends and then back to him. "Well, then, I guess I might actually believe you now. Neighbor." And with a nod of good-bye to them all, I started descending the stairs carefully.

"That's Jo?" Nate asked loudly, as I disappeared from view, his voice carrying all the way down to me, and I couldn't help but prick my ears up to listen.

"Shut up," Cam hissed. "Let's get the rest of the stuff in."

"Christ almighty, you weren't kidding, were you? How fucking long are those legs?"

"Nate . . ."

"How can you stand it, mate? If you're not having a crack at her, I am."

Cam's growl reverberated down to me. "Get in the fucking flat!"

His door slammed and I jumped, stalling on the last landing. What the hell had all that meant? What had Cam said about me?

The simple style of the restaurant with its soft wood and soothing beige and cream decor should have at least added a semblance of calm to the situation.

But nope.

I sat across from Becca and Cam, Malcolm at my side, and prayed that I was the only one feeling the cloying tension at the table. We'd ordered and eaten our appetizers, and all the while Becca and Malcolm kept the conversation afloat. As we waited for our main course to arrive, I shifted uncomfortably under the silence that had fallen over the group.

Since the moment I'd arrived with Malcolm, I'd been desperately avoiding looking at Cam. He'd been on my mind all day, and I swear my pulse had not slowed since discovering he was our new neighbor. All the worst scenarios played out in my head. Cam hearing my mum, Cam discovering why my mum was so bloody noisy sometimes, Cam letting it slip to someone important to me . . . say, Malcolm.

And yes, if I was honest with myself, I was also worried that Cam's already low opinion of me would be completely obliterated by the truth of my mother's situation. Why I cared what he thought, I couldn't work out. I didn't know him. I didn't really know what kind of man he was.

"I love your dress, Jo. Malcolm has such good taste, doesn't he?" Becca smiled over the top of her wineglass.

I managed a small smile in return, not sure if she was being catty or genuine. "I love your dress too." *I* was being genuine. Becca was wearing a dark gold sequined dress with a high neckline and short skirt. It looked expensive and classy.

Malcolm was dapper as always in a three-piece suit with an emerald green tie to match my dress and Cam . . . well . . . Cam was Cam.

Although I avoided his direct gaze, I couldn't help but check out his attire. His only concession to formal wear was a pair of black suit trousers—black suit trousers he had worn with a printed tee, a worn black leather biker jacket, and his engineer boots. Out of politeness, he'd taken off the leather jacket at the dinner table.

Somehow I couldn't help but admire him. He was dressed the way he wanted to dress and he didn't give a damn what anyone else thought. That's probably why he was so bloody attractive no matter what he wore.

"Your shoes are cute too." Becca grinned. "I was eyeing them as you walked across the room."

Cam snorted, pushing his fork into his napkin in absentminded boredom. His mouth tilted up at the corner. "Malcolm, I just love your tie. It does magnificent things for your eyes."

Malcolm grinned at his drollness and pointed at Cam's tattoos. "I like the art. What does the black script say?"

I leaned forward. I'd wanted to know this from the moment I'd met him.

"'Be Caledonia,'" Becca answered, eyeing Cam's arm in irritation. "And don't bother asking him what the hell that means, because he won't tell you."

I wasn't even surprised anymore at the warm shock of tingles between my legs at the way Cam's lips curled in amusement. Apparently, anything he did turned me on. Our eyes met for a second and I lowered mine quickly, flushing.

"Well, what about the dragon?" Malcolm continued. "Does that have significance?"

Cam nodded. "I was *significantly* drunk when I got it."

"Oh, no." Malcolm laughed. "One of those."

"One of those. I was twenty-two, dating an older woman who happened to be a tattoo artist. We got drunk, I ended up in her chair, she asked me what tattoo I wanted, I said surprise me . . ." He shrugged.

I laughed at the thought of him coming out of the chair to find he had a fierce dragon on his arm. "So she gave you a black-and-purple dragon?"

Cam flashed his knickers-dropping smile at me. "She was big into fantasy. I should have remembered that before I agreed to sit in her chair."

"It's an amazing piece of artwork."

"Well, Anna was an amazing artist."

"Stop, or I might get jealous," Becca interrupted, laughing, but her laugh sounded fake. There was no "might" about it. She took a sip of her wine and turned her direct gaze from her boyfriend to me. "So, Cam told me about the happy coincidence."

Malcolm glanced at me. "What happy coincidence?"

"Oh, Cam's new flat . . . It's in Jo's building. The flat below hers, in fact."

"Really?" Malcolm shot me a teasing look before smirking at Cam. "You'll have to tell me what it's like. Jo refuses to let me near it."

I squirmed under Cam's curious look, his eyes asking, *What in the hell kind of relationship do you two have?* "It's just like anywhere in Edinburgh."

"Very informative, Cam, thank you. You're as bad as Jo."

"Did it take you long to move your things in?" Becca asked just as the second course arrived.

Cam waited until we'd all been served and had begun to tuck in before he replied. "All day."

"You know, it might have taken less time if you'd bothered to get rid of all those comic books."

"I've already said no to that suggestion," Cam replied to her lazily.

Becca shook her head and turned to us, clearly frustrated. "He has hundreds of them in plastic seal, in box after box. It's ridiculous. I know I should get it, because I'm an artist, but I totally don't."

Malcolm nodded at her. "I admit to never understanding the fascination with comics."

"I don't know." I found myself speaking up, thinking about the worlds Cole had created, and the worlds he had shared with me through his love of comics and graphic novels. "I think there's something compelling about them. Most of them are really just about ordinary people rising to the extraordinary. We read books like that every day. These ones just have cool pictures to illustrate what the words can't."

I wanted to avoid Cam's reaction to my opinion, but the heat of his gaze drew mine and when our eyes met, they held. And locked. I felt my breathing grow shallow at his soft smile, his warm, inquisitive eyes. "Joss says your brother draws and writes his own."

The thought of Cole loosened my lips into a more relaxed smile. "He's very talented."

"I'd love to take a look at them sometime."

"I think Cole would like that." I didn't know why I said that. I didn't want Cam anywhere near Cole or my flat. It was the way he was looking at me. Like he saw something he liked and it had nothing to do with my pretty face, long legs, or perky boobs. Words that had tumbled out of my mouth had pleased him and I was basking in his good opinion.

I was such an idiot.

"Jo?"

My gaze was ripped from Cam's at the voice.

No. I tensed. *It can't be.*

I shifted around in my seat and looked up into the eyes of someone very familiar. An unexpected ache flared in my chest as a rush of memories exploded over me.

Oh, God. Was someone just being particularly cruel today? I mean, how many coincidences could a person deal with in one day?

"Callum?" My eyes searched my ex-boyfriend's handsome face. I hadn't seen him for about a year. We'd bumped into each other a number of times since breaking up three years ago but never somewhere where we could talk.

I noted a couple of lines around his eyes that hadn't been there when we'd dated, but they only added to his attractiveness. Not a strand of his silky dark hair was out of place, and his suit was cut exquisitely for his perfect physique. The short brunette at his side was a fresh-faced beauty about my age.

"Jo, it's good to see you." He took a step away from his date and I thought I saw a momentary flicker in his eyes. I stood up from the table and was immediately enveloped in his hug. He hadn't changed his cologne and it sparked sensual memories. Sex with Callum had been the best I'd ever had—nothing kinky or exceptionally adventurous, but earthy and satisfying. Sadly, I wondered if that was what had kept us together so long.

Callum's hands had slid familiarly around my body as he drew me into the hug and now one of them was pressed low on my back and the other just touching my ass. "I've missed you," he murmured, giving me a squeeze.

I laughed nervously, pulling out of his embrace. "I've missed you too."

A throat cleared and I twisted my head to see Malcolm staring up at us, his eyebrows elevated to his hairline.

"Oh, Malcolm, this is Callum Forsyth. Callum, this is my boyfriend, Malcolm Hendry."

Malcolm half stood so he could lean over and shake Callum's hand. Callum eyed him carefully, murmuring a polite "Hello" before sliding his gaze back to me.

"You look amazing."

"Thank you." I flicked a look at his date, wondering if he was going to introduce her. Following my gaze, Callum seemed to suddenly realize she was there. "Oh, this is Meaghan. My fiancée."

Wow, what a way to greet an ex-girlfriend in front of his fiancée. I almost sent him a chiding look. "Nice to meet you."

"You too," she answered politely, smiling sweetly up at Callum.

If I was her I'd have been pissed off if my fiancé had just had his hand on another woman's ass. If I was her I'd be—

Rubbish, Jo. I chastised myself. *You're talking absolute rubbish. If it had been you, you would have pretended you hadn't seen anything so it wouldn't cause an argument and upset him.*

As I stared at my ex-boyfriend and his new fiancée I saw that nothing had changed. She might be short and brunette, but she was likely just another version of me. That look of longing in Callum's eyes perhaps attested to our great sex life and nothing more, because . . . he hadn't *known* me.

I was the perfect girlfriend. Thinking back, I couldn't remember a time we'd ever gotten into a fight. Why? Because I never argued. I always agreed with him or curbed my tongue. I didn't care what we did as long as it made him happy. I was the epitome of congenial blandness.

And when I finally hadn't catered to his every whim, when I'd put my family's needs over his, he'd kicked me to the curb.

A shudder rippled through me and I took a step back from Callum, all those warm memories evaporating. Did Cam see that when he looked at me with Malcolm? Was I like that with Malcolm? We never argued. I always agreed . . . but that was the way to keep him, right? I shot a look down at him and saw he was frowning at me. I wanted this man to propose one day, right? It didn't matter whether he was proposing to the real me or not.

My gut churned.

Right?

It didn't matter.

. . . right?

I looked back at Callum with a tight smile. "I'd better get back to dinner. It was nice seeing you after all this time, and nice meeting you, Meaghan." I nodded at them and slipped back into my chair.

I knew they were gone when Malcolm's gaze returned to me. "Are you okay?"

"Fine."

"Who was that?"

"Ex-boyfriend."

Becca choked on a giggle. "A handsy ex-boyfriend."

"Too handsy," Cam muttered, and I looked up, only for our eyes to clash. I couldn't tell what was going on behind his. Was he angry?

"Yes, well," Malcolm replied tightly now. "He certainly didn't care that his fiancée was standing right next to him."

Did you care? Malcolm, did you care? I shot him a look and almost swore at the way he was looking at Cam. Not Callum. Cam. I frowned, totally confused. "Are you angry?"

With that careful look at Cam, Malcolm smiled at me and slid his arm around the back of my chair. "It's my bed you end up in at the end of the night, sweetheart. I've got nothing to be mad about."

I smiled weakly at him, taken aback by his uncharacteristic comment, and then chanced another look at Cam. His plate seemed to hold a great deal of interest for him, and since I couldn't read his eyes, I read his body. His jaw was locked tight, his fist was curled around his fork until his knuckles were white, and his shoulders had tensed.

Cam was mad now?

Jesus, what were we playing at with each other?

CHAPTER 10

"Where are you going?" Malcolm slid his arm around my waist and halted my progress out of his bed.

I grew still, confused. This was the part at the end of the night when I always left.

"Stay. Stay with me tonight."

Dinner had been a strange affair after Callum's appearance. Malcolm seemed off, his behavior taking a surprising turn as he acted both cocky and proprietary toward me, and Becca's mood had soured along with Cam's. I was grateful when Malcolm called it quits, taking me home to his flat. However, as soon as we were in the door, he was on me, his kisses hard and demanding, his need immediate and intense.

We ended up having sex on his living room couch. It was the first time we'd had sex outside of his bed.

I wanted to find it exciting, but it hadn't been. It had felt like a claiming, and with my mind all over the place, it was not a claiming I'd been into. After months of praying for this moment, I couldn't believe I was questioning whether I wanted it or not.

Malcolm had carried to me to his bed after the couch sex, where he'd made love to me tenderly, sweetly . . . but no matter how much I tried, I couldn't switch my brain off, my thoughts buzzing around in my head like too many trolleys in one supermarket aisle—they were relevant, but they weren't going anywhere that made sense.

"I feel like you're someplace else tonight." Malcolm tugged on my waist, pulling me closer. "I'd feel better if you stayed, but only if you want to."

I took a deep breath, trying to remind myself that this was exactly what I wanted. So Malcolm didn't know me as well as he thought he did. That was a good thing. And anyway, Cole was staying at Jamie's. The only one I had to worry about was Mum, and really that was just a case of hoping she didn't burn down the flat.

I relaxed, cuddling into Malcolm. "Okay."

He wrapped his arms tighter around me, stroking my arm soothingly. "I wish you'd tell me what's wrong."

I tensed. "Nothing is wrong."

"You keep saying that, but I don't believe you."

I scrambled around for some excuse. "Things are just difficult with Mum at the moment."

"You could let me help."

At his kindness, I melted against him, pressing a tender kiss to his throat. "You are helping. Being with you helps."

He kissed my hair. "You weren't with me tonight. Not the first time or the second time. And altogether that would be the third time."

Oh, God. He knew I hadn't come again. If sex with me was terrible, would Malcolm dump me? I tensed.

"I'm not criticizing. I'm worried." He pulled away from me and tipped my chin up so he could look into my eyes. "I care about you, Jo. I hope you care about me."

I nodded quickly, sincerely. "I do care about you. It's just been a difficult few weeks, but I promise it's going to get better."

He pressed a soft kiss to my lips and snuggled us down under his duvet. "Let's start with getting you a proper sleep. You work too hard."

I held on to him, letting his patience and kindness act as a balm to my harried nerves. I was just drifting off when he said quietly, "You seem to get on okay with Cam?"

My eyes popped open at the question. "Not really."

"Hmm." His hand slid down to cup my hip, pulling my body into his. "I'm not sure about him. I don't like the way he looks at you. And I don't like that he's living in such close proximity to you."

My body wanted to grow tense at the suspicion in Malcolm's voice, and it took everything I had to remain relaxed. His behavior tonight had been so strange. "You were a little off tonight. I thought it was because of Callum's appearance . . ."

Malcolm grunted. "No. You were uncomfortable around him. Anyone could see that. No, that didn't bother me."

However, Cam had. Malcolm's slight possessiveness tonight and the claiming of me on his living room couch hadn't been about Callum. It had all been about Cam. He'd seen the way Cam had been looking at me and it had ignited his inner Alpha. And although Callum had touched my ass in front of Malcolm, that hadn't bothered him because I hadn't reacted.

But Cam had bothered him.

Because I *had* reacted.

I nuzzled against Malcolm, trying to force my pulse to slow. "He rubs me the wrong way too." I tried to cover up my attraction, making excuses for my response to Cam. "To be honest, we barely speak a word to each other at work."

I hadn't even realized Malcolm had been tense until I felt his muscles relax against me. "I'm going to see about getting him a job in graphic design. For Becca's sake."

Yeah. For Becca's sake.

It took a while for me to fall asleep after that conversation.

My eyes slammed open, my heart beating hard against my ribs. I had sensed something was wrong.

Where was I? I tried to blink the fog of sleep from my eyes so I could focus.

Why was I so bloody warm?

Malcolm. I was in his room.

My eyes traveled down to the arm that was slung over my waist, and I turned my head over my shoulder to see Malcolm sleeping soundly behind me.

My eyelashes fluttered against the bright light streaming in through the crack in his blinds.

What time was it?

Lifting his arm as gently as possible, I eased out of the bed and tiptoed over to where my watch lay on his black lacquered Oriental cabinet.

"Balls," I hissed, gaping at the time. It was past noon. On a Sunday. Cole would have come home early in hopes that I was taking him to the Nicholses' for Sunday dinner. And I wasn't there. Where was my phone? Where was my dress?

Shit, shit, shit.

"Jo?" Malcolm mumbled and my gaze flew back to the bed, where he was staring at me sleepily. "Where are you going?"

"I slept in. I'm supposed to be home for Cole and my mum by now."

"Fuck," he mumbled. "What time is it?"

"Quarter past twelve."

"It feels earlier."

"Well, it's not," I replied, exasperated. I wasn't quite sure at whom. I dashed across the room and planted a quick peck on his cheek before hurrying away. "I'll phone you later!" I called, grabbing my dress from his bedroom floor. I found my shoes, knickers, bra, and bag in his living room, and as I hurriedly dressed I called for a taxi on speakerphone.

It was there in no time, and I dashed out of the duplex, shivering against the blast of cold air coming off the water, before I dived into the warm confines of the cab. I took the opportunity to check my messages.

I had one from Joss asking if I would be at lunch today.

And, bloody hell, I also had a text from Cole that he'd sent hours ago. I'd missed it. It seemed Jamie's parents had had a huge argument, so Cole had gotten a taxi home last night.

Balls!

In the flustered, muddled mess I was in, Sunday lunch was not a good idea. I texted Joss back to let her know we'd be skipping it this week.

When the taxi pulled up to the flat, I tore up those stairs in my five-inch heels, not caring about the noise clacking like nails against steel all the way through the building. I shot a glower at Cam's door as I passed, and then threw myself up the last few stairs, bursting through my front door, only to be welcomed by the sound of Cole's laughter. Laughter that was followed by deep masculine laughter.

"Cole?" I stormed from the hall into the living room and stopped dead in my tracks.

My little brother was sitting on the floor, surrounded by his drawings, laughing up into Cameron MacCabe's face. Cole's eyes were lit up in a way I hadn't seen in a long time, and for a moment all I could think was how much it hurt that he didn't look that happy more often.

And then the fact that Cam was in my flat registered.

Cam was in my *flat*.

My flat, where my mother *lived*.

I felt sick.

"Jo." Cole jumped to his feet, his eyes dimming. "I was worried."

"I'm sorry." I shook my head, gesturing with my phone. "I didn't get your text until twenty minutes ago."

"It's okay." He shrugged. "Everything's okay."

Cam stood up, smiling at Cole. That expression completely dissipated when he turned to face me, the softness melting into absolute nothingness. "Jo."

"Cam, what are you doing here?" I asked breathlessly, my eyes darting toward the hall, thinking of Mum hidden away in her room. Maybe I could get him out before she made an appearance.

He strode past Cole, patting his shoulder almost protectively, before moving toward me. "Let's talk. Out in the hall."

Dumbfounded, I watched him pass me.

"Now, Jo."

I flinched at the demand in his voice, annoyance taking over my bemusement. How dared he speak to me that way? I wasn't a bloody dog. I narrowed my eyes on Cole. "What happened?"

"Johanna, now," Cam snapped.

My spine straightened. He might as well have whacked me across the ass with a belt. I gave Cole a look that promised retribution for letting Cam into the flat, and then I turned on my heel and followed Cam out into the hall. He'd walked down the first flight of stairs.

I threw my hands on my hips, giving him attitude as I glared down at him. "Well?"

"Would you come here?" His authoritative voice drew my gaze to his features—they were tight, his blue eyes blazing sparks at me. Someone was seriously pissed off. "I'm not shouting up there to you."

With a huff of annoyance I tore off the heels that were hurting me and threw them back into the flat. My bare feet touched the icy concrete as I hurried down the stairs toward him, and that seemed to wake me up. It also made me fully aware of what a disheveled mess I was. "What? Why were you in my flat?"

Cam leaned into me, our faces almost on eye level. That soft curl of his upper lip was gone again, pinched against his lower lip. His gorgeous cobalt eyes were bloodshot today, and he looked even more tired than he had yesterday. Despite his obvious and mysterious irritation with me, I couldn't help but want to fall against him, feel those strong arms wrap around me, and inhale the scent of Cam and bay rum.

"Maybe first you'd like to tell me what kind of sister leaves her wee brother alone all night to deal with an alcoholic mother who's a bit too quick to raise a hand against him. Hmm? What kind of sister would leave a kid to that so she can spread her legs for someone who probably doesn't know the first thing about her," he hissed, his eyes flashing with disgust. "Just when I think I'm completely wrong about you, you prove me right with your utter selfishness."

I couldn't breathe.

What did he mean, she was quick to raise her hand against Cole?

"I had to help Cole out last night. I heard shouting coming from the flat and I went up to see if you were okay. You were gone. And he was left alone with *that*." Cam couldn't have looked more disappointed in me if he'd tried. In fact, he seemed enraged by the disappointment of me. "You should be fucking ashamed."

Words failed me.

I could feel the tears welling up inside me and I pushed them back, refusing to let him make me cry. His attack seemed to boomerang around my head and it took me a moment to gather myself, to come to a decision about how to react.

My first thought was of Cole.

What does Cam mean? Fear and a sleeping anger burned in my stomach.

As for Cam, he was going to think what he liked about me. He had a proven record of jumping to conclusions and ripping me apart. As much as I was attracted to him, I knew without a doubt that I wouldn't be able to like this man. He so easily hurt me.

And he didn't deserve a response.

I turned away with what I hoped was a quiet dignity, but Cam wouldn't even give me that.

His grip pinched my upper arm as he tugged me back to face him, and the blood drained from my face as the forceful aggression triggered memories.

"Useless little bitch, give me that." Dad grasped my arm, his fingers bruising as he pulled me toward him, ripping the TV remote from my hand.

I froze in fear, anticipating the next blow.

"Always in the fucking way." His breath stank of beer as he leaned into my face, his own face red with alcohol and anger. His eyes flashed. "Dinnae you look at me like that!" His hand raised and I braced myself, my bladder letting go in fright before he backhanded me, sending me flying against the floor, my cheek blazing with red-hot pain that stung my eyes and nose. I felt wetness soak my pants. "Get out of my sight before I give you a proper leathering."

I whimpered, trying to see through the tears.

"Get up!" He moved toward me and I scrambled along the floor . . .

"Let me go," I whispered in panic. "Please let me go."

Cam's hand immediately fell from me. "Jo?"

I shook my head, my eyes refocusing on him. I could see he'd paled too, the disgust gone from his eyes and replaced with a frustrated concern.

"Jo, I'm not going to hurt you."

I made a scoffing sound. Too late. "Stay away from me, Cam," I managed shakily and this time when I turned to leave him, he let me.

I found Cole standing in the hallway, and from the undiluted anger in his boyish features I knew he'd heard every word of my tongue-lashing from Cam. He shook his head, his fists clenched at his side. "I'm sorry," he said as I shut the door behind me. "He helped with Mum and then . . . he was interested in my work, my comics. It was stupid. I thought he was cool. I'm really sorry, Jo."

I leaned back against the door, still trembling. I had questions and I wasn't sure I really wanted to hear the answers to them. "Why did you let him in?"

Cole heaved a sigh, running a hand through his hair. "I got home late and I must have woken her up. She was in one of her moods. She was yelling and I couldn't get her to stop. And then I heard a banging at the door and then Cam was calling your name. He was going to wake up the whole building, so I answered the door to see who the hell he was."

My jaw clenched. Cam knew the truth about Mum.

Could my life get any crappier? "Well, now he knows everything about me."

As if remembering what he'd overheard Cam saying to me, Cole's eyes narrowed in vengeful slits. "He knows fuck all."

"Language."

Cole just stared at me, and while he did I searched his face for marks. Was that redness on his cheekbone or just the light? My chest tightened with the weight of my emotions. "He says . . ." I struggled, flexing my shaking fingers. "He says she hit you."

"It was nothing." Cole shrugged.

He *shrugged* and my entire world tilted dangerously. "Mum hit you? Has she hit you before?" I felt the angry tears prick the corner of my eyes and Cole caught sight of them.

This time when he answered me, his mouth quivered a little. "Just slaps, Jo. It's nothing I can't handle."

I clutched my stomach, feeling sick, and the tears spilled over my lids.

No. No! NO!

I sobbed and fell back against the door.

I thought I'd done everything that was in my power to protect him from the physical and emotional pain of a parent's abusive hands. And it seemed I hadn't done nearly enough.

"Jo." I felt Cole approach me tentatively. "This is why I didn't say anything."

"You should." I tried to breathe through my tears. "You should ha-have told me."

His arms came around me and as so often of late, I found myself being comforted by my baby brother instead of the other way around.

Eventually the tears stopped and I moved to the living room, where Cole brought me a cup of tea. As the hot drink spilled into my stomach, it seemed to stoke the flames of my seething rage against my mother.

It had been one thing to neglect Cole.

It was another thing entirely to have physically abused him.

"How many times?"

"Jo . . ."

"Cole, how many times?"

"It's just been the past year. A few slaps here and there. She says I look like Dad. I haven't hit her back, though, Jo, I promise."

I remembered the muttered comments of late about Cole's resemblance to Dad—the bitterness in those comments, the blame, the resentment. I should have seen it. Worse, I remembered a bruise he'd had around his right eye and cheekbone months ago. He'd told me Jamie had clipped him when they'd gotten overly exuberant during a video game fight. I stared at his cheek. "The bruise?"

He knew what I was talking about. His gaze dropped to the floor, his shoulders hunched. "She was hysterical. She kept hitting at me and I was trying to get away without hurting her back, but I fell against the corner of the kitchen unit."

Growing up with an aggressive father had made me skittish of confrontation, of arguments, of anger. I became passive. I didn't anger easily. Until I met Cam.

Even then, I didn't think I'd ever felt the kind of rage I was feeling now.

Cole had always felt like my kid. He was *my* kid.

And I hadn't protected him.

"I'm going to watch some TV for a while," I told him quietly, trying to deal with this new information.

"Jo, I'm really okay."

"Yeah."

He sighed and got up. "I take it we're not going to the Nicholses' today."

"Nope."

"Okay. Well . . . I'll be in my room if you need me."

I don't know how long I sat there staring blankly at the television, vacillating between walking into my mother's room and smothering her with a pillow and just packing Cole's and my bags and running for it, hoping that Mum's threats were empty. At a sound behind me, I blinked and turned around. Nothing was there.

I thought I'd heard the front door open.

Now I was going crazy.

Exhausted by the tumult of emotions I'd gone through in the last twenty-four hours, I flopped back against the couch and closed my eyes. I needed to shower and change, but I was afraid to move toward my mum's room. I was afraid that passive old me was about to lose my cool—big-time.

A while later, the worst happened.

Mum's door creaked open and I sat up, my muscles growing taut as I watched her appear in the hall. Her hair was all over the place and she was clutching her fuzzy pink robe around her as she shuffled into the kitchen holding an empty bottle and a mug.

Blood whooshed in my ears as my body stood up with no command from me to do so. It was as if I was stuck inside my head but no longer in control of what my limbs did. With my heart slamming against my ribs, I followed her into the kitchen.

She turned at the sounds of my footsteps, and leaned against the counter, putting the mug down. Her smile was weak as she said, "Hi, sweetie."

Looking at her, all I could recall was the utter humiliation I'd felt at the hands of my father with his quick fists and hateful words. I lacked any self-worth because of that man.

How dared she try to do the same to Cole—try to undo all I'd done to protect him from ever having to feel that way? It was a singular kind of pain to have your parents find you worthless, find you so unlovable that they could hurt what nature told them they should protect. I'd never wanted Cole to feel that pain . . .

. . . and this bitch had gone and done it.

With an animalistic cry of deep, gnawing rage, I flew at her. My body slammed hers against the counter, her head snapping back against the upper kitchen unit, and I took satisfaction in her wince of pain.

How does it feel? How does it FEEL?

My hand reached up to grip her loosely but threateningly by the throat and she stared into my face with round, appalled eyes.

I leaned into her, trembling from my reaction, shaking with betrayal.

Yes, betrayal.

She'd betrayed us for gin.

She'd betrayed me by hurting what I loved most.

I sought to catch my breath, my chest rising and falling rapidly, and I flexed my hand around her throat. "If you ever . . ." I shook my head in disbelief. "If you *ever* touch Cole again . . . I will kill you." I pushed against her. "I will fucking *kill* you!"

Her eyes flared and she nodded rapidly, gulping in fear. I glared into her eyes, somehow unable to remove my hand from her throat.

I felt a touch on my arm. "Jo?"

Slowly but surely, the world came back to me and I shuddered, relaxing my grip as I turned to my left.

Cole stood at my side, the color leached from his face, staring at me as if he'd never seen me before.

Oh, God.

I looked over his shoulder only to find Cam standing in the kitchen doorway, his expression grim.

Oh, God.

When I turned, Mum was cowering against the kitchen counter.

What am I doing?

Shame flooded me . . . and I ran.

I flew past Cole, pushed past Cam, ignoring him as he called out to me. Throwing myself out the door, I hurried down the stairs in my bare feet, not knowing where I was going, just knowing I had to get away from the person I'd just become in that kitchen.

Something gripped my arm, wrenching me to a stop.

Cam's face blurred before me, and I pulled away from him, trying to escape, but his arms seemed to be everywhere. I struck out at him, grunting and swearing at him, and the more I struggled, the more soothing his voice became.

"Cam, let me go," I pleaded, exhaustion draining the strength from my limbs. "Please." The sob broke before I could stop it, and then I was crying, my hard, pained, loud, tear-filled cries muffled quickly against his throat as he enfolded me in his warm arms.

I fell against him, letting him hold me, my tears soaking his T-shirt and his skin as his arms hugged me tight against him.

"Let it out," he whispered comfortingly in my ear. "Let it out."

_____

In their own time my jagged tears stopped, and my breathing became easier as Cam's body heat and strong embrace provided a balm against the pain I was in.

It occurred to me that I'd had an emotional breakdown in front of the one person in the world I hadn't ever wanted to.

And he had been kind.

I pulled back, abruptly letting go of Cam, but his hands still clasped my upper arms lightly. Not quite able to meet his gaze yet, I looked to the left, and movement drew my attention. The gasp caught in my throat as I tilted my head up to find Cole standing on the stairs, deep lines furrowing his forehead and his eyes dark with concern.

Cam's hands rubbed up and down my shoulders in a gesture of comfort and I could no longer avoid his gaze. Our eyes met and I felt overwhelmed with emotion.

Humiliation.

Shame.

Anger.

Gratitude.

Anxiety.

Fear.

"I'm sorry," I mumbled, my eyes sliding back up to Cole. "I better take Cole inside."

"No."

Surprised, I found my gaze drawn back to Cam. His expression was troubled but determined as he shook his head at me. "Come into my flat. I'll make you some coffee."

"I have to talk to Cole." My little brother had witnessed my attack on our mother. I was terrified of what he must think of me, and I needed to somehow explain.

"You can talk to Cole later. First you're going to take a minute for yourself."

I thought of Cole in the flat alone with Mum and my stomach flipped. "He's not going back in there without me."

"Here." Cam finally let go of me so he could pull his wallet out of the back pocket of his jeans. I watched warily as he removed a twenty-pound note and held it up to Cole. "You think you could phone some pals to come and join you at a movie at the Omni Centre?"

Eyes pinning Cam in place, Cole took the stairs down to us with an air of authority that stunned me. Every day was another progression into manhood—especially days like this. When he reached Cam, his eyes were full of understanding and maturity, and he took the note carefully. "Aye, I can do that."

"But—" My protest was cut off by Cole, who shook his head at me like a parent to his child. My mouth slammed shut more from surprise than anything else, and I watched with a mixture of pride and worry as he narrowed his eyes on Cam.

"Can I trust you with her?"

Cam heaved a deep sigh, but he answered Cole as if he was speaking to a man on equal footing. "I know I deserve that, but I promise from now on I'll treat your sister with the respect she deserves."

I was truly dumbfounded by the exchange. The fact that I was already a shell-shocked mess didn't make it any easier to understand what was passing between them, and it was probably why I allowed Cole to take money that I knew Cam must need and walk out of our building. That's also why I let myself be manhandled into Cam's flat.

His flat, like ours, was a rental, and although decorated in neutral colors it was definitely in need of a repaint. Cam's furniture was practical and comfortable, with very little thought to style, except for his huge black suede couch and matching armchair. I found myself ushered to the couch and I sat down numbly, staring around at the space that was still cluttered with packing boxes.

"Tea? Coffee?"

I shook my head. "Water, please."

When Cam returned with a glass of water for me and a coffee for him, I watched him settle into the armchair just across from me and my heart began to gallop.

What was I doing here? Why was Cam being so nice all of a sudden? What did he want? I should get back up to the flat and face the consequences.

"Jo." His deep, raspy voice brought my chin down. I'd been staring at the ceiling and hadn't really even realized it. When I looked at Cam, I felt my body tense. His eyes were searching my face as if he was desperate to dive inside me and unearth all my secrets. My breath caught at the intensity of his look. "What the hell happened to your life, Jo? How did you get here?"

A bubble of bitter laughter escaped from my lips and I shook my head at him. I asked myself that question every day. "I don't trust you, Cameron, so why would I tell you anything?"

Regret replaced his concern, and there was no denying the genuine remorse in his eyes. "That's fair. And I can't even begin to tell you how shit I feel about going off on you about Cole. He came down here to set me straight." He suddenly threw me a rueful grin that kicked my heart into high gear. "I swear I thought he was going to take a swing at me."

That wasn't particularly good news to my ears, which Cam must have sensed, because he grew somber quickly. "You never have to worry about that kid being disappointed in you, Jo. He loves you to bits. And what we just witnessed in the kitchen—that's nothing for you to be ashamed of. That was a mum protecting her kid. Because that's what you are to him. More of a mum than a sister—I realize that now." He made a sound heavy with regret. "I feel awful about the way I spoke to you. I feel shit that you found out about your mum hitting Cole that way."

My eyes dropped to the floor and I couldn't speak. I couldn't respond to his apology—partly because the ungracious side of me was thinking, *Good. I'm glad you feel like shit.*

"You need to talk to someone. Out in the hall, that was because you've been bottling up God knows what for months . . . years? Jo, please talk to me."

Instead I took a sip of water, my fingers trembling—from adrenaline or my emotional fear of Cam, I couldn't tell you.

"Fine." Movement from Cam drew my gaze back to him and he was leaning forward in his chair, his expression seeming more open than I'd ever seen it. "Maybe it'll help if you get to know me a bit better."

My response was a humorless snort. "What? Were you a therapist in another life?"

Cam made a face. "I've never been accused of that before. You know, usually it's the woman asking me to open up to her? The first one I'm actually interested in hearing about and she's shutting me down. Not good for my ego." He gave me a coaxing smile and I remembered the night I'd first seen him, watching him give Becca that smile and thinking I'd do anything that smile asked of me.

Funny how a couple of weeks could change it all.

Cam saw my eyes darken and his expression fell. "Okay, Jo, ask me anything. Anything you want to know."

I raised an eyebrow. *Anything?* So he was serious about wanting to help, was he? Well, I knew one way of finding out. My eyes fell to the

tattoo on his arm, the one with the black script that read BE CALEDO-
NIA. Becca's lilting voice echoed in my head . . .

"*. . . don't bother asking him what the hell that means, because he won't
tell you.*"

"Jo?"

I looked up from the tattoo to his rugged face. "What does the ink
mean? 'Be Caledonia'?"

The left side of his mouth tilted up as his eyes glittered at me.
"Well played."

I was already braced for disappointment. There was no way Cam
cared enough about me to divulge the secret behind his tattoo. My
question would prove that his interest was mere curiosity and then I
could go back to hating that he knew more about my life than he
should.

So when he relaxed back into his armchair, his eyes never leaving
mine, I was more than taken aback when he replied, "It's something my
dad said to me."

"Your dad?" I asked a little breathlessly, still astonished that he'd
offered up an answer. What did that mean?

Cam nodded, taking on a faraway look that told me he was back
somewhere in his memories. "I grew up in Longniddry with a doting
mum and a caring dad. I've never met two people who loved each
other more, or who loved their kid more than they loved me. Not to
mention that my dad's brother, my uncle I once told you about, was
like a second father to me. He was always there for me. We were a
close-knit group. When I hit my teens, though, I went through what
everybody goes through. You're trying to find out who you are and
you're struggling to stay true to that person when the people around
you seem so different from you. You're asking yourself, is it me? Pu-
berty makes you a really moody fucker, but for me it was only exacerbated when my parents sat me down when I was sixteen and told me
I was adopted."

That I had not been expecting. My mouth dropped open, "Cam . . . ," I muttered sympathetically, drawing his sharp gaze.

He gave me a small shake of his head, as if to say, "I'm fine now."

"It messed me up then. Suddenly, there were two people in the world who had abandoned me, who, for whatever reason, didn't love me enough to want to keep me. And who were they? What were they like? If Mum and Dad weren't my real parents, then who the fuck was I? The way I laughed had nothing to do with Dad like I thought it did . . . Their dreams, their talents . . . the possibility of all their kindness, intelligence, and passions passing on to me was gone. Who was I?" He gave me a sad smirk. "You don't realize how important it is to feel like you belong somewhere, that you're part of a family legacy, until you don't have it. It's a huge part of your identity growing up. It's just a huge part of your identity full stop, and I guess I was in quite a bit of pain for a while after I found out the truth.

"I acted like a dick—skipped school, got high, almost destroyed my chances of graduating with the qualifications I needed to get into the College of Art at Edinburgh Uni to do graphic design. I insulted my mum, ignored my dad. I constantly thought about finding my birth parents. I couldn't think of anything else, and in the interim I seemed intent on destroying everything I had been, in the hopes of finding who I reckoned I was supposed to be.

"A few months later I took my dad's car for a joyride. Luckily, the police didn't catch me, but a wall did. I totaled the car and my dad had to come out and get me. I was drunk. Shaken up. And once my dad finished verbally annihilating me for putting my life and everyone else on the road's life in danger, he took me for a walk on the beach. And what he said to me that day changed my life."

"Be Caledonia," I replied softly.

"Be Caledonia." Cam grinned, love in his eyes for the man who was his dad. "He said that Caledonia wasn't a name we'd given to our land, to Scotland, but the name the Romans had. I was used to him spouting off random stuff about history, so I thought I was in for some boring lecture. But what he said that day changed everything for me—he put it all in perspective.

"You know, the world will always try to make you into who it wants you to be. People, time, events, they'll all try to carve away at you and make you think you don't know who you are. But it doesn't matter who they try to make you, or what name they try to give you. If you stay true, you can chip off all their machinations and you're still you underneath it all. Be Caledonia. It might be the name someone else gave the land, but it didn't change the land. Better yet, we embraced the name, keeping it but never changing for it. Be Caledonia. I had it inked on my arm when I was eighteen to remind me every day of what he said." He smiled ruefully. "If I'd known how many people were going to ask me what it meant, I wouldn't have put it somewhere so bloody visible."

My eyes had welled up again as I watched Cam's face relax with humor. My chest ached with a fullness I'd only ever rarely felt, and I realized that it was gladness. I was glad for him. I was glad he had that kind of love in his life. "He sounds like a great dad." I knew if I'd had that kind of love in my life I would have turned out so differently.

Cam nodded, his eyes lifting to smile into mine. "I have a wonderful mum and dad." His gaze drifted upward to the ceiling, and even at that angle I could see it darken. "Sometimes it takes days like today to remind me of that."

"You're going to phone them as soon as I leave, aren't you?"

He threw me a shy grin, and my chest squeezed at the little splotch of color high on his cheeks. "Probably," he muttered.

"I'm happy for you, Cam." I nervously straightened the dress I was still wearing from last night's dinner. "I can't imagine what it's like to wonder who your real parents are. But to a certain extent I understand feeling abandoned by the two people in the whole world who are supposed to want me. It's not the best feeling, is it? I would have swapped what I had for what you had in a second."

Cam's eyes pinned me to the couch again. "And what exactly did you have?"

My hands trembled as I smoothed my dress over my legs again. "You know, the only person who knows anything real about my life is Joss."

"Not Malcolm? Not Ellie?"

"No. Just Joss. I don't want anyone else to know."

"That is a helluva lot to be carrying around by yourself."

"Cam." I leaned forward, my watery eyes searching his face, my pulse speeding as I struggled to come to a decision on whether to trust him or not. "I . . ."

"Jo." He leaned forward too and my whole body tensed under his sober regard. "What I just told you, about the adoption and about the tattoo—only a handful of people in this world know about them. Mum, Dad, Peetie, and Nate. And now you. You and I are starting over today. I'm not some asshole who has judged you over and over again and got you wrong every single time. Trust me. Please."

"Why?" I shook my head, completely confused by his interest. I mean, I knew that we were sexually attracted to each other, even if we wouldn't admit it out loud, but this was something else. This was different . . . more intense—and I hadn't thought anything could be more intense than the way my body came alive around Cam.

He gave a jerk of his head. "Honestly, I don't know. All I do know is that I've never treated anyone the way I've treated you, and I've never met anyone who deserved it less. I like you, Jo. And whether you want to admit it or not, you need a friend."

Those bloody tears swam toward the corners of my eyes again, threatening to spill over. I sucked in a deep breath, looking away from him, my eyes catching on the large desk in the corner of the room. A drawing board was propped up on it. There was a sketch on it, but I couldn't make out what it was. I squinted at it as I procrastinated over whether or not I should tell him anything.

"Where's your dad, Johanna? Why are you raising Cole?"

"I don't know where he is." I glanced back at him, wondering if my eyes were as haunted as I felt inside. "He was abusive."

Cam's jaw immediately clenched, and I saw his fingers grip his coffee mug tighter. "To you and Cole?"

I shook my head. "I protected Cole. Cole doesn't even remember him or know that he was abusive to me."

Cam swore under his breath, dropping his gaze so I wouldn't be subjected to the full force of his anger. Somehow that anger felt nice. It was nice to have someone else feel it. What I was telling him, not even Joss knew. "How long?"

"Since I was little." The words seemed to pry open my lips and spill down my chin. Although confused, I didn't dare stop them. "Until I was twelve. He was aggressive, violent and stupid. That's definitely the way to sum up Murray Walker. He spent a good time away from the house, which allowed us to breathe a little, but when he was there he'd hit me and Mum. But Cole . . . I always got Cole out of the way when Dad was in a mood or I'd distract him from Cole so he'd go for me instead."

"Jesus, Jo . . ."

"Cole was two. Dad could have killed him with one blow, so it was all I could do."

"What happened to him? Your dad?" Cam almost spat the word, as if the man had no right to carry the title. And he didn't really, did he?

I curled my lip in disgust as I thought about Dad's greatest moment of stupidity. "Assault and armed robbery. He got ten years in Barlinnie Prison. I don't know if he served all his time, or when he got out—all I know is that by the time he did we'd already left Paisley with no forwarding address. Mum never told anyone from the old life where we were going. Neither did I."

"Was your mum always the way she is?"

"She drank, but not like this. She still functioned."

"I take it she started after your dad went to prison?"

"No." I scoffed bitterly, knowing exactly why she'd started. "Not that she was a great mum or anything, but she was better than she is now. No." I closed my eyes against the dull pain in my chest. "She went downhill for another reason.

"Growing up, I had one person in my life I trusted. My uncle Mick. He wasn't my real uncle. He was my dad's best friend when they were kids. Uncle Mick was a good guy, though. Straight as an arrow—made a good living as a painter and decorator. But he was friends with my asshole of a father. I never really found out why they were friends, but I got the impression they went through a lot together as kids. Although Dad pissed him off, Uncle Mick couldn't seem to let go. Whenever he could, he'd check in with us. He used to take me to work with him sometimes." The ache intensified as I felt the loss of him again. "He didn't know Dad hit me. Dad was careful in front of him. I think he was always a little wary of Uncle Mick. That changed when I was twelve." I shuddered as the memories washed over me.

"It was a Saturday and Dad was drinking while watching the football. Mum was at work. I made the mistake of walking past the television at an important point in the game. He backhanded me and I was on the floor . . ." I sucked in a breath, staring at Cam's carpet, feeling the pain all over again. I'd never felt anything like it. The bite, the sting, the heat . . . "He took off his belt and hit me . . . I can still see the look on his face, like I wasn't human to him, let alone his daughter." I shook myself and lifted my gaze to Cam's. He had grown pale, his features stretched taut with emotion he was trying to control. "I guess I was lucky that Uncle Mick turned up when he did. He heard me screaming and came crashing in. Uncle Mick was a big guy and, well . . . he put Dad in hospital that day. He was arrested, but neither of them mentioned Dad's assault on me for fear the social services would get involved. Dad just dropped the charges and Uncle Mick walked away with a fine.

"Dad disappeared. Next thing we heard was that he'd been jailed for armed robbery. While he was inside, Uncle Mick was around a lot more, helping out. For the first time in my life I had an almost twenty-four/seven parent who really cared. He even had a good influence on Mum." I huffed, the resentment welling up again. "Too good."

Cam guessed. "Your mum was in love with him."

I nodded. "I think she always had been, but as far as I know nothing ever happened. Uncle Mick cared about her but not like that."

"So what happened?"

Someone took him away from me. "Just a little over a year later, Uncle Mick left for America."

"America?"

"Years ago he'd had an affair with an American student. She was studying at Glasgow University for a year and they were together for a good few months. But she left and Mick didn't follow. Fourteen years later Mick was contacted by his thirteen-year-old daughter, a daughter he never knew he had. He flew over there to meet her, get DNA testing rolling, hash it out, I imagine, with his kid's mum. He came back for a while, but the results came in and the kid was his . . . so he left everything behind to go be with her."

Seeming to sense how much that had ripped me up inside, Cam whispered, "I'm sorry, Jo."

I nodded, feeling the emotion claw at my throat. "He told me he would have taken me and Cole if he could have." I coughed, trying to force the pain back down. "He e-mailed me, but I stopped responding and eventually his e-mails stopped."

"And your mum fell apart?"

"Aye. I think he broke her heart. She started drinking more than normal, but things didn't get really bad until we moved here. She was fine for a while, had a good job, but then she put her back out of commission and couldn't work. So she got drunk instead, and then she got drunker. Until eventually she wasn't even a functioning alcoholic."

"And you can't take Cole away from her because he's not legally yours and if the social services ever found out about your family situation, they'd most likely put him into care rather than let you have him . . ."

"Or worse . . . they'd contact my dad."

"Fuck, Jo."

"Yeah, you can say that again. I dropped out of school at sixteen, got a job, tried to keep us afloat, but it was really rough. There were days it took everything I had to buy Cole a tin of beans. We were checking down the sides of the couch for lost coins, measuring out how much milk we were using. It was ridiculous. Then . . . I met someone. He helped me pay the rent and put some money aside for a rainy day. However, he got bored after six months, so it wasn't really all I'd thought it had been."

"But it showed you a new life. You started dating men with money to get by?" Cam's body tensed as he asked the question.

I turned my head from him and even though there was no longer any censure in his question, I still felt ashamed. "I've never dated a guy I wasn't attracted to, or that I didn't care about." My eyes found his and I prayed for him to believe me. "I cared about Callum. I care about Malcolm."

Holding up his hands, Cam stopped my worries with a gentle look. "I am not judging you. I promise."

I raised an eyebrow.

He grunted. "Anymore. Or ever again." He shook his head, his brows dipped in consternation. "You must have thought I was such a self-righteous prick."

I chuckled. "I do believe I may have actually called you that."

His eyes brightened. "Good girl, by the way," he said approvingly. "Giving me what for."

I smiled a little shyly. "I usually hate confrontation, but I did quite enjoy putting you in your place."

My words had the opposite effect than what I'd intended. He didn't laugh. Instead he was grave. "Earlier in the hall, I grabbed your arm . . ."

I looked away as I remembered my reaction. "I tend to freeze if someone gets aggressive with me. Just a reflex from years with my dad."

"I didn't mean to be aggressive."

"I know."

"You know I'm a martial artist."

As my eyes ran over his lean but roped physique, I was so busy checking him out that I didn't call him on his seemingly abrupt change of subject. "Makes sense."

His answering smile was more than a little cocky and I rolled my eyes, making him laugh. He shook his head, trying to return to being serious. "Judo. Nate and I both go to classes. You should come with me, Jo. Learning self-defense might help—it could give you back a little control."

"I don't know." My stomach jumped uneasily at the thought. "I work during the day Monday to Wednesday anyway. I don't have a lot of spare time."

I had surprised him again. "You have another job?"

I gave a huff of laughter, thinking I understood his surprise. "Believe it or not, I never ask Malcolm for anything he gives me. I accept gifts he chooses to give me, but that still leaves me with bills to pay. Plus I have to put money aside for when Cole decides what university he's going to. Oh, speaking of—let me get my purse so I can pay you back the money you just gave Cole."

"Forget it." Cam shook his head, and catching the stubborn tilt to my chin, he narrowed his eyes. "I mean it."

Hmm. I would just have to find a way to pay him back later in such a way that he couldn't say no.

As if he was reading my thoughts, our eyes locked in a battle of wills, and slowly but surely the familiar tension thickened, heat creeping between us. My eyes dipped to his mouth, to that soft, curling upper lip I wanted to nip . . . amongst other things. I wondered what his mouth tasted like, how it would feel brushing butterfly kisses down my neck, tugging my nipple into its heat . . .

My body tightened, fire tingling in my cheeks and between my legs. I snapped my gaze back up and found that Cam's own eyes had darkened, his body coiled with the tension.

I stood up abruptly. "I better go."

Cam smoothly got to his feet as well. "Are you going to be okay going back up there?"

For a while he'd actually managed to make me forget that I'd attacked my mum not too long ago. I found myself shocked all over again. "How do I even . . . ?"

"First . . ." Cam approached me carefully and I had to contain the little shiver of want that rolled over me again when his rough hand grasped my chin to lift my eyes to his. When our eyes met, the pull between us grew stronger. I wanted to curl my nails into his skin, latch on and never let go, and the overwhelming need shook me to my very core. How had it happened that one conversation had changed everything? This Cam in front of me was someone new, someone good, someone I felt close to—closer to than anyone. And I found that I wanted in deeper, not satisfied with merely "close."

The realization made me a little dizzy.

"You get that guilt out of your head," Cam ordered softly. "Don't dare apologize to her. Anyone would have done what you did. Look at what your uncle Mick did when he found out your dad was beating you. It's instinct to protect those we care about. Sometimes instinct makes us do things we'd never imagine we're capable of doing."

"Violence should never be the answer."

"Aye, in a perfect world. But sometimes animals don't understand anything but their own language."

"I don't want Cole to think what I did was right."

"He doesn't," Cam assured me. "What you did was human. He thinks what you did, you did out of love." His hands dropped to curve around my shoulders and he tugged me a little closer, causing my breath to hitch. The expression in his eyes, the one I couldn't quite understand, didn't help my frayed nerves any. "That kid could have been brought up like you—without a parent, without proper care and affection. Jo, you saved him from that. And he bloody well knows it."

I felt the weight of today's revelations settle on me, and I suddenly, desperately, wanted my bed. "Thank you, Cam."

"Nothing you told me leaves this room. I promise."

"Ditto with what you told me." I stepped back, needing a little physical distance from him. Something awful suddenly occurred to me. "I don't know how I'm going to ever be able to leave Cole alone with her again."

"He's a strong kid. He'll be fine."

I blew out a breath. "Yeah, but will I?"

Cam smiled at me as if I was completely clueless. "Jo, you are now officially the strongest woman I know. Have a little faith in yourself."

Silence stretched between us as I processed his words. It was the nicest thing anyone had ever said to me, and I wondered how someone who had been so unpleasant to me could do such a three-sixty. "Why were you really such a dick to me?"

Cam's chin lifted a little, telling me he hadn't expected the blunt question after our "heart-to-heart." "I don't know . . . I just . . ." He ran a hand through his messy hair, his ring glinting in the light. He had such beautiful, masculine hands. "At first when I saw you with Malcolm, I just assumed you were like my uncle's ex-wife."

"Why?"

He grinned and gestured to me. "Because I didn't think a girl like you would be interested in an older guy like Malcolm unless he had money."

"A compliment and insult in one. Well done, Cam."

"I do try."

I made a face at him. "So after that . . . ?"

"Well, I realized pretty quickly you weren't stupid, and it just pissed me off that a bright, attractive woman didn't think she was worth anything more than being some rich guy's fancy piece."

"And then?"

He gave me an unamused look at my interrogation. "Then I thought I was wrong. You genuinely seemed to care about Malcolm. However, Callum turned up at the dinner and I took one look at him, a younger version of Malcolm, and I realized you *had* done this before."

I glanced away. "I see."

"But really—" My eyes flew back to his at his softened tone. "It just pissed me off that you're this completely different person around those guys."

"A different person?"

"Yeah, with Joss and everyone, with me, you're someone else, some- one real. With Malcolm, with Callum, with the guys you flirt with, you're different. You're *less* than you really are. And that fucking giggle . . ."

I laughed outright.

Cam's lips twitched. "You're aware of it?"

"Joss made me aware of it. It drives her nuts. Sometimes I do it just to annoy her."

Cam laughed. "Well, it works. It's irritating as hell."

A feeling I couldn't quite name took hold of me then. Cam really did like me. For me. Sans fake giggle. Just like Joss. "I'm going to go, Cam. But thank you for today."

He eyed me warmly, hope glittering a little mischievously in his gaze. "I'm forgiven, then?"

I nodded without needing to think about it. I was already feeling more free for having confided in him, and since we both had done some confiding it felt like a balanced exchange. I wasn't anxious about having trusted him, and that just blew my mind. "Clean slate."

"Friends?"

I almost laughed at that paltry description of what I felt for this stranger who had become my confidant. "Friends."

CHAPTER 12

I had showered and changed into my pajamas and was feeling a little better—Mum hadn't come out of her room—by the time Cole returned home. He stopped by the couch and squeezed my shoulder before heading into the kitchen to grab a snack.

"We're okay?" I asked as he came back in to flop down on the floor.

"We're okay." He shrugged, staring at the television with a casualness I was sure he wasn't feeling. "Are you okay? Was Cam okay?"

I smiled, ignoring the stupid flutter of butterflies in my stomach at the thought of Cam. "He was great. What did you say to him earlier? He mentioned something about you looking like you were going to hit him?"

Cole grunted. "If I had, he would have deserved it. Didn't need to, though. Dude's a decent guy—felt like shit when I told him how wrong he was about you."

"Language." I threw a cushion at him and he batted it away with a murmured apology. "And why did you go down there to set him straight? It wasn't like I was desperate for him to see me in a better light."

Cole looked at me, and I saw his green eyes had gone a forest color from some unnamed emotion. "Nobody gets to think that about you, let alone say it out fu—" He caught himself before he swore. "Out loud."

I wanted to cry, because right then my brother was making me feel pretty loved and pretty cool, but I thought crying would just make Cole roll his eyes. "Okay," I whispered and he gave me a little nod before turning back to the television. "Comedy Channel?"

I changed the channel for him just as my phone rang. Handing Cole the remote, I got up and followed the ringtone into the kitchen where I'd left my purse.

It was Joss. I felt a little relieved it wasn't Malcolm—I didn't even want to touch on why. "Hi," I answered quietly.

"Hey, you." Joss's rich, husky voice was soothing to my nerves and I realized I'd missed seeing her at lunch today. "I'm just checking in. You okay?"

"Um, not really."

"You sound like shit."

"Well . . ."

"Okay, I'm coming over."

"Joss, you don't have to."

"I have a bottle of wine here. Are you going to argue with me and a bottle of wine?"

I smiled. "I wouldn't dream of it."

"Smart lady. I'll be there in ten." She hung up and I rolled my eyes. I always knew there was a secret "momma bear" hiding underneath all Joss's prickliness.

When she arrived, she took one look at me and shook her head, her brows drawn together. "Jesus C, Jo, what's happened now?"

I stepped aside to let her in, nodding at the bottle of wine in her hand. "Let's crack this open first. We're both going to need it."

Cole greeted Joss with a brusque nod and headed into his room to give us some privacy. Joss got comfortable on the end of the couch. "Hit me with it."

My mouth twisted at the irony of her word choice. "Well, now that you mention it . . ."

When I was finished, I had to body tackle her to the couch so she couldn't barge into my mum's room and give her a beatdown, and then I had to spend five minutes assuring her that Cole and I were okay.

Her eyes were still flashing a little wildly as she took a sip of wine. "So Cam was there for you?"

"Yeah. He was very kind, actually."

Her eyebrows rose at my expression and then she gifted me with one of her gorgeous smiles. "Oh, I recognize that look. I see that look on Ellie's face every time she gazes at Adam."

"Whatever," I muttered, refusing to let her catch sight of my eyes in case they just confirmed her suspicions.

"You are so crushing on Cam and I didn't even have to do anything."

"I'm not crushing on Cam."

"I know what that look means."

"We're just friends." I stared at her now. "Joss, I like him, but we have partners, and I . . ."

Joss sighed. "You still want the security that Malcolm can give you."

I didn't need to answer—we both knew she was right.

"Does Cam give you butterflies?"

I nodded.

"Are you aware of every move he makes?"

Another affirmative.

"Does he enter your thoughts at the slightest provocation?"

"Mm-hmm."

"You are so screwed."

"I am not." I huffed indignantly. "I'm perfectly in control of the situation."

"Yeah." Joss snorted. "So was I until I found myself pinned to Su's desk. Eighteen months later and I'm picking out bedsheets with Braden and worrying if he doesn't text me at least once from work to let me know how his day is going—as if he can't tell me when he gets home. I can't get to sleep without him beside me. Me? Can't sleep without a guy in my bed? I'm addicted, Jo. And it started out with that look you've got."

"I'm glad for you, Joss. I really am. But it's not the same thing. I care about Malcolm. I'm just physically attracted to Cam. It's nothing."

Joss burst out laughing and I watched in complete bemusement as she shook with her own hysterics.

"What?"

She waved me off, trying to catch her breath. "Oh, man, nothing. Nothing." She looked at me again and then gave a furtive chuckle as if she knew something I didn't. "I'm just having déjà vu."

For the first time ever, I pretended to be sick at work. I told Mr. Meikle I was coming down with a migraine, and since I was pale with worry for Cole, it didn't take much convincing for him to let me leave early, although he grumbled the entire time I packed up my things.

I managed to get back to the flat just as Cole was getting home from school. He stopped in the hallway when he stepped inside the flat, his lips pinched as he watched me kick off my work shoes.

"Well, you can't pull a sickie every day," he said, deducing exactly what I'd done and why. "You'll just have to trust that I can take care of being in the flat alone with her. Plus, I really think you scared the crap out of her."

At that exact moment Mum's bedroom door opened. She peered out at us, her lip curling in hostility as her eyes clashed with mine. She made a grunting noise before using the wall to help her along to the bathroom. As soon as the door shut, I turned back to Cole.

"Apparently, I *can't* trust you to be alone with her."

He winced at the reminder that he had kept her abuse from me. "I just didn't want to upset you."

I harrumphed at that and strode into the kitchen for a cup of tea. By the time I'd made it and nestled into the couch with my book, Cole had settled down on the armchair with his homework and Mum had gone back into her bedroom.

We sat there for an hour before I decided to get up and put on some dinner. I was just coming out of the kitchen when I heard a knock at the door. For an awful moment I thought maybe I'd finally stretched Malcolm's patience and he'd turned up at the flat. He'd texted me today and I'd texted back, but I hadn't encouraged conversation. Had he decided to show up to see what was going on?

My heart was pounding stupidly hard as I reached for the door, and it flipped over in my chest when I saw who stood on the other side of it.

"Cam." I smiled, more than happy to see him.

He was wearing his usual uniform of print tee and jeans and I wanted to haul him in out of the freezing-cold stairwell. He gave me a quick smile. "All right?"

I stepped aside. "Come in."

His smile widened and he slid past me, his shoulder brushing mine and causing inappropriate thoughts to tumble through my overworked brain. "Can I get you a coffee?"

"Aye, that would be great." He followed me, throwing a wave to Cole. "Hey, bud, how are you?"

Cole grinned at him. "Good. You?"

"Yeah, not bad." He trailed me into the kitchen.

"What do you take?"

"Milk, no sugar."

I set about making it, fully aware of his eyes on my every movement. My cheeks felt incredibly warm under his perusal, and I hurried to get his drink ready. "You're working tonight, aren't you?" I said, handing him the mug.

"I am. But I wanted to drop something off first." He took a sip of his drink. "Mmm, good coffee."

I laughed softly. "The way to a man's heart."

His grin was wicked. "Only an easily pleased man," he retorted, suggesting he was anything but easy to please.

"Yeah, I can guess what it takes to please you, Cam, and this is a PG-13 household."

He threw back his head and laughed, causing another flutter in my chest and my own smile to widen. "Good thing the flat downstairs is open to R-rated situations."

I flushed and shook my head. "Moving on . . ."

"What? Punters in the bar say worse than that to you and your comebacks are always good."

He *had* been paying attention. I shrugged. "They're not my friends."

His eyes softened. "I'm still your friend, then? You haven't changed your mind?"

"No, I haven't changed my mind."

"Good." He pulled something out of his back pocket. "Because I want you to trust me enough to give this to Cole." Cam held out a key. I raised an eyebrow at it. "A spare key to my flat. I want him to use my place when you're not around. It's a safe place for him to be so you're not worrying every second of every minute that you're not with him."

That key was the best present anyone had ever given me.

Ever.

"Cam"—I looked from the key up to him—"are you sure? I mean, it's not too much of an imposition?"

"Not if it helps you out."

I reached for the key, but instead of just taking it, I curled my hand around it and his fingers. He tensed with awareness and I poured my gratitude into my eyes. "This is the best present I've ever gotten."

Cam's eyes roamed my face, his mouth curled up at the corners. "A key: the way to a woman's heart."

"Only an easily pleased one."

He laughed again.

"What's so funny?" Cole's voice snapped us out of our little bubble. I pulled my hand back from Cam's and held up the key to Cole.

"Present."

"Oh?"

"I'll explain in a minute." I turned to Cam. "Would you like to stay for dinner? Mac 'n' cheese."

"How can I say no to that?"

"You can't. I won't let you." I handed the key to Cole. "Take Cam into the sitting room—he'll explain. Dinner will be ready soon."

They left me to it and for a moment I could only stare at the cupboard, my insides all trembling and fluttering from my interaction with Cam. He was thoughtful and considerate and trying to prove what a good friend he could be, and that just made his hotness even hotter. I wondered, not for the first time, what he'd be like in bed. His grin alone made me tingle—imagine what his tongue could do.

My phone buzzed, snapping me out of my sensual haze.

Malcolm.

Guilt immediately washed over me as I pressed the ANSWER button. "Hey, Malcolm."

"Sweetheart. How are you?"

"Just about to put out dinner for me and Cole." I winced at the omission of our guest. "Can I call you back?"

"Of course. Talk to you soon."

I hung up and shoved my phone in my back pocket with shaking fingers.

Seriously. What was I playing at?

Cam stopped by early before work the next day and walked me to the bar. I found that now that we understood each other Cam was pretty easy to talk to. He tried once more to persuade me to go to judo with him, but I put him off, still not keen on the idea of having someone slam me into a mat or whatever it was judo involved.

"Can you imagine me?" I scoffed as we neared the bar. "I'd be screaming about breaking a nail within five seconds."

Cam gave me a look as he held the wrought-iron gate to the basement stairs open for me. "See, that's the kind of bullshit other people believe. I know better."

"Oh, you do, do you?"

"You were sitting chewing a nail last night after dinner."

"Yeah, but I filed it and repainted it for work this morning."

He flashed his teeth at me. "Whatever, Walker. I know the truth."

"Evenin', Jo, Cam," Brian greeted us as we came down the stairs. He stood beside Phil, who was grinning at me like always.

"Hi, guys."

"Brian, Phil." Cam nodded at them.

As I made to pass them, Phil stopped me with a hand on my arm. He ran his eyes down my body. "Still with Malcolm?"

"Persistent Philip, I am still with Malcolm."

He winked at me. "Persistence will win in the end."

"And so will an STD," Cam put in drolly, gently pushing me forward with his hands on my back so that Phil had to let me go. "But you already know that, right, Phil?"

I tried to stifle my giggle as we walked into the bar to the sounds of Brian howling with laughter and Phil swearing at him. "It was only that one time. Fuck! I'm never telling you anything again, Bri."

"Euch," I whispered to Cam. "That was more than I needed to know."

"Correction: That was the *one* thing you needed to know."

I laughed again and we sauntered into the staff room, barely getting a "hello, good-bye" out of Su, who came racing out of her office at the sight of us and disappeared as quickly as she'd materialized.

"It amazes me that anything gets done around here," Cam said, shrugging out of his jacket. "She's never here when she should be."

I grunted at that, completely used to Su's physical absence and as always grateful for it.

The bar soon started to fill up. As usual on a Tuesday, there weren't many customers, but we were kept relatively occupied.

We weren't busy enough to diminish our attraction to one another, however. For some reason, being behind the bar together seemed to heighten the tension. Was it the confined space? I didn't know. All I did know was that I spent half the time with one eye on my work and the other on Cam.

Joss was right. I was absolutely aware of every move he made.

And speaking of Joss, I wasn't at all surprised when she stopped in at around nine thirty. I was surprised she was alone, but she explained that Braden was working late and Ellie and Adam were on a date.

"So you were bored and thought you'd come to work?" I asked, sliding her a Diet Coke as she settled onto a stool at my end of the bar. I didn't think so. I thought she was worried about me.

Joss just smiled and then nodded in greeting to Cam, who had just noticed her presence, but he was too busy talking to a customer to come over. No, not a customer. My eyes focused more carefully on the girl he was grinning at so flirtatiously. Becca and a friend. She handed him his aviator watch and Cam leaned over and pressed a soft kiss to Becca's lips.

I felt an ache rake across my chest, unfamiliar and brutal.

My eyes slid back to Joss and she had one eyebrow raised at me. "What you're feeling . . . it's called jealousy. It's a vile emotion, I know. However, it also tells you that Cam is definitely more than just someone you're attracted to."

"We barely know each other."

"From what you've told me, you know each other better than al-most anyone else does."

Somehow, this was the truth. I leaned forward on the bar, frowning at my friend. "Yeah, how did that happen?"

"How did what happen?" I turned my head to see Cam approach-ing, fastening his watch on his wrist. Becca and the other girl were gone. He waited for an answer, his eyes curious on mine.

I decided to hedge. "You really are a nosy bugger, aren't you?" I teased.

Cam tipped his head to the side, contemplating me. "Deflection?" His eyes glittered as if something had just occurred to him. "You were talking about me, weren't you?"

I wanted to wipe that cocky smile off his face.

Joss groaned. "You and Braden should be forced to join a club for men who need to get over themselves."

My eyes slid to her in amusement. "Blatant displays of egotism will be punished in the form of making them wear Speedos in freezing-cold conditions."

"And possibly withholding food."

"No. Sex. Withholding sex."

Joss bit her lip. "I don't know if that would work for me."

I eyed her incredulously. "Are you telling me you couldn't go without sex for a few days?"

"I don't think so."

"Where is your willpower?"

My friend took a swig of her Diet Coke. "Hey, you haven't had sex with Braden Carmichael."

No, I hadn't, although I almost blushed remembering I'd definitely tried to get myself into the position to do so. "Yeah, but I've had perfectly good sex and I could still abstain for a few days."

"Perfectly good sex?" Cam interrupted us, drawing both our gazes. His voice was low with some unnamed emotion. "Abstain?" His now heated eyes ran the length of me before returning to meet mine. "Then *he* isn't doing it right."

My heart puttered to a stop before choking and wheezing. When it got back up to speed, it took off in a drag race. All that sexual heat rolled over me and I felt my knickers grow damp with want.

"Jesus C," Joss croaked. "Now I'm turned on." She jumped off her stool, checking her phone. "I think I'll go home and see if Braden's back from work."

And just like that she left us simmering in our sexual chemistry.

I smiled weakly at Cam. "How's Becca?"

A few customers approached the bar and we both moved to serve them. As we were preparing their drinks Cam answered tightly, "Becca's fine. How's Malcolm?"

"Fine." He'd taken me for lunch during my break from work that day and I'd managed to convince him that everything was hunky-dory.

"Cole text yet to say if he's home?"

I found myself grinning like an idiot at his concern, and my customer grinned back at me, clearly thinking the look was for him. I quickly handed him his change and turned to Cam. "Yeah, he's home."

His eyes crinkled at the corners, adding another one of his expressions to my favorites. "Good."

The rest of the night flew by. We worked, we talked, we joked, but the sexual undercurrent remained. When we walked home after our shift, we did so in utter silence. I could say it was just tiredness, but my whole body was vibrating like a tuning fork just strolling beside him. We said good night at his door, and as I took the stairs to my flat with his eyes on my back, I wished, not for the first time, for a different life—that Cam was single, that Malcolm wasn't a part of my life that I cared about, and that for once I could do what I really wanted to do.

And what I really wanted to do was Cameron MacCabe.

I checked on Cole and found him sleeping peacefully in his room. I even checked on Mum just to make sure she hadn't choked on her own vomit or anything like that, and I found her snoring away. That done, I changed into my pj's and crawled into bed. But I couldn't fall asleep.

My blood felt as if it was on fire in my veins, my nerves were sparking at the very ends, and I couldn't get the smell of Cam's cologne out of my nostrils.

I was so turned on, it wasn't funny.

How different would my night have been if Cam had followed me into Su's office when I'd gone in there to leave her new stock information? What if he'd come up behind me, pushed my hair off my neck, and pressed his hot mouth to my skin as his hand skimmed around my waist and down to the buttons on my jeans . . .

. . . if he'd undone them, his long fingers sliding inside, beneath my underwear . . .

My own hand smoothed over my stomach, slipping under my pajamas and knickers so I could bring myself to climax, fantasizing about Cam screwing me against Su's desk.

I muffled my moan as I came and once the tremors stopped, I curled into my side, guilt cascading over me once again.

I was a terrible girlfriend.

CHAPTER 13

A truth I hadn't been willing to face pushed its way to the forefront of my life over the next few weeks. The truth was, for a number of years now every day had been the same—had been constrained, dulled, vivid colors muted beneath the shadow of a wall. And behind that wall I walked in the same uniform every day—if I wanted to be really melodramatic, I'd call it a dull orange jumpsuit. But as the days of those few weeks flew by, I felt that uniform melting away, shredding into tatters and scraped from my body as I climbed the wall to the other side.

The wall was moving further away now, the shadow lifting, the colors brightening.

All because I was spending time with Cam.

We hung out as much as possible on weekdays. Every night, in fact, he'd stop by for coffee or dinner before his work shift, even if I was out with Malcolm. We walked back and forth to work together, and had a laugh with Joss during our shifts. I didn't see him on the weekends because he worked, trained at judo class with his friends, and hung out with Becca. Last time, he'd taken Cole to watch the class, encouraging Cole to do more physical activity, and surprisingly, my brother was embracing the idea. My ears were bleeding from hearing about judo.

For me, Cam was a confidant. I told him more about my life and my hopes for Cole's future. For Cole, Cam was a soul mate. They drew comics together, they discussed comics together, they liked the same music, the same movies, and from what I could read between the lines, Cam also answered all those questions Cole wouldn't dare ask me.

We became this family unit, bonding quickly and strongly.

My feelings for Cam only grew deeper and I was in a constant battle with my conscience, arguing with it, pretending that it didn't mean anything. Along with the emotional stuff, my body was almost at the breaking point for want of him. I don't know how I managed to hide it from him, but I did. I didn't want anything to destroy our friendship.

That didn't mean I didn't find other outlets for my pent-up sexual frustration, and that outlet only added a whole other level of guilt and shame to my already considerable stack. I hadn't seen Malcolm as much as I usually did, but three of the four times I did see him, we had sex . . . and the three times we had sex I . . .

. . . I did the unthinkable. I closed my eyes and imagined Cam.

I came each time.

Malcolm took this to mean he and I were back on track and whatever had been bothering me before was dealt with.

I was an awful, *awful* person.

Yup. My world was full of color. Red for want. Yellow for shame. Green for jealousy.

Yes, the green-eyed monster had also reared her ugly head in the last few weeks. Every time Cam mentioned Becca's name I felt that little ache in my chest, an ache that ruptured into a full-blown bleed on Sunday.

Cole and I had had lunch with the Nicholses and had come home in a good mood. Cole had gone downstairs to invite Cam up for coffee and I was humming away like an idiot, my stomach already a riot of fluttery winged creatures in anticipation of seeing him, when Cole came back into the flat unaccompanied.

I frowned at him as I poured Cam's coffee. "Is he just coming?"

Cole shook his head, his brows drawn together in what I took for bemusement.

"Not in?"

He shrugged.

Oh, dear God, the shrugging had returned. "Well?"

He leaned against the kitchen counter and sighed before he shot me a questioning look. "Are you and Cam just friends?"

I coughed up the lie quite easily these days. "Of course. I'm with Malcolm. Why?"

Two spots of color appeared high on Cole's cheeks and his mouth quirked up at the corners in amusement. "Because it definitely sounds like Cam's too busy shagging some noisy bird to want to have coffee with us."

My whole body froze as I stared at my brother, my heart pounding, a horribly uneasy feeling in my stomach as jealousy seized hold of me.

"Jo?"

I frowned, grasping at a reason for my freeze. "Don't say 'shagging' and don't say 'bird.' Not 'bird,' 'chick,' 'piece.' We're 'women,' or 'ladies,' or 'girls.'"

Cole grunted. "Thanks for the vocab lesson."

I stared after him as he took off for the living room, my good mood annihilated by the thought of Cam and Becca having sex.

I guess in the end I couldn't really cope with all the color, and the following Thursday, before the crack of dawn, I stripped the wallpaper in the sitting room. I was taking time to find some calm. The night before I went on a date with Malcolm, but I ended up getting him to drop me off early at the flat, after making up some excuse about not feeling well. I hurried upstairs to check the Internet, found the sale I was looking for, reserved what I needed from the local store, and began priming the walls.

When Thursday morning broke, I got Cole ready for school, ignoring his grumblings about the stripped walls, and then I headed out to pick up what I'd reserved: three rolls of wallpaper. I also bought some paste and a box of doughnuts.

As soon as I changed into my paint-covered jeans and tee, scraped my long hair back into a ponytail, and put on my headscarf, I felt better. Calmer already. I was just putting up my pasting table when Mum appeared in the doorway.

We stared at each other.

We hadn't spoken since my attack in the kitchen almost three weeks before.

Her tired eyes swept the living room—the dust sheets, the rolls of wallpaper, the bucket of paste. She grunted. "Again?"

Taking cue from Cole, I shrugged in reply.

Mum sighed and shook her head wearily. "Any food?"

"There's leftover pasta from last night. Can you heat it up without burning down the flat?"

She waved off my caustic comment and moved toward the kitchen a little unsteadily. "I'll eat it cold."

A little while later she returned to her room. That was good. Despite what I considered my civility in light of the circumstances, I still found it hard not to throw a punch anytime I thought of her hitting Cole. Honestly, that's all I really saw now when I looked at her.

I switched on my music but kept it low so as not to disturb Alcomum and began to hang the new wallpaper. It was cream with very faint champagne, silver, and chocolate stripes. I'd have to get new cushions for the couch and change the floor lamp, but I didn't care. Decorating always zoned me out and I needed to zone out big-time. I started at ten and by eleven I was feeling completely relaxed and sated from having eaten two doughnuts. I was in the middle of hanging a sheet of wallpaper, thinking that the kitchen cabinets could do with a repaint, when there was a knock at the door.

Turning on my stepladder, my hands high above me holding the wallpaper away from the wall, I yelled, "Who is it?"

"Cam!"

Nope. He wasn't going to destroy my calm. I took a deep breath and looked back at what I'd accomplished so far. I was on my last piece of wallpaper and the room looked brighter and fresher already. "Come in!" I lined up the paper and used the brush to smooth the top of it to the wall.

Two seconds later I heard him ask behind me, "What are you doing?"

Ignoring the effect of his voice on my body, I slid the paper slightly, checking its position before smoothing down another section. "I'm wall-papering."

"By yourself?" I could hear the incredulity in his voice.

I nodded, taking a step down the ladder so I could smooth the middle section. It was lining up exactly. Practice did make perfect. "Who do you think decorated this place? The wallpaper, the paint, the sanded floors . . ." I finished off the piece and stepped back, smiling at the new look.

Turning to Cam, I was surprised to find a slightly dumbfounded look on his face as his eyes searched the room and then came back to me. "Do you know how bloody hard it is to hang wallpaper? You just did it like a pro."

I made a face at him. I didn't see what the big deal was. "Uncle Mick taught me."

"When you were ten?" he asked, smiling in curiosity. "When did you start this?" He nodded at the folding table.

"An hour ago."

Those gorgeous eyes of his widened. "And you're done already? Jo, this place is really nicely put together. It looks professional. You know that, right?"

I grinned at the compliment, feeling a flush of pleasure that he thought so. "Thank you. It drives Cole nuts. He almost had a fit when he saw the stripped walls."

"Actually"—Cam took a step toward me—"the reason I came by was because of Cole. I got this weird text from him saying, 'Jo's wallpapering. She only does that when something's up. Do you know what's going on?'"

Traitor. I sighed, looking away from Cam. So it had gotten to the point where Cole was now going to our neighbor for help, even when it concerned me. Was I to have no secrets?

"Well?"

I shrugged. "Every now and then it helps me relax." I tried to placate him with a smile. "Cam, you of all people know my life is stressful. I just do this to relieve it."

Seeming to have mercy on me, Cam gave me a slow nod. "Right." He looked at the floor now, his eyes running along it to the paintwork on the skirting board. Without saying a word he disappeared and turned toward the kitchen. I heard him in the kitchen and then watched him appear, passing the doorway to head along to the bedrooms and bathroom. I heard three doors open. Bathroom, Cole's room, and my room.

Cam returned to the living room to encounter my "look," featuring raised eyebrows and arms crossed over my chest. His lips twitched at it. Mine did not. "Are you done, you nosy bugger?"

He grinned. "You have a lot of books."

I harrumphed.

"Explains the vocab."

"Excuse me?"

"You're very articulate. Well read."

Why did Cam's compliments always have to be the best? It was very irritating to someone who was trying to get him out from under her skin.

"You're also talented."

Astonishment jolted through my body. "Me? Talented?" Was he high?

His arm swept around the room. "Jo, you should be doing this for a living."

"Um, doing what?"

"Painting and decorating."

I laughed at the absurdity of it. "Oh, okay. Who in their right mind would hire a high school dropout with no experience to be a painter and decorator? Let's face facts. I'm useless, Cam."

His eyes instantly hardened, narrowing on me and pinning me in place. "You are not useless. Don't talk about yourself like that in front of me. It pisses me off." It was lucky he had no intention of waiting on me to speak, since I didn't know how to reply or react to the warm fuzzies in my chest. "You're good at this. Really good. I think Nate knows someone with his own company. I could see about getting you an apprenticeship."

"No. I'm twenty-four. No one hires a twenty-four-year-old apprentice."

"They do if it's a favor for a friend."

"Cam, no."

"Jo, come on, at least think about it. You enjoy it and you're good at it. It's better than working two jobs and dating—" He stopped himself, blanching when he realized he'd almost crossed the line.

Well, not really "almost." He had crossed it. I clenched my jaw, forcing back the sting of tears in my eyes as I realized he still saw me that way—the bimbo after the rich guy's wallet. I wiped the paste off the folding table, deciding to ignore him.

"Jo, think about it. Please."

"I said no, thanks." I couldn't imagine anyone would ever want to hire me, and the humiliation of rejection didn't sound like a lot of fun.

"Jo—"

"Cam, why are you here?" I cut him off sharply. I immediately regretted my tone, but there was no taking it back.

He blew out the air between his lips, his eyes searching mine, and as if he couldn't find what he was looking for, he took a step back. "No reason. I better go. I've—"

"Jo!" My mum's voice cut him off this time, her shrill shriek making us wince.

It was the first time she'd called for my help since the incident. I sighed heavily and dumped the paste brush back in the bucket. "Cam, stay. I'll see to Mum. You make yourself a coffee. Maybe get me a tea while you're at it."

"Jo!"

"I'm coming!" I shouted and Cam seemed taken aback. "What?" I asked as I moved to pass him.

He smirked. "Never heard you raise your voice."

"You've obviously never seen me approached by a spider."

Laughing, Cam waved toward the door. "I'll get the coffee."

Feeling relieved that he'd decided to stay, I hurried to get whatever Mum needed over and done with.

To my surprise she was lying in her bed, not seeming to be in any kind of "situation" after all. Oh, God, I hoped she hadn't lost control of her bladder. That had happened before. "What?" I asked, hovering in the doorway.

"Who is that?" she asked loudly, nodding her head to indicate behind me. "I've heard his voice lately. Who is it?"

It was the first time Mum had really ever taken an interest in anything outside of her gin-soaked, wasted existence and I couldn't help but reply, "That's Cam. He's a friend."

"You fucking him?"

"Mum," I snapped, flinching at how loudly the question had been asked.

"Well?" she asked with a sneer. "Look at you! Standing there, judging me. Get that look oot yer eyes, girl. You think yer better than me. Accusing me of hitting Cole, thinking I'm nothing. Well, look in the mirror, girl, 'cause yer nothing too!" As her eyes sparked with her contempt, I knew this was what she'd been waiting on. This was her payback for my attack. Humiliating me in front of Cam. "Yer useless and that piece oot there will walk away when he gets bored with what's between yer legs!"

I slammed the door shut, my whole body shaking as I leaned my forehead against it, trying to control my breathing. A few seconds later I heard her start to cry.

"Jo?"

I sucked in my breath at his voice and turned slowly around to find him standing in the hallway, his eyes glittering with anger. He took the few steps he needed to be close to me and he said loudly, so Mum would hear, I imagine, "You are not useless. You are not what they say you are."

I glanced down at his tattoo.

Be Caledonia.

When my eyes traveled back up to his and I saw pain in his eyes for me, I knew that Cam was the only guy who had ever *seen* me. And even more important, he saw beyond what I could see. I was *more* to Cam.

I wanted to grab his hand, lead him down the hall to my room, strip myself bare before him, and let him take everything I could give him.

And take everything he could give me.

Instead of doing what I really wanted to do, I gave him a platonic but grateful smile. "Let's have that coffee."

CHAPTER 14

The following Saturday everything I was avoiding feeling, everything that wasn't being admitted out loud, came to a head.

The week before, Malcolm had invited me to a party that Becca's flatmate was hosting. The party was to be held in their place in Bruntsfield and Malcolm had said he'd put in an appearance. However, he didn't want to feel like a fish out of water, so he'd practically begged me to accompany him. I wasn't really looking forward to seeing Cam and Becca in action together, but since I'd been unfaithful to Malcolm in my head, I thought it was the least I could do for him.

The morning of that Saturday I was up early because Mum had woken us up smashing empty bottles of gin in the kitchen sink. I'd gotten to her before she did too much damage, wrapped a few plasters around little cuts on her hands, held her while she curled into me and bawled like a baby, and finally accepted Cole's help getting her back into bed. The muscles in her legs were wasting away—it was a wonder she could even walk. Cole and I had given up trying to get her out and about, and seeing the damage I began to feel guilty.

Trying to shake off the grim sadness that always overwhelmed me when Mum found a way to let us know she was just as angry at her addiction as we were, I thought I'd spend a rare Saturday morning reading while Cole hurried down to Cam's flat. Since I was still trying to weigh whether we could afford the expense of Cole taking up a martial art, Cam had started training lessons with him on Saturday mornings. Cole loved every minute of it, and honestly, I think Cam was enjoying teaching what he'd learned.

I was immersed in the translation of a romance novel by one of my favorite Japanese writers when the doorbell rang.

It was Jamie, Cole's friend.

As soon as I opened the door, the short, slightly chubby kid turned beetroot. I bit my lip, trying not to smile. "Hi, Jamie."

"Hi, Jo." He gulped, his eyes looking anywhere but at my face. "Is Cole in? He was supposed to meet me outside fifteen minutes ago."

Clearly Cole had lost track of the time. I stifled my aggravated sigh and stepped out of the flat, shutting the door gently behind me—I had been at a really good part in my book. "Let me take you to him."

After I knocked on Cam's door, he yelled for me to come in. I left Jamie waiting outside and entered the flat to find Cam and Cole standing in the center of the living room beside a mat. All of the furniture had been pushed to the edges of the room. Cole was grinning, perspiration running down his neck, damp patches all over his T-shirt. Cam was wearing a T-shirt and joggers, not looking that much the worse for wear.

I raised my eyebrows at Cole. "Did you forget about something?"

He frowned instantly. "No."

"Tell that to the kid on Cam's doorstep."

"Oh, sh—" He stopped himself. "I forgot Jamie."

"He's waiting."

Cole hurried to grab his socks and trainers. "Cheers for the lesson, Cam."

"No probs, bud."

"You better wash and change your clothes before you go out!" I called after him as he disappeared into the hall. "And text me to let me know what you're doing—" I slammed my mouth closed at the sound of Cam's front door shutting. I turned back to Cam. "Why do I bother?"

He threw me a crooked smile—my fourth favorite after the lip twitch—and curled a finger, beckoning me to him. "Care to take up where he left off?"

I immediately took a step back, shaking my head. "I don't think so."

"Come on." He suddenly grew serious. "I've seen the way some of the customers are with you, and Joss told me she's had to rescue you more than once in the past from an overeager punter. This will help you learn to deal with the way you freeze up."

I imagined it might be pretty nice to be able to handle aggressive assholes by myself rather than relying on protective friends. But training with Cam? No. That would be fanning the flame.

"No, thanks."

Cam sighed but gave in. "Fine. You want a cup of tea?"

I nodded and followed him into his kitchen, trying to keep my eyes on anything but his muscled shoulders and tight ass. I didn't try very hard.

Standing by his kitchen counter, I was lost in thought about the evening ahead of us as Cam made the tea and coffee, when I caught movement out of the corner of my eye. I glanced toward it and nearly had full-on heart failure at the size of the spider clinging to Cam's kitchen tiles.

"Oh, my God!" I squealed, skittering back away from it, a lump of fear in my throat the size of Canada.

"What—what?" Cam spun around, his eyes wide on me.

I stared round-eyed at the spider. "Get rid of it or I won't be able to move." I wasn't kidding. I was literally frozen with fear. I don't know where my phobia of spiders originated, but it was bad enough that we had to invest in spider repellents that plugged into the sockets in our flat. We got the rare few spiders nevertheless and Cole always took care of them.

Cam looked from me to the spider and then back to me again. I could see the beginning of a smile start to curl the corners of his mouth.

"Don't even think about laughing. It's not funny."

His gaze softened as he seemed to finally realize the extent of my fear. "Okay. Stop panicking. I'll get rid of it." He reached into a cupboard and pulled out a pan.

I scowled. "What are you doing? Don't kill it!"

Cam froze, cocking his head in bemusement as he gazed at me. "Why don't you want me to kill it? I thought you were frightened of it."

"I am *terrified* of it," I corrected him. "But what does it say about humans as a species if we go around killing things just because we fear them?" *Not anything good, that's what.*

Cam's gorgeous eyes warmed even more and I found myself forgetting the fear and falling into his gaze.

"What?" I whispered, feeling my chest swell at the way he was looking at me. No one had ever looked at me like that before.

He shook his head. "Nothing. You just . . . Nothing."

"Cam?"

"Mmm-hmm?"

"The spider."

He blinked a little rapidly before pinning the spider with his gaze. "Right." He lifted the lid off the pan. "I'm not killing it. I just needed something to put it in."

As he rescued the spider from me and me from the spider, I crammed myself into the corner of the kitchen, scared that Cam wouldn't move quickly enough and the spider would somehow launch itself across the room at me. I had no reason to fear. Cam had the spider in the pan in record time and I watched with growing relief as he took it to the kitchen window and deposited it outside.

"Thank you," I breathed.

Cam didn't reply. Instead he shut the window carefully, put the pan by the sink, and turned around to gaze at me.

Suddenly the air felt electric between us, like it always did while we worked side by side at the bar. I'd done my darnedest to make sure those moments were confined to the bar, trying to feign ordinary interaction outside in the real world.

Today there would be no feigning.

I held my breath at the intensity in Cam's eyes as he slowly began to make his way toward me. When he closed the distance that would be considered socially acceptable between two friends who both had partners, I was just about to question him, stall him, but then my breasts brushed his chest and the words got sucked right back into my mouth along with all the air in the room. I felt his hands in a gentle embrace around my upper arms, his aftershave familiar and intoxicating, and the heat of his body made mine languid.

I hadn't been able to meet his eyes, and so I was looking at his throat when he leaned in and pressed the sweetest kiss to my forehead. A yearning, deep and expanding, burst open in my chest and I melted into him, feeling his lips chase a delicious shiver across my skin. He replaced his mouth with his own forehead. I closed my eyes as he closed his and we rested against one another, breathing each other in.

I was filled with such longing, a longing only intensified because I knew it was reciprocated.

"Cam," I whispered, wanting him to pull away and needing him to never leave.

He groaned and gently slid his forehead down the side of mine, his nose skimming my cheek, following my jaw, and coming to rest in a nuzzle against my throat.

I held my breath, waiting.

His hot lips touched the skin there. One brush. Two.

And then I felt the wet, erotic touch of tongue and I shuddered, falling against him. My nipples pebbled against my thin shirt, begging him to go further.

A sharp, piercing ringtone shattered the air between us and I jerked back, coming to my senses. Cam cursed, his jaw clenched so tight it was close to shattering. He reached for his phone on the counter beside us and then blanched as he read the caller ID. He shot me an unfathomable look. "Becca," he stated grimly.

I gulped, not believing that I'd let him touch me, that we'd been seconds from hurting two people who didn't deserve to be hurt. More than that, I was shocked at how much I hadn't even cared—my need for Cam was that selfish.

This was not good.

If it was anybody else, I would have suggested it was time to put some distance between us. But this was Cam. I needed Cam.

"I better go. Malcolm is picking me up in a few hours." I straightened my shirt and tightened the band holding my ponytail in place. I couldn't meet his gaze.

"So we're back to pretending there's nothing between us?"

My spine stiffened at his curtness and I looked up, only to flinch at the anger I saw in his eyes.

Shit.

I couldn't lose Cam's friendship. It was the best thing that had happened to me since Cole. "Cam, please don't. I'm with Malcolm and you're with Becca."

His mouth opened to respond, but I fled his presence before I was forced to hear what he had to say.

All day I felt I might be sick at any moment. I could barely do anything, really only taking time to reply to Cole when he texted me that he was staying at Jamie's house that night. I dressed uncharacteristically casually for the party, pulling on a skintight black miniskirt and a print tee from Topshop. I paired them with knee-high boots with a fleecy lining so my legs wouldn't freeze and a dark faux fur jacket I'd gotten at a sale and usually wore with something dressier.

Tonight I wasn't in the mood to sparkle. I wanted comfort, youth—

I wanted to be me in some tiny way. I shook the entire time I was dressing, wondering what Cam was doing, wondering if he was ever going to speak to me again. I could still feel his hot mouth against my throat, burned there along with the tingling sensation of his tongue. Why did he want us to face our attraction when we were both with other people? Did he want to leave Becca? Did he want me to leave Malcolm?

And the biggest question of all was, could I?

Could I walk away from a man who cared about me, who could provide me with security and safety? Could I risk it for Cam? If I did, what would happen if it just turned out to be physical between us? No emotion, just spark.

My head pounded from overload.

Malcolm waited outside my building, beside our cab, and I almost came to a standstill at the look on his face as he eyed my outfit. When he was done with the once-over, he gave me a small smile before pressing a quick kiss to my lips.

"What is it?" I asked, frowning, sensing that something was off and not liking it. My stomach was already in upheaval over facing Cam again; I didn't need to worry about Malcolm too.

Malcolm ushered me into the cab and as we pulled away, he perused my legs before looking back up at my face. "You look very young tonight."

I glanced down at my outfit and pursed my lips. I looked my age tonight. I looked like me. "You don't like it," I muttered.

He gave a huff of laughter. "Sweetheart, you look sexy as hell, but you look like a young wild child dating a grumpy older man."

Something in his voice drew my gaze and I caught the flicker of unease in his eyes. He seemed worried. Cam's face hovering so close to mine flashed across my eyes and the guilt was crushing. "You're not a grumpy older man. You're my sexy older man."

His shoulders relaxed. "As long as you think so."

"I won't wear this again."

"Good," he murmured, leaning down to kiss my cheek. "I prefer you in the dresses we bought. They make you look older, sophisticated."

I would never have let a comment like that bother me before, but tonight it rubbed me a little raw. I faked a smile and let him squeeze my hand, wishing like hell I was back in my flat alone with a good book.

When we pulled up to Becca's building my stomach almost revolted and I sucked in a gasp to hold back the queasiness. Malcolm turned sharply to me, his brows drawn together. "Are you okay?"

"You know, I've been feeling off," I lied. "I think I'm fighting a bug or something."

"Do you want to leave?"

YES, YES, YES!

"No." I nodded at the bottle of wine in his hand. "Let's at least go up and have a drink."

The party was in full bloom when we arrived. The huge flat had the rough needs-a-good-repaint-scrub-and-tidy-up look that many of the old student flats in Edinburgh had. Becca didn't seem to mind the clutter, or the ripped carpets, chipped woodwork, and yellowing walls, and neither did her guests. Her artwork was plastered across as much of the wall space as possible, and the guests didn't seem to mind that either.

I admit to having to blink a little against all the stripes and splashes and colors. They reminded me of those nonsensical images you're supposed to stare at until a real image appeared in them.

"Mal, Jo!" Becca called as we entered the large open living space. She rushed past her friends and threw herself into Malcolm's arms. When she pulled back she clapped her hands like a little girl. "You brought the good wine."

"I did." Malcolm grinned at her as he handed it over to her.

I eyed Becca carefully, analyzing her like I had never done before. There she stood before me, with her wide, pretty smile, her intelligent eyes full of sparkle. What was it about her that made someone like Cam take notice? Suddenly I was uncomfortably aware of all Becca's positive attributes and I hated the jealousy they elicited in me.

Becca's own eyes flickered over my outfit and she smiled brightly. "Jo, you look great."

"Thank you," I replied softly, feeling guilty as sin for almost . . . well . . . whatever it was Cam and I had almost done.

"Cam!" She twisted around and gestured through the crowd. "Come say hello."

I felt the pulse in my neck start to throb as Cam approached. I must not have masked my reaction sufficiently, because Malcolm slid a hand around my waist, curling me into him. He bent to whisper in my ear, "What's going on? You look tense."

Oh, crap. Oh, hell. I was blowing this. I sucked in a deep breath and then turned to him, deciding it best to play it like I was worried I'd upset him. "I shouldn't have worn this."

Malcolm grimaced and touched my cheek affectionately. "Don't worry. I would never have said anything if I thought it would make you uncomfortable. You look beautiful. You always do."

As I gazed up into his kind eyes I felt even worse about myself. I decided to make him happy as recompense, even at the sacrifice of my own self-respect. "I don't like disappointing you."

His eyes warmed at that—in fact it was safe to say they heated and I felt myself drawn tighter against him. "You haven't. But I will look forward to undressing you later."

More than ever I felt choked by my own lies. I'd created this person I thought Malcolm wanted me to be—I was who *he* wanted me to be. In other words, I wasn't me. And even as unhappiness crashed over me at the thought, I faked a giggle and he grinned.

"Uh, hullo." Becca chuckled and we both whipped our heads around to face her and Cam. "Need a room much?"

Cam's eyes bored into me with barely leashed fury, his features stretched taut with his discomfort. I felt that look like a punch in the gut and found myself wanting to pull away from Malcolm and fall to my knees in apology before Cam.

Or run like hell from both of them.

In other words, I was a bloody mess.

To my relief, Cam was distracted by Becca as she urged him to help her greet more guests. I was left alone with Malcolm, left alone to try to assure him that I was all right. That *we* were all right. I laughed at his jokes, I touched him affectionately, and I gave him my whole focus, even when we found ourselves in a group talking with Cam and Becca. Even when I felt the heat of Cam's gaze on me, I devoted my attention to Malcolm.

An hour later I felt exhausted by the effort and excused myself to use the bathroom in the hallway near the front entrance. I had just slipped inside and was shutting the door behind me when it was forced open again. I stumbled back, astonished, as Cam quickly stepped inside and slammed the door behind him. He locked it and then faced me.

I wished I'd worn heels. In my flat boots I was only five ten and Cam had two inches on me. It wasn't much, but he was built of solid muscle and when he was powered by seething anger, he might as well have had a whole foot on me.

Trembling, I gestured to the door with a jerky hand. "What are you doing? Someone could have seen you."

His blue eyes snapped cold fire at me. "Malcolm, you mean."

"Or Becca," I reminded him through clenched teeth. "Remember her? Your girlfriend?"

Cam ignored me and I shivered as his gaze drifted slowly down my body, then climbed back up. I tingled all over. His lips quirked up at the corner as our eyes met. "You look gorgeous tonight. I've never seen you like this."

As we continued to stare at each other in silence I felt my heart race and my breathing speed up. I had to get out of there before I did something unbelievably stupid. Hoping I looked suitably determined and pissed off, I closed the distance between us. "Let me out of here, Cameron."

He held his hands up in surrender and stepped aside, but as soon as I reached for the lock I found my back flattened against the door, Cam's body pressed against mine, and his hands braced on either side of my head, imprisoning me.

"Wha—"

"Hush." His breath whispered against my lips and he lowered his hands until they circled my waist. "You feel this too. You've felt it since the night we met."

I couldn't find my voice, lost in a mixture of exultation that I hadn't been alone in this from the beginning and anxiety that we were doing something wrong and we'd be caught. I licked my lips nervously.

He took it as an invitation.

My gasp was swallowed by his kiss, his mouth hot as his tongue slid against mine. Stubble scratched my skin as he deepened the kiss, and his right hand glided up my side, over my ribs, until it came to a rest at my breast. His thumb brushed the underside deliberately. My skin immediately caught fire and I reached for him, my arms curling around his neck, drawing him closer. I moaned into his mouth, my heart hammering as my senses went on overload. I could taste coffee on his tongue, smell the scent of his skin, feel his heat, his strength. I was surrounded. And I wanted more.

I forgot where we were.

Who we were.

All I cared about was climbing inside of Cam.

Our grip on each other was almost painful, our kiss hard, wet, desperate.

Right.

Cam groaned, the vibration reverberating in my chest and soaring downward between my legs, and I writhed against him. He got the message, pressing his body deeper against mine, his erection digging into my lower stomach as his legs spread mine farther apart. I whimpered with a want that was out of control and Cam pulled back to stare at my swollen lips. I'd never seen a man so lost in a sexual fog and my sex clenched at the knowledge of the power I had over him, my knickers damp as my body grew ready for him.

Cam nipped at my bottom lip, and then licked the same spot. "I've fantasized a million times about this mouth," he told me hoarsely before crushing my lips against his again.

The embrace was even more out of control than the last one, and when I felt his warm fingers against the inside of my thigh, I deepened the kiss, urging him onward to explore. When I felt his fingers go beneath my underwear, I almost exploded.

His fingers slipped torturously slowly inside me and I cried out against his mouth, my hips jerking against his hand.

Cam dragged his mouth from mine, panting against my neck. "If we don't stop, I'm going to fuck you right here."

Those words were like a cold shower and I pitched back under the icy blast—guilt and shame I'd never felt before spraying down on me as Cam lifted his head to look at me.

Slowly, as he took in my expression, the sexual haze dissipated from his eyes and I felt the loss of his fingers. "Jo . . ."

I shook my head at him and pushed against his shoulders, trying to fight back the tears. "We can't do this. What are we doing?"

The muscle in Cam's jaw twitched and he abruptly released me, only to grab me by the upper arms, his expression raw with some unnamed emotion. "I'm ending it with Becca. Tonight."

Tonight? Now? The blood rushed in my ears as panic set in and I realized what he really meant . . .

"I know. It's shit, I know. But I can't go on like this. I'm not the guy who cheats on his girlfriend. And I can't continue to be the guy who fucks his girlfriend wishing all the time she was someone else."

Elation and fear washed over me in equal measure. "Cam, I . . ."

"You want this. I know you do." He pressed his forehead against mine and I closed my eyes, breathing him in. "Will you leave Malcolm?"

My muscles locked and I knew Cam felt it, because his grip on my arms tightened.

"Johanna?"

The truth was, I didn't know the answer to that question. Walking away from Malcolm wasn't just about me. It was about me and Cole and our future.

"You're telling me you're going to stay with that guy?" Cam asked harshly, shaking me a little. "You're going to go through the rest of your life standing at his side at parties, laughing that stupid bloody fake giggle, with your eyes contradicting your mouth every time it opens." He pulled back and I almost flinched at the distaste in his eyes. "That girl you were out there is not Jo. I don't know who that is, but she's an arse who pisses me off. She's fake, she's simpering, and she's a fucking bimbo. She's not you."

We were silent, our breathing uneven and loud as we worked to calm the tension between us. Hurt by his words, and yet in agreement with them, I found my mind whirling as I tried to weigh my options, the consequences, what was right and what was wrong.

I took too long to answer.

Cam let go of me and I shivered, feeling instantly cold. I wanted to die at the look he gave me.

Without another word, he reached past me to unlock the door and I found myself unceremoniously moved aside as he wrenched it open and disappeared into the party.

Tears clogged my throat, but I refused to let them travel to my eyes, my hands clenching at my sides. I could handle this without the waterworks. I knew I could.

Moving on shaking legs, I slumped against the sink to stare at my reflection and then gasped in horror. My cheeks were flushed, my eyes bright, and my skirt was still rucked up a little from where Cam had slipped his hand between my legs. I gasped again, remembering his fingers in me, and I gripped the sink so tight that my knuckles turned white. My nipples were peaked against my shirt and the color was still high on my cheeks.

I had to get myself under control or everyone would know what I'd been up to.

I gave myself ten minutes and as I returned to Malcolm's side, I saw Cam out of the corner of my eye shoving his way through the crowds of people toward the exit. The front door slammed loudly not too long after.

"You okay?" Malcolm's voice pulled my head around.

"He's a bastard!" Becca could suddenly be heard over the hum of music and voices. Malcolm and I twisted around to find her. She was in the corner, being comforted by her friends.

"Do you think he dumped her?" Malcolm asked in my ear. "While you were in the bathroom they were arguing."

Ashamed that I knew the answer all too well, I couldn't look at him. "Looks like it."

"You okay?" he repeated.

"I'm not feeling this party." I shrugged.

"Yeah, and it looks like Becca is about to kick off." Malcolm sighed. "Would it be awful if we snuck out?"

I threw him a weak smile. "It would be great."

He held my jacket and I shrugged into it. Two seconds later I let him pull me out of the flat. Without a word we walked down Leamington Terrace to the main road on Bruntsfield Place and waited for a taxi to approach with its light on. When we had no luck, Malcolm took out his phone. "I'll just call us one. We'll go back to my place for a while, yeah?"

I thought about heading back to his place with him, of him leading me up to his room like he always did, undressing me slowly and pushing me back on the bed . . .

It left me cold.

It made me feel sick with guilt.

Like I was cheating . . .

Malcolm had just put the phone to his ear when I found myself blurting out, "Stop."

Taken aback, Malcolm immediately lowered his phone and switched it off. His eyes washed over my face and whatever he saw there made his lips pinch tight together. He took a moment and then he asked, "What's going on?"

My practicality had taken a run and jumped off the nearest cliff. My emotions were fully in charge as I replied, "I can't go back to your place."

And then he surprised the hell out of me. "Because of Cam."

After working so hard to control them earlier, I felt those blasted tears hit my eyes. "I'm so sorry."

Malcolm heaved a sigh and I saw pain flicker in his gaze as it searched my face. "I really care about you, Jo."

"I care about you, too."

"I see the way he looks at you. The way you look at him. I knew there was something . . ."

"I'm sorry."

He shook his head, holding a hand up to stop me. "Don't."

"I feel awful."

"I can see that."

"I never slept with him."

His jaw clenched and then relaxed enough for him to reply, "I know. You're not that kind of girl."

Fingers quaking, I pushed up the sleeve on my jacket and unfastened the Omega watch he'd given me for Christmas. When he made no move to take it, I lifted his hand and placed the gift in the palm of it, curling his fingers around it. "Thank you for everything, Malcolm."

When he looked up from the watch, a piercing ache emanated from my chest at the dejection I saw in his face. "He's just a kid who doesn't know what the hell kind of gift he's getting in you, and when he's done, when he makes the mistake of throwing you away, I hope you'll come back to me." He stepped toward me and I froze as he dipped his head to press a sweet kiss against my cold lips. "We could be really happy."

I didn't take a breath until he put some distance between us. He threw up a hand and I turned to see he was flagging down a taxi. It did a U-turn and pulled up at the curb. Malcolm opened the door for me. "I'll be here when he's done with you."

I left him standing on the street, as the taxi took me back to London Road.

I'd broken up with Malcolm.

Oh, my God.

I felt heavyhearted. I felt remorseful. I was worried I wasn't doing the right thing. However, overriding all of that was this desperation to find Cam, to tell him I did feel what he felt. For the first time in as long as I could remember I was going after what I really wanted. Perhaps tomorrow I would lament the decision, but tonight I just wanted a taste of something really good and pure for once.

I almost threw the fare at the taxi driver, then rushed into the building, my boots slapping carelessly against the concrete as I hurried up the stairs. I was just rounding the stairwell to Cam's landing when I heard a door open. As I reached the top of the stairs, he came into view, standing barefoot in his doorway, waiting for me.

Overwhelmed that just the sight of him made my chest so full of emotion that it hurt, I stumbled a little toward him, my boots just clipping the doorstep.

Cam didn't say anything. Every inch of him was solid with tension as he looked at me.

"Cam—"

My words were swallowed by motion as his hand clamped around my wrist, wrenching me hard against his body, his mouth slamming down on mine. I instantly wrapped myself around him, and my fingers curled in the hair at the back of his neck as I licked and sucked and flicked my tongue against his, our kiss so deep I didn't even realize I was inside his flat until the door crashed shut behind us.

Cam broke the kiss to pull back, his hands shoving my jacket off my shoulders. I let it drop to the floor, exhilarated in *feeling*—my breasts were swollen, my skin burned, and I was surprised once more to realize I was already wet for him from just a kiss and anticipation. "Cam . . . ," I whispered urgently, needing some part of me touching him at all times. I slid my hand up under the bottom of his tee, feeling silken, hard, hot skin against my palm. "I broke up with him."

He nodded, his hands on my waist as he yanked me to him, my breasts brushing his chest deliciously. I shivered and Cam smiled, fully aware of the power he had over me. In reaction to his cockiness, my hand glided back down his six-pack and out from under his shirt and didn't stop its descent. He sucked in his breath as I rubbed him through his jeans, watching the color on his cheekbones rise. "I got that, baby," he said with a groan. "You wouldn't be here otherwise."

"Are we really doing this?" I whispered against his mouth.

His hands squeezed my waist, and I looked up into his eyes. They were almost navy with scorching heat. "We're really doing this. No backing out." His lips skimmed my jaw until his mouth stopped at my ear. "I'm going to fuck you so hard, sink so deep inside of you, you'll never work me out from under your skin. Never."

Tingles exploded all over my body at his words.

I reached for his mouth. I loved the taste of him, the feel, the way he kissed, like I hoped he screwed. I sucked his tongue hard and he shuddered, his growl urging me on, until it descended into the wettest, dirtiest kiss I'd ever experienced.

My back slammed up against the wall as he crashed us into it. "I can't wait," he told me breathlessly.

I shook my head, my chest heaving against his, telling him silently I couldn't wait either.

I felt his warm, rough hands on my outer thighs as they brushed my skin, pushing my skirt up to my waist. With an almost animalistic grunt, Cam curled his hands around the fabric of my knickers and tugged, the sound of it tearing away from my body and the sudden air between my legs increasing the heat between us to a combustible level. He'd just ripped my underwear off! Holy hell!

That was seriously hot.

I thought I would feel exposed, uncomfortable, standing there with my skirt at my waist, the most private part of me on display for him. I felt neither.

All I felt was urgency.

Our lips collided, biting, nipping, licking, as we both reached for the closure on his jeans. He shoved them and his boxers down to his ankles, freeing his cock, and I watched as he took his wallet out of his back pocket and pulled a condom out of it. As he rolled it up his straining dick, I gasped. It was big, but I had had big before. That wasn't what the gasp was for. The gasp was for the girth.

"Oh, my," I breathed, feeling the trickle between my legs incite my already excited state.

"Why, thank you." Cam flashed me a cocky grin that made me laugh—laughter that ended with a gasp as he gripped my legs, spread them, and thrust up into me.

"Cam!" I cried out in pleasured shock, his throbbing heat overwhelming me. Every feeling, thought, all my focus were on the sensation of his thickness inside me, and I struggled for breath as my body tried to adjust and relax. It was as if every nerve in my body was inflamed, and a minuscule shift between us sparked a tug of delicious tension I immediately sought more of.

Cam, however, held still against me, breathing heavily as though he was attempting to gain a little control. My body wasn't for it. I wanted more and I wanted more now. I pushed my hips against him and his grip on my thighs became almost bruising. "Wait," he said hoarsely. "Give me a minute. I've wanted this for ages and you feel bloody amazing. Just give me a minute." As I heard this erotic confession, my inner muscles clamped around his cock and he inhaled sharply. His head drew back in surprise as his eyes collided with mine. "Baby, do that again and I'm not going to last."

I shook my head, my fingers digging into the muscles of his back. "I don't care. Just move, please just move. I need you."

His control snapped.

As he hauled my legs up, my body took his lead and I wrapped my legs around him. Holding tight to him, I panted with excitement as he pounded us into the wall, thrusting into me hard, gliding in and out of my snug channel, the wet slap of flesh against flesh spurring us toward climax.

I felt his thumb press down on my clit and I blew apart, my cry of release triggering Cam's. He threw his head back, his eyes on me, his muscles strained as he let out a guttural grunt, my sex pulsing around him as he shuddered inside me in climax.

He fell against me, his lips on my shoulder, his chest against mine, my arms still locked around him. He turned his head and kissed my neck. "Do you know how many times I've imagined these long, gorgeous legs wrapped around me as I fucked you?"

I shook my head, still not recovered enough to speak.

"Every day. And none of the fantasies were as good as the real thing."

I smiled softly at that as he raised his head to kiss me. He made to pull back, but I chased his mouth, my hands sliding up his back to his nape, holding him to me as I kissed him with an ardor that hopefully clued him in to the fact that I wasn't nearly done. I leaned back and raised my eyes to his beautiful ones. Someone naughty and a little bit wicked had crept inside me. I wanted him again. And I wanted him just as raw and hard as I'd just had him. "Do you know how many times over the last few weeks I lay in my bed and touched myself thinking about you?"

His breath sputtered and I felt his dick twitch inside me. "Jesus," he breathed, his eyes dilating. "Keep talking and you're not going be able to walk tomorrow."

I grinned up at him, squeezing my inner muscles around him again. "That's the plan."

CHAPTER 15

Cam pressed a soft kiss to my mouth before he leaned back and pulled out of me. The fever hadn't quite left me, but I did feel the heated fog drift to the edges of my brain, allowing reality to settle in.

I'd dumped Malcolm tonight.

And then I'd had sex with Cam against his hallway wall.

Amazing sex.

Mind-blowing sex.

"Going to be a difficult act to follow" sex.

Cam-and-I-were-together-now sex.

The churning worry in my gut was overwhelmed for a moment by giddy butterflies. Weeks of daydreaming about him—and now it was no longer a fantasy. We were doing this.

All of a sudden I felt weirdly shy.

"Keep thinking those thoughts, whatever they are." Cam grinned, reaching out to smooth my skirt down for me. His eyes remained trained on mine as he took off the used condom and pulled his jeans up. "Stay right there."

Before I could reply, he wandered off down the hall, disappearing into the bathroom. I heard the flush and then he was sauntering back toward me with his jeans still unzipped, his eyes hot on me. "Is Cole staying at Jamie's tonight?"

I nodded, my heart banging away in my chest.

When Cam drew to a stop before me, he held out his hand to me. "Good. You can stay the night, then."

I'd never been turned on by a guy with tattoos, but as I drank in the sight of his arm, my eyes following the curling script of his BE CALEDONIA tattoo, I felt a rush of possessiveness over his ink—that one in particular. Somehow, it was mine too, and I wanted to follow every detail of it with my tongue, laying claim to it.

A flare of emotion blazed through my chest as he squeezed my hand, then led me to the back of the flat, to the master bedroom. I looked around as he walked us inside. I hadn't been in his room before. I was entering his private domain.

There wasn't much to see.

A king-sized bed with a pale blue duvet set, mostly bare walls except for a large framed print of two Stormtroopers getting into a DeLorean, a chest of drawers, a wardrobe, and a couple of bookshelves filled with books and DVDs. It was clean and tidy, just like the rest of his flat, I mused, trying to ignore my racing heartbeat. We'd just had sex, so the thought of having more sex shouldn't have sent my pulse skyrocketing. But it did.

Cam let go of my hand as he reached the bed and he turned to face me. In one smooth movement, he pulled his T-shirt over his head and threw it on the floor.

I swear I started to drool at the sight of him half-naked.

Yes, I had been right when I fantasized about this moment. Cam was pure, lean, solid muscle. I followed the lines of his six-pack to the sexy cut of his hips, my cheeks blazing.

I had been waiting for him to drop his jeans and let me ogle the rest of him, but instead, he sat down on the edge of the bed and looked up at me. "So . . . what would you like to do with me?"

Um, that seemed like a silly question, no? Was my panting and drooling not an indication of what I'd like to do with him? "What?"

He shrugged casually, as though we were sitting down to tea and not getting ready to repeat the hall sex but this time on a bed. "If we're doing this, you're going to be straight with me. In every way—including in bed. I'm not some guy you're trying to hold on to for dear life—accommodating him and forgetting about yourself and what you want. We're in this together and I just took what I wanted. Now *you* take what *you* want. So what do you want?"

My first thought was to jump on him and ravish him. Everything he'd said was perfect and it took me a moment to remember that this was real. Had I finally found someone who actually gave a shit? Like . . . *really* gave a shit?

I tried to stop myself from getting carried away on a floating cloud with one oar called hope and the other called dreams, but it was difficult when he was being so bloody wonderful.

So, okay, I wasn't some naive girl. I certainly knew Cam wasn't a perfect man—he'd proven that when we first met—but I was beginning to wonder if he might possibly be just a little bit perfect for me. Finally, I'd found a guy who wanted to be with me—the real me. And not only that—he was actually encouraging me to be a bit self-indulgent.

What he'd asked caused me, to my bemusement, some embarrassment. I wasn't a prude. I'd had plenty of sex with a few different men. However, none of them had ever asked me to talk about sex with them. No questions, no likes, no dislikes. Now Cam wanted me to communicate with him about sex, and I found myself grinning to cover my timidity. "You don't seem like the kind of guy who lets a girl take the lead much."

"I'm not the kind of guy who lets the girl take the lead much. I'm not the kind of guy who talks this much either. But I need to make sure your head is in the right place. It's too important. So as much as I want to strip you naked and bend you over my desk, tonight I'm leaving it up to you." His eyes darkened. "The desk can wait."

I was unbelievably turned on by the thought of Cam taking me against his desk. Sounded orgasmic to me. I licked my lips, eyeing him as he waited patiently for me to decide what we'd be doing next.

As I drank in his half-nakedness, I tingled all over with anticipation.

He was right. The desk could wait.

"Strip," I ordered quietly.

Cam stood up, his eyes never leaving mine as he pushed his jeans and boxers down his legs, his hard-on saluting me as he kicked himself free of his clothes. He stood before me completely unabashed by his nakedness, and I took a moment to sear the sight of him like this into my memory.

With shaking fingers I pulled off my own T-shirt, and pulled off my boots. My skirt followed them and lastly I unsnapped my bra, dropping it onto the pile of clothes at my feet.

I shivered as Cam slowly took me in, his dick throbbing, the color heightened again in his cheeks. When his blue eyes met mine, I inhaled sharply at the raw need in them.

"You're stunning," he whispered hoarsely. "No man can possibly deserve you."

Holy . . .

Wow.

My stomach actually somersaulted.

"Cam," I whispered back. The sheer emotion provoked by his beautiful words clogged my throat. It seemed that Cameron MacCabe was a bit of a romantic. I shook my head, not knowing how to respond to this side of him. Instead, I gestured to the bed. "Lie down on your back."

I noticed a muscle tic in his jaw at my order and had to curb my smug smile. No, Cam was definitely not used to letting the woman take the lead. Since I had a feeling that this was going to be a rare gift from him, I decided to take full advantage. I waited, my eyebrows raised expectantly, and Cam responded by lying back on the bed.

His hard-on didn't diminish under my command, though, straining and awaiting my attention. He stared at me, his hands crossed casually behind his head. *Well?* his eyes asked.

Ignoring the slight tremor in my hands and legs, I approached him slowly, my slender hips swaying from side to side, my perky breasts bouncing a little, and I kept the feminine satisfaction from my expression at the way his body tensed, all cocky relaxation coiling into anticipation.

I crawled up his legs, noting that his chest began rising and falling a little faster. My own breathing grew shallow as I stopped at his erection.

"Jo . . ." He groaned as my head dipped.

I didn't dislike going down on a guy, but it had never been my favorite thing. I found, however, that I wanted to taste Cam. I wanted to own him in every way that I could.

I wanted him to burn with me.

His scorching hardness passed between my lips and I felt his thighs tense under my fingertips. My tongue trailed along a vein on the underside of his cock and his breathing stuttered before seeming to stop entirely as I began to suck, bobbing my head so my mouth slid excruciatingly slowly up and down his length.

"Jesus," he growled through gritted teeth. "You keep that up— ahh—baby, I'll come and this will all be over."

Well, I didn't want that.

After a little more teasing, I released him and gazed at him from under my lashes, taken aback by how much I'd enjoyed that, how much my own body had responded to it. Finding the anticipation a total aphrodisiac and wondering where foreplay had been all my life, I kissed the sexy cut of definition in his left hip, my lips tracing a path along his torso as I crawled up his body. Knees on either side of his hips, I shivered as I felt his cock against inner thigh. I pressed my lips over his right nipple, my tongue flicking, my moan muffled against his body as I felt his rough hands cup my breasts, my own nipples pebbling, eager for his touch. When his thumbs brushed them, I shuddered, a sigh escaping from between my lips.

"You're sensitive," Cam murmured in satisfaction, squeezing my nipples between his fingers and thumbs. I barely had time to recover from the streaks of white-hot lightning that shot toward my groin before his right hand coasted down my stomach, heading between my legs.

As two fingers slid into my slick passage, my back arched, giving his left hand better access to my breast, and my hips surged against his right. I panted for breath, not caring that Cam had taken over.

Really, I was astonished he'd lasted as long as he had.

"Jesus," he grunted this time, his lower body bowing up off the bed. "Take me inside you. Condom in the drawer . . ."

I reached blindly through my sensual fog, yanking his bedside drawer open. Once we had him sheathed and ready to go, we guided him together to my entrance, the muscles in my legs shaking with need.

I slammed down on him and we both cried out, Cam's hips jerking up in reaction.

We found a torturous rhythm quickly and with my hands braced on the bed beside his thighs, I leaned back slightly so his cock thrust into me at the most delicious angle. I moved slowly, building toward an exquisite orgasm.

My gaze never left Cam's face as I moved, feeling sexy and powerful at his glittering expression, watching the way his blue eyes darkened on my breasts, on my hair swinging across my back. His hands gripped my hips, urging me on; his jaw clenched as the heat between us increased and a light sheen of sweat covered our skin.

As I approached climax all I was aware of was the coiling pleasure low in my belly, the sound of my uncontrolled breaths and mews of pleasure, the intoxicating smell of sex . . . and then I heard Cam hoarsely asking me to come. Pure bliss took me over, and I closed my eyes, reveling in it as my body moved faster up and down his length, rushing toward climax.

Lights exploded behind my lids as my orgasm shook through my entire body. My muscles clenched around Cam, wave after wave of pleasure pulsing around his cock.

Cool air whipped over my skin as Cam flipped me unexpectedly to my back, my eyes flying open as he pressed me into the mattress, holding my hands imprisoned above my head. His features were strained with uncontrolled need, and as he crushed his mouth against mine he began to stroke deep inside me, his movements rough and hard. He groaned into my mouth, the noise vibrating through my whole body, and I felt the stirring of another orgasm.

When his lips left mine, I stared up in wonderment, our gasps seeming to echo all around us as I pushed up against his thrusts. He let go of one of my arms, his hand disappearing between our joined bodies, and as soon as his thumb pressed down on my clit I flew apart, my scream filling the flat.

"Jo!" Cam cried out, eyes wide with wonder as my climax drew a staggered, seemingly soul-deep release from him. He collapsed on me, his face buried in the crook of my neck, his hand relaxing around my arm. His cock continued to twitch inside me, and I enjoyed the lingering pleasure it brought.

It was as though I'd melted into a puddle in the mattress—I couldn't feel or move any of my limbs. I was floating on utter gratification. I was sated air.

"Wow!" I breathed, wanting to curl my fingers in his hair but unable to remember how to move.

Cam nodded in agreement against my skin.

After a little while he pulled up, bracing his weight on his arms beside my head. His features were completely relaxed, his eyes soft and languid. "I've never come so fucking hard before," he confessed quietly.

Sweet satisfaction washed over me and gave me the strength to lift my arm. I stroked Cam's muscled back, then slid my hand into his hair, running my fingers through it soothingly. "Me either. In fact, up until now I thought multiple orgasms were a myth."

He laughed, his thumb sweeping affectionately across my cheek-bone. "You'll stay here tonight?"

"If you want me to."

His expression changed, becoming more serious—pensive even. "There's nothing I want more."

Smiling, I realized I believed him.

I didn't know if I trusted him completely yet, but at least I knew that in that moment I believed him. I drew his head down to mine, pressing my mouth to his for a kiss sweetened not just by the satisfaction of great sex but by emotion as well. When I let him up for air, I grinned at him, feeling a bit like a kid who'd found out Santa Claus was real after all. "You'll have to tell me if I snore."

He frowned. "No one's ever told you before?"

"I've had a sleepover once and I didn't stick around in the morning to ask."

"You mean you've only stayed with a guy once?" I knew by the hardness in his eyes that he'd drawn the right conclusion as to why that was.

I shrugged, turning my head away, embarrassed that I'd brought it up now and worried what he'd think. "Yeah."

"Jo?" He touched my chin, turning my head so I had to meet his gaze. "They were dicks. All of them."

"Let's not talk about them."

"We'll talk, just not now." And with that ominous warning, he withdrew from me and went to get rid of the condom. When he re-turned from the bathroom seconds later he pulled the duvet down underneath me so I could crawl onto the sheets, and he slid in beside me, covering us. I rested on my side, my head on his pillow, my nose inhaling the smell of his cologne, my heart suddenly racing again as I realized I didn't know what to do.

It became quickly apparent that I had no reason to be anxious.

Cam's strong arms wrapped around my waist as he snuggled in behind me, my naked bottom pressed to his groin, his legs entangling themselves in mine. "Night, baby." His voice rumbled in my ear and I felt my stomach flip at the possessiveness in those two words.

Smoothing my hands down over the arms that held me close, I burrowed back against him and let myself melt. "Night."

My butterflies actually woke me up, my eyes blinking open to find my cheek pressed against Cam's bare chest, my arm thrown across his stomach, and his hand resting on the curve of my waist as I lay curled into him. The fluttering in my stomach only worsened.

Cam must have seeped into my subconscious, all my concerns and exhilaration waking me. There was my excitement at being with him, and yet the anxiety over throwing away a secure relationship with Malcolm for this passionate but nevertheless somewhat shaky relationship I'd developed with Cam. Unlike any man I'd met, he could rile me, piss me off, argue with me until we were blue in the face . . . all of which screamed "disaster waiting to happen!"

Yet I had to weigh that against the unbelievable chemistry between us, the awe-inspiring sex, his concern and consideration once he'd stopped being a prick, his patience, and how down-to-earth he was. I loved that he could admit when he was wrong, that he saw things in me no other man had, and that he had taken time to get to know Cole. I liked Cam. I really liked him, and I knew as I lay there that I would have lost the tiny sliver of self-respect I'd had left if I'd walked away from those feelings, if I had given up on them because of another man's wealth and what it could bring me and Cole.

Cole.

I tensed a little, fretting at the thought of my brother. I didn't have nearly enough saved for his future. I needed to go job hunting again, see if I couldn't find something that paid better than Meikle & Young's.

"Whatever you're thinking, I'm not sure I'm going to like it," Cam murmured sleepily.

I tilted my head back in surprise, my eyes meeting his drowsy gaze. "What?"

He squeezed my waist. "You were warm and relaxed, and then I felt your whole body get tense. What's up?"

"Worrying about my job. Worrying I should try to get something that pays better than Meikle's."

"Never mind better pay. How about someone who treats you better?"

I made a noise of agreement.

"So is that what you do first thing in the morning? Worry?"

Smiling at him, I nodded. "If you're sticking around you'll need to get used to it."

He tightened his embrace. "If I'm sticking around, I'll do my best to make bloody sure you never have to worry again."

My breath caught. Damn, I hoped it wasn't going to become a habit of his to say romantic crap that robbed me of speech all the time. "Smooth talker," I answered a little hoarsely, and his lips twitched with amusement, as if the arrogant bugger knew that his words liquefied my insides.

"What time is it?"

"I don't know. I gave Malcolm back the Omega watch."

"That was good of you."

"It was the right thing to do." I winced, feeling a wave of remorse wash over me. It somehow didn't feel right to be luxuriating in the heat of Cam and the happiness he brought me, while Malcolm was home hurting over my betrayal. "Do you feel guilty?" I mumbled against his warm skin, my fingers absentmindedly stroking the lines of his abs.

"It's difficult to feel anything but hard when you're touching me, baby," Cam answered gruffly.

I chuckled despite myself. "Insatiable, are we?"

"Apparently around you."

"More sweet talk. Am I required to repay you in some way for it?"

"Now why would you assume you had to pay for it?"

I grinned teasingly. "Well, you're not known for being sweet to me, Cam."

His chest rose under my cheek as he gave a little huff of annoyance. "How long am I going to pay for being a bastard to you?"

"Oh, I don't know. I think it might prove useful as leverage in the future."

His playful growl filled the room as he rolled me onto my back. At the sudden move, I giggled up into his now alert eyes, letting him pin me to the mattress. He nudged my legs apart. His face was still relaxed from sleep, the sexy curl of his upper lip soft and begging for attention. "Do you want to know why I was such a bastard?"

"You've already told me why—ah." I ended on a gasp, feeling him hard and nudging insistently between my legs. My legs widened instinctively as he moved slowly against me, teasing me.

"Truth?" He lowered his head, kissing softly along my jaw until he found my ear. I shuddered at the tiny nip he gave the lobe, at the lick of his tongue against the bite. My chest heaved and my breasts brushed tantalizingly against his chest. My chest rose and fell in fast, shallow movements.

At the press of our bodies, Cam froze for a second, a guttural moan falling from his lips to land on a breath against my neck.

I brought my knees up, inviting him to take what we both so desperately wanted him to. He reached for the chest of drawers and rummaged around, then pulled out a condom.

As Cam put on the protection his usually cobalt eyes were almost black. "Truth?"

"Truth," I whispered on a nod.

"I wanted you and I couldn't have you."

My lips parted in amazement at the confession. "That's why you were a bastard to me?"

"I didn't want to want you so badly, so when it appeared that you were someone I could never respect or want, I held on to that and ran with it. But you kept blowing all my preconceptions to smithereens, and I just kept wanting you more."

As Cameron gazed deep into my eyes I felt a weight bear down on us, like a cocoon wrapping around us, protecting the connection that was developing so deep and fast between us. "I guess that means your bastard days are behind you," I replied, my words barely audible under the gravity of emotion.

His brows drew together. "Meaning?"

"You can stop wanting me now that you have me."

Light twinkled mischievously in his eyes as he grinned at me. "I don't think that's possible. To stop wanting you, I mean."

Without warning, before I could even reply to *that*, he pushed into me and I cried out, my hands digging into the muscles in his back as my body grew reacquainted with his thickness. His breath whispered over my lips just before he kissed me, his tongue teasing mine as he pulled out of me a few inches before sliding back in.

His kisses were hot and sweet as he slowly made love to me, pushing us toward another shattering release.

We had just gotten out of his shower—where I'd finally found my chance to study the ink on his arms with my tongue—and we were in the kitchen making tea and toast when my phone rang. I found it in the pocket of my faux fur jacket, still lying in the hall from last night when Cam stripped me out of it.

A picture of Joss giving someone behind me a sly grin popped up on my phone screen as it rang. I'd taken it at the bar months ago, not realizing Craig was doing some absurd "sexy" dance behind me as I snapped Joss's picture. I smiled. "Hullo?"

"Hey, you," she answered casually. "How are you?"

"I'm fine." *More than fine! I just had life-changing sex with Tattoo Guy!* I grinned, trying to contain my giddiness as I wandered back into the kitchen, where Cam stood by the kettle, shirtless and all mine. "You?"

"Good. You sound weird."

"Weird?"

"Yeah. Weird."

"I don't know what you're talking about." Cam glanced up at me and smiled, the corners of his eyes crinkling sexily. I grinned again. "I don't know what you're talking about at all."

"Hmm." Clearly Joss was unconvinced. "Are you and Cole coming to lunch today?"

I hesitated. I had a lot to do today. I had to tell Cole about me and Cam, and it was time to put the clothes Malcolm had bought me on eBay. Just the thought of it made my stomach lurch with guilt about how things had ended between us.

"Butter or jam on your toast?" Cam asked loudly.

I sucked in my breath.

"Was that Cam?" Joss asked quietly, more than idle curiosity in her tone.

"Yes."

"At nine thirty in the morning? Asking about toast?"

"Mm-hmm."

"Oh, my God, you fucked him."

I rolled my eyes. "Well, just say it like it is, Joss."

"I take it you dumped Malcolm first before you got it on with Tattoo Guy. Poor Malcolm. Oh, well."

An unexpected warmth flooded my chest at Joss's summation of the situation. She hadn't asked me if I'd cheated on Malcolm. She'd just assumed I'd been good enough to be straight with him. It was nice to know she thought so well of me. "We broke up last night." I was suddenly very aware of Cam's inquisitive eyes on me. "Look, we'll talk about it later."

"Bring Cam to lunch."

Okay, what? "What?" I tried to squelch the hint of hysteria in that question.

"If you're seeing him now you should bring him to lunch. Elodie won't mind."

"You never asked Malcolm to lunch."

Cam shot me another questioning look.

"Well, if I'd thought the lunch would be as interesting as this one is definitely going to be, I might have."

"We're not coming to lunch just to entertain you."

Suddenly the phone was whipped from my ear and I watched wide-eyed as Cameron held it up to his own. "Joss, hey, it's Cam. We'll be there. Time?" He nodded at whatever she said. "Cool. See you then."

I took the phone from him and gestured between us. "I don't know what just happened here, but we'll talk." I lifted it to my ear. "Joss."

"Nice phone voice, huh?" She chuckled.

"Funny. Apparently we'll see you at lunch."

"See you then. Oh, and Jo?"

"Yeah?"

"Was he good?"

Laughter fell from my lips before I could stop it, remembering how I'd pestered Joss about Braden after I found out they had slept together. Payback was a bitch. "What was it you said to me? You can have him when I'm done."

Her groan caused my smile to widen. "I'm such a bitch. Never tell Braden I said that. Please?"

"I promise."

"Good. If you break that promise, I'll find a way to lock you in a room with Ellie and her romantic drama collection."

"You know, some of us don't find that an excruciating prospect."

"Fine. I'll take up smoking just to drive your cravings nuts."

"You have a severely sadistic side. Anyway, I don't have any cravings."

"Even when you smell cigarette smoke?" she asked smugly.

Damn. It was true. Anytime I got a whiff of cigarette smoke, my eyes closed in torture and I had to hunt down the nearest stick of gum to quell the need for nicotine intake. "Your point is moot considering I'm not going to tell him."

"Moot? Nice word choice. The brain is certainly working well for a Sunday morning conversation. He must have really started those engines, huh?"

"Good-bye, Joss. Oh, and you tell anyone about me and Cam before I get a chance to and I will tell Braden." I hung up with a satisfied smirk.

Cam was staring at me as he held out my mug of coffee. "What was that about?"

"I have some information she'd like me to keep quiet. She threatened to torture me with cigarette smoke if I ever give her up."

He frowned, pushing a plate of toast toward me. There were slices spread with butter and others with jam. I took some sugary goodness. "You used to smoke?"

"Quit almost six months ago."

"Thank God," he muttered.

His words caused a pang of anxiety at the thought that something as insignificant as being a smoker would make him less attracted to me. Would it be so easy to diminish his attraction in the future? I covered my insecure thoughts with a forced chuckle. "What? Would that have been a deal breaker?"

The corner of his mouth quirked up cheekily. "Nah. I'd have convinced you to quit somehow. Just glad I missed the withdrawal. That must have been fun for Cole."

My whole body relaxed at his answer and when I laughed it was for real this time. "I wasn't that bad."

"Yeah, yeah, I'll get the real story from Cole."

"Speaking of . . ." I muttered and scrolled through my phone until I found his number. Cole's phone rang three times before I heard his voice.

"What's up?"

"You on your way home?"

"Five minutes away."

"Okay. I have something to talk to you about." I smiled at Cam, but inside I was a little nervous about Cole's reaction to me and Cam being together.

"That doesn't sound good."

"We'll see."

He grunted and I rolled my eyes.

"See you soon."

Another grunt and then he hung up. I sighed. "Someone should have written a book by now about interpreting teen language. I was never that monosyllabic."

Cam grinned into his mug. "I'll bet."

I smacked him playfully. "You know what I mean."

He shrugged. "He's a teenage boy. As far as teenage boys go I think you guys have good communication between you."

Guessing he was probably right, I nodded and reached for another slice of toast. "Well, let's see how my communication skills hold up when we try to explain this to him."

As Cam dumped his mug in the sink, he flashed me a wolfish grin. "Oh, I'd say from all that screaming you did last night and this morning, those communication skills are pretty sharp."

"You're such a cocky bugger."

"Then stop with the screaming. It only inflates my ego. Among other things."

"Fine. From now on I'll be quiet as a church mouse."

Laughing, Cam reached for me, tugging me against his chest as I took the last bite of my toast. He kissed me, getting crumbs and jam on his lips. "I dare you to try to keep quiet. Go on. It'll make things even more interesting."

Resting my hands on his chest, I leaned into him, feeling him harden against me through his jeans. I bit my lip, smiling a little as I stared at his sensual mouth. "I accept that dare." My eyes flicked to his, laughing at him. "It's not like it won't be a win-win situation."

His arms tightened around me. "Going to make me work for it, huh?"

"You'll enjoy the labor."

His grin widened and he shook his head. "I can't believe we waited this long."

Still smiling, I nodded in agreement. "It's definitely fun so far."

Although Cam was still smiling back at me, something grave entered his expression as he held my gaze. "Yeah, baby. It's definitely fun so far."

CHAPTER 16

There was a sense of unreality as Cam threaded his fingers through mine and brought my knuckles to his lips. The soft brush against my skin was like a greeting and goose bumps popped up all over my body to say hello back to him. He led me up the stairs to my flat and the whole time I gazed at him in surreal wonder, the concrete steps like marshmallow clouds beneath my feet. How could it be that sex had not had such a "girly" effect on me but this arbitrary act of handholding did? For a moment, the beauty of it allowed me to forget where he was actually leading me.

Mum.

Fiona was sitting on the couch watching television when Cam and I entered the flat. As soon as I heard the muffled sound of voices filtering into the hall from the sitting room, my whole body tensed with the realization that Cam was about to come face-to-face with her since he'd helped Cole out the night I'd stayed at Malcolm's.

Yay.

Seeming to read my body language, Cam pressed a reassuring hand to the small of my back, guiding me into the room.

She was lounging on the armchair in her ratty robe with her thinning hair wet. To my surprise I realized that she had obviously taken a shower without being coerced by me. She had a hot mug in her hand and it shook as she raised it to her lips, watching us as we slowly made our way farther into the room.

"Mum." I gave her a brittle nod and Cam's hand coasted around my waist, his strong arm hugging me into his side.

The slight widening of Mum's eyes told me she hadn't missed the deliberate move. "You've been here before?" She asked it quietly, with mild curiosity but no accusation, as I had been expecting. Clearly she'd forgotten Cam and his presence that awful night.

"Cameron MacCabe." Cam acknowledged her gruffly, giving me a squeeze.

She made a mumbling noise, her bloodshot eyes darting back to me. "No one was here this morning."

Burrowing deeper into Cam, my hand clutching the back of his shirt like a little girl, I nodded again. "Cole stayed at Jamie's."

"I fell." Her mouth pursed. "I fell. My back is killing me. No one was here to help. If you're going to be gallivanting around, that little bugger should at least be here to help."

The insult to my brother was like a steel rod sliding into my spine. I straightened sharply, taking a step away from Cam. My eyes narrowed on her, and I tried to squelch the hurt in my chest—the hurt I felt anytime she did or said something so selfish and uncaring, so lacking in parental concern. "Did the gin not help you back up, Mum? Funny, it seems to help you with everything else."

Her rugged cheeks were peppered with visibly broken veins and the little color that was in them leached out completely at my comment. "Don't you get smart with me because *he's* here."

Taking a deep breath, knowing that if we continued at this pace, we'd end up in a huge argument in front of Cam, I softened my tone. "Cole and I have lives, Mum. You need to watch out for yourself more now, okay?"

Waiting for a reaction, I stepped back so I could at least feel the heat of Cam behind me. I was grateful to him for keeping quiet and letting me deal with Mum in my own way. She got shakily to her feet, setting her mug on the table. "I just needed a bit of help," she answered quietly, hitting me in the chest with her words. Guilt wormed its way inside, despite my urgent battle against it.

I sighed heavily. "If you're really desperate, phone me next time." I could have punched myself for giving in.

"I will, darling." She shuffled past us, her eyes on the ground. "Nice meeting you, Cameron." It was the nicest she had been to me since I confronted her about hitting Cole. Remembering how much I distrusted her, I felt deep regret at being even slightly polite to her. *I shouldn't have given in*, I thought bitterly.

Cam grunted in response to her, doing a fair impression of Cole.

I waited until she'd disappeared from the room, until we heard her bedroom door closing, and then my eyes slid to Cam. "Well?"

His features had hardened. "She's a manipulative cow and she knows just how to play you." At that he turned on his heel and disappeared into the hall, heading toward the kitchen.

I followed him, my heart thumping in my chest. "I told you how she is."

"Yeah, one minute a bloody witch, the next completely normal and nice. It's deliberate. When she's a witch, you stand up to her. When she's nice, you give in and she knows it. She's playing you."

Knowing that he was right and not really wanting to get into it with him on what had started out as the best morning ever, I began helping him make tea and coffee. We returned to the sitting room, having come to an unspoken agreement to put thoughts of my mum aside, and we both sat down on the couch. As soon as I did, Cam pulled me over his lap so that my legs straddled his thighs.

"What are you doing?" I asked, my lips twitching with laughter.

"Getting comfy." He reached past me and grabbed our mugs, handing me mine.

I took it, completely bemused by our proximity. We were so close I could see coppery striations in the cobalt blue of his irises. "You're comfortable like this?" I watched him as he casually took a sip of coffee, his other arm around my hip, his hand resting on the curve of my ass.

"Extremely," he murmured.

Shrugging, I relaxed into him, taking a sip of tea.

And that was as long as I got to relax. The sound of the front door opening moved me into instant action. I attempted to dive out of Cam's arms.

He stopped me effortlessly with *one* arm.

"What are you doing?" I hissed, my eyes narrowed on him, my heart thumping hard at the thought of Cole's walking in on us wrapped around each other without an explanation first.

"Um, what's going on?"

Too late.

I closed my eyes briefly, shooting Cam a death look when I opened them and then peering past his head to smile apologetically at my brother, who took up a good portion of the doorway with his height and increasing frame. His green eyes were narrowed on the back of Cam's head. They shifted to me. "Is this what you wanted to talk about?"

I nodded and tried once again, unsuccessfully, to clamber off Cam's lap as Cole strode into the room. He walked past the sofa to the armchair and Cam smiled at him before sipping his coffee, completely relaxed except for the arm that bound me tight to him.

Cole sighed and dropped into the chair. "You two together, then?"

We answered in unison.

Unfortunately not with the same answers.

"Yes."

"We'll see."

As Cole's eyebrows rose, his eyes bright with amusement, Cam turned his head sharply to glare at me. "We'll see?"

Bugger. Now he thought I didn't want this. I *did* want this. I just didn't want him to feel pressured in case that scared him off. "I don't want us to feel rushed."

"Bullshit. You don't want me to feel rushed. I thought we talked about that."

I gaped at him. Cam wasn't known for his intuitiveness when it came to me, but apparently the more he got to know me, the more he saw. Was I becoming predictable?

I didn't know how I felt about that.

"If you're looking for my approval, you have it," Cole muttered as he stood up again. He shot Cam a quick smile as he passed us. "Seems like you know what you're doing."

"Oh, funny." I took umbrage to my brother's droll comment, rolling my eyes at the sound of his chuckle as he disappeared down the hall into his room. My eyes slid back to Cam's face only to find him grinning at me. "Don't even think about becoming a tag team."

He laughed, his eyes crinkling in the way that melted my insides. "Wouldn't dream of it." He put his mug down and then mine, before wrapping his arms around me. I slid my arms around his neck, settling closer into him. "That went well."

"It went how every conversation with Cole goes lately."

"And what way is that?"

"Quickly."

I felt Cam's shoulders shake underneath me. "He's a guy. We like to get straight to the point."

Enjoying the mix of contentment and excitement I felt in his arms, I pressed my body deeper into his, feeling his erection grow against my butt. I brushed his mouth lightly with my own, glorying at the hitch in his breathing. "You took a while to get to the point this morning."

The glitter in his eyes was the only warning before I found myself thrown back on the couch. Cam gripped my thighs, pushing my legs open so he could settle between them. I wrapped my long legs around him and he kissed me, slow and deep. We made out for a while like two teenagers. It was bloody brilliant!

As his strong hand glided up my outer thigh, I breathed in his familiar scent and wished we didn't have to go to lunch. Reading my thoughts, he finally pulled back, and I couldn't stop myself from tracing my fingers along his lips. He really had the most distracting mouth of any man I'd ever met.

Continuing our conversation as if five minutes of lip-locking hadn't just happened, I whispered, "I didn't mean that as a bad thing. I meant it as a very, very good thing."

"Then I'll make sure to take my time getting to the point in the future."

"I said I was cool with it, not that I wanted to see it," Cole grumbled above us.

We both jerked our heads around to see Cole standing by the couch, glaring down at us, a plate of sandwiches in one hand and a glass of Coke in the other.

"Oi, what are you doing?" I huffed at my brother, pushing Cam off of me. "We're going to lunch. You're going to spoil your dinner."

"Wow," Cam said lightly as he sat up. "I just got a glimpse into the future."

"What?"

He laughed, shaking his head as he turned to Cole. He gestured to the sandwiches. "I'll take one of those."

Cole held the plate out and Cam casually took a sandwich.

I stared at them both, munching on their snacks, ruining their appetites. "God. Now there's two of them."

That only made Cam and Cole share amused, secret "guy club" smiles.

A sense of warmth—beautiful, relaxing, contented warmth—radiated out from my chest, enveloping my entire body in a kind of happiness I'd never felt before.

The feeling absolutely terrified the bejesus out of me.

. . .

I spent the bus ride to Stockbridge talking. I don't think I stopped to breathe once. Cole sat behind us with his earphones in, listening to an audiobook, so he was completely oblivious to my record-breaking non-stop chatter at Cam as I laid out the benefits of keeping our relationship on the down low. I honestly didn't know why I wanted to keep it quiet. I thought it might have something to do with making sure there were few witnesses to my heartbreak if this went south, but I wasn't going to tell Cam that. Instead I rambled, and rambled, and rambled at him.

He may have been sick of the sound of my voice by the time we got off that bus, but at least I knew my point had been made. We were keeping our relationship quiet.

"Jo and I are together now."

Ten minutes had passed since we'd gotten off the bus and we were standing in Elodie Nichols's living room with the entire Nichols family plus Adam, Braden, and Joss staring at us. Cam had made that little announcement in response to Ellie's "So how are you?"

As Joss would say, I felt sucker-punched. I shot Cam a disbelieving look. "Did you not hear a word I said on the bus?"

He gave me that wide, appeasing grin that did naughty things to my insides. "I have selective hearing, baby." He clutched my hip, trying to pull me close. "Good thing too or my brain might have melted out of my ears. I didn't know it was possible for a human to say that many words per minute."

I looked at my friends, who were all staring at us with sly grins on their faces. "Cam and I just broke up."

Cam laughed, hugging me even tighter into his side.

I huffed, trying to wriggle free. "What are you doing?"

"Getting back together with you."

The sound of barely stifled chortles made my cheeks redden. Oh, God, we were being "cute" in company. My eyes slid to Joss. Sure enough, she had a superior smile on her face. There was no way to win this round, but I could lessen the cuteness. "Fine," I mumbled ungraciously, relaxing against him.

Elodie and Clark, who had been introduced to Cam only three minutes ago, started firing questions at him about being a graphic designer, about growing up in Longniddry, and about his parents, until I eventually left him sitting beside Cole and enlisted Hannah in making an escape. Since I couldn't feel the heat of Joss's stare, I took this to mean that she was just happy Cam and I were together and didn't need to know the details. Ellie was a different story. She would want to know absolutely everything. Her eyes bored into me, and I could almost hear her telepathic orders for me to look at her. That was when I started shooting Hannah "save me" looks.

My little savior shot to her feet. "I have to show Jo something. *Alone*," she said pointedly, giving her sister a look that allowed no room for argument. She got that look from Elodie.

"But—"

We were already out of the room before Ellie could say a second word.

Trying to muffle our giggles, we fell into Hannah's room. "You are the best person in the whole world." I grinned at her.

Hannah smiled in response as she flopped down on her bed. "You know you're going to have to face the inquisition soon though, right?"

"I know. I'd just rather face it later rather than sooner."

Suddenly Hannah's cheeks flushed a little red. "He's really hot."

Laughing, I moved to sit beside her, feeling my own cheeks heat as I remembered this morning and last night. "He is that."

"I won't ask about Malcolm or anything, but . . . I heard Ellie speaking with Joss and they said Cam's not really your usual type. I guess that doesn't matter if you're happy."

I loved this kid. Truly and deeply. "I'm happy today. Scared. But happy. Cam has convinced me to do something just for me, rather than for me and Cole." I remembered all the security that had walked away with Malcolm last night and I felt a stab of fear and anxiety. In an effort to ignore it, I nudged Hannah with my shoulder. "So how is Marco?"

Heaving a massive sigh, Hannah fell back on the mattress and stared at the ceiling, avoiding my eyes. "He's talking to me again."

"Why aren't you more excited about that?"

"Because the tool is acting like nothing happened. Like we're just friends. Not to mention there is this girl in the year above me who's been telling everyone she hooked up with him at a party last weekend. She's really pretty."

"Well, considering you're beautiful, I think you have one over on her." Hannah made a noise of disbelief and I patted her knee. "One day you're going to look in the mirror and see what I see."

"A geek who needs an attitude readjustment?"

I made a face. "What?"

"I got in trouble this week. Mum and Dad aren't happy."

My painfully shy Hannah had gotten in trouble? "What?" I repeated in disbelief.

"My PE teacher had a go at me because I refused to get into an all-girls team against an all-boys team at basketball. I told him that it's scientifically proven that boys are stronger and faster than girls and that to put all girls against all boys was setting the girls' team up for failure. He said that I was being unfair to my own sex. I said I was being realistic and that I thought that he was deliberately favoring the boys over the girls. He reported me and, while our head teacher told him that all basketball teams during classes should be mixed from now on, the head teacher also called Mum and told her I needed an attitude readjustment."

Choking down my amusement as I caught the twinkle of bedevilment in her eyes, I shook my head at her. "What happened to the crippling shyness?"

She somehow managed to shrug lying down. "I just feel like being shy is getting in my way."

"Is this because of Marco?"

"No, not just that. Although I'm getting the impression I'm not really 'cool' enough for him—"

"Then he's an idiot."

"It's more that I missed out on joining the debate team because I was too shy to speak up. And I know I'd be really good at debate."

"I think we all know that."

She threw a cushion at me and continued as if I hadn't spoken. "And I missed out on the Christmas dance this year because my friends and I felt too self-conscious going alone together. And I wrote this poem that really means a lot to me and I wanted to enter it into this regional competition but I didn't because—"

"You were too shy." I patted her knee again. "So you what? Just woke up one day and decided not to be?"

Hannah sat up, her eyes filled with wisdom beyond her years. "No. I kissed a boy I really like and he rejected me. If I can handle that, I'm pretty sure I can handle opening my mouth in front of people I've gone to school with for years and saying what I want to say."

I nodded slowly and then gave her a reassuring smile. "For what it's worth, you are the coolest person I know."

"Even cooler than Cam?"

Cam was that smart, geek-like, hot guy who marched to the beat of his own drum. Yeah. He was so cool I could die from his coolness, but I wasn't going to admit to that like a besotted teenager. I snorted, getting up off the bed. "Oh, please, he only thinks he's cool."

"He's really cool, isn't he?" Hannah grinned at me over her shoulder as she opened her bedroom door.

I followed her out, all fake superiority gone. "Yeah. Just don't tell him I said so."

"Tell who?" Ellie was suddenly in my face as if she'd appeared out of nowhere. Within seconds, Hannah and I had been herded back into her bedroom by Ellie and Joss.

Joss gave me a sympathetic smile. "I tried to stop her."

I sucked in a breath, waiting.

And then Ellie began peppering me with her rapid-fire questions.

Lunch actually couldn't have gone any better. Cam was well-mannered, gracious, intelligent, interesting—all the things I knew he was and could be, but I was glad to see that the Nicholses and Joss and Braden could see that too. I also loved that they noticed how close he was to Cole already. They sat together at the table and whenever conversation wasn't directed at either one of them, they had their heads together, talking quietly about the book Cole was listening to. Apparently Cam had recommended it.

Since Cam shared Braden's and Adam's dry senses of humor, I had no worries that the three guys wouldn't get on. Braden kept shooting me these teasing smiles that somehow translated into "I'm happy for you." That was nice. It really was. However, it just amplified the little ghost of anxiety floating around me, groaning at me about what would happen if this "thing" with Cam fell apart.

I'd never received that awful pity and sympathy other people did when they broke up with someone, because no one had ever really taken my feelings for my boyfriends seriously—whether they were serious or not—yet I knew that in this situation there would be agonizing sympathy if Cam walked away, and I wasn't sure I could handle that.

There I was, already imagining the demise of our relationship.

I needed my head checked.

With Cam's strong, slightly callused hand in mine, his body close, his voice full of warmth and affection as we strolled down London Road with Cole, I knew I needed my head checked. This was good. We'd only just started and it was *good*. I wasn't going to let my mistrust poison this. I wasn't.

I squeezed Cam's hand as we walked into our building, his deep voice echoing up the stairwell as he told me about a couple of jobs he'd seen advertised in the paper.

"You should definitely apply for them," I responded, frowning at Cole, who walked upstairs ahead of us, his shoelace flapping against the concrete. He was going to get himself killed. "Cole, tie your shoe."

"We're nearly at the flat," he argued.

"Tie your shoe."

We all stopped and waited for him to follow my instruction.

"Happy?" he grunted, continuing upward.

"When you speak to me like that, baby boy, how can I not be?"

I could hear Cam choke on his laughter behind me, so when we turned onto his landing I was looking back at him. That's why I slammed into Cole.

"What the . . ." My voice trailed off as I turned sharply to see what the problem was.

The problem was Becca, standing in front of Cam's door with a carrier bag in her hand.

"I want my stuff back." She thrust the bag out at Cam, who stepped in front of us to approach her. "Here's your shit. You were always careful not to leave much with me, so there's only a book and your MP3 player." Ouch. The hallway fairly echoed with her bitterness.

Guilt immediately assailed me and I pressed close to Cole, who leaned back into me, his stance almost protective. He'd met Becca only once, but he knew who she was and what this situation meant.

Cam calmly took the bag from her. "What stuff did you leave?"

She sneered at him. "You don't even care, do you? You broke up with me and then you went home with *her*." She pointed at me like I was trash. "Yeah, Malcolm filled me in." Her eyes glittered now as she turned to face me. "Don't worry, slut. Malcolm and I made each other feel better last night. Hope that lessens the guilt."

"Enough," Cam snapped, stepping into Becca's space. He bristled with anger and Becca was smart enough to slam her mouth closed. "Don't ever speak to her like that again. Understood?"

Her eyes narrowed. "Just get me my stuff."

"I'll look around the flat and whatever I find of yours, I'll send to you."

"But—"

"I'll send it, Becca. We're done here."

It was cold of him, but I understood his reaction. I imagined he didn't want a scene in the hallway where our neighbors could hear and, worse, where Cole could hear. Intimidating her into leaving seemed like the safest option. I moved out of her way as she passed me, but she stopped as she reached me.

"Are you going to fuck every man I fuck?"

I flinched. "Watch your language."

Becca looked at me as if I had just crawled out from under a rock. "You're an idiot for walking away from Malcolm Hendry for *him*. Everyone knows Cameron MacCabe only fucks around with a girl for a couple of weeks before moving on. You downgraded big-time. But that's your mistake." She shot Cam a snide smile that I knew merely covered her hurt. It had always been clear that Becca was more into Cam than he was into her. "I think I'll upgrade." Her nasty smile was just for me as she leaned in to whisper, "I might give Malcolm a call."

The three of us watched her leave in silence, and finally, trembling a little, I let Cole lead us up to the flat. He shot me a worried look before disappearing into his bedroom, and I felt more than heard Cam follow me into the kitchen.

The heat of him enveloped me as he pressed against my back, stilling my hand on the kettle before wrapping his arms around my waist. I slid my hands over his and leaned into him. "You okay?" he asked softly, genuine concern in his voice.

I shrugged, not really sure what I was feeling. "I guess. I feel bad."

"If it makes you feel any better, I never made any promises to Becca. We were very casual."

"Malcolm and I weren't."

Cam's arms tightened. "Did it bother you? What she said about her and Malcolm last night?"

I didn't know. I thought it did. I just wasn't sure if it was because I still had feelings for him or because my vanity was pricked. "It just reinforced the truth. It wasn't real between us."

The touch of Cam's warm lips on my jaw sent a delicious shiver down my spine and I momentarily forgot everything. "Where am I sleeping tonight?"

My skin grew warm just at the prospect of tonight. "My bed is too small for us to share but I can't leave Cole alone. Why don't I come down to see you? I won't be able to stay, though."

"That's fine, baby. Listen, I said I'd meet Nate for a drink." He pulled back and turned me in his arms. "I'll see you back at my flat tonight?"

"Yeah. Around eleven thirty?"

"I'll be there." He dipped his head to press a light kiss to my lips, but I reached up to cup his jaw, drawing his mouth back to mine. I deepened the kiss, my tongue teasing his, my fingernails scraping gently along his stubbly jawline until my fingers clenched in the hair at his nape. I kissed him until he had to pull back to draw breath.

Eyes a little wide and unfocused, Cam nodded and reluctantly let me go. "Let's make it ten thirty."

CHAPTER 17

"I was thinking we should both get checked out so we can stop using condoms. You're on the pill, right?"

My hair whispered across the pillow as I turned to look at Cam lying next to me, his skin glistening with a faint sheen of sweat. I was still panting from our exertions and it took me a minute to process what he'd asked. "Yeah. I'll get checked this week."

"Me too. I should be fine. I got checked before Becca and she and I always used protection."

"A little friendly advice." I sighed, looking up at the ceiling. "Don't talk about your sexcapades with another woman seconds after having sex with your current woman."

"No need to be jealous, baby. You're a ten—she was a five. Maybe a six on a good day."

I rolled my eyes, pretending not to be satisfied that Cam thought I was a better lay than Becca. "And definitely don't score them."

Cam laughed, rolling onto his side so he could pull me to him. He tried to kiss me, but I was still slightly pissed that he'd mentioned Becca, so I covered his mouth with my hand. He kissed it and said something, but it was muffled against my skin.

I pulled my hand back. "What was that?"

His eyes roamed my face, a small smile playing on his lips. "I said I'm sorry."

"Good."

Dipping his head, his eyes serious, Cam spoke, his lips grazing mine. "You ever try to keep this mouth from me again and I'll find very creative forms of use for it as punishment."

I shivered. This side of him in bed was a real turn-on. "It's my mouth. It's up to me who gets near it."

"True," he acquiesced, his hand trailing down my hip to wind up between my legs. I jolted involuntarily at the press of his thumb on my clit. "But last night you agreed that we were together, and being to- gether means that mouth belongs to me. I don't like people hiding my things." He ended that pronouncement with a roguish grin. His thumb circled my clit and I gasped, clutching his wrist, urging him on.

I wanted to call him on his crap, but I couldn't speak. Couldn't think. My body had already been treated to a tremendous orgasm and was now positioned on the precipice of another.

I came quickly, I came hard, and I came with a cry that Cam qui- eted against his mouth. His kiss was wet and dirty, and its purpose was to swallow my climax and stamp me with his ownership.

The bastard was lucky I was feeling equally possessive.

Gripping his head tight, I kissed him back just as voraciously and when he moved to catch his breath, I nipped his lip. Hard.

He hissed, his eyes widening, his tongue flicking out to lick the hurt.

"If mine is yours, yours is mine."

He liked that. I could tell by the way his eyes crinkled at the cor- ners. "Deal."

I liked that too. I liked that I felt comfortable enough to be myself with him. My thumb caught the nip in an affectionate gesture of half- hearted apology. "I need to go." I moved to roll away from him, only to be drawn to a halt by his arm across my waist.

"Stay. Just for a little while."

Worry immediately caused my whole body to tense, obliterating all my happy thoughts about us as a couple. This felt an awful lot like déjà vu—me hurrying home to Cole, leaving an annoyed man lying in bed. Before, it had mattered on some level that I not upset my relationship. With Cam it mattered on *every* level. My brows drew together in confusion and anxiety. I'd assumed things would be different with Cam. That he understood. Only seconds ago I was "Miss Comfortable" and now I was back to being who I was suddenly very sick and tired of being.

"What?" He tugged on my waist, trying to urge me closer. "What's causing this?" His fingers traced my frown lines.

"Nothing."

"It's not nothing." With an effort, he forced me to turn completely back to him. "Your muscles are locked up tight. Why?"

On the one hand, I wanted us to be okay. To be open. To be real. On the other hand, I didn't want him to think I was questioning him so soon into this. I didn't want to leave his bed pissed off at him and vice versa.

I chewed my lip, taking far too long to think it over.

"Jesus, Johanna." He pulled back before I had a chance to say anything, his eyebrows dipped in anger. "I'm not bloody *them*." He threw the sheets off of us as he moved to leave the bed.

Dammit! "I'm just worried," I huffed, feeling my cheeks heat at the coming confession.

Cam grew still, twisting his head to look at me over my shoulder. "Go on."

I made a face at his bossiness and sat up, drawing my knees to my chest in a subconscious need to protect myself. "I'm worried you'll get bored with the fact that I can't . . . accommodate you. Because I have Cole and"—I braced myself, wondering how he'd react to my next piece of brutal honesty—"he'll always come first."

In seconds I was flat on my back, Cam looking down at me, his eyes soft again, and better yet, they were filled with understanding. "You never have to worry about that. I get it. I understand. Cole comes first. Of course he does. He's a bloody kid who needs you. I'm not going to get bored or pissed off. And frankly if I do, you should dump my ass."

Something shifted in my chest, something huge and overwhelming and scary. That something was my feelings for Cam. They were settled inside me now, held in place by an immovable anchor. "Are you for real?" I asked, giving him a weak smile, trying to cover how emotional I felt.

Cam smiled back at me as he placed a soft kiss on my mouth. "Completely real, baby. But if you need proof . . ." He pressed his knee between my legs, nudging them open, the wicked look in his eyes telling me I wasn't going anywhere just yet.

After everything Cole and I had been through, it was almost difficult allowing myself to feel this happy. I was high on Cameron MacCabe, and although most of me loved it, this small part of me, the small part that couldn't let go of the past, was terrified by it. Fortunately for us both, I'd watched Joss almost destroy her relationship with Braden over that exact thing, and I had no wish to follow in her footsteps. It was only two days in, and I was guessing it would take a small miracle to make me walk away from Tattoo Guy.

What it would take for him to walk away was a different story, but I was determined to try to kill that kind of negative thinking before it spoiled everything for me. I was also resolved not to rock the boat, so when Malcolm texted me on Monday morning while I was at work, I didn't tell Cam.

So of course I also didn't tell him that I texted Malcolm back.

Malcolm had proven himself to be a good guy. A gentleman. A friend. It didn't matter if he'd found solace in the arms of Becca. All that mattered was that he'd been kind to me when we were together. I wasn't sure I was ready to lose that, so when he asked if I was okay, I told him I was. I apologized again, and I asked him how he was.

I'll be fine, sweetheart. I miss you. I'm glad we can still talk. x

There was no measuring my feelings of guilt when I read that text.

Friends?

Of course. Let me know if you need anything. I hope you're happy, Jo. x

Cut me to the quick.

Yeah. You too. x

Cam may or may not have been okay with Malcolm texting me, but I thought it was too soon to broach that subject, especially after the night before and my little confession and all its drama.

I saw him later before he had to go to work and I didn't say a word.

Tuesday night was our first night working together as a couple. We agreed at the outset that we wouldn't curb our flirtations with customers, since that increased our tips. I wasn't looking forward to it, but it made sense for us both. Tuesday night was one of the quietest nights we'd ever had. No flirtations, no incidents.

Thursday night was a little different.

It started off with Phil working the door.

Just as he had done Tuesday night, Cam held my hand all the way to work and all the way into the club when we got to work. He led us down the stairs to the entrance, his warm hand tight in mine, and the first thing we heard was, "You're with this idiot now, eh? I've got more money than him."

While Phil thought this was funny, I tried desperately to ignore the hurt.

My hand slipped out of Cam's and with a small smile at Brian, I went on into the club, Cam's harsh voice echoing down the hall as he growled at Phil. "You. Watch it."

I didn't wait for Phil's reply. Sufficiently pissed off, I hurried past Joss, ignoring her greeting.

"What's wrong?" she called after me, her light footsteps following mine into the staff room.

Shrugging out of my coat, I tried to turn the seething down to a simmer.

"Jo?"

"You can blame Cam," I replied sourly.

"What did I do?" Cam marched into the staff room, heading for his locker. His expression was as dark as mine as he turned to face me. Joss sidled up next to him, her eyebrows drawn together in confusion.

I glared at them both. "You were right before." I directed my words at Joss. "I let people think the worst of me. And I could handle it. But Tattoo Guy came along and told me to ask more of myself, and suddenly snide comments from people I thought liked me—but it turns out they thought exactly what you said they thought of me—hurt me. So, thanks, Cam. Now I'm a bloody walking open wound."

There were a number of appropriate responses to my rant. Joss grinning at Cam and then smacking him heartily on the back was not one of them. "You are my new favorite person."

I gave points to Cam for looking at her like she was nuts. I gave him some more for pulling me into a hug. I wrapped my arms around him, finding the feel of his hard, solid, safe body soothing. I breathed him in and snuggled deeper when his arms tightened around me.

"Why all the long faces? This is good news," Joss insisted, completely serious.

Moving my chin so I could rest it on Cam's shoulder and glare at her, I warned, "I am this close to ending our friendship."

Nowhere near intimidated by my threats, Joss's expression turned mulish. "I'm sorry someone hurt you. Point me in their direction and I'll give them a beatdown they won't forget in a hurry. But this is good, Jo. Cam has done what I've been trying to do for a year. He woke you up."

Cam pulled back, smirking at her. "That's a little cheesy, Joss."

It was like he'd told her she'd stepped in dog poo. Her nose wrinkled and she shuddered, a look of absolute self-disgust falling over her pretty features. "I have got to stop letting Ellie choose what we watch on movie night. It's causing me to acclimate to heartfelt emotion." She turned on her heel, muttering something under her breath about Jason Bourne.

"Nicely done," I murmured to Cam, impressed at the way he'd so easily dispatched Joss. His lips brushed my cheek in response and I turned to look into his eyes. "You sure you want to be seen with a girl everyone thinks of as one step above a paid escort?"

It was clearly the wrong thing to say, as evidenced by the tic of the muscle in his jaw as he clenched his teeth. He gripped my chin so I couldn't look away. "Don't. Don't even consider thinking of yourself in those terms. And don't ask me stupid questions. If anyone ever says anything like that to you . . . tell me. They'll not be saying it for long."

Cam had gone all alpha male on me but I wasn't even processing it. Despite his portrayal of the overprotective boyfriend, I couldn't forget that only weeks before, he'd accused me of the same thing Phil had. I wanted to forget. I really thought I had. But it seemed it was still there, niggling away at me under layers of denial.

Eyes dimming of their anger, mouth slackening to exasperation, Cam sighed as he let go of me. "Is this about me? About before?"

I shrugged, not wanting to lie outright.

"Are you ever really going to forgive me for what I said when we met?"

I shrugged again. Cole would have been so proud. "It's forgiven."
Just clearly not forgotten.

"But not forgotten."
Mind reader.

Heaving another sigh, Cam took hold of my hips and pulled me close, dipping his head to kiss me softly. His right hand coasted up under my tank top, his cool hand on my bare skin sending shivers rippling over me. I felt my nipples pebble as his hand cupped my bra, his thumb tracing the swell of my breast. My knees shook and I gripped Cameron's waist tightly. "You've not forgotten," he repeated roughly. "But you will." He crushed my mouth against his, his kiss almost painful in its demand. I didn't care. It was fair to say that at this point I was absolutely addicted to the taste and feel of him.

"Customers!" Joss yelled from behind the bar.

We jolted apart, Cam reluctantly pulling his hand out from under my top and smoothing it back in place. "You go out first."

I glanced down at the bulge in his jeans and grinned. "Take your time."

He growled at me playfully in response as I passed him, adding a taunting swing to my hips.

After the first two come-hither smiles Cam sent to customers, I stopped looking at him. I was aware of him, as I was always aware of him, but determined to shut out actual hard evidence of the flirting.

Combating it with my own flirting might have worked, but every time I attempted to flirt with a customer, I could feel Cam's eyes burning into my skin, and it put me off my game.

My growing irritation finally came to a head when there was a lull at the bar. I threw a dish towel at Cam. "Our tips jar is suffering because of you, buddy."

Cam had caught the towel before it hit him and was now laughing as he wiped up some spillage on the bar top. "What did I do?"

"I can feel you watching me. I can't flirt with you watching me."

His deep chuckle tickled all my good-for-nothing places and I hated that I found the cheeky grin he gave Joss so bloody hot. "Was I doing anything?"

Joss shrugged. "I have no clue what you were doing, but keep it up. The fake giggle"—she gestured lazily at me—"has disappeared, so I'm happy."

Another tag team? I crossed my arms over my chest, hoping my body language was a warning to back off. "The fake giggle is not that bad."

My friend grunted in disagreement. "It sounds like Miss Piggy has a machine gun stuck in her throat."

Roaring with laughter, Cam didn't even feel the heat of my glower. But watching him laugh as Joss's apt description took hold of me, I had to stifle my own amusement. I couldn't encourage them or I'd have Cole and Cam against me at home and Joss and Cam against me at work.

Harrumphing at them both, I turned to greet our next customer. He was male. Tall. Pretty cute. As I poured him a draft, I asked him about his night, laughing and flirting with him for a good five minutes before his friends called him back to their table. I will note that I did all this minus the fake giggle.

Since Cam had already provided evidence that he was a fairly possessive guy, my intention was to piss him off and put him in his place.

I spun on my heel, expecting to face his annoyance. Instead he was leaning back against the bar, smirking at me. "Nice try."

Damn. I was dating Mr. Unpredictable. The bloody idiot did not respond to any situation the way I expected him to. How on earth was I meant to navigate these waters if I didn't know the depth of them?

Bugger.

This really was going to be a relationship unlike any of my others.

The next words out of Cam's mouth just reinforced that realization.

"Let's go to my mum and dad's for a weekend."

I blinked rapidly, taken aback by the suggestion, ignoring Joss, who was hovering on the edges of our conversation, pretending to fix the napkin holder.

"What?"

"Three weeks from Saturday, it'll be my Saturday off work. We'll go then. Stay the night. You, me, and Cole."

"Dude, he wants you to meet the parents," Joss said under her breath. "Think carefully before you give him an answer. The parents. Already." She shuddered at the thought.

"Jo?"

I glanced back at an expectant Cam. "I can't leave Mum."

"I can check in on her," Joss offered loudly.

My mouth fell open as I stared at her in total bafflement. I whispered to her, "I thought you just said to think carefully about meeting his parents."

"I did. You didn't say you didn't want to. You offered up an impediment and I offered up a solution." When she turned away I caught the start of a sly grin on her face.

"You're twisted," I hissed.

Cam flicked the towel at me, bringing my attention back to him. "Well?"

I smiled tremulously. "Sure. Why not?"

Fuck.

CHAPTER 18

For weeks after discovering Mum had hit Cole, I couldn't go near her, could barely talk to her, and I swam in a muddy pond of bitter resentment and guilt. However, spending my nights with Cam when I could, whether that time involved the best sex of my life, or quiet time reading a book while he and Cole worked on their graphic novel together, changed me. It chipped away at my bitterness.

The weight I'd always carried on my shoulders hadn't disappeared completely, but it was lessened. When I walked down the street my steps felt lighter, my breathing easier. I no longer felt old and tired.

I felt young. Excited. Charmed. Almost . . . content.

I'd also decided to try to relax more about our financial situation. As difficult as that was, I did give in to the expense of sending Cole to judo lessons with Cam. It meant the boys were out on a Saturday morning, one of the few times Cam and I could actually spend time together, but I didn't care. It sounded so cheesy, but seeing Cole come through that door, smiling at Cam, being happy and having a guy to talk to . . . it gave me a kind of peace I never thought I'd have.

Cameron MacCabe. You charmer, you. You're changing my life.

I rested my hand on the parcel I'd just finished wrapping, smiling stupidly as I remembered last night. Well, technically this morning.

Both Cam and I had returned from work, feeling more buzzed than tired, and he'd finally taken me against his desk like he'd been promising. It had been slow, sensual, teasing, bloody fantastic sex. I swear I was getting through my days on a rush of endorphins. I think that's what made it easier to say good-bye to some very pretty things. I stroked the brown paper of the package. Inside was my favorite Donna Karan dress—one that Malcolm had bought me. It had sold well on eBay and it was time to send it to its new home.

Blowing air out between my lips in boredom, I eyed my eBay pile. I'd sold a few things but I still had to take photographs of a couple of items and post them on the site. The profits were paying for Cole's judo lessons, so it needed to be done. I had to crack on. Next up, a pair of Jimmy Choos. Staring at them, I realized I was going to need one of the boys to help me with this. The gorgeous six-inch heels were made up of a lot of spaghetti ties. Off the feet, they didn't look like much. On the feet, they looked sexy as all hell. I'd have to be wearing them in the photographs, which meant I'd need someone to take photographs for me.

Bundling them into my arms, I left Cole's room and stopped outside Mum's door. Loud snoring from within assured me everything was normal with her, and I headed out of the flat and downstairs to Cam's. Cam and Cole had texted me after their judo class to let me know they were going to Cam's to work on the graphic novel.

From the sounds of machine-gun fire coming from Cam's flat, I realized I'd been bullshitted. They were playing *Call of Duty*.

I walked in without knocking and slipped quietly into the sitting room. Cam, Cole, and Nate were sitting on the couch, Nate and Cole holding the controllers. Peetie was in the armchair directly facing me. I'd met Nate and Peetie a couple of times since Cam had moved in, but I still hadn't really spent that much time with them, mostly because when they were over they played video games, only really interacting with me when I took the time to feed them snacks.

Peetie saw me and waved, drawing Cam's attention. He turned and flashed me a welcoming smile that hit me in the gut, waking up all those annoying little butterflies fluttering around in there. "Hi, baby."

I raised an eyebrow at his flat-screen. "This is working on a graphic novel?"

"Nate and Peetie came over with us after class." As if that explained everything.

"Hi, Jo!" Nate called over the sounds of gunfire, his eyes flicking to me briefly. "Did you bring sandwiches by any chance?"

That was me. Sandwich lady. "No." I held my shoes up to an inquisitive Cam. "I need you to take a picture of me wearing these."

Cameron eyed them and then raised his eyebrows. "Whoa." He held up his hands, gesturing to his friends. "Not in front of the boys."

I narrowed my eyes on him. "Not *that* kind of picture, you sex-craved pervert."

"Eh, before anyone says anything else," Cole interjected loudly, "remember her wee brother is in the room."

Cam grinned and stood up. "Is this for eBay?"

Handing him my camera, I nodded, and then began taking off my shoes and strapping on the Jimmy Choos. Once they were on, I lifted my leg to eye them, turning my ankle to the side, feeling their loss already.

"Baby, if you love them that much, keep them."

I pouted. "I can't. They cost a ridiculous amount of money. It would be stupid to keep them."

"Fuck, man," Nate breathed, his attention suddenly on the shoes and my legs. "Don't let her sell those." His heated eyes devoured me. "Those are shit hot."

"I will seriously hit you," Cam warned him darkly.

Nate shrugged, threw me a cheeky grin, and turned back to the television screen. "Not my fault your girlfriend is so bloody fuckable."

Cole slammed his shoulder into Nate before Cam could retaliate. "Dude, that's my sister."

"And dude, watch your language." I tried not to blush. Ignoring Nate's unrepentant smile, I turned my feet so Cam could get a good shot of the shoes. My eyes fell on Peetie, who was texting someone. From what Cam had told me, I figured it was probably his fiancée, Lyn. Peetie was wrapped around her little finger, apparently. He seemed like a nice guy. A balance to Nate's unpredictable, blunt, Jack-the-lad persona. Nate was gorgeous—not rugged sexy like Cam, or rough-around-the-edges hot like Braden. He was movie-star-stunning, with his thick black hair and even blacker eyes, and he knew it.

My gaze moved to Cole, who was starting to look more and more like our father every day. My dad may have been a brute and an asshole, but he'd been a good-looking one. Once Cole realized he was a good-looking kid, it would depend on the influences in his life to how he would react to it and to girls.

I did not want him to become a Nate.

"I hope you three aren't corrupting my brother."

Nate huffed. "You kidding? If anyone's doing the corrupting, it's him."

Cole grinned at that and I felt a weird mixture of happiness and worry. Over the last few weeks I'd noticed a difference in him. He still grunted and shrugged a lot and was definitely destined to be broody, but he'd actually begun to converse with people other than Cam and me, and I took that as a good sign. Hanging around Nate, however, might turn him cocky. Or, hey, hanging around Cam might turn him cocky.

"Done." Cam handed me my camera with a quick peck to the lips.

"Thank you." I had just bent to unhook the strap at my ankle, when Cam's mouth brushed my ear.

"Be here tonight, waiting for me in nothing but those shoes."

My skin flushed hot at the thought and I quickly glanced over at

Cole and the boys to make sure they hadn't heard. They were completely oblivious. My eyes met Cam's dark gaze and I nodded in agreement.

A phone buzzed and we reluctantly broke eye contact.

Cole held up his phone. "Me. I've got to go. Guys are waiting for me at the cinema."

"We're not finished," Nate complained.

Peetie chuckled. "Nate, mate, when you try to convince a teenager to spend time with you playing video games, it's time to reevaluate your life."

We laughed, earning us the middle finger from Nate.

"I'll be home in a few hours," Cole informed me with a small smile before he left the flat. That smile warmed me up better than a mug of hot chocolate.

"Actually, you guys should go too." Cam moved toward them, making a shooing gesture.

Peetie stood up with a knowing grin. "Sure, no problem. Lyn wants me to meet her on Princes Street anyway."

Grumbling, Nate switched off the console and telly. "You're both whipped."

"Did you see the shoes?" Cam asked smugly, making me blush. If I didn't know he had plans to screw me imminently, I did now. And so did his friends.

Nate did some more grumbling, making me blush harder with a "Lucky bastard."

"See you soon, Jo." Peetie nodded at me as he passed us.

Punching Cam on the arm, Nate advised, "Watch those heels on your back. Those fuckers can hurt."

I groaned in mortification as Cam laughed.

"Wear protection." Nate winked at me. "And have fun, kiddies."

As soon as the door shut behind them, I glowered at Cam. "We're not having sex."

His mouth fell open. "Why not? I threw them out. We have a couple of hours of uninterrupted sex time."

"Yeah, but now they know that's what we're doing."

"And what difference does that make?"

"I don't know. But it makes some kind of difference."

Cam cocked his head to the side. "Female logic. It needs its own decipher code."

"We should invite Peetie and Lyn out for dinner with us."

"Okay, maybe it's just Jo logic." Cam chuckled at me jumping topics on him.

I shrugged, heading toward the fireplace to pick up a photo frame Cam had on the mantel. It held a photo of him, Nate, and Peetie dressed up as superheroes for Halloween. Cam was Batman. *Of course he was.* "I just thought it would be nice to get to know your friends better. They are like your brothers."

"Okay, that sounds good. I'll talk to him about it."

"I'd say we should invite Nate, but bringing a girl to dinner with his friends might be the kind of signal he wants to avoid sending out to one of his . . . companions."

Cam grunted. "And you'd be right."

Studying the photo of Nate dressed as Iron Man, I frowned. He really was incredibly good-looking. And there was something about him. Behind all the bluster there was something else. It was in his eyes. They were kind. "Is he completely against all relationships? It's a shame if so." I turned to smile softly at Cam. "He really does seem like a nice guy."

"He is." Cam nodded, seeming very serious all of sudden. "But . . . he lost someone."

An ache pierced my chest as I processed what Cam wasn't saying. "A girl?"

Looking away, I could see that whatever it was that had happened had also affected Cam. "It was a while ago, but it changed him."

Stunned, I shook my head, looking back at the grinning Nate in the photo. "You just never know what hurts people are living with, do you? We're all so good at hiding them."

"You're the master."

Yeah, I wasn't going to disagree with that.

Lost for a moment, staring at the photo, feeling a deep sympathy for Nate and for the love that had been taken from him, I didn't hear Cam move until he was standing right behind me. The heat of him, the smell of him, drew me out of my melancholy thoughts and my fingers fell from the picture frame, my body growing hot in anticipation of him.

His hands rested on my hips for a moment and that was all I needed to feel a quiver of excitement low in my belly. Strong fingers curled into the hem of my jumper and slowly he began to pull it up. The movement demanded that I raise my arms above my head and I did so, the room silent except for our soft breathing and the rustle of clothing. Darkness descended over me for a second as he tugged the jumper up over my head, cool air whispering across my skin, kissing it into goose bumps.

I shivered, letting my arms fall slowly as my jumper hit the floor.

Cam's warm hand grazed my back gently, sweeping my hair over my shoulder. Tenderly, his fingertips brushed my skin, following the strap of my bra down my shoulder and along my upper back.

I felt a slight tug and my bra loosened, descending to the floor with Cam's slight nudging. Another shiver moved through me and my nipples grew tight with arousal. I shifted a little, my underwear rubbing against me, damp with excitement.

He tortured me with his touch, his deft fingertips skimming my waist, my ribs, the curve of my breasts. I moaned, my head falling back, my back arching, my breasts begging to be touched. My silent pleading was ignored as Cam's gentle exploration moved down my stomach, his hands coming to a stop on the waistband of my skirt.

Taking a step closer, so that his front was pressed against my back, Cam hooked his thumbs in the fabric of my skirt and pants and pushed down. Rather than letting them drop, he kept hold of the material with his palms pressed against it, capturing it against my body, as his fingers trailed down my bare skin. He followed the movement, slowly lowering himself to his haunches, his teasing caress coasting down my outer thighs, past my knees, down my calves, until his thumbs brushed my ankles.

Struggling to control my breathing, I shakily stepped out of my clothes. His heat rushed back up my body as he stood.

He stroked the cheeks of my ass and I would have stumbled forward into the mantel if he hadn't wrapped an arm around my waist, pulling me back into him. Something hard nudged my buttocks and I didn't need his sudden stutter of breath to tell me it was his arousal.

Warm lips barely touched my shoulder, and then his arm was gone but not his warmth.

The sound of a zipper behind me made me slick with anticipation, my breathing growing louder in the quiet of the room. Clothes whispered and I saw his T-shirt fall to the floor out of the corner of my eye, and then the fabric of his jeans was gone against my behind, the throbbing, naked heat of his cock digging into the curve of my butt.

And then that was gone too.

Confused, I twisted my head over my shoulder, my gaze dropping to the rug in front of his empty fireplace. Naked, hard, Cam looked up at me with searing eyes. He lay there, knees bent, arms behind him, palms pressed to the floor.

He held up a hand, not saying a word, and I turned to take it. Positioning myself over him, I blushed, trembling, as I stood there with my feet on either side of his hips, so vulnerable and open to him.

Cam tugged on my hand, and I followed the motion, lowering myself to my knees, the rug a soft pillow against them. Taking his erection in hand, Cam guided it to my entrance, and as I lowered myself farther, he filled me, sliding into my wet channel with a satisfaction that made us both gasp. I clasped his shoulders and eased back up ever so slightly, the delicious friction causing a pool of coiling tension in my lower belly. My lips parted in a delighted exhalation, and my eyes hooked on Cam's as my hips began to undulate against his in perfect rhythm.

It was intense, watching the pleasure escalate in his eyes as he watched it in mine. My skin began to burn and I tried to move faster, chasing climax, but Cam slowed me, gripping my hips to falter my movement. His eyes washed over my face, taking in every tiny detail, making me feel more naked than I'd ever felt before.

I shook my head, silently telling him to stop. His grip on my hips hardened. I couldn't look away. I wanted to look away. It was so much. Too much. Feeling tears prick my eyes, I leaned forward, crushing my breasts against him, wrapping my arms around his neck, my lips in his hair as I rode him with torturously slow strokes.

Feeling a gentle tug on my hair, I let him pull me up, my back arching under his hold. Warm, wet heat captured my nipple as he took my right breast into his mouth, his other hand squeezing and fondling the left, pinching my nipple between forefinger and thumb. A cry fell from my lips as a sharp surge of pleasure shot between my legs, and I clutched the nape of his neck tightly, moving faster whether he wanted me to or not.

His mouth moved, pressing wet kisses over my breast, and I slammed down on him, needing more, needing everything. He groaned against my skin, his fingers digging into the muscles in my back.

"Cameron," I breathed as the tension built and built, my hips moving faster against his. "I'm close. So close . . ." Wanting his mouth when I came, I tugged gently on his hair, drawing his face up to mine, my lips falling on his, my tongue sliding deep into his mouth for a kiss made up of eroticism, of pure longing.

The tension snapped inside me. I came with a muffled cry in his mouth, and my muscles momentarily locked around him as my sex clenched his cock, wave after wave of pulsating pleasure cascading over me. I fell against him completely, my forehead on his shoulder as he pumped into me a few times before the wet warmth of his release exploded inside me, his hard grunt in my ear as he came, causing my inner muscles to pulse around him a few more times.

We stayed there for a good while, wrapped around each other.

Not saying a word.

Not needing to.

Cam groaned. "I have to move in an hour."

We were lying on the rug, the faux fur blanket from his couch that Becca had bought as a moving-in gift now thrown over us. My head rested on Cam's chest, my legs tangled with his, as his fingers teased through my hair.

"Boo to work," I said with a pout, tracing the tattooed curlicues on his right arm.

"I know. I could stay here forever."

I smiled against his skin, utterly delighted. "You know, the only thing that would make this more perfect would be a real fire in that fireplace."

He gave a huff of laughter. "I'll light some candles next time."

"Very nice. Has anyone told you you're a bit of a romantic?"

"Nope. That's definitely the first time I've been called that."

Surprised, I tilted my head to look into his face. "Seriously?"

"Seriously." His lips twitched. "You think I'm romantic? Baby, that doesn't say much for those assholes you've dated."

I grinned back at him. "Actually, you have your moments."

With soft eyes, he gave my shoulder a squeeze. "You make it easy."

"See!" I cried softly, my eyes glittering with utter contentment. "That was romantic."

"It was?"

"Yes. Surely, you've been romantic with ex-girlfriends?"

Why, oh, why did I ask that? Did I really want to hear about the ex-girlfriends?

Thankfully, Cam sidestepped the question. Unfortunately, he sidestepped it by asking one. "So was Malcolm romantic? That Callum guy?" There was a definite edge to the question, so I thought I'd best tread carefully. But honestly.

"Callum could be very romantic. All hearts and flowers and shit like that."

Cam grunted. "Shit like that?"

I shrugged, feeling okay talking about it now that I was wrapped in the arms of something real. "Looking back, it all seems fake. We were together two years. He met Cole a few times. Never met Mum. I saw him every other weekend when I could. He sent me flowers, bought me nice things, went all out on Valentine's Day. I met his parents but knew very little about them. Hung out with some of his friends and knew even less about them. I don't know if I even knew *Callum*. I know for a fact he didn't know me. So, yeah . . . shit like that. I'd take hot sex against a desk with a guy who knows exactly what he's getting into—pardon the pun—over flowers and chocolates any day."

I chanced a glance up at Cam and saw him smiling widely at me. "I think I'm having an earthy influence on you, Johanna Walker."

I grinned back. "I think so too."

He rubbed his calf against mine and pulled me even closer. "And Malcolm?"

"He had his moments. Again, I didn't know much about him and he seemed happy with that. I knew he had an ex-wife, that his mum had passed but his dad was alive. He had a brother he was really close with but not close enough with to introduce me. He didn't know me at all like he thought he did . . . but he was a true gentleman."

I felt Cam tense beneath me for a second before letting air out between his lips. "You cared about him."

After pressing a reassuring kiss to his chest, I nodded.

That silence fell over us again, the one that seemed so full of words unspoken, so full of emotion, charging the air between us. Understanding what it meant, I felt my chest compress with the gravity of the emotion. To stop myself from saying the words too soon, I stupidly asked what I didn't want to know. "Have you ever been in love?"

When he heaved a huge sigh I tried not to react physically, and when he answered quietly, "Yes," I tried not to be sick.

It was stupid, of course, to feel pain in my chest, to feel my stomach flip and my brain scream *Noo!!!* but I couldn't help my reaction. Cameron had been in love.

Taking a moment to make sure my voice was steady, I sucked in another breath and then asked, "When? Who?"

"Do you really want to know this?" His voice was gruff.

"If you want to tell me, I want to know."

"Okay," he answered gently, his hand sliding down my arm in a caress. "It was a long time ago. I met her ten years ago when I was eighteen. Her name was Blair and we met in our first semester of uni."

Blair.

And he'd loved her.

Already I was envisioning some tall, dark-haired beauty with intelligent eyes and cool self-possession like Joss. I pushed those imaginings aside. "What happened?"

"We were together for three and a half years. I thought we'd get engaged, buy a house, get married, churn out some kids. I thought she was it."

Was that a knife he was twisting in my side? I held still, trying to squash the intense jealousy and hurt I felt at his revelation.

"However, Blair was offered a placement at a university in France to do her postgraduate degree in French literature. So I broke it off with her. I broke it off with her before she could break it off with me because I knew she was going to choose France and she knew I would never leave Scotland. I couldn't leave my parents or Nate and Peetie behind. She was going to end it, so I just made it easy for her."

There was so much in that confession that my throat closed with anxiety. I didn't say a word, just threaded my fingers through his and waited for the pain to ease.

It didn't.

A while later, we showered together and then Cam left me to go to the bar. I found myself heading up to the flat in a fog of absolute despondency. I'd tried to pull myself out of my gloomy mood, giving him easy smiles and soft kisses, telling myself that he had not once given me reason to believe that he wasn't in this with me, that he didn't feel what I felt when we were together.

I'd almost convinced myself as I entered my flat, but when I shut the door I came face-to-face with Mum. She swayed on her bare feet, her nightdress hanging like a sack on her gaunt frame. Her unfocused eyes and unstable feet told me she hadn't taken it easy with the drink today. Today she'd wanted to get well and truly pissed.

"Whereyebeen?"

Not in the mood to talk to her, I replied shortly, "With Cam," and moved past her, on my way to my room.

"Where'd go?"

Assuming she was asking where he'd gone, I looked back over my shoulder. "Work."

"Bar," she scoffed. "Bit of a loser, eh?"

Since I worked at the bar too, I tried not to take that personally. "Actually he's a graphic designer, Mum."

"Mmph, fancy bugger, eh?" She gave a wee laugh and headed toward the kitchen. "What the fuck he doing wi' you?"

I froze.

"Get bored wi' you, wee lass. No smart enough for him."

Backtracking up the hall, I hurried into the bathroom and locked myself in, listening to my insecurities eat away at me. They sounded an awful lot like Mum when she was drunk.

But she was right, wasn't she?

Cam had been in love with a girl who had been intelligent and interesting, heading off to Europe to do a postgraduate degree in French literature.

He'd been in love with someone who was obviously my complete opposite.

Worse, it hadn't ended because he stopped loving her.

It ended because of his fucked-up abandonment issues.

I stared in the mirror, searching for something, something interesting, something unique, something that made me someone that Cam *needed* to be with.

I couldn't find anything.

A sob rose up out of my mouth and I let the tears fall.

Today I'd fallen in love with Cameron MacCabe. But how could I ever expect him to love me back when *I* couldn't find anything in me worth loving?

CHAPTER 19

"I have pancakes," Helena MacCabe announced brightly, reaching for her husband's plate. I immediately put my own clean plate on top of Cole's and grabbed Cameron's too.

"I'll help." I smiled politely.

Helena and Anderson MacCabe had been nothing but friendly and open with me and Cole since we'd arrived at their house yesterday, but I still couldn't shake off my nervousness.

It wasn't just because they were my boyfriend's parents and I wanted them to like me. It was because they were *Cam's* parents— parents he adored—and I wanted them to think I was good enough for their son.

The last week had been strange. At the beginning of the week I'd still felt insecure and weird over Cam's announcement that he'd been in love with this exotic-sounding Blair person, but since he spent all his spare time with me, and was even affectionate at the bar—seeming unable to keep his hands off of me for more than five seconds—those insecurities started to fade into the background until finally I was barely even aware of them.

As Saturday approached, and Cole and I readied ourselves for a night in Longniddry, I grew more and more anxious about meeting

Cam's parents. I confessed this to him and he thought it was adorable. He appeared to be completely confident that they'd like me.

So was Malcolm.

We'd still been texting, and on Wednesday he'd called me to talk for the first time since the split. It had been awkward at first, but tension eased between us when he told me he was dating someone. The said someone was older than me and had a kid, and Malcolm felt a little out of his depth with her. I told him to spoil the working mother of one and he'd win her over in no time. He told me to just be myself and I'd win Cam's parents over in no time. I had gotten off the phone wondering which "myself" he was talking about, since I didn't think I'd ever introduced him to the real one.

On Saturday morning Cam had rented a car to drive us out of the city and before I knew it we were driving down the main street of Long-niddry, passing quaint cottages with their beach-colored bricks and red-slate roofs and the local pub, which looked well-frequented, but I hadn't been able to enjoy the idyllic prettiness. It was a cool spring day and the sun was out and the little village was fairly busy. But me? I was too busy gnawing my lip. Despite both Cam's and Malcolm's assurances, little mini-versions of me had started freaking out together in my stomach. I could feel them kicking and screaming in there.

We turned left at a roundabout, I knew that, and Cam had pointed out the grand red stone gatehouse to the Gosford estate, babbling on about something his father had told him about it. Cole had replied, so I gathered he was actually listening. I, on the other hand, was just trying not to upchuck.

When we pulled into a well-groomed housing estate and parked in front of a medium-sized whitewashed house with a red roof, I lost my ability to breathe. Cam laughed at my reaction, giving me a quick, hard kiss before ushering us out of the car and into his parents' house.

They had been lovely so far. Helena, or Lena, as she preferred to be called, was warm, kind, and dry-witted, and Anderson—Andy—was quiet, friendly, and genuinely interested in me and Cole. Their dog, Bryn, was an energetic fourteen-month-old King Charles puppy who immediately fell in love with Cole, and vice versa.

We'd gone to the local inn for lunch together, where we chatted about work, my work, Cam's work, their work, and Cole's talent for drawing and writing. I gathered Cam had told them something about Mum because they trod very carefully around the subject. Surprisingly, I didn't mind if they knew. Cam was obviously close to them and shared a lot about his life with them. If that included me and my life, I could only take that as a good sign for our relationship.

That night we'd watched some telly with them and Cole had been drawn into a history program Andy was watching, finding Andy's knowledge about historical events completely fascinating. He had multitasked, listening to Andy while tormenting the life out of Bryn, who loved every minute of the attention. I'd sat in the kitchen with Cam and his mum while she pulled out old baby photographs that I giggled over. Cam had been a funny-looking preadolescent. It was so cute.

It was all so normal.

So perfectly ordinary.

It was wonderful.

At bedtime, Cole took the couch and Cam and I crashed in his old bedroom. His old bedroom had been completely preserved from his teen years: posters of bands looking a decade younger plastered over his walls, cutouts from film magazines, as well as his own drawings. Like his sketches now, they consisted of cool little cartoon paradox people. He tended to draw cartoon people in an action that was completely at odds with their physical appearance. I'd stolen one of his recent drawings, sketched on a napkin at work. It was a cartoon mercenary—big, bulging muscles, leather vest, motorcycle boots, chains, bullet clips strapped around him, headscarf, guns in holsters and a knife tucked into his boots. In his hands was a big open box of chocolates in the shape of a love heart and as he ate them he wore this dreamy, goofy smile on his face. It was now my bookmark.

Cam's old room just exploded with his teenage personality and I loved it. I felt like a teenager myself as we began quietly making out on his bed. I'd stopped before it got too hot and heavy, refusing to have sex under his parents' roof. He had not been pleased by this, but considering that he had the squeakiest mattress on planet earth, I would not be moved on the subject.

Cuddling up with him to just fall asleep had been nice anyway. Sweet. A little bit emotional. Safe.

I'd woken up contented, to the smell of breakfast.

After stuffing us with a huge breakfast that included amazing haggis fritters, Lena was now determined to kill us. Or me. The boys looked perfectly happy with the idea of scarfing down pancakes.

"Maybe I'll sit these out," I told Lena with a wry smile. "I'm pretty full."

"Nonsense." She grinned back at me as she dumped the plates by the sink. "If you can eat all you want and still keep your beautiful figure, then you should."

Glowing under her compliment, I rinsed the plates quickly and then put them in the dishwasher. By the time I turned around, Lena had already piled a mound of pancakes onto two plates.

"Grab the syrups." She nodded to the bottles of golden and chocolate syrup.

I followed her back into the dining room and sat down, watching as everyone dug in, ignoring Bryn, who wandered from one seat to the next, her gorgeous brown eyes begging someone to drop a piece of pancakey goodness. I took one pancake to be polite, tore a piece off, and dangled it surreptitiously under the table. A gentle doggy mouth gobbled it up, licking my fingers for good measure. I immediately reached for one of the napkins in the center of the table, ignoring Cam's knowing smile.

"Cam said he's applied for a graphics job in the city," Andy told Lena as she settled down at her own place.

"Oh, that's good, son. What company is it for?"

"It's a Web site company," Cam replied after swallowing a mouthful of food. "It's not much more money than the bar, but I'd be doing what I enjoy."

"And it's better than having to commute to Glasgow or move down south," I added, my chest squeezing at the thought of Cam leaving.

"True," Lena agreed.

"I won't be moving," Cam assured us—or me, rather, smiling at me with heat in his eyes that was unbelievably embarrassing in front of his parents. "I like my neighbors too much."

I blushed, smiling.

"Dude," Cole muttered, shaking his head.

"What do you mean, dude?" Cam asked, affronted that Cole had insinuated he wasn't cool. "That was as smooth as you get, bud."

"Aye." Andy nodded, cutting a hearty bite of pancake soaked in syrup as he winked at his wife. "Learned it from the best."

Before we left for the day we decided to take Bryn to the beach. It wasn't a perfect beach. It was typical of the area, covered in pebbles, mussels, icky seaweed, and seagulls. Bryn immediately took off after the gulls, diving into the cold water without a care, doggy tongue dangling from her mouth in absolute delight. It was cute that she thought the seagulls were playing with her when in truth they were barely aware of her presence until she yipped at them to say hello and frightened them into moving along. Almost like what Braden must have thought of me when we first met. I'd gushed all over him like an idiot, so determined to land the perfect man that I'd been blind to his infatuation with Joss.

As I strolled with Andy at my side, Lena, Cole, and Cam off in front, playing with Bryn, I wondered who that person was that had acted like such a fool over a guy. I didn't recognize her. I didn't know her and I never wanted to meet her ever again.

Thanks to Cam, I didn't think there was a remote possibility that I would.

"He's happy," Andy suddenly said, his voice low so it wouldn't carry on the wind that was whipping my hair past my cheeks.

I tucked it behind my ear, throwing him a quizzical look. "Cameron?"

Andy nodded, giving me a smile, one that reached his eyes, one that was full of a surprising amount of affection. "I knew from the way he spoke about you on the phone that you were different. Meeting you, though, seeing you together, I know."

Confused, I slowed down while my heart sped up. "Know what?"

"My son has always been a private person. He has his family and Nathaniel and Gregor, and that's always been enough for him. There have been girlfriends, obviously, ones he was close to, but he's always kept his circle tight, excluding them and not even realizing it." Andy grinned again, his eyes on Cam, who was walking with his arm wrapped around his mum's shoulders, grinning down into her face. "Not you, though. You're in. And Cameron is . . . well, I don't think I've ever seen him this happy."

My heart lurched, my breath stuttering as I focused on Cam, loving the way he moved, powerful, at ease with himself, confident. Not to mention his easy affection with people, his ability to reveal how he felt about someone without caring what anyone else thought. "You think?"

"Yup." Andy nudged me with his shoulder, a move Cameron had obviously unconsciously developed from watching his dad. "I'm glad he met you, Johanna."

All the tension melted out of my shoulders and I relaxed. "Me too," I whispered, unable to mask my feelings.

Before Andy could ask me whatever probing question was brimming in his eyes, my phone rang. I apologized and tugged it out of my jacket pocket. It was Joss.

My heart stopped.

Mum?

"Hello?" I answered a little breathlessly.

"Hey, you." Joss's voice was quiet, unsteady.

I felt sick. "Is everything okay? Is Mum okay?"

"God, yes." She hurried to reassure me. "I'm actually calling to tell you something."

That sounded slightly ominous. "Something?"

"Well . . . Braden proposed to me yesterday."

WHAT? "Oh, my God."

"I said yes."

"What?" I laughed happily, hearing her throaty and quite obviously pleased chuckle on the other end of the line. "I'm so happy for you! Congratulations, hon, and tell Braden I said 'about time!'"

Her laughter warmed my frozen cheeks. "I will. Look, Ellie is already planning a dreaded engagement party, so, um, we'll talk when you get back. Hope 'meeting-the-parents weekend' has gone well."

"Very well. Not as well as your weekend, obviously."

"Yeah. Well, he paid a cabdriver to be in on it and he proposed in Bruntsfield in the cab just where we met. He pulled out a ring, told me he loved me and that he'd try not to fuck it up if I tried not to fuck it up, so how could I say no?"

I snorted. "You couldn't. Sounds like the perfect proposal for you."

Her voice softened. "Yeah, it kind of was."

"So happy for you."

"Thanks, Jo. I'll see you soon?"

"Soon."

We hung up and Andy looked at me with a quirked eyebrow. "Good news?"

I nodded. "My best friend just got engaged. She doesn't have any family of her own, so this is amazing for her." Suddenly tears pricked my eyes at the thought of everything Joss was gaining, and I laughed a little weepily, feeling like an idiot.

"What's going on?" Cam approached, his eyebrows drawn together in a glower. "Why are you upset?"

"I'm not upset." I waved him off with a goofy smile and held up my phone. "That was Joss. She and Braden just got engaged."

Cam grinned, hooking an arm around my neck to draw me into his side. "Come here, sappy girl. The brisk coastal wind will dry those tears."

I cuddled into him. "Don't you think it's great news?"

He nodded, his eyes bright on me. "I think it's brilliant news. She's a good girl, deserves to be happy."

God, he was lovely sometimes.

"And Braden is a brave man. I'll need to buy him a pint when we get back."

Andy grunted at our side. "A pint for a soldier going off to war."

Cam's shoulders shook. "Exactly."

"For a general surveying his battlefield and using logic against an illogical foe."

"Yep."

"For a warrior about to head into the mouth of the dragon's cave."

"Definitely."

"For—"

"Okay, okay, funny men," I interrupted with a huff. "Who needs a coastal wind to dry the eyes when I'm in the presence of the MacCabe sense of humor?"

Andy shot me a wry smile and then turned a full-blown grin on Cam as we drew closer to Cole, Lena, and Bryn. "You better keep this one, son."

CHAPTER 20

"Hello, beautiful." A deep, familiar voice brought my head up from the letter I was shoving into an envelope.

Greeted by the sight of Malcolm standing in the doorway to Mr. Meikle's reception area, I smiled. My heart thudded a little faster as he smiled back affectionately, all class and polish in his designer suit. "Malcolm," I replied warmly.

His dark eyes glittered as he strolled casually into the room toward me. "It's good to see you."

I stayed frozen awkwardly in place for a moment as I decided what I should do, how I should greet him. Malcolm waited on the other side of my desk, his eyebrows raised in question.

After seeing his name on the appointment sheet today, I'd felt my stomach start to do flips. We'd been texting, but this would be the first time we'd seen each other in person since the breakup. Now that he was here in front of me, I didn't know how to react.

Laughing a little at my own nervousness, I pushed back from the desk and rounded it, my arms open. He immediately drew me into a tight hug that I reciprocated, surprised by how glad I was to see him. I had to pull away, however, when his hands started sliding slowly down my back. My cheeks were flushed with guilt for letting Malcolm get close enough to touch me in any way that was remotely more than friendly.

It had been two weeks since the Saturday with Cam's parents and Cam and I had been dating each other for just over six weeks. Six weeks didn't sound like long, but it felt like forever. Long enough for me to know that this was the kind of flirtatious interaction with another guy that *would* piss my boyfriend off.

"You look good." I gave him another quick smile to cover my abrupt departure from the hug.

"You too. I take it you're well?"

I nodded, and sat back in my chair, looking up at him with genuine interest. "And you?"

"Yes. I'm good. You know me."

"And how's your single mother of one?"

He laughed drily. "Ah, over. We didn't quite fit."

"Oh, I'm sorry to hear that."

"And Cameron?"

My cheeks heated again and I had to force myself to meet his eyes. "He's good."

Malcolm frowned. "Still taking care of you?"

"He is."

"Good." He blew air out between his lips, glancing around, I think attempting to appear casual. "I take it he's met Cole and your mum?"

Crap. More guilt washed over me and I found myself choking on the answer. I suddenly felt panicked that if I told him the truth, that Cam knew more about my life than I had ever let Malcolm know, I would hurt this man even more than I already had.

My silence at his question seemed to provide my answer. His eyes dimmed as he watched me. "I'll take that as a yes."

"Malcolm!" Mr. Meikle boomed as he threw his office door open. "Joanne didn't tell me you'd arrived. Come in, come in."

It was the first time I'd ever been grateful to my harsh employer.

238 · SAMANTHA YOUNG

He'd saved me from having to answer to that wounded look on Malcolm's face.

The entire time Malcolm was in Meikle's office I watched the door like a hawk, chewing on my lip, my knee bouncing up and down with my anxiety as I waited for him to reappear. I spent twenty minutes building myself up to his reaction and in the end he walked out the door, threw me a casual smile, and told me he'd talk to me soon. Then he left.

I wilted against my chair, the tension draining from my body.

"Johanna."

I snapped around, surprised not only that Mr. Meikle had gotten my name correct but also that he had uttered it in a tone that was scathing, even for him. He stood in his doorway, his eyes narrowed on me, his expression almost incredulous. "Sir?"

"You broke up with Malcolm Hendry?"

My fingernails bit into the palm of my hands at the inappropriate question while my brain cursed Malcolm to hell. "Sir."

"You silly girl." He shook his head, almost as if he felt sorry for me. My heart began to thump in preparation for the insult I knew was coming, my blood already heating with anger. "A girl with your limited talents should think more carefully in future before throwing away the opportunity to attach yourself to an affluent man like Malcolm Hendry."

His unkind attack slapped me back into the past.

"Get out of my way!" Dad bellowed, kicking out at me, catching my buttocks with his work boot as I passed. I stumbled, humiliation and pain making me whirl around and glare at him in defiance. His face darkened and he took a menacing step toward me. "Dinnae you look at me like that. Dinnae you! You're nothing. Absolutely worthless."

The memory, summoned by Mr. Meikle's condescension, pinned me in my seat. My skin grew hot with renewed humiliation. It's hard to believe you're anything but worthless when a parent spends most of your formative years telling you you're useless. A big nothing. I knew I'd carried that with me. It didn't take a genius to understand why I had such low self-esteem, or why I had very little belief in myself.

Or why I probably never would.

However, I'd grown so used to thinking that way about myself that when others thought it too it didn't seem *wrong*. Although Joss had spent the last few months attempting to make me see that it was wrong, it had never fully gotten through to me.

Until Cameron.

He wanted me to demand more of myself. He got angry when I didn't, and furious when other people belittled me. He told me in little ways almost every day that he thought I was special. He chipped away at my insecurities about my intelligence, my personality, and although they were still there, they had been suppressed by his support. Every day they were squashed deeper and deeper into the caverns of my worries.

Cam said I was *more*.

How dared anyone who didn't know me at all try to tell me I was *less*?

I pushed back from my desk, my chair careening into the metal filing shelves behind me with the force of the action. "I quit."

Mr. Meikle blinked rapidly, the color on his cheeks deepening to a rosy red. "Pardon?"

Glowering at him, I pulled my bag up off the floor and yanked my jacket off the coat stand near my desk. Standing in the doorway to his reception area, I kept my eyes on him in defiance as I put my jacket on. "I said, I quit. Find someone else to hiss at with your viperous tongue, you short old windbag."

I spun around on trembling legs and left him spluttering in my wake as I hurried out the door, down the stairs, and out the main entrance. Adrenaline pumped through me as I marched down the street fueled by ire and self-righteous indignation.

Cool air blew through my hair and across my cheeks until the fire began to wane and my trembling increased.

I'd just quit my job.

The job Cole and I needed.

The breath whooshed out of me and I stumbled against a wrought-iron fence, struggling to get air into my lungs. What were we going to do? We couldn't survive on my wages from the bar, and jobs weren't exactly easy to come by. I had some money put away, but that money was for Cole, not for me to burn through while I tried to find a new job.

"Oh, fuck," I muttered, tears pricking the corners of my eyes as I pushed myself off the fence, looking back the way I'd come. I could feel the eyes of passersby on my face, as they sensed my distress and probably wondered if I needed help. "I need to go back." I took two steps back toward the office, then stopped, clenching my fists at my sides.

I was halted by pride.

Me? Halted by pride?

I gave a huff of hysterical laughter and clutched my stomach, fighting the urge to be sick.

I couldn't go back. Meikle wouldn't even take me back after what I'd just said to him.

"Oh, God." I pushed a shaking hand through my hair, gulping in as much air as I could.

And then it hit me.

This was Cam's fault.

My attraction to him had caused me to dump a wealthy, kind, handsome man who I knew cared about me. And now I'd quit my job! And for what? Because Cameron was charming enough to make me feel special, to make me feel better about myself? What about something real? What about telling me he loved me, huh?

It had been only six weeks, but I knew I loved him. Shouldn't he know he loved me? It wasn't like he wasn't capable of it. He'd fucking loved Blair!

More tears trembled on my eyelashes. I was mucking up my life because of him. Making impulsive, stupid decisions that were going to wreck any hope of a financially secure future for Cole.

Oh, God . . . Cole.

I'd let him get close to Cole too.

Who did that?

Who played Russian roulette not only with their own emotions but with their bloody kid's?

I had to do something. Quickly. I needed space. Time to reevaluate before it was too late.

I needed to see Cam.

Despite my alarming pace, the usually forty-minute distance that I covered in twenty-five minutes still seemed to take forever, and I had to stop myself from walking down to Joss's flat on Dublin Street when I passed it. Perhaps talking this over with a friend would help, would clear up all my confusion, but I feared that Joss, who was Team Cameron, would only convince me I was being hysterical.

And maybe I was.

In fact, somewhere inside, I was pretty sure I was, but the anger and panic were overruling logic at the moment.

Logic that Joss probably would have used to talk me around. But Joss was hiding out from Ellie at the moment because Els had gone overboard with plans for the engagement party that was to take place in two weeks. With her brain ready to explode from Ellie in celebration mode, Joss had told me the other night at work that she had taken to not answering her door during the day. Five weeks of planning for a party? If I were Joss I'd be in hiding too.

With no one to talk me down and my emotions rocketing all over the place, I stormed into my building and stomped up the stairs, breathless by the time I reached Cam's flat. I may have pounded on his door harder than was necessary.

"Jesus Chr—" Cam cut his words short at the sight of me as he opened the door to find me there, disheveled and out of breath. "Jo? What are you— Why aren't you at work?"

My eyes skimmed over him. He was kind of dressed up for Cam. The Diesel T-shirt he wore looked new and was a little more tight-fitting than his usual tees, sculpting the lean lines of muscle in his strong body. And were those new jeans? My eyes dropped to the black Levi's and I was almost relieved to see he was wearing his scuffed black engineer boots. Why was he semi–dressed up?

He looked hot.

It was such a turn-on when he gazed at me with those warm blue eyes, even when they were all worried and concerned as they were now. "Jo?" He stepped out of his flat, reaching for me.

I wanted to lean into him, to let him hold me against him, to breathe him in, to feel his lips on my skin. I wanted that forever.

No, dammit! I drew back, taking him by surprise. I needed space. Every time I was near him, he just befuddled my brain.

He frowned, dropping his arm. "What's wrong?"

I suddenly had an overwhelming desire to start crying. I held it at bay and looked anywhere but at him. "I quit my job."

Silence fell between us for a moment and then he replied, "That's good."

My glare skewered him to the wall behind him. "No. It's not good. It's not bloody good, Cam."

"Okay, baby, calm down. Obviously something has happened." He sighed heavily and ran a hand through his hair. "And I'm about to make it either better or worse. I need to tell you something."

Shaking my head, I took a step up the stairs that would lead me to my flat. "I don't want to know. Cam"—I took a deep breath, reaching far inside me for the strength to say it—"I need space to think."

He looked stunned, almost like I'd hit him. "Space?"

I nodded, chewing my lip to hell.

And then Cam's eyes darkened, his whole expression growing taut with coming anger. I began to gnaw my lip as he took a menacing step toward me. "Space from me?"

I nodded.

"Fuck that shit," he growled, his hands reaching for me before drawing back with restraint. "What the hell happened today?"

"You did," I replied as calmly as I could.

His eyes only blazed bluer. Apparently my being calm only exacerbated his anger. "Me?"

"I keep making these rash decisions and being completely selfish and that's not fair to Cole."

Cam screwed up his face. "Rash decisions? Am I a fucking rash decision? Is that what you're saying?"

"No!" I cried, aghast at the hurt in his eyes. "No. I don't know." I threw up my hands, so confused I just wanted the floor to open up and swallow me whole. "Are you? Are we? I mean, what are we doing here? I keep expecting—"

"Expecting what?"

"You to just wake up one day, realize you're bored out of your skull, and end it."

A very tense silence fell between us again, and I watched with growing nervousness as Cam struggled to control his frustration. Finally he met my gaze and asked quietly, "Have I ever given you that impression? That I'm just messing around? I took you to meet my parents, for Christ's sake, not to mention what I've just done today. That bullshit is in *your* head and I didn't put it there, so what is going on?"

I threw up my hands again, tears glistening in my eyes. "I don't know. I quit my job and being angry at me only took me so far, so I had to be angry at you! And I'm on my period, so I might be a little emotional." I sucked back tears.

His lips twitched now, the anger easing from his expression.

"It's not funny!" I stomped my foot like a petulant child.

With a grunt, Cam answered by hauling me off the stairs and into his arms. I automatically wrapped my arms around him and buried my burning face in his neck.

"No more talk about needing space?" he asked hoarsely, his warm breath on my ear.

I nodded in agreement and his arms tightened.

"Why did you quit?"

I pulled back and he eased me to my feet, although he didn't let go of me. Now that I was this close to him I didn't want to let go either.

Jesus, I was such a mess.

"He found out I dumped Malcolm and he said some horrible things to me."

Cam's face clouded over. "What horrible things?"

I shrugged. "Basically he said I was stupid for dumping a rich man when that was about as good as my life would get."

"I'm going to kill him. First, you're going to report him for misconduct, and then I'm going to kill him."

"I don't want anything else to do with him."

"Jo, he crossed a line."

"Yeah, he did. But I don't have the luxury of time to go through the rigmarole of seeing him brought to some kind of meager justice. I have to find a job."

"Braden."

"Nope." I pinched my lips together.

Cam shook his head. "You are so bloody stubborn." And then he kissed my pinched mouth open, his lips light at first and then pressing harder, drawing me deeper into his demand for more.

When he finally let me up for breath, his expression was almost pained. "Don't do that to me again, okay?"

Feeling ashamed of my behavior, and vowing to be absolutely sure about a decision before throwing something as important as a breakup Cam's way, I pressed another kiss to his lips, my hands cupping his bristly cheeks tenderly, hoping he understood more in that kiss than I was willing to say. "I'm sorry," I whispered.

"You're forgiven." He squeezed my waist.

Smoothing my hands down his new T-shirt, I puckered my brows in thought. "Why are you dressed up? And what did you mean, 'not to mention what I've just done today'?"

"Ah." Cam pushed me back a little. "There's someone here to see you."

CHAPTER 21

You would think that after witnessing my crazy emotional drama Cam would have been considerate enough to prepare me for who was in his flat waiting for me.

But no.

He wanted it to be a surprise.

Feeling a little nervous about whatever unknown thing awaited me, I followed him into his sitting room.

My eyes immediately were drawn to a young woman rising from Cam's couch. Shorter than me but taller than Joss, she stood there, all curves and ass and amazing hair. For some reason, my immediate thought was that this was Blair. I stared into exceptionally light hazel eyes, so light they were almost gold, and felt my throat close up. Some might say the woman was slightly overweight, but all I processed was the big boobs and curvy ass, which looked good on her. Her jet-black hair cascaded down her back in an amazing riot of soft waves. Thinking this woman was Blair, and hating her on sight, I didn't realize for a while that the rest of her features were kind of plain. Her hair, eyes, and figure gave the impression of extraordinary.

Then she smiled.

She had a knee-knockingly great smile. "Jo?"

And an American accent.

Uh . . . what?

"Johanna?"

The gruff voice drew my gaze to the left, and my eyes widened at the sight of the large man standing next to Cam's fireplace. The weight of his light hazel eyes on me made me stagger back in shock. I'd been so consumed with jealousy, thinking the woman was Blair, that it hadn't even registered how familiar those exotic eyes were.

"Uncle Mick?" I breathed in shock, my eyes running the length of him.

He looked older now, gray peppering his dark hair and beard, but it was him. A tower of a man, standing at six and a half feet tall with huge shoulders, he still looked as fit and healthy as he had eleven years ago. Everyone had always said Uncle Mick was built like a brick shithouse. He still was.

What was he doing here?

"Jo." He shook his head, giving me a grin that made me feel homesick. "I always knew you'd be a knockout, lass, but just look at you." His accent threw me for a moment, the sharp, abrupt inflection of Scots softened slightly in certain words by an American drawl. His accent was Joss's in reverse.

Still dumbstruck, I could only say his name again. "Uncle Mick?" I glanced back at Cam, my mouth open in wonder, my heart in my throat. "What is going on?"

Cam stepped forward and took my hand in reassurance. "You told me Mick's surname, that he'd moved to Arizona, and you showed me old photographs. Mick has a Facebook account, and I tracked him down on there."

Facebook? I looked back at Mick incredulously, still not believing he was here. Everything that had been good about my life as a child was standing in front of me and I didn't know whether I wanted to run face-first into his chest or turn on my heel and flee.

"Cam and I got to talking and he told me how difficult things have been for you, darling. I'm so sorry." Mick's voice was low, as though he were talking to a frightened animal. "I'm so sorry I wasn't here."

I gulped and for the hundredth time that day tried desperately not to cry. "Why are you here?"

"We came back a few years ago to Paisley for a short visit, but no one knew where you'd gone. I saw your dad."

I winced at the thought of my father. "He's still there, then?"

Mick nodded, taking a step toward me. "I'm glad Fiona got you away from him. I'm glad he has no clue where you went and is too stupid to find you."

I felt my nose sting with the tears I could no longer hold back. "So you came all the way here to see me?"

He grinned. "You're worth the plane ticket, baby girl."

Baby girl. He'd always called me that and I'd loved it. It was why I called Cole "baby boy." The sob rose out of my mouth before I could stop it, and seemingly done with being patient, Uncle Mick made a rough noise and crossed the room to pull me into a bear hug. I hugged him back, breathing him in. Mick had never been one for aftershave. He'd always smelled of soap and earth. The ache in my chest intensified as I reverted to a ten-year-old in his arms.

We stood together for a good while, until my crying finally trailed off, and then Mick eased me back, his light eyes—eyes I'd loved more than any other eyes in the world until Cole came along—bright on me. "I've missed you."

I laughed in an attempt to curb another crying jag. "Missed you, too."

Clearing his throat and shifting uncomfortably under the weight of emotion between us, Mick turned to look back at the young woman. Although he introduced her, I no longer needed to be told who she was. Her eyes gave her away. "Jo, this is Olivia, my daughter."

Olivia's eyes were shining with tears as she took a step toward me.

"It's nice to meet you, Jo. Dad has been talking about you for years, so I almost feel like I know you. God, was that as cliché as it sounded?"

I smiled weakly, not quite sure how I felt about her. Watching the way Uncle Mick gazed adoringly at his daughter, I was happy for him. Happy he'd found his own family. But the thirteen-year-old girl inside me resented Olivia—resented her for being what had taken Mick away in the first place.

I tried to quash that feeling, knowing it was useless and childish and petty, but it was there no matter how much I didn't want it to be.

"After coming to Paisley and not finding you, we tried Facebook too, but you don't have an account. We thought we'd found Cole, but we couldn't be sure, and Dad was worried that you didn't want to hear from him anyway."

I looked up at Mick, my hand curling on his arm. "I'm sorry for losing touch. It was childish."

"Baby girl, you *were* just a child."

"Cam was pretty sure you'd want to see Dad." Olivia smiled gratefully behind me and I turned to face Cameron.

"I can't believe you did this," I whispered softly, knowing and not caring at the moment that everything I felt for him was shimmering in my eyes.

Cam's knuckles brushed along my jaw affectionately. "Happy?"

I nodded, choking on the lump in my throat. I was happy. Just having Mick in the room . . . I felt safe.

We settled around Cam's coffee table while he made us refreshments. I sat between Mick and Olivia, surprised by Olivia's friendliness and enthusiasm. I'd have thought she'd be mad at me for having had her dad for the first thirteen years of our lives, but she seemed anything but mad. She seemed glad for her dad that they had found me.

"How long are you staying?" I asked Mick as he relaxed against the cushions, his long arm draping across the back of the sofa behind me.

His eyes drifted to Olivia as he replied, "We don't know yet."

When Cam rejoined us the questions just started pouring out of my mouth.

I was saddened by some of the answers and my resentment toward Olivia began to diminish. I wasn't the only one who hadn't had it easy.

Mick had moved to Phoenix to get to know his daughter, and there his affair with her mother, Yvonne, rekindled. Mick worked for a few contractors over there, he and Yvonne got married, and they were a happy family. Until Yvonne was diagnosed with stage IV breast cancer. She passed away three years ago, leaving Olivia and Mick all alone in the world. Yvonne's mother and sister lived in New Mexico, but they weren't that close to them.

"We thought of Cameron's e-mails as a sign," Olivia told me quietly. "Perhaps we just need a break from Arizona . . ." She shrugged. "It just seemed like the right thing to do to come here and see you and take a breath."

I frowned. "But what about your lives there? Uncle Mick's business? Your job?"

"Things haven't been the same for us in Phoenix for a long time," Mick replied softly. "We both thought a break might do us good." I gathered from the sadness buried in the back of his eyes, he meant things hadn't been the same for them since Yvonne's death. Mick smiled softly down at me. "Do you fancy coming on a wee walk with me, Jo? We'll talk."

It was the most bizarre day. I walked by Mick's mammoth side and for the first time in my adult life I felt physically small. He kept close to me, but I could see his eyes drinking everything in as we strolled all the way to Leith Walk and continued onto Princes Street. Uncle Mick stared at the Balmoral Hotel across the road from us as we passed it.

"I missed this place. Edinburgh wasn't even my city and I missed it. I missed everything here."

"I can't imagine anywhere more different from Scotland than Arizona."

"Yeah. Ain't that the truth."

"You were happy, though?"

I felt his eyes return to my face as we dodged the busy foot traffic. As soon as we were side by side again he began to speak. "When I had Yvonne and Olivia, aye, I was happy. But there wasn't a day that I didn't think about you, Cole, and Fiona. I have two regrets in life, Jo. One is missing out on the first thirteen years of Olivia's life, and the second is not being there for you when you needed me. Especially now that I know what you've been going through."

"Did Cam tell you everything, then?"

"He told me about Fiona. How hard you've had to work. He told me you've raised Cole and that he's a good kid. Things have been tough, but I'm glad you've found someone who cares about you, baby girl."

Remembering my earlier freak-out at Cam, I felt another rainfall of guilt begin to drop on my head. I had to make it up to him.

"I would like to see Fiona."

"I don't know if that's a good idea."

"I need to see for myself. She was never the easiest person, but she was my friend."

I sighed, wondering what kind of drama Mick's appearance would kick off in my tiny flat. However, the man had flown thousands of miles to see us. I couldn't say no. "All right."

"And I'd like to meet Cole."

"Okay."

"I don't how long we're going to be here, but I'd like to spend as much time as possible with you."

I threw him a wry but worried grin. "That shouldn't be a problem, since I quit my job today."

Curled up in Cam's lap on his couch, I stared at his television in silence.

Uncle Mick and Olivia had left as soon as we returned to Cam's, and not long after that Cole had arrived home and I'd had to explain everything to him.

Cam had insisted we have dinner with him and when I'd gotten up to leave so Cole could shower and do his homework, Cam had insisted even harder that we stay. Since I still wasn't happy leaving Cole alone in the flat with Mum for any length of time, I'd agreed to stay as long as Cole took his shower at Cam's.

"You've hardly said a word." Cam suddenly spoke up, his fingers trailing a lazy caress down my arm. "Earlier you said you were happy I contacted them. Are you still happy?"

"Aye," I assured him. "I feel a kind of peace knowing that he's okay. And Olivia seems nice." I twisted my neck to look into his eyes. "Thank you."

He shrugged and looked back at the telly. "I just want to make you happy."

My stomach rolled out another somersault. "You do."

"Really? The earlier drama was definitely just an emotional . . . female . . . thing . . . ?"

I wanted to laugh, but in the end the crap I'd pulled out in the hall wasn't funny. "I'm sorry for doing that. It wasn't nice. I was pissed off at Meikle and at myself and I twisted it all in my head so I could blame someone else. Someone more accessible to my rage."

Cam grunted. "So naturally that someone is me?"

I stroked his chest affectionately. "Sorry."

He looked down at me carefully. "Would this be a bad time to tell you I got a job?"

Taken aback, I pushed up off of him. "In graphic design?"

"Yeah."

Delight for him surged through me and I found myself grinning like an idiot. "Where?"

"Here. I got my old job back. Their restructuring hasn't gone over well and they realized they'd left themselves a man short. They can't handle the workload without another designer. My boss put in a good word for me." He shrugged. "It's a gamble to go back with them, but it pays well and I'd be doing what I love to do."

I leaned into him, placing a soft kiss on his mouth. "Cam, I'm so pleased for you. When do you go back?"

"Monday." His arm tightened around me. "Su's unhappy with me for not giving two weeks' notice, but I can't risk losing this offer."

"Su will manage. I'll probably take on more shifts." My mouth turned down at the thought of working more backshifts.

"You know, if you took Braden up on his offer this wouldn't even be a problem."

"I said no. I'll find something. Don't worry."

He shifted under me, tensing. "You're so bloody stubborn. You're always all concerned about Cole and providing for him and making sure he's going to be okay. I bet half of what happened out in the hall this afternoon was because of him and you feeling like you'd let him down. If you're so concerned about him, then take a bloody job when it's offered to you."

I pulled out of his embrace, my cheeks burning at being spoken down to like that. I stretched out on the other side of the couch and reached over for the television remote, bumping up the volume of the sci-fi program we were watching. Not only was I annoyed by his tone, but I was annoyed that he was absolutely right.

His weary sigh filled the living room.

"Fine," I grumbled. "I'll call Braden tomorrow."

Silence greeted me, so I shot him a quick look before focusing back on the television. The overbearing bastard was trying not to smile. "Good. I'm glad to hear it."

"Are you deliberately trying to be a smug bugger?"

He snorted. "How did I go from being the guy who brought your family back together to being a smug bugger? How did we go from cuddling to you sitting as far from me as possible?" He grabbed my calf. "Come back."

I kicked out at him. "Stop it."

"Fine, I'll come to you."

I squealed as he launched himself over me, pinning me to the sofa. "Get off!" I laughed as he buried his nose in my neck, his fingers tickling my waist.

"Will you be nice?" he muttered against my skin.

I pouted. "I'm always nice."

Cam lifted his head and kissed the pout right off my mouth and what had started as playful quickly gained heat. I held him to me, his chest pressing against my sensitive breasts as he deepened our kiss.

When his hips began to thrust gently against me, his hard-on nudging between my legs, I tore my mouth away from his, feeling as if my whole body was going to burst into flames. "Don't," I breathed, gripping his hips to still his erotic motion. "We can't do anything and I'm horny as hell. Don't torture me."

"Yeah?" Cam's grin was wicked as his hand coasted up my waist to cup my breast. He squeezed it, setting off a weird mixture of painful tenderness and a bolt of lust to my sex.

"My eyes!" Cole yelled.

Cam and I jerked apart, and I twisted my head to see my brother standing in the doorway in his pajamas, his hair falling in wet locks across his forehead. His forearm covered his eyes. "I'm fucking blind," he growled and turned around, bumping into the wall before remembering to drop his arm. After that he stomped out of the flat, the door slamming in his wake.

Horrified, I looked up into Cam's face, my eyes wide. "I think I should let him get away with using the 'f' word on this occasion."

Cam snorted, laughter spluttering as he dropped his head to my chest, his whole body shaking with amusement.

I felt an irrepressible giggle escape me despite my mortification for myself and Cole. "It's not funny. We've scarred him. I better check on him."

Cam shook his head, his eyes bright with mirth. "You're the last person he wants to see right now."

"But he's upstairs with Mum."

"I'm sure he's barricaded himself in his room and is doing anything he can to burn the image of me dry-humping his sister out of his mind."

"Why do you have to be right about everything? It's exceptionally annoying."

He just smiled.

"No, I mean it. Either you're going to have to stop or you're constantly going to find yourself on the wrong end of the couch."

"Good." He flashed that heated smile at me again. "I like the making-up part."

I abruptly kissed him hard, liking that answer and too love-fogged to care that he now knew just how much his cockiness could turn me on. When I finally let him up for breath, I brushed my thumb across his mouth, hoping I got to keep that sexy curl of his lip forever and ever. "I am grateful for today. For everything. For handling me with care and for going out of your way to bring Uncle Mick to me."

His eyes lit with affection and sweet tenderness as he searched my face slowly, seeming to memorize each feature. "Anytime, baby."

I cuddled him close and we lay in silence for a few moments. Brushing his hair through my fingers, I asked tentatively, "Cam?"

"Aye?"

"I know you said you gave up on the idea of looking for your birth parents, but after seeing what happened today with Mick . . . are you sure?"

"That was different." His breath whispered across my collarbone. "You and Mick had a relationship. I don't know the people who gave me up. Honestly, I no longer need to know them. I have everything I could ever want for in Anderson and Helena MacCabe. I don't need reasons or excuses because . . . well . . . no matter how good they are, it's never going to change the fact that I came second to those excuses. They abandoned me. Doesn't matter if their reasons are logical, practical . . . It will never change how I felt when I found out the truth. So what's the point?"

I ran my hand down his back soothingly, wanting to draw him inside me, where he was loved more than he even knew. "They missed out, baby. They missed out big."

CHAPTER 22

Cole had been given the full rundown about Uncle Mick already. He'd been only three years old when Mick left, so he couldn't remember him, but he seemed okay about meeting him, having learned enough from me over the years to know that I'd once thought the guy walked on water.

Telling Mum had been a different story. I'd actually feared telling her, afraid that the news would cause her to kick off. To my surprise, she accepted the news with calm and agreed to come out and speak to Mick when he arrived.

I thought I even heard her take a shower while I clicked through the job site on Cole's computer.

By the time Cole arrived home from school, my palms were sweating. Mum had been unruffled earlier, but that might change when she set eyes on Mick. The knock at the door caused my heart to skip a beat. I don't know why people described that in romance novels as if it was a good thing. When your heart skips a beat, it makes you breathless—you feel a little sick, and definitely out of sorts.

"You made it." I stretched my lips into a weak smile as I opened the door to Uncle Mick and Olivia.

Olivia chuckled. "Are we that bad?"

"No, no, no." I hurried to reassure them, stepping aside to let them in.

"It's not us she's worried about," Mick murmured to her, and I threw him a knowing but weary smile over my shoulder as I led them into the sitting room.

"Just take off your jackets. Make yourself at home. Can I get you tea or coffee? Water, juice?"

"Coffee," they answered in unison.

I nodded, all nervous energy. "No probs."

But Cole's appearance in the doorway stopped me in my tracks. I put my arm around his shoulders and led him back toward Mick and Olivia. "Cole, this is Mick and his daughter, Olivia."

Mick grinned at him and stuck his hand out. Cole took it tentatively. "Nice to meet you," he murmured, letting his hair hang in his eyes so he didn't have to look directly at them.

"You too. Jesus, you're the spitting image of your dad when he was your age."

"He's nothing like Dad," I said tersely.

Olivia's eyebrows rose and she shot a look at her father before she said admonishingly, "Way to go, Dad."

Looking uncomfortable, Mick sighed. "I didn't mean it like that."

Way to go, Jo. "I know." I waved him off, feeling bad for my waspishness. "I'm a little sensitive around that subject."

"Understood."

"Cole, I'm Olivia." She stuck her hand out and Cole's cheekbones flushed a little as they shook hands. "It's good to meet you." She glanced around the sitting room, her eyes brimming with approval. "You guys have a really nice place."

"Jo does all the decorating." Cole surprised me as he informed her about that almost enthusiastically. "The wallpapering, painting, sanding . . . everything."

"I'm impressed."

I felt Uncle Mick's smiling eyes on me. "All my teaching stuck with you, eh?"

Embarrassed, I shrugged. "I like decorating."

"Aye, we know." Mum's voice had me sucking in my breath as we all turned to watch her shuffle into the sitting room. "You do it often enough." Cole and I exchanged glances, utterly taken aback by her appearance. She hadn't just showered; she'd gotten dressed. Her hair was blow-dried smooth, she had some makeup on and she was wearing a pair of skinny jeans that were loose on her frail body, and a black silk shirt I'd bought her for her Christmas even though I never thought she'd wear it. To us she looked better than she had in ages, but when I glanced back at Uncle Mick I could see the shock in his eyes at her appearance.

He stepped past us and towered over Mum, who gave him a small smile. "Fiona. It's good to see you."

She nodded, her mouth trembling a little. "It's been a long time, Michael."

"Aye."

"You look almost the same."

"You don't, darling," he replied softly, something like anguish in his voice.

Mum lifted her shoulders in a gesture of resignation. "I did what I could."

Uncle Mick didn't say anything, but I could see from the hard set of his jaw that he didn't think she'd done enough. We would be in agreement on that one.

"Dad." Olivia moved to his side, taking his hand reassuringly, and I felt the last of my resentment toward her disappear. How could I resent someone who so obviously adored Mick?

Uncle Mick tightened his hand around his daughter's. "Fiona, this is my girl, Olivia."

And just like that it all went to pot.

Mum pursed her lips as her eyes drifted over Olivia. "Aye, she looks like that American piece you had a thing with."

I squeezed my eyes shut in mortification and heard Cole's low groan beside me.

"Fiona," Mick scolded her.

"Dad, it doesn't matter."

"Pfft." Mum looked past her to me. "You told me it would just be him. I'm going back to bed. Leave me some dinner later."

I nodded, my muscles tense as we waited for her to leave. When her bedroom door slammed closed, I sighed. "Sorry, Uncle Mick. That's about as good as it gets with her. Olivia, I'm sorry . . ."

"Forget it." Olivia waved me off. "It's not a problem."

"I can't believe that's the same woman." Mick shook his head as he strode across the room to take a seat, his body seeming heavy with the shock. "I just can't believe it."

I thought of how Mum had actually behaved fairly well, at least until she saw Olivia but I didn't want to tell Mick that. "Believe it."

Like a turtle that had poked its head out for a little sunshine only to discover that it was raining, Mum retreated back into her shell even worse than before. She rarely left her room, a crate of alcohol was delivered to the flat, and the only way I knew she was alive was that the food I'd leave for her disappeared. Anytime I knocked to check on her, she grunted at me to go away.

I wanted it to be black and white. I wanted to hate her for hitting Cole and not give a shit whether she lived or died, but I found I just couldn't abandon her entirely.

Cam said there came a time when we had to let some people go. There was no helping them, and attempting to would just pull you into the mire with them.

It was easier said than done. Despite all of our ugly encounters, she was my mum and there was still a part of me that wanted her to care more about us than she did about herself. I knew I had to let her go. I knew it. For Cole and also for me. When it came time to leave her, I would. But I would take the guilt with me.

Uncle Mick had said he wanted to spend as much time with me as possible and he hadn't been lying. That Saturday Cole, Cam, Olivia, Mick, and I met in the Grassmarket for a pub lunch. I learned that Olivia had been a librarian in the States, but much like Cam, she had been made redundant due to budget issues. Olivia was warm and funny and extremely hard not to like, and I could envision her getting along well with both Joss and Ellie.

Lunch was fun and I could tell Mick approved of Cole and Cam's close friendship, as he kept shooting me looks that said as much. We took a stroll down the busy spring streets of the city, wandering up Victoria Street to George IV Bridge, and then taking Olivia down the Royal Mile. I took some photographs of her and Mick standing on the Mile and then more as we traveled back toward New Town. We walked along Princes Street Gardens and I got some great shots of them together by the Ross Fountain with Edinburgh Castle towering over them in the background. It was a good day. A relaxing day, and as I walked behind them, Cam's arm around my waist, I forgot about all my worries for a while.

On Sunday, Elodie was in her element. Having heard from Ellie about Uncle Mick and Olivia, she'd invited them for lunch. When we arrived, it was to discover Elodie had found a second table somewhere and placed it at the end of the one that was already there. Their flat was filled with conversation and laughter as everyone chatted away, getting to know them. I watched Olivia and felt a lump in my throat when I saw the delight on her face, the flush in her cheeks, and the spark in her eyes. Ellie had pounced on her almost immediately and I could tell they'd already glued themselves to each other. Ellie had a way of doing that with people.

Seated at the table next to Joss, she nudged me and leaned in to whisper, "Did you ever think you'd be a part of something like this?"

I glanced around at all the faces, my eyes coming to a stop on Cam, who was laughing at something Braden had said. I turned back to her, shaking my head. "Never in a million years."

She smiled, and I was taken aback by the emotion in her eyes as she looked down at the simple diamond engagement ring on her finger. "Me either."

"You okay?"

Joss nodded. "More than."

I grinned at her and was just about to crack a joke to ease us out of such seriousness when Braden called, "Jo, you need a job?"

I rolled my eyes and shot Cam an impatient look. "I was going to ask him."

"Well, you were taking your time about it."

Sighing, I nodded at Braden, my cheeks flushing at having to ask. "If you have a part-time position available, I'd appreciate it."

His light blue eyes searched mine and I felt vulnerable under his scrutiny. Braden had a way of stripping a person bare, as if he could see into the very depths of them. I didn't know how Joss had withstood him so long before eventually owning up to her feelings for him. Surely he'd known all along. "Jo, come to us whenever you need us, please."

I gulped but nodded.

"I'll set something up tomorrow, see if we can't get you started on Tuesday."

"Thank you," I whispered gratefully.

When conversation started up again, Joss chortled under her breath. "He's scary, right?"

"Braden?"

"Yeah. He sees more than most people." She eyed me carefully. "Is there something going on with you we don't know about? Are you and Cam okay?"

I thought of all my insecurities and the fight I was having with them on a daily basis. "Just finding our feet with each other."

"Sure. Well, I think he's pretty cool. I mean, before you met him you would never have taken a job from Braden."

"Yeah, don't rub it in."

"Jesus C, woman, I didn't think anyone was as proud or as stubborn as I am."

"Well, you were wrong," I answered drily.

Joss laughed. "Yeah, and now you have your very own caveman to . . . shake out some of that stubbornness."

I felt my cheeks warm at the thought of Cameron shaking out my stubbornness tonight. Good times ahead.

Joss snorted. "Just keep that thought to yourself."

CHAPTER 23

There are times in life when there is so much going on you may feel as though you don't even have a chance to take a breath. You wake up, you get washed and dressed, the day is a blur of events, work, activities, chores, and then before you know it, your exhausted body is melting against your pillow and mattress. Then, in what feels like two seconds later, your eyes are forced open at the sound of the alarm clock. That's how my life was for the next few weeks.

Because there was so much going on, I let go of my neurosis for a night and stayed in Cam's bed until morning. It was the Wednesday after the weekend with Mick and Olivia. As soon as the alarm went off, I groaned, shoved back the covers, and jumped out of bed.

Apparently Cameron found the way I got out of bed very amusing.

I watched his naked shoulders shaking as he pressed his face into his pillow.

My heavy eyelids and nervous anticipation of my second day working at Douglas Carmichael & Co didn't add up to a whole lot of patience. "It's not that funny."

Cam pulled his sleepy, grinning face out of the pillow. "Baby, you're hilarious," he said in his sexy, sleep-roughened voice. I wanted to dive back under the covers with him, but I had to get ready for work.

"If I don't jump out of bed right away I'll fall back asleep. What you're doing . . . I can't do that."

He pushed himself up to look at me, the tenderness in his eyes stopping me in my tracks. "You're fucking adorable. You know that, right?"

His ability to make me blush was ridiculous. No one got under my skin the way he did, or made me feel less like myself and yet more like myself. I looked away as I wandered out of the room to the bathroom, "I'm going to be adorably late."

That was as much one-on-one conversation as we got out of each other over the next two weeks. That first week we'd both started our new jobs (well, Cam had started back at his old job), Mick and Olivia invited us out for dinner, came over to Cam's for dinner, took the three of us to the cinema, spent alone time with me and Cole while Cam hung out with Peetie and Nate, and generally crammed as much time in with us as they could. I willingly spent that time with them, unsure when they'd be returning to the States. I couldn't imagine how expensive their hotel bill at the Caledonian was. Mick said Yvonne had inherited money from her grandmother—part of the contention between Yvonne and her family—and that she'd left that money to Mick and Olivia when she passed. It wasn't "forever" kind of money, and the trip to Scotland was eating its way through it. I knew Mick well enough to know he wouldn't want to continue to waste his money on hotel bills.

As much as I found Olivia easy to be around, it was Mick's company that I craved. Like a real dad, he refused to let me pay for anything, he gave me fatherly advice, and teased me mercilessly, just as he had when I was a kid. Being around him brought back that feeling of safety, security, and of being accepted for who I was. He also examined all the work I'd done in the flat and reemphasized Cam's point that I had a talent for it. I'd never been told by anyone that I had a talent for anything and now two of the most important men in my life insisted I did.

It was pretty bloody brilliant.

During the second week I saw less of Mick and Olivia. He had decided that he wanted her to see a bit of her heritage, and so he'd booked them into an inn in Loch Lomond and they'd disappeared for a few days. That left me to focus on getting the hang of my new job. It wasn't too difficult. Braden had set me up as an administrator and I helped out at reception as well. It was a much livelier place to work, with estate agents in one room and administrators in another. Everyone was always coming and going, and there were a number of young, good-looking guys who worked as estate agents and liked to flirt with the admin staff.

Their reaction to my arrival had been almost comical. A new toy to play with! Except my inner flirt had lost a lot of her flair since meeting Cameron. Yes, I could smile and banter with the best of them, but the heated come-on in my eyes and the promises in my teasing smile had disappeared. I was no longer constantly looking for a backup plan. I didn't want a backup plan.

All I wanted I had, in one annoyingly right, somewhat arrogant, kind, funny, patient, tattooed man.

In a new pattern of working Monday, Wednesday, and Thursday at the estate agency and working my usual Tuesday, Thursday, and Friday nights at the bar, I saw Cam very little, as he'd started a new project at work that was eating into all his spare time. He had returned to evening judo classes, and so I saw him when he popped up to the flat to collect Cole for class. I had gone to him on Wednesday night, but he had fallen asleep on top of his drawing desk by the time I'd gotten there. I'd had to gently wake him up and make sure he made it to his bed. He'd wrapped a surprisingly strong arm around my waist and pulled me down onto the bed with him. I let him, enjoying being close to him even if he was unconscious. When his arm relaxed, I managed to slip out without waking him up.

By the time Saturday came around, I missed him. I didn't want to be that needy, cloying girl, and I hadn't thought I was. But I missed not seeing him as often, and I was used to spending time together talking

and laughing, sitting in comfortable silence, or having the most incredible sex.

It had only been a week.

Christ, I was addicted.

That Saturday was the night of Joss and Braden's engagement
party, and since I'd cleaned out my wardrobe by selling most of my nice
dresses on eBay, I was going shopping for a new dress on my new,
smaller budget.

To my surprise, Cameron offered to accompany me.

It became apparent very quickly that he hated shopping.

"Why did you come?" I asked him, laughing as I found him brood-
ing in the corner of Topshop.

He immediately took my hand and led me out of the shop. "Because I miss you," he told me, completely unabashed at the confession.
"If I have to endure this to spend time with you, then so be it."

Deciding his valor deserved a kiss, I laid a hot one on him right in
the middle of Princes Street. When his arms wrapped tight around me,
holding me as close as I could get, I decided it might have been a bad
idea. By the time we pulled back, letting immature catcalls from a
group of prepubescent boys insisting that we "Get a room!" ricochet off
of us, our skin was on fire. We hadn't had sex in a week. That was a record for us. A dry spell we both apparently wanted to end, and end soon.

Now was not the time. "Tonight," I whispered against his mouth
and reluctantly let him go.

I tried not to put him through the torture of shopping for too long.
We went into one of my favorite high street stores on Castle Street, Cam
complaining loudly about the pop music blaring out of the sound system
because it was so deafening that it was almost impossible to hear one another, while I grabbed a bundle of dresses to try on. The lady at the
changing room entrance tried to stop me from taking Cam in with me,
but I charmed her, explaining that I needed my boyfriend's advice since it
was a very special evening, *wink, wink*. She could take that *wink, wink* any

way she pleased, and she did, grinning and letting us pass. To my delight, I found the largest changing room empty and dumped all the dresses inside. I pointed to the stool outside the curtain. "You can sit there."

Cam sighed and folded his tall body onto the stool. When I grinned down at him, his lips twitched. "That's the first time I've actually heard you call me your boyfriend."

I scrunched up my face in protest. "Uh-uh."

"Mmm-hmm."

"Really?"

He grinned. "Really."

I braced myself as I asked, "How did it sound to you?"

His smile softened and he nodded. "Very nice."

We shared a moment and I found myself growing all glowy inside. "Okay," I sighed, attempting not to seem like an adoring teen in love. "I'll try to be quick."

After shutting the curtain, I hurried out of my clothes and into the first dress. I thought it was too short. Cam agreed. "This is easy." I smiled and dashed back behind the curtain. There was a succession of "no" and "maybe" verdicts until I finally tried on a dark blue lace pencil dress, classy and elegant but so body-forming that it was sexy too.

"What do you think?" I twirled around for Cam as I came out from behind the curtain.

His eyes drifted from the tip of my toes to my face, growing more heated as they did. Then he merely nodded.

I raised an eyebrow in question. "Good?"

When he just nodded again, I shrugged and dipped back behind the curtain. I stared at my reflection for a moment. *Well, I like it.*

I was just about to reach for the zip, when the curtain ruffled behind me and Cameron slipped inside, pulling it closed behind him. I felt my heart begin to speed up, my skin already flushing with anticipation. I didn't need to ask him what he was doing. I knew that look on his face all too well.

Suddenly it didn't matter that we were in a changing room, in a store, in public.

Cam slid his hand along my jaw, to the back of my nape, drawing me toward him for a kiss that literally made all my nerves snap. I trembled against him as though it was our first kiss, exhilarating in the deep, wet heat of his mouth, tasting him and the mint he'd been chewing earlier. I clawed at him and we stumbled over my pile of clothing, my back hitting the mirrored wall. Cam pulled back, his lids low, his mouth swollen. "Turn around," he demanded in a rough voice in my ear, so I could hear him over the music. The heated coarseness of his tone caused my body to react as though he'd slipped two fingers inside of me. My chest rising and falling with excited breaths, I spun around. He yanked the zip on the dress down and began peeling it off my body. I watched him in the mirror as he threw it onto the pile with my own clothing. "Buy it," he advised and I shivered at the feel of his breath on my skin as his warm hands coasted around to squeeze my naked breasts. Biting my lip to curb the moan I was desperate to release, I arched into his touch, my hands on his as he pinched my nipples. I could feel his chest against my back, his breathing uncontrolled as he pushed my underwear down. They fell to my thighs and I hurriedly shoved them farther down, kicking them out from around my ankles as the sound of Cam unzipping met my ears.

While his clothes rustled, his black trousers falling to his ankles, Cam slowly glided two strong fingers into my channel and I leaned against the mirror for support, my eyes on him. He watched his fingers moving in and out of me, fascinated and excited, and it only made me wetter.

"Cam," I moaned softly, and as if he heard me his head came up, his eyes meeting mine in the mirror. They flashed at the expression on my face.

He pinned me against the mirror, one hand flat above mine while the other cradled my hip.

He glided into me with a stifled grunt and I swallowed my gasp.

As he began to move, I pushed back against his slow thrusts, and our eyes stayed connected in the mirror as he fucked me.

As the tension began to build inside me, Cam grasped my hips, his cock so deep inside me it was almost painful. Abruptly he lowered himself to his knees, pulling me down with him. Poised over his lap, my hand still pressed to the mirror, his hands caressing my breasts, I began to move against his strokes. I felt his cheek against my back as we chased climax, my orgasm spurred on by the low, needy, guttural noises he was making in the back of his throat.

Sensing that I was about to come, Cam drew up behind me, his hand moving from my breast to cover my mouth. The tight heat co-cooning my skin and muscles combusted and I exploded around him, my cry of release muffled against his palm.

Cam followed me to release seconds later, my eyes watching him in the mirror as he stiffened, the muscles in his neck straining. His mouth opened in a silent groan as his hips jerked against my ass and he came, the warm heat of his release flooding me.

"Fuck," he whispered, resting his head against mine.

"Um, everything all right in there?" the shop assistant called loudly. Her sudden interruption filtered through the curtain, so close that we tensed against one another.

Oh, my holy hell! I'd forgotten where we were. "Yes," I answered, my voice breaking with postcoital exhaustion and embarrassment that I'd gotten so lost in this man, I'd forgotten we were screwing each other on the floor of a changing room.

"Do you need me to fetch another size, or is the dress okay?"

Go away! My wide eyes met Cameron's in the mirror and he gave me no indication of what I should do. He was still inside me, for Christ's sake. I almost laughed at that and glanced back at the curtain. "Everything's great. In fact . . . it's a perfect fit."

At the innuendo, Cameron collapsed against my back, his laughter muffled in my hair, his shoulders shaking with amusement. It also caused him to jostle inside me, setting off little aftershocks of lust.

"Okay . . ." Her voice trailed off as she wandered away from the curtain.

"Do you think they heard us?"

He gave a low bark of laughter. "I don't give a shit."

And he meant it.

With tender gentleness, he eased out of me and helped me to my feet. Hands cupping my cheeks, he drew me against him for a languorous, sensual kiss that made my chest ache with emotion.

I love you.

I cleared the thought from my eyes as Cam pulled back to gaze at me.

"Luckily we finally chose a dress because there's no way I can try anything else on before I have a shower."

Something darkly sexual heated in his eyes and I knew he was thinking it was hot that I had to walk home with his sweat on me and his seed inside me.

"Joss is right," I murmured. "You're all cavemen."

Cam didn't take offense at that. Instead he took his time helping me dress, his knuckles brushing all my sensitive bits until I had to slap his hand away so I could get dressed without wanting to maul him again.

My cheeks were blazing as I handed the dresses I didn't want back to the suspicious sales assistant. I couldn't look at Cam because every time I did he shot me a wicked grin that made me want to giggle with equal parts exhilaration and mortification. As soon as we stumbled out of the store with my new dress, I fell against Cam's side, laughing hard as he wrapped his arm around me.

"I can't believe we did that," I breathed.

"Aye, can't say I've done that before."

"You better not tell Nate and Peetie." My warning didn't hold much of an impact since I was still grinning like a fool.

"Why not? That's a bloody good sex story."

My cheeks warmed again and Cam laughed, snuggling me against his chest as I giggled. I was so caught up in happy la-la land with him that what happened in the next few moments was even more of a crashing, cold bump back to earth.

Cam stopped abruptly and I grabbed him to keep my balance, my head pulling back to study his face. The color had leached from it and his eyes were wide with utter shock. "Cam?" I whispered, feeling something hard begin to form in my stomach. I followed his gaze to the girl who was standing in front of us, her pretty eyes just as wide as Cam's.

"Cameron?" she breathed, taking a step toward us, apparently not even aware that I was there.

"Blair," he answered hoarsely.

I felt my head spin at the sound of her name, my eyes immediately examining her, processing everything about her. To my surprise she wasn't at all what I'd been expecting. I'd pictured her in my mind as this tall, exotic stunner with an air of mystique. Instead she was shorter than Joss, her body slim and petite. She wore a T-shirt with a band on it over a long-sleeved white top, ratty jeans that fit her well and boots quite like Cam's. She had short black hair that framed her cute pixie face. Her wide brown eyes were her best feature, framed by long black lashes. Shock mixed with longing haunted those pretty eyes, and I felt my hand fist around the material of Cam's light jacket.

"It's great to see you." She gave him a sweet smile.

Cam nodded, clearing his throat and shaking the deer-caught-in-the-headlights expression from his eyes. "Uh, you too. How long have you been back in Edinburgh?"

"A few months. I thought about looking you up, but I wasn't sure . . ." Her voice trailed off as she finally registered that I was burrowed into Cam's side. She took me in, a crestfallen expression on her face, disappointment in her eyes. Disappointment in Cam? For choosing someone like me?

I bristled at the thought and Cam's arm tightened around me. "No, you should have," Cam surprised me by saying.

Blair's whole face lit up. "Really?"

"Yeah." Cam dropped his arm from around me to pull his phone out of his pocket. "Here, give me your number and we'll arrange to catch up."

What?

I watched them as they exchanged numbers, Cam's head bent over hers, and my brain just started screaming at me. What the hell was going on? He was arranging to get in contact with the ex–love of his life! What effed-up reality was this?

To make matters worse, he hadn't even introduced me.

I stood there, attempting to appear calm and unconcerned.

He laughed softly at something she said and she gazed up at him like he was some kind of miracle. He was a miracle. He was *my* miracle and if he didn't introduce me I was going—

"Blair, this is my girlfriend, Jo," Cam said as he tucked his phone away. He gave me a reassuring smile that I didn't return.

"Nice to meet you." I managed to give her a small smile while inside I was flinging every swearword I could think of at her.

She didn't smile back. "You too."

When our gazes met, we had a silent conversation with each other. *I resent you*, she said. *I think I hate you*, I replied. *He was mine first*, she answered. *He's mine now*, I growled.

Thick tension fell between the three of us until Cam broke the silence with a few polite questions.

After arranging to speak to one another soon, we left Blair to walk home via Princes Street. To my growing panic, Cam didn't reach for me again. We walked home side by side, not touching and not talking. He seemed to have disappeared somewhere inside himself and I feared that place almost more than I feared anything else.

CHAPTER 24

Cole knew there was something wrong as soon as I returned to the flat. I kept insisting it was nothing, which pissed him off. I knew this because he told me to my face it pissed him off. I retaliated with a lecture on swearing, which he informed me pissed him off even more, so by the time I was dressed for the party, I was mad at Cam for being an inconsiderate dimwit, terrified that I was facing the end of my relationship, and upset that my wee brother had left to stay with Jamie for the night without saying good-bye to me.

In other words I was really in the party spirit.

My depressed thoughts weren't eased any when I hurried down to Cam's flat to pick him up and he barely registered my dress. The dress he'd found so hot pre–Blair encounter that he'd ravished me in a public dressing room.

I felt my chest tighten with anxiety as he remained quiet during the taxi ride with Olivia and Uncle Mick. Even Olivia commented on it, asking him if he was all right.

Of course he insisted he was, though we all knew (we, as in I) that he had been thrown for a loop by the arrival of his ex-girlfriend, aka the only woman he had ever loved.

We arrived at Joss and Braden's flat on Dublin Street to find the party already in full swing. Hannah and Declan were staying with friends tonight, so Elodie and Clark were free to stay as long as they wanted. Elodie was completely smashed already—and Elodie smashed was just a heightened version of Elodie sober. She kept moving around all the guests asking them if they wanted a refill and when they said yes, she proceeded to overfill their glasses with a loopy "Oopsie!"

Cam, Olivia, and I settled in a corner with Adam and Ellie. I tried to keep up with the conversation, and attempted to appear as if everything was all right, laughing along with the others as Adam pointed out the growing strain on Joss's face as she was forced to mingle. At one point we watched as Joss attempted to remove her hand from the grip of the wife of one of Braden's professional acquaintances as she peered at the engagement ring. Joss tugged politely a few times, but when that didn't seem to get through, she actually swatted the woman's hand off hers and then smiled prettily as if nothing had happened, leaving Braden choking on laughter while she excused herself.

We were all laughing, and I turned to Cam to share a smile with him, only to find his head bent over his phone.

"You okay?" I asked, looking down at the text message he was typing and feeling that ugly compression on my chest again.

He glanced up and gave me a barely there smile. "Yeah, you?"

"Fine. Who are you texting?"

"Just Blair. She wanted my address."

"Hmm." I nodded, hoping my fury wasn't evident in my eyes. I turned away from him, cursing him to the moon and back.

Come to a party for my friend's engagement as my bloody date and stand there not paying attention to anything anyone's saying, tapping away at your bloody phone, talking to an ex-girlfriend you casually mention you were in love with, and expect me not to be bloody well pissed off, you bloody swine, you utter—

"So, Jo, how are you liking the new job?" Adam asked me, interrupting my inner diatribe against my boyfriend.

"Oh, good."

Adam waited for me to say more, but I couldn't make my brain work. While my blood was hot with anger, my chest hurt, and my melancholy thoughts took up all my head space. Realizing he wasn't going to get anything else out of me, Adam engaged Olivia in conversation and I ignored the worried looks Ellie kept shooting me.

I glanced around the room, wishing I could just escape, lock myself in the bathroom and cry. But that seemed awfully melodramatic, considering Cam hadn't actually done anything wrong. It was my insecurities that were making me feel this way, right?

I caught Uncle Mick's eye across the room and smiled. He grinned and then turned back to Clark. The two men were so different, one a scholar, one a manual laborer, and yet they seemed to get on incredibly well with each other. I was glad. It was nice of Joss and Braden to invite Mick and Olivia to their engagement party, but I had worried that they would feel out of place.

Turned out the only one feeling out of place was me.

I listened with half an ear as Ellie managed to engage Cam in conversation. Although he chatted with her about the new project he was creating the graphics for, an independent chocolate shop that was opening in Edinburgh, I could hear the lack of enthusiasm in his voice. I knew him too well. I knew his mind was off somewhere else tonight.

Was it really my insecurities telling me his mind was on Blair? Or was it my instincts?

I needed the opinion of a blunt, straightforward, honest couple.

Sweeping the crowded sitting room, I couldn't see Joss and Braden anywhere. I excused myself and headed out into the empty hallway, then proceeded to check the kitchen, where a large group of people had congregated. They weren't there either. I checked the bedrooms. Both empty.

Wondering if they'd gone outside for some fresh air, I headed down the hall toward the door and that was when I heard the deep, rumbling chuckle.

I halted, my eyebrows at my hairline as I turned to face the bathroom door.

No.

They wouldn't.

Would they?

"Oh, wait, I think my leg cramped up." Joss snorted and then giggled. Actually giggled. I didn't know she could do that.

"How did it cramp up?" Braden murmured.

"Well, I don't know if you know this about me, baby, but my body isn't a pretzel."

My mouth fell open and I muffled a laugh into my hand despite myself. What position had he gotten her into?

"Do you want me to massage it?"

There was a moment of silence and then . . . "Oh, yeah, right there," she moaned.

"Fuck," Braden huffed. "You'll set me off again."

"Seriously?" she asked incredulously. "I just moaned."

"That's all it takes, babe."

Joss giggled again. I decided it was a nice sound.

And then I realized I was creepily eavesdropping on their sex-in-the-bathroom-at-their-own-fricking-engagement encounter. I knocked on the door.

"Uh, just a minute!" Joss yelled.

"It's me," I called semi-loudly through the door. "Are you decent yet?"

"Um, not yet. Wait." I heard clothes rustling and then a muffled "oof" before something clattered to the floor. "Are you trying to kill me?"

Braden laughed. "You were the one that wanted to fuck in the bathroom."

"Ssssh!" Joss hissed. "Jo is outside."

"I think she knows what we're up to."

"She does," I offered helpfully.

Braden laughed.

The door swung open. Braden stood over me, his hair mussed, and his shirt tucked messily back into his trousers. Joss was hopping on one foot behind him, trying to get her shoe back on. Her cheeks were flushed and the French knot in her hair was a little more than worse for wear.

"Really?" I asked, glancing around to make sure we were still alone. "The bathroom during your engagement party?"

Joss rolled her eyes at me. "What, like you've never done it somewhere a little risqué?"

My cheeks bloomed bright red as I remembered how risqué it had gotten with Cam just this morning. God, it seemed like a lifetime ago already.

Bloody Blair.

Braden scrutinized me and nodded smugly at Joss. "She's definitely done it somewhere risqué."

Joss grinned, finally getting her shoe on and coming to a standstill. "I do believe you're right, Mr. Carmichael. Look at those pretty cheeks blush."

I sighed impatiently, trying to cover my embarrassment. "I didn't hunt you down to talk about risqué sex." I brushed past Braden and motioned to him to shut the door.

He raised an eyebrow but complied. "Everything all right?"

Trying to keep a lid on my emotions I laid it out for them. The story of Cam and Blair, and now her sudden reentrance into his life and Cam's troubling reaction to it.

"Should I be worried?" I chewed on my lip, glancing from one to the other.

Joss looked at Braden. "What do you think?"

Braden winked at her. "I think I'm looking pretty good right now."

Joss smacked him across the arm for the both of us. "Not helpful, you smug idiot."

He grunted, still smiling cockily, a smile that slipped when he turned to me and saw that I was not in the mood for his humor at the moment. He sighed, his eyes softening. "Jo, you've nothing to worry about."

It was exactly the reassurance I'd been looking for, but I needed more. "Really?"

"Look, Cameron just bumped into a girl he has a history with. It's going to affect him. It doesn't mean he still has feelings for her. If Joss and I were out for a stroll and we bumped into my ex, I'd probably be feeling a bit off for the rest of the day as well, but not because I'm still in love with the bitch."

I raised my eyebrows, wondering what the history was there. I shot Joss a look. "Clearly."

Joss caressed Braden's arm in comfort. "She *is* a bitch."

I sighed this time. "So, you think I'm jumping the gun?"

"Yes," they answered in unison.

"I must say, though"—Joss shook her head as if in disappointment—"it shows a serious lack of intuition when it comes to women that Cam wouldn't realize that him planning to meet with an old girlfriend would bother you."

Braden snorted at Cam's lack of smoothness. "Agreed."

I pouted a little. "Agreed." I made a face. "Sorry for dumping this on you at your engagement party. That was more than a little selfish. God!" I threw up my hands. "This relationship is turning me into a schizo!"

Joss threw me a sympathetic smile. "Welcome to my world."

When I returned to the party it was to discover that Cam had gotten surprisingly drunk, shockingly fast. He never drank to the point of being drunk and as the evening wore on, the little that Braden had done to reassure me was obliterated by the state Cam ended up in. Mick had to help me put him in a taxi and then help me up to the flat with him.

I bade Mick and Olivia good night, stripped Cam out of his clothes, put water and aspirin beside his bed, and crawled in beside him to stay with him and make sure he was okay.

I didn't sleep.

I felt like I was standing on top of the world's tallest building, staring out on all that the world had to offer, waiting for that gust of wind to come along and blow me down, ripping me from the best view I'd ever had.

When I turned my head on the pillow to study Cam sleeping, a part of me thought I might hate him a little. I hated him for making me love him so much and for making me feel this horribly uncertain. I'd spent my whole adult life depending on men for financial security, and now I'd traded it in for Cam. I'd thought I was doing it for all the right reasons, but it seemed to me I'd traded financial security for emotional security and the risk hadn't paid off.

Assured that the drunken twat would be fine, I got up out of his bed and pulled on my boots.

Maybe I should try just depending on myself for a while.

CHAPTER 25

Where are you? x

I looked down at Cam's text, sighed a little, and then quickly texted him back.

Took Cole out to lunch with Mick and Olivia. Hungover? x

"I know it's none of my business, but you seem a little out of it," Olivia observed softly as she strolled beside me.

Uncle Mick and Cole walked ahead of us and I could see Mick chatting away quite animatedly to Cole. We'd gone for lunch at the Buffalo Grill, this amazing Tex-Mex place behind the university. Now we were walking off our burgers with a nice Sunday stroll down the Meadows. We weren't the only ones enjoying the large park behind the uni. Friends and families had descended upon it, playing football and tennis, chasing playful dogs, and in general hanging out and enjoying the fair spring weather while it lasted. I'd decided this morning that I didn't really feel like facing Cam or our problems. Instead I'd pounced on Cole as soon as he'd gotten home and then called Uncle Mick to suggest lunch. I'd found myself breathing a little easier as soon as Cole and I stepped out of our building and had been trying to enjoy myself until Cam had intruded upon my thoughts with his text.

My phone buzzed before I could respond to Olivia's comment.

Cam's reply:

A wee bit. You okay? x

"Just a second, Olivia," I muttered apologetically, before replying that I was fine and I'd see him when I got back.

"Is that Cam?" She nodded down at my phone.

"Aye." I'd sadistically hoped he was suffering the worst hangover ever. He couldn't even give me that. "I've never seen him that drunk before."

"Is he okay?"

I studied her for a moment. We didn't know each other all that well, so I didn't know if I could confide in her. I'd gone to Joss and Braden for help because I trusted them to be honest, but the welcome advice they'd given me had been blown to smithereens by Cam's dive to the bottom of a bottle last night. I did feel the urge to talk to someone else about it, but Olivia? I just didn't know her that well.

As if she sensed the turn of my thoughts, she gave me an understanding smile. "I get it. You're not sure you can talk to me. That's cool—but you should know I'm really good at dispensing advice and keeping secrets. If I hadn't become a librarian I most certainly would have become an advice columnist by day and a spy by night."

I chuckled. "Well, that's good to know. Truthfully, I don't even know what to say. I don't know if it's all in my head or if there really is a problem."

Olivia cleared her throat. "You're obviously distressed about something and . . . well . . . I learned a hard lesson in the past about ignoring something just because I thought it was all in my head."

Momentarily distracted, I asked tentatively, "What happened?"

Her unusual eyes narrowed and I noted that she unconsciously clenched her hands into fists. "Mom. She was weird for a while before we learned her diagnosis. She was snippy, short-tempered, impatient. This was a woman who was pretty much the most laid-back person I knew. My gut told me something was seriously wrong, but I didn't press her about it. And I should have. If I had I might have gotten her to go to the doctors about the lump in her breast. Instead she was so frozen in fear, by the time she finally found the courage to do something about it, it was too late."

"God, Olivia, I'm so sorry."

She shrugged. "I live with that guilt every day, so whatever your gut is telling you, don't ignore it."

I was so busy scrutinizing the dark shadows lurking in her eyes that I sidestepped Olivia's advice completely. "Does Uncle Mick know how you feel about your mum's death?"

"Yeah." She nodded. "He worries. But I'm okay."

"If you ever want to talk . . ."

Olivia smiled sadly at me. "Thanks, Jo. I mean that. You've been really cool about me being here, and I know that can't be easy. I can tell by the way you look at Dad that he's important to you, and after seeing what your mom is like, I kind of hate myself for taking him away from you when you so obviously needed him."

"Don't ever feel that way. You're his daughter. And *he* needed you. I understand that. 'Teen Me' didn't, but 'Adult Me' gets it. And 'Adult Me' is finally all right with it." I watched Mick laugh at something Cole said. "But it's nice to have him back for a while."

"Cameron must really care about you to have gone to all the trouble of finding us?"

There was a question within her question, and I knew Olivia realized that whatever was troubling me was about Cam. I felt the need to confide in her forcing its way to the fore. I'd spent so long bottling everything up and keeping it to myself, I guess I was kind of tired of shouldering every little problem in silence. "Cam and I bumped into his ex-girlfriend yesterday."

Olivia sighed heavily. "Ah."

"He told me a while back he'd been in love with this girl Blair. They broke up because she left to work at a university in France, not because they fell out of love. Now she's back and they're already exchanging text messages. You must have seen how subdued and weird Cam was yesterday after it, and then you saw how bloody drunk he got—and he never gets drunk. So now I'm thinking the worst. Blair's back and Cam's head is all messed up because he still loves her."

"Whoa, okay, that's a lot." Olivia threw her shoulders back and began counting down her points on her fingers. "One: You don't know he still loves her. Two: Bumping into an ex you have real history with will mess with anyone's head. Three: He doesn't get to just start up a friendship with this woman without discussing it with you, which brings me to four: You have to talk to him about it. Otherwise the uncertainty is just going to eat away at your relationship like a virus."

I nodded. "You're right. You are good at this."

"I know. So are you going to take my advice?"

"I have a little insecurity problem, so it might take me a while to gather the nerve to approach him about it."

"In other words you're afraid he's going to turn around and say that he's in love with this Blair person."

I frowned. "You might want to add mind reader to your résumé."

"Yeah, I think we've established that I am awesome." She grinned cheekily.

I smiled back. "Agreed."

Just as quickly as her grin had appeared, Olivia grew serious again. "Find the courage to talk to him, Jo, or it'll blow out of proportion."

"Courage?" I furrowed my brow. "Do you think I can download that from the Internet?"

"It wouldn't surprise me. But it'll probably come with strings attached and a whole host of nasty ramifications."

"So I'm going to have to steal it from someone else, then?"

"What do you mean, steal courage? Johanna Walker, you're one of the bravest, strongest people I've ever met, and that's saying something— I come from Arizona, where about six million people willingly live in torturous heat between May and September."

"Cam says he thinks I'm strong, too," I murmured disbelievingly.

"Girl, talk to him. I cannot believe that a man who looks at you in a way that actually makes me think that being in a relationship might be pretty sweet could possibly be in love with someone else."

I sucked in a deep breath. "Okay. I'll talk to him."

Olivia smacked me on the back, making me wince. "That a girl!"

A few hours later I said good-bye to Uncle Mick and Olivia on Princes Street with plans to meet them for dinner during the week, and then I dropped Cole off at the Omni Centre, where he was meeting up with his friends. Before I left, he grabbed my arm.

"Jo, you okay?" he asked, his eyebrows drawn together in concern.

I marveled that I was now looking my brother in the eye. I wished he wasn't so tall for his age; it would at least allow me to pretend he wasn't growing up if he still looked like a wee boy. However, height or no height, nothing could diminish his intuitiveness. It was a part of who he was; it was a part of our relationship—he knew me too well. I shrugged. "I'm okay."

Cole stuck his hands in his jeans, hunching over, his head bowed toward me, his eyes searching mine. "Is there something I should know?"

"I'm just feeling a little off. It's a girl thing," I reassured him with a soft smile. "Now go. Hang out with your friends and be immature. Responsible," I added hurriedly, "but immature."

He made a face. "Do those two go hand in hand?"

"If your immaturity can lead to consequences, then it's irresponsible."

Cole grunted. "You should write that shi—stuff down."

"I heard the 'shit' in there, baby boy, and I'm stealing the last Pop-Tart as punishment."

"Harsh, Jo." He shook his head, backing off with a smile. "Harsh."

I rolled my eyes and gave him a little wave before I left him there, hoping to use the walk back home to bolster my courage.

By the time I was standing outside Cam's door I was pretty sure I was ready to call him on his bullshit. Having already texted him to let him know I was on my way, I didn't bother to knock. "It's me," I called as I stepped inside and shut the door.

"In here."

I followed his voice to the sitting room and was surprised to find that Nate was with him. Even more surprising, the telly wasn't on. Glancing down at the coffee mugs and the half-eaten sandwiches from the local deli, it was clear that Nate had stopped by for a chat.

My heart thumped.

Uh-oh. That couldn't be good, right?

"Hey, Nate." I smiled tremulously.

"Jo. Looking gorgeous as always, babe." He grinned at me, dusting the crumbs off his fingers.

I didn't know how to greet Cam. After our encounter with Blair, he hadn't touched me. Cam, who didn't seem to be able to breathe without touching me, hadn't placed a single fingertip upon me. No handholding, no waist squeezing, no affectionate neck nuzzles. I didn't think I'd been in his company once since we started dating without him giving me a neck nuzzle.

Not really feeling in the mood to be rejected by his sudden disinclination to touch me, I didn't go over to him to kiss him like I normally would. I just stood there awkwardly, gazing at him. He didn't look the least hungover, the lucky bastard. "How are you feeling?"

Cameron didn't answer me right away. In fact, for what felt like the longest moment, he sat there cradling his coffee mug in his hand as his eyes roamed my face, drinking in every single feature. Slowly, a smile

DOWN LONDON ROAD · 287

stretched his lips, the tenderness in his gaze causing an ache to blossom in my chest. "A lot better, baby. A lot better."

There seemed to be more behind his words than an update on his physical health. I just couldn't work out what it was.

"Well, my work here is done." Nate clapped his hands on his knees and stood up.

I followed his movements, completely confused. "What work?"

"Oh." He shook his head, smirking like he had a secret. "Feeding Brewery Boy over there." Still smiling, Nate approached me and pressed a soft kiss to my cheek, his dark eyes glittering happily as he pulled back. "Always good to see you, Jo. Catch you later."

"Bye," I answered quietly, stunned by his affection, confused by his and Cam's mysterious behavior, and wondering what the hell I'd walked into.

"See you, mate," Cam called to him, and Nate waved to him, then left us in the quiet emptiness of the flat.

My nose wrinkled in bemusement, I turned back to Cam. "What was that all about?"

Cam shook his head, setting his mug down on the coffee table. "He just came around for a chat." His lips tilted up at the corners. "Why are you still over there when I'm over here?" He curled a finger, beckoning me toward him with a sexy confidence that immediately set off little green flags in all my erogenous zones. The revving of my sexual engines purred in my ears, the flags waving, ready to drop . . .

I physically shook myself, attempting to remind myself that I came here to talk to him, not to throw myself at him at the first opportunity. Just because Cam was suddenly feeling all nice and affectionate didn't mean I had to give in to him. I wanted answers about his behavior yesterday.

Didn't I?

"Jo?" Cam raised an eyebrow. "Get over here, babe."

"No." I jutted my chin out, my eyes narrowed on him. What kind of game was he playing with me? "If you want me, come and get me."

A low growl was the last thing I heard before he moved, at surprising speed for a hungover person. One minute he'd been in the armchair; the next he was on the other side of the room, his body pressing me back onto his work desk. Manhandling me a little roughly, he gripped my thighs, wrapping my legs around his hips so he could grind his erection into me. I clung to him, my hands on his waist, my head thrown back in instant pleasure as he nuzzled my neck.

"Cam," I groaned, trying to remember what the point in my visit had been as he thrust his hips, the denim around his hard-on rubbing against the seam between the legs of my own jeans. I panted, wet and needful. *What was going . . . what were we . . . what?*

I felt his tongue on my throat and ground harder against his movements.

His lips peppered kisses up my neck to my ear. "I missed you this morning," he whispered hoarsely.

"You did? I thought you'd be too hungover to notice." My hands slid up his back to wrap around his neck, my fingers curling in his hair as I angled his head so I could look in his eyes and see if I could discern the truth in them. I took a deep breath, terrified that what I was about to say might conclude with experiencing the abject loss of Cam in my arms. "You were off yesterday. After . . . Blair . . ."

Cam nodded carefully, running his hands up and down my outer thighs in what appeared to be a reassuring gesture. "I was taken aback to see her. I got lost in my thoughts for a while."

"You got drunk." I smiled weakly. "Are you sure everything is okay? That . . . we're okay?"

His eyes gentling, Cam grasped my chin in his hand. "Baby, we're more than okay." He kissed me, pulling me closer, deeper, and I relaxed into him with a groan. God, I wanted to believe him more than I'd ever wanted to believe anyone in my life.

His tongue teased my lower lip as I felt his fingers on the button of my jeans. I pulled back, anticipation and arousal knocking the rest of the questions I had out of my head. He'd reassured me we were okay. That was enough. I licked my lip where his tongue had just been and held his scorching gaze as he unbuttoned me. After the last button was popped, Cam cradled my hips and slid me forward gently so that my ass was hanging precariously off the edge of his desk. His warm fingers slid inside my waistband and I held on to the desk, lifting my hips up to give him better access as he eased my jeans down my legs. They came off, along with the red flats I was wearing.

Teasing me, Cam slowly pulled my underwear down my legs and when they were off, he stuffed the knickers in the back pocket of his jeans.

"You're such a perv."

He laughed quietly, watching me as I watched him unzip his jeans. He shoved them and his boxers down to his ankles, his eyes never leaving my flushed face as he slowly stroked his cock.

I squirmed, my legs unconsciously widening.

Cam stepped forward, his jeans rustling around his ankles, and just when I thought he was about to slide inside me, he lowered himself to his knees and pushed my thighs apart, insinuating his face between my legs.

"Oh, God," I groaned, throwing my head back at the electric touch of his tongue on my clit. I grasped his hair, holding on, rocking gently against his mouth as he licked me and spurred me toward climax.

And then he sucked on my clit. Hard.

I cried out, coming against his mouth in an explosion of light and heat. My muscles were just relaxing when he stood up, gripped my hips, tilted them upward, and slammed his dick inside me so deep it was almost painful. I gasped, clinging to him as my inner muscles pulsed around him in little aftershocks.

His grip on my skin was bruising, his movements rough, hard and frenetic, but I didn't care. Already the tension had started to coil inside me again, and my sputtered breaths and cries for more mingled with his animalistic growls and grunts.

I was hot.

Too hot.

I wanted to rip off my T-shirt and his, but that would mean stopping, and nothing could stop me now.

One hand left my hip to grasp the back of my head, and then he crushed his mouth over mine, a panting, gasping slide of lips and tongue . . . no finesse, just a wild need to mimic with our mouths what his dick was doing to my insides. He tilted my hips up more, dislodging my mouth from his as I held on. His eyes were dark with possessiveness as he pounded into me.

I felt like my entire body must be glowing with fiery fractures, as each thrust pushed me toward breaking point.

And finally . . .

I shattered.

The orgasm came in wave after wave, and I was so caught up in the extraordinary moment I barely even heard Cam's growled "Fuck!" as he climaxed, jerking against me as he came hard.

My hand slipped on the desk as my muscles liquefied, and Cam's arms came around my waist, holding me up as he continued to pant into my shoulder.

It was the roughest sex I'd ever had, a kind of pleasure-pain experience. I didn't know if my body's epic response had been to the rough sex or to the possessive, seemingly unearthly need Cam had appeared to be driven by, a need to have me, to claim me. He was always a little like that during sex, but this had been . . . different.

Almost desperate.

"Did I hurt you?" he asked quietly, sounding remorseful.

I shook my head against his shoulder, the material of his T-shirt, damp with sweat, rubbing against my cheek. The smells of his aftershave, the sea breeze detergent he used, and his fresh sweat were comforting. "No."

"You're sure?"

"Positive." I laughed a little. "Although I could sleep for a month now."

He snorted. "Me too." He pulled back, smiling softly, tenderly, as he brushed his knuckles down my cheek. "Nothing feels as good as being inside you."

And there he went, pushing back all my insecurities. "Nothing feels as good as having you inside me."

His kiss was warm and sweet, so soft in comparison to the sex we'd just had . . . like whatever had happened between us had reassured him and taken the edge off.

I remembered Andy telling me he'd never seen Cam so happy as he was with me, and I suddenly felt stupid for having doubted us. For having doubted him. Like a contented kitten, I leaned back on my elbows and watched as Cam pulled his jeans back on. He told me to stay there. He disappeared out of the room and returned a few minutes later with a washcloth. Up until then I'd still felt a little embarrassed whenever Cam helped me clean up after sex, but something had just changed between us and I felt secure again. If possible, even more than I had. I no longer felt embarrassed. I felt . . . powerful.

I widened my legs with a come-hither smile and his blue eyes flashed at my wickedness.

"Sexy as fuck," he muttered, pressing the cloth between my legs.

My eyelashes fluttered shut at the coolness of it, and I lifted myself a little to help him. Warm lips closed down over mine, his tongue pushing into my mouth. The cloth disappeared, and I cried out into his mouth as two thick fingers slid inside my swollen passage.

I couldn't take anymore.

I shook my head, moaning as I pulled away from him. "I can't."

Cam disagreed. He pumped his fingers in and out of me, watching my face intently. I had thought that after that huge climax it would take some time to work me up to another, but my body was still tautly strung, and his penetration along with the torturously gentle flick of his thumb against my clit sent me crashing headlong into another orgasm.

It was gentler, but my skin was almost burning with overuse. "You're trying to kill me."

Cam kissed me again, and I felt the cloth back between my legs.

I was still trembling when he helped me off the desk and eased my jeans back up my legs. I didn't even bother asking for my underwear. I knew what the answer would be.

After a little while, we were settled on his couch. I lay between his legs, my back against his chest as we watched a movie. I felt relaxed for what felt like the first time in days. I couldn't actually believe that it was only yesterday we'd bumped into Blair. It felt like it had been preying on me for weeks.

Cam laughed loudly at the telly and I turned my head to smile up into his face. "You're definitely in a better mood today."

His arm tightened around me. "Things are good today. Incredible sex, great company, and good friends. Which reminds me, did I tell you I'm having a party next week?"

I smiled and shook my head.

"Aye, I was telling Nate and Blair about it. I'm inviting everyone around to the flat next weekend. Invite Olivia."

All I heard was ". . . and Blair about it."

"Blair?"

Cam nodded, looking back at the television, his concentration on me waning. "I spoke to her this morning just before Nate got here. Thought it would be nice for her to catch up with Nate and Peetie."

"I thought you said it was a shock seeing her yesterday?" I was trying to ignore the banging of my heart against my chest and I really hoped Cam couldn't feel it.

"It was. But it was a good shock. Bumping into Blair was just what I needed—" Cam snorted at the screen. "What the hell is he going to do with that?" His focus on the movie cut him off in midsentence. What did he mean, "Bumping into Blair was just what I needed"?

And just like that I was back at square one.

Now was the time to ask him outright how he felt—in plain English—about having Blair back in his life. What did it mean for us? How did he feel about Blair? Was he still in love with her?

Oh, God. Was that what the happy, rough sex was all about?

I felt my chest tighten and I couldn't breathe.

Was his good mood due to his conversation with Blair? Was he transferring possessive, lovey-dovey thoughts for her to me because I was here and willing?

Or were my big, fat, illogical, psychotic insecurities rearing their ugly heads again and twisting everything around?

"You okay?" Cam asked softly, running his hand up and down my arm.

Tell him! Ask him!

But I was terrified. If I asked and he did still love Blair, Cam would feel compelled to tell me the truth and I would have to get up out of his arms and never return to them again.

How pathetic that I could willingly sit with him in a lie just to feel his breath on my ear?

"I'm fine," I whispered softly, snuggling against his chest. I closed my eyes. "Just tired."

His fingers brushed through my hair and I punched back at my insecurities. *The sex earlier, the cuddling now—that couldn't be about anybody but me.*

Cam cares.

He really cares.

"Jo? I know when something's wrong with you. Your whole body goes tense."

Dammit!

I sighed and pulled back, leaning my hands on his chest as I looked up into his familiar and wonderful face. My stomach was suddenly a riot of butterflies. "I'm just wondering if I should be worried that the love of your life is suddenly back in it?"

Cam's eyebrows slammed together. He looked completely baffled by my question. "I never said she was the love of my life. I said we used to be in love. *Used* to be. We're both different people now. Well, I am at least." He traced my lip with his thumb, his eyes following the movement before finding their way into mine. "You've got nothing to be worried about. I told you that. You believe me, right?" His hand slid to the nape of my neck, his strong grip bringing my face even closer to his. "You trust me?"

When Cam gazed at me like that, with such intensity and sincerity, it was hard to reply with anything but a quiet affirmation: "I trust you."

CHAPTER 26

As though Cam sensed that I needed a little reassurance, he texted me more than usual over the next few days despite how busy he was. We were both busy. To the delight of both me and Cole, Uncle Mick and Olivia had decided to stay in Edinburgh indefinitely. I spent time helping them search for flats online and sending them links to decent ones during my quieter periods at work, since Uncle Mick was preoccupied with looking into setting up a painting and decorating business in Edinburgh. I'd put him in touch with Braden as a start for building a profile and contacts, but Mick also had a lot of stuff to figure out financially, and Olivia and I were happy to let him get on with that while we searched for flats. I was a little surprised when Olivia informed me that we were looking for two flats, but she insisted that she'd been relying on Uncle Mick too much lately and it was time she took back control of her life—starting with renting her own place.

On top of that, I found myself playing referee with regard to Joss's wedding plans. Ellie still hadn't given up her hopes of turning Joss into a romantic, and Joss, in my effort to talk her out of homicidal thoughts, needed a reminder every now and then that she loved Ellie and would be greatly upset with herself if she "accidentally" offed her maid of honor.

So, a little overwhelmed that week and unable to see Cam as much as I would have liked, I thought it was nice of him to keep in contact with me so much during the day, and even lovelier of him to stop by on Thursday to take me for a long lunch.

I was seated behind the reception desk waiting for him when he strode into the estate agents office wearing his worn jeans, boots, and ragged Def Leppard T-shirt, looking sexy and cool and utterly at home in his own skin. I watched my colleague Anna, who worked in admin with me, stop in the middle of her conversation with Ollie, one of our agents, to slaver over Cam as he strolled past her.

My face split into a big grin and I hurried around the desk to greet him. I should have been embarrassed by the long kiss he smacked on me, but I wasn't. I was just so pleased to see him.

"Hey, you," I murmured, pulling back to affectionately stroke his scruffy cheeks.

His eyes drifted down my body and were filled with more than a little appreciation when they returned to my face. "You look good, baby." I was wearing a black high-waist, calf-length pencil skirt with a sleeveless white silk blouse tucked into it. On my feet were four-inch black-and-white stilettos that took me a couple of inches above his head. He clearly didn't care. "Very sexy secretary."

"My God, is this the boyfriend?" Ryan, one of the younger estate agents, asked teasingly from behind Cam.

Cam turned with a raised eyebrow, taking in the good-looking guy in his well-cut suit. Ryan was exactly the kind of guy I would have dated pre-Cameron, and I think Cam knew it. I felt the instant tension in his body.

I pressed closer to Cam, understanding after my own recent bout of insecurity and jealousy (neither of which had completely gone away) how much it helped to be reassured by your partner. To make it clear that I was with Cam and Cam alone, I curled an arm around his waist. "Yes, this is Cameron."

Cam nodded at Ryan, still appraising him.

Ryan grinned in response. "We all thought you were a phantom, mate." His eyes shot over Cam's shoulder to me and a decidedly flirtatious spark flared to life in them. "We just thought Jo was pretending to have a boyfriend to keep us all off her back."

Oh, God.

"Pardon?" Cam murmured, and I felt his hand slide down from my waist to cup my hip, pulling me even tighter against him.

Ryan laughed, holding up his hands. "Ah, don't worry. We know she's taken. You're a lucky bloke."

I heard Anna giggle nervously when Cam's face remained intimidatingly impassive. I decided it was definitely time for lunch. "Well, we're going now," I announced cheerily, reaching across my desk for my purse. "See you in a bit."

With his arm still around my waist, Cam led me out of the office and we walked in silence up the hill past Queen Street Gardens. By the time we got to the restaurant, this delicious little place on Thistle Street, I'd received three grunts in response to the three questions I'd asked him about work.

When we had settled at our table, he sat and looked at me for a moment and then said quietly, "I must have counted at least five guys in there, all our age."

Trying not to get pissed off at him, since I'd acted like a jealous shrew (at least inwardly) on the weekend, I nodded.

"And I take it they all flirt with you like that wee git was."

I shrugged. "You've seen guys flirt with me, Cam. They flirt at the bar all the time."

"That's different. Friendly banter gets you tips there."

"I didn't say I flirt back with these guys. That's why Ryan cracked a joke about you being real. They've never seen you, but I talk about you all the time." I leaned forward. "You asked me to trust you. I'd appreciate it if you'd trust me back."

After a moment, Cam relaxed and leaned an elbow on the table, running his hand through his hair in frustration. "I'm just tired. Sorry. Not in a great mood."

I reached over and took his other hand. "It's okay. You're allowed to be in a shitty mood."

"Not today. We haven't seen each other since Monday. I'm not going to spend our lunch together snapping your head off because you're too fucking gorgeous for your own good."

Pleased, I laughed, and the mood between us relaxed. By the time the food arrived we'd caught each other up on everything that had happened that week.

"I think Cole has been missing judo," I said. Cam had been too busy to attend class, so Cole had missed out too. Consequently he'd seemed restless and bored all week. When Cam didn't answer, I looked up from my salmon to find him texting. "Something wrong?"

He shook his head. "Nah, it's just Blair."

And just like that, a dark cloud rolled over our table and burst, drenching me in cold, wet miserableness. I waited a couple of seconds, but he continued to text. My patience snapped. "Can you text her later? We're supposed to be spending time together."

"Sorry." He flashed me a look of concern before hitting SEND and tucking his phone back in his pocket. "She left her Kindle at my flat last night."

I felt like he had just kicked me in the stomach. His casual announcement knocked the breath out of me and it took me a moment to pull myself together. "She was at your flat last night?"

Catching the accusation in my tone, Cam's eyebrows knitted together. "Is that a problem?"

My blood heated and I had a sudden vision of throwing my salmon and potatoes in his face and screaming, "Yes, it's a fucking problem!"

Instead, I pushed my plate back and gave him a look that suggested he was a complete and utter dunce. "Let's see . . . you were alone in your flat last night with your ex-lover. Why on earth would that bother me?"

"We've been over this. We're just friends."

"And if I have a problem with that?"

"You said you trusted me."

I leaned over the table, keeping my voice low, trying not to cause a scene. "Ten minutes ago you acted like a possessive asshole in my place of business over a couple of guys flirting with me. How can you not see that inviting your ex-girlfriend over to your flat and not telling your current girlfriend is a huge bloody problem?" My voice rose on the last three words and people turned to look. Cheeks burning, I stood up from the table. "I'm going back to work."

"Johanna." Cam stood to stop me, but I'd already grabbed my bag and moved toward the doorway, leaving him in my dust, knowing he couldn't follow me before paying for our meal.

I was so upset I couldn't return to work immediately. I let myself into the Gardens and sat on a bench tucked behind a tree, and I sniffled away to myself.

Being with Cameron had turned me into an emotional wreck.

My phone rang. It was Cam. I ignored him.

And then I got a text.

Baby, I'm sorry. You're right. I would have been pissed off, too. Come by the flat after work so we can talk. I hate fighting with you. x

I swiped the tears out of the corner of my eyes before I picked up the phone to text him back.

Okay. x

That was all he was getting. After all, I was still hurt and severely pissed off at his inconsiderate assholery.

. . .

Although I'm not one of those people who infect everyone else with their bad moods, I was so lost in my own thoughts for the rest of the day that my colleagues gave me a wide berth, sensing my misery. I didn't know what I would say to Cam when I saw him. Was I going to get over the whole Blair thing? I didn't think so. Was I going to make him choose between me and her? I wanted to, but that just made me the shittiest person ever. I couldn't dictate to Cam who he was and was not friends with.

By the time I knocked on his door I felt ill with uncertainty.

He opened the door, looking relieved to see me. I gave him nothing, brushing by him briskly. I strode into his living room and the first thing I saw on the coffee table was her effing Kindle. I dumped my bag and threw my phone on the table beside it. "She's not picked it up, then?"

"Jo . . ."

At his plaintive tone, I spun on my heel and raised an eyebrow at him. "You know, I was willing to believe it was just me. Just me and my stupid insecurities. But having her over here without telling me, that was really crap of you, Cam."

It had been a long time since I'd seen Cam look guilty. The last time, in fact, had been when he realized he'd been wrong about me, when we'd sat in this room and I'd trusted him with my life story. He had the same look on his face now. "I am sorry I didn't tell you. But it was completely innocent."

I bit my lip, feeling my stomach roil with emotion. "I have a problem with her," I confessed.

"She hasn't done anything wrong. Jo, Blair and I were friends before we were a couple, and I'm just catching up with an old friend. That's it. You need to grow up about this. "

I hated him. Right then, I actually physically hated him.

"Don't speak to me like that, you condescending dick."

"Jo—"

"Why didn't you tell me she was here last night?"

"I didn't hide it from you. I told you at lunch. If something was going on I wouldn't fucking tell you, would I?" His voice began to mimic mine, rising in frustration.

"You said you loved her."

"*Loved*. Past tense."

Ignoring his growing impatience, I crossed my arms over my chest and attempted to drive my point home. "You didn't break up because you fell out of love, Cameron. You broke up because you were scared she was going to leave you. You were scared she wasn't going to choose you and so you walked away first."

Anger sparked in his eyes and he took a few steps toward me, bearing down on me. "You don't know shit."

For once I wasn't daunted. I was too pissed off. "I know I'm right."

Cameron cursed under his breath and looked down at the table where her Kindle was. "This conversation is insane."

Before I could respond to that non-answer to my non-question, my phone rang. I was about to turn around to pick it up and shut it off when I froze at the look on Cam's face. His eyes had narrowed on my phone, studying it, it seemed. Gently brushing me aside, he reached to pick it up. As he stared at the screen, his jaw clenched, the muscle in his cheek popping as he lifted furious eyes to my face.

My heart suddenly began to pound in my chest.

Cam turned the phone toward me. The screen read MALCOLM CALLING. "What's *he* doing calling you? What? Did you go running off to him at the first sign of trouble?"

I flinched at the accusation. "No. We talk sometimes."

Wrong thing to say. "You've kept in contact with him and you didn't tell me?"

Uh-oh. I shrugged.

Cam gave a huff of disbelief. "I'm standing here getting grilled about Blair and you've been keeping Malcolm from me? Why? Why not tell me?"

I threw up my hands, wondering how on earth the argument had turned on me. "Because it doesn't matter. He's just a friend."

His expression turned glacial, jealousy and anger and *disgust* in his eyes.

And his next words broke my heart.

"No. *Blair's* just a friend. *Malcolm's* a rich fuck who still has a hard-on for you, and he lets you dangle him on a string. Got a problem with me hanging out with Blair? Think I'm keeping her around in case you and I don't work out? Well, what's to say you're not ready to spread your legs for Malcolm if what we have goes south?"

I guess that's the problem when you really get to know someone. We learn all their triggers and emotional buttons, and unfortunately, in times of war, we press them. The button Cam pressed had direct access to my tear ducts, and salt water spilled down my cheeks in anguished silence. I took a step away from him, feeling sick. I ignored his remorseful expression, concentrating on those ugly words and what they meant.

They meant he had never stopped thinking of me as a shallow gold digger. He'd never believed that I could be more than that. Not really. Did that mean he'd never meant anything he'd said to me?

The pain wouldn't allow the silence to hold and I lost control of a sob.

"Fuck, Jo." He swore hoarsely, trying to reach for me. "I didn't—"

"Don't touch me." I ripped my phone out of his hands and seized my purse.

"Jo, I didn't mean it." He grabbed my arm. "I was just—"

"Let go!" I screamed in his face, wrenching myself away from him, frightened that if I let him touch me, I'd give in to him as I always did. I sagged with grief as I backed away.

"I didn't mean it." His eyes were bright with a panic I couldn't quite process.

"What are we doing?" I shook my head. "Is this worth it? Is it worth the way I've been feeling the last few weeks? I feel raw all the time, like my heart has been laid out on a butcher's block and you're hammering away at it. I thought it was me. I didn't feel smart or interesting enough for you. I kept thinking, 'Any minute now he's going to wake up and wonder what the fuck he's doing with me.'"

Cam sucked in a breath. "No—"

"I thought it was me," I repeated. "That my insecurities were the problem. Not you and Blair. But then last night, you hanging out with her . . . not telling me, not talking to me about it, expecting that I would be okay with it? And maybe not telling you about Malcolm wasn't right either. But none of that really matters in the face of this." I wiped a hand down my cheek, trying to clear the stream of tears. But as I began to speak again, more poured out. "You said you wanted me to see that there was so much more to me than even I realized. No one had ever told me I was smart or talented or brave, or that I deserved more than what I'd asked for. Until you. And it turns out you never really believed that. You always believed that deep down I'm just this shallow girl that would fuck her way to a gold mine."

"No," he argued, taking hold of my arms to shake me. "I was just pissed off. It came out wrong. I didn't mean it." He tried to pull me into a hug, but I struggled against him. "Baby, stop, just stop. I can't—"

I pushed at him and shoved at him until he let me go, and I glared into his face with every shred of my tattered self-respect. "You said it. It means it's in there somewhere." And then I threw out, "And I saw the way you reacted to Ryan."

As he dragged a hand through his hair, Cam's expression changed from remorse to agitation. "Well, he is the kind of stupid prick you'd go for."

I shook my head in disbelief. "You really think that after everything between us, he's the kind of guy I'd go for?"

"You really think that, after everything, I'd cheat on you with Blair?"

"You cheated on Becca with me." I winced as soon as the words were out of my mouth. That was a low blow.

Cam huffed, looking at me incredulously. "And you cheated on Malcolm with me."

"Is that what you really think?" I repeated his words back at him. I felt more tears tremble on my lashes and I hated that he could reduce me to this sniveling mess. "That I've been holding on to Malcolm in case this ends?"

He shrugged, his expression stony. "Do you really think I've been waiting on someone better to come along? That I'm using you?"

I wiped my nose with the back of my hand and looked away, unable to stare into his eyes as I answered hoarsely, "I think you never stopped seeing me as *that* girl. The one you didn't respect very much."

"Then maybe you really aren't that smart after all." His tone was cutting, horrible.

I didn't think anyone had sliced me as deep with their words as he had. And I hated that he had that kind of power over me.

He sighed and I finally looked at him, watching as he rubbed a hand down his face and turned away from me. In a weary voice he suggested, "Maybe you better go before we say more ugly shit we don't mean."

I didn't answer him in words.

I just left.

CHAPTER 27

I had difficulty finding sleep that night. I finally drifted into unconsciousness in the wee hours of the morning and was awoken at ten thirty by the loud *bing* of a text notification on my phone.

It was from Uncle Mick, reminding me that I'd agreed to go flat hunting with him. That was fine. Probably better to keep my mind off my fight with Cameron anyway.

I'd swayed back and forth on the whole thing during the night. Part of me felt like our argument was ridiculous, that it was ludicrous to be feeling this much pain over misunderstandings. I wondered if they were all misunderstandings of my own making. Three times I almost picked up the phone to call Cam, to talk it through, to try to make sense of all the drama. I'd watched crap like this on the telly, read about it in books, and although I'd enjoyed the angst of it all, I'd rolled my eyes and thought of how it never really happened in real life. People weren't that stupid.

Well, we were.

I was.

In the end I didn't call him. I decided my wounds were still too fresh to talk to him just yet. Since I was sixteen years old I hadn't been without a boyfriend, and during the months in between relationships,

I'd been on the hunt for a boyfriend. I'd spent so much time believing Mum and Dad, believing I was nothing, that instead of putting effort into fighting the hateful crap they'd fed me all my life, I'd bought into it and thus clutched onto men I believed had all the attributes I lacked.

Cam had been different from the start, but I'd still launched myself into a relationship with him. I'd begun to rely on him. More than that, I'd begun to rely on his opinion of me as a person to make me feel better about who I was. I was more than a little cut up inside at the thought of losing that good opinion—or worse, that he'd never really had a good opinion in the first place.

I shook my head at that thought. Even though my mind was all over the place because of him, I couldn't bring myself to believe that he'd never seen more in me. Everything he'd done for me, all the looks he'd given me, the affection, the tenderness, it couldn't be fake. I knew it couldn't be fake.

Maybe taking a day away from each other to calm down was best. We could talk it out tomorrow.

Chest aching, I nodded to myself. That sounded like a plan.

I got up out of bed to see Cole off to school. He took one look at me and he knew. "You and Cam have a fight?"

"Bloody clairvoyant," I muttered irritably under my breath as I passed him to make some tea.

"I'll take that as an aye."

I grunted.

"Is it bad?" He suddenly sounded worried and very much like a little boy.

I looked at him over my shoulder. Cole was trying to act cool, like a fight between Cam and me was no big deal, but I knew he would be anxious about what it meant for his friendship with Cam. I shook my head at him. "We'll be fine. It's nothing that can't be fixed."

Relief glinted in his eyes as he gave me a sympathetic smile. *Sympathy from Cole. I must really look like crap.*

I closed my eyes. God, I hoped Cam and I could fix this.

I loved him.

Heaving a heartfelt sigh, I opened my eyes and squealed.

Spider.

On my mug.

"Cole!" I yelled, frozen on the spot.

"Spider?" he asked casually, his footsteps coming closer.

He knew my squeal so well.

"Mug."

I never moved a muscle as Cole calmly tilted the mug out our kitchen window, depositing the spider on the sill, much as Cam had done with the humongous spider that had been in his kitchen. I felt a wave of longing at the memory of that day and tried to squash it just as quickly as it had risen.

Cole gestured the mug at me and I made a face. "Bin it."

He rolled his eyes. "Just wash it in hot water."

"If you think I can put that mug to my mouth without forever remembering that those spindly, hairy—eeeeeh"—I shuddered—"legs were on it, you're mental."

With another eye roll, he threw the mug in the bin and I slumped with relief.

Damn all the spiders of the world. They were putting a serious dent in my road to independence. When Cole came over and kissed my hair before going to school, I knew I had progressed from looking like crap to just looking pathetic. Still, his affection gave me the warm fuzzies and for a moment I forgot my worries about Cam.

I hurried in the shower and got dressed in something comfortable for flat hunting with Uncle Mick. As I was passing Mum's bedroom, I sighed in exasperation. Mum hadn't popped her head out of her bedroom for days, and the only reason I knew she was alive was because I heard her snoring. It occurred to me as I stood in our quiet flat that I hadn't said a word to her in a week. Not one word. *Maybe that's a good thing*, I thought with a surprising amount of sadness. Maybe I would never learn to think more of myself if I continued to let Mum get close enough to poison my attempts. And maybe if I thought more of myself, I wouldn't feel so irrational over Cam's friendship with Blair.

Then again, maybe that was just wishful thinking.

Uncle Mick and I were lying on the hardwood floor of the two-bedroom flat on Heriot Row. A street that was mere minutes away from Dublin Street, it skirted the north side of Queen Street Gardens. More importantly, it was just around the corner from Jamaica Lane, where Olivia had just signed a lease on a one-bedroom flat above a coffee shop. It was all coming together for her. Proving it's *who* you know once again, Clark managed to get Olivia an interview at the university library. They'd been impressed with her postgraduate degree in library science from the States as well as her six years of work experience. They had taken her on, on a temporary contract to be reviewed for permanency in six months' time.

She seemed happy. Nervous but happy.

Mick was worried.

Since Olivia had started her new job today, I'd offered to accompany Mick to see the unfurnished flat that was so close to his daughter's new home. Unfurnished wasn't ideal, but the location was. The rental was under the Carmichael banner, so Ryan was the one viewing the flat with us. When we suddenly lay down on the floor, our eyes studying the level of craftsmanship in the decor, Ryan had stared at us wide-eyed and then said, "Uh, I'll wait outside."

Uncle Mick and I used to lie like this when he took me on jobs with him. During our lunch break we'd lie down on the dust sheets and talk nonsense to one another. Today, I wasn't in the mood for nonsense. I was in the mood for answers.

"Are you going to tell me why you keep hovering over your adult daughter like she might disappear or shatter into a million pieces at any second?"

Mick heaved a sigh, rolling his head to the side to look at me. His golden eyes were soft with affection for me, but I could still see that glimmer of sadness at the back of them.

"I'm a father. I worry, baby girl."

"Is it because she's carrying all this guilt about Yvonne?"

"She told you that?"

"Yeah."

"My girl is tough, just like you, and she's going to be okay. I know that. But I'm her dad and she's moved to a new country, left all her friends behind, and is starting over. I want to make sure she's okay, and I'll worry if I can't be near her. So what if I have to put up with bad paintwork in order to do that?" He gestured to the main wall, where the paint had dried in uneven brushstrokes. "Something happens, she needs me, she calls me, and I'm literally seconds away."

"So you're taking this place, then?"

"Aye." He sat up, pulling me with him. "Fancy a trip to IKEA?"

I grinned. "Lucky for me today was payday." Mick looked confused. "I can go a little accessory mad when I shop at IKEA."

"Ah." He chuckled and helped me to my feet.

As I dusted off my bum, I became aware of the heat of Mick's sudden and intense scrutiny.

I looked up and raised an eyebrow at his grave expression. "What?"

"I'm worried about you, too." He brushed my hair off my face, stroking my cheek with his callused thumb. "You look tired."

Shaking my head, I gave Mick a glum smile. "I had a fight with Cam."

He frowned. "About what?"

And so I laid it out for him, telling him about Blair and my insecurity over their friendship and my worry that Cameron would never really respect me the way he would respect someone like Blair.

"All that's going on in your head?" Mick asked in disbelief.

Confused, I nodded slowly.

"Jesus Christ, woman. I doubt very much Cam was thinking any of the shit you threw at him last night. It probably felt like it came out of nowhere. You know, men don't think like women."

"Well . . ." I pulled a face. "That's because you have the emotional capacity of a shot cup."

Mick huffed in amusement as we met Ryan outside. "I'll take it, son." He nodded at him.

"Great." Ryan beamed. "Let's get you back to the office so we can sign all the forms."

We followed Ryan down the street as he talked at someone on his phone. Everything about him was so polished, so rehearsed. I actually couldn't believe that only four months ago I would have been attracted to the douche bag.

Douche bag?

Oh, Christ, I was spending too much time with Cole these days.

"Back to my earlier point," Uncle Mick suddenly said, drawing my gaze away from Ryan's well-tailored jacket. "I think you're overthinking the whole thing. I think you'll find that boy cares a great deal about you and would be willing to compromise. And I can tell you for a fact he didn't mean what he said last night. You know we all say shit we don't mean when we're angry."

"You think he cares a great deal about me?"

Rolling his eyes (someone else was spending too much time with Cole, too), Mick sighed. "Of course he does. Jesus Christ, girl. Get your head out of your arse."

I'd been planning on popping down to Cam's before my shift at the bar that night, but when I tried his door there was no answer. Since he hadn't texted me or called me, I thought perhaps it was a good thing anyway. Maybe he needed time away from me to cool down.

I received a text from Joss before heading to work, explaining she wouldn't be in tonight because she'd caught a bug that Declan had picked up at school and couldn't keep anything down.

Lovely.

She said Sadie was covering for her.

Brian greeted me cheerily at the door to the bar and introduced me to our new doorman, Vic. He was this huge, hulking Polish guy I wouldn't want to mess with. I smiled hello at Vic and got a stoic nod back. I raised an eyebrow at Brian. "What happened to Phil?" Not that I would miss him.

"Left us for greener pastures," Brian replied with a shrug.

Mimicking his shrug, I went inside to find Sadie and Alistair working behind the bar. Su still hadn't found a replacement for Cam, so Alistair was back to covering the shifts that he could. Sadie was a twenty-one-year-old postgrad student who usually worked Monday nights. She seemed like a cool girl. She was outgoing and funny and very smart. We'd only worked together a few times, so I didn't really know her that well, and tonight would be busy so I didn't imagine that would change in any way.

Three hours later the place was packed. The three of us were worked off our feet and I hid in Su's office during my break since the sound level was much quieter in there. I also obsessively checked my phone, but Cam still hadn't gotten in touch. Biting my lip, I wondered if I should be worried, but then it occurred to me that I hadn't contacted him either, and maybe he was sitting looking at his phone, worrying about why *I* hadn't texted *him.*

God, I hoped so.

When I got back to the bar, it was so busy I thankfully didn't have time to dwell on my relationship. In fact my head was so into work that when the guy first pushed his way to the front of the bar and leaned across it, I didn't recognize him. I shot him a quick, irritated look, not having much patience with anyone who shoved himself to the front of the queue, but I hurried down the bar to get a beer for my customer, not registering who he was. It wasn't until I stretched back up from the fridge and realized he'd shoved his way down to the end of the bar to be near me that I took the time to really look at him.

Gray-blue eyes stared at me out of a rugged, older man's face. His hair was cropped close to his head, but I could see the sprinklings of gray among the dark strands. There were attractive lines around his eyes, and his face hadn't softened with age. It was still rough-hewn. His powerful shoulders and chest suggested he was still as fit as he'd ever been.

Those hard eyes glittered at me and I felt my world flip upside down.

"Dad?" I mouthed, disbelieving that he was standing at the bar in front of me.

I wanted to run. I wanted to hide. No. I wanted to run home, grab Cole, and then hide.

"Jo." Murray Walker leaned across the bar. "Good to see you, lass."

I found myself stumbling toward him, the pounding noise of chatter and music fizzling to a quiet murmur. I put the beer on the bar with a trembling hand.

Murray eyed my shaking fingers and smirked as he turned his gaze back on my face. "Been a long time. You're all grown-up. You're even prettier than your maw was."

"Hey, can I get served?" an irritated girl beside Murray asked. The irritation melted to fear when Murray whipped his head around to glare at her.

"What are you doing here?" I asked, loud enough to be heard over the music, hating myself for the quiver in my voice.

"Been trying to find you for fucking ages, ever since I got out." He grunted, his face twisting into that familiar expression of hate. "Bitch took off and didn't tell me where you were going. Then I did a google search on you the other week there and where did you crop up but in a picture with a multimillionaire from Edinburgh. The article said you worked here. It was an auld article like, but I thought I'd try my luck." He flashed me a grin that didn't reach his eyes.

My whole body was shaking now. The blood was rushing in my ears, my pulse points throbbing and my stomach churning. I clasped my hands behind my back, trying to still the tremors. "Wh-what do you want?"

Murray's eyes narrowed and he leaned over the bar. I instinctively moved back. "I want to see my son, Jo."

It was my worst fear realized.

I feared it more than I feared Murray Walker.

"No."

He curled his lip at me. "What?"

I shook my head, eyes blazing. "Never. I'll not let you near him."

He huffed, seeming amazed at my audacity. He slammed a hand on the bar with a twisted smile. "I'll let you think on that very carefully, lass. See you soon." And just as quickly as he'd appeared, he melted back into the crowd.

The noise, the music, came flooding back and I staggered against the bar in absolute shock.

"Jo, you okay?"

Blinking rapidly, seeing little dark spots all over my vision, I turned on unstable feet to find Alistair peering into my face in concern. "I feel—"

"Whoa." He reached for me as I swayed toward him. "Okay, you're taking a break."

"Too busy . . . ," I murmured.

Something cold was pressed into my hand as Alistair led me toward the staff room. I glanced down at the bottle of water. "Sadie and I have this, so just take a minute or two. You're probably dehydrated. It's hot in here tonight. Go on, drink up," he insisted, and then once he was sure I was obeying his order, he hurried back out to the bar to help Sadie with the customers.

My heart was still pounding. I gazed at the wall. Trying to process what had just happened.

Murray Walker was back.

He was still a mean bastard.

And . . . Cole. He wanted to see Cole. I shook my head, bending over on a gasp as tears pricked my eyes.

No. Never.

Fuck.

What was I going to do?

I took a taxi home that night, terrified that Murray would be waiting outside the bar for me. He wasn't. Still . . .

I lay in bed staring at the ceiling.

This could break me. I could curl up and cry and become that little girl he'd abused. I could run to Cam.

But Cole was mine to protect. He'd always been mine to protect. And anyway, Murray was just playing with me. He'd had no interest in wanting to see Cole when he was in Cole's bloody life, and now he'd come to me. Not Mum. Me.

Then I did a google search on you the other week there and where did you crop up but in a picture with a multimillionaire from Edinburgh.

The bastard didn't want Cole. He wanted money.

He was going to blackmail me for money.

Stupid asshole. I didn't *have* any money!

I shook my head and turned on my side, pulling the covers tight around me. I'd just tell him that Malcolm and I were over and I didn't have access to his money anymore. I was pretty sure that then he'd go slithering back into his little hole in Glasgow.

That was it, settled then. There was no need to tell anyone about this. Murray would be gone before I knew it.

Sleep evaded me for another night.

CHAPTER 28

Thankfully Cole put my subdued behavior the next morning down to the reigning silence between me and Cam.

"You should talk to him," my little brother had advised as if it was the most obvious solution in the world. I'd just nodded at him and promised him I was nipping down to see Cam before work tonight.

Cam still hadn't texted me.

Then again, I still hadn't texted him.

Zombified from lack of sleep, I didn't do much that day. When I popped out for some groceries I felt as though eyes were following me the entire time, paranoid that Murray had found me again. I hurried home and stayed in the flat for the rest of the day.

When I was sure Cam would have returned home from work, I threw plenty of concealer on the dark circles under my eyes and walked down to his flat on shaking legs. I didn't know what to say to him, where to start . . .

I'd worked myself up into such a nervous mess that it was sort of deflating to discover that he wasn't home.

That had not been an outcome I'd imagined when I'd been guessing as to how our conversation would go. Mostly I hoped it would conclude with a lot of apologies from both of us, Cam agreeing never to see Blair again and then taking me wildly on his couch.

If he wasn't home, none of those things would happen.

A little nonplussed, I moodily returned to the flat. Cole was having dinner at Jamie's after school and returning home later that night. He was of course under strict orders to inform me when he got back to the flat. Strict orders or not, he had been getting a little lax lately with keeping me informed. Well, with thoughts of Murray riding me, baby boy would not be getting away with radio silence tonight. I'd be on his back like hair on a gorilla.

Determined to at least see Cam's face (I missed the asshole, god-dammit), I knocked on his door on my way out to work. Again there was no answer. I pressed my ear against the door, but there was no sound of movement, no sound of the television, no music.

Where was he?

I glanced at my phone as I left the building, wondering if I should text him, make the first move, and it vibrated in my hand. My heart leapt into my throat as the message envelope blinked at me. Relief rushed through as I swiped the lock screen away and saw Cam's name.

> **Think maybe it's time we talk, baby. Can you come down to the flat tomorrow morning? Please. x**

I sucked in the fresh air, feeling at least one weight lift off my shoulders. I nodded, as though he was there in front of me, and quickly sent him a reply.

> **I'll be there. x**

I was just getting on the bus for work when my phone vibrated again.

> ☺

I chuckled and settled into my seat. A smiley face. A smiley face was always a good thing, right?

Joss was still unwell, so I was working with Sadie and Alistair again. Alistair inquired immediately if I was feeling better, and I lied and told him I was fine. It was nice of him to ask. Alistair was a sweet guy. I was glad, however, that we'd been so busy the night before that he hadn't noticed Murray's appearance. If Alistair had seen the interaction between us, he would have known something was wrong and he would have peppered me with questions. He was a sweet guy, but he was also a nosy bastard, and if I hadn't given him answers, which I wouldn't have, he would have sought out Joss for them. Joss would then be involved and well . . . she had a way of unearthing all of my secrets.

It was just as busy as it had been the night before, and I was a jittery mess. I got drink orders mixed up, I dropped not one but two glasses, and in general caused Alistair to raise his eyebrows so many times he could have been mistaken for a Muppet.

When the time for my break arrived, I couldn't have been more relieved. I threw back water, staying away from anything with caffeine in it, since it would probably only make my nerves worse, and I pulled out my phone. Cole still hadn't texted me.

I rang him.

"Uh, hullo?"

"Uh, hullo?" I sniped. Sometimes worrying could turn me a mite crabby. "You were supposed to text me when you got home. Are you home?"

I heard him sigh heavily and had to stomp down on my aggravation so I didn't scream at him. "Aye, I'm home. And when are you going to start talking to Cam again so you can stop being a total—"

"Finish that sentence and die."

Silence governed on the end of the line.

I scowled. "Are you still there?"

He grunted in response.

"I'll take that as a yes." I tugged on the end of my ponytail, wrapping my hair around my fist. "You locked the door, right?"

"Of course." He sighed again. "Jo, is there something else bothering you?"

"Nope," I answered quickly. "Just, you know, I worry, so next time I ask you to text me, text me."

"Fine."

"Okay. I'll see you in the morning."

With another grunt he hung up.

As I blew out the air between my lips in relief that he was home and safe, I noted the envelope in the top left-hand corner of my phone screen. I clicked on the unopened message. It was from Joss.

> The Reign of the Vomit is over! Hope you're not missing me
> too much ;)

I choked on a weak laugh and texted her back.

> Are you telling me you're well enough to be working but
> aren't? Tut tut, Mrs. Carmichael, tut tut. x

Two seconds later my phone binged.

> I was well until you called me that :\

> Better get used to it x

> Fuck!

I laughed for real now, shaking my head. She was worse than a bloke. Poor Braden had his work cut out for him with that one.

Feeling somewhat better, I returned to the bar, praying the evening would be over quickly. For the next few hours I couldn't help but scan the crowds for Murray's face, but as the night wore on and he didn't show, I started to feel antsy. Part of me had wanted him to appear so I could get our confrontation over with. The sooner he realized I wasn't with Malcolm anymore and didn't have the kind of money he was after, the quicker he'd get the bugger out of Edinburgh.

Last night I'd called a cab to pick me up at the door of the bar, but tonight I was feeling defiant. I was still angry at myself for reacting to Murray like I was ten years old again and defending myself against his fists. I didn't want him to know I was frightened of him. I didn't want him to think he had that kind of power over me. I wanted him to think he'd never left a mark on me.

So I (in retrospect, stupidly) took my usual route home—walking to Leith Walk in hopes of grabbing a taxi with its light on once I got there.

I stood on Leith Walk for five minutes, waiting for a taxi to turn down the wide road. The only one that did was mobbed by a small group of guys. As the taxi drove away, I stood there for a minute, listening to two drunken girls across the street shout names at one another.

I was starting to get uneasy standing there alone. It never usually bothered me because Edinburgh was still so alive at this time in this area—people were still out and about, witnesses to halt any nefarious intentions of a creepy stranger. But I had goose bumps and the hair on the nape of my neck prickled. I whipped my head around, scanning back up the road I'd just walked down. I couldn't see anyone watching me.

With a weary huff, I decided to just walk home. It was a fair wee walk at this time and I didn't particularly enjoy walking down the very long London Road, but I didn't want to hang around anymore.

I was just about to turn the corner onto Blenheim Place when something made me look back. Call it a sixth sense, a chill down the spine, a warning . . .

My heart shot up into my throat.

A dark silhouette was a few yards behind me. I recognized the lope. Growing up, we called it the "hard man" lope. The gentle but forced swagger of the shoulders, chest puffed up, steps deliberate. It was usually adopted by men when they were going into some kind of "battle." My dad had walked like that all the time, though. Then again, every second of every day he'd treated life as one big battle and everyone as an enemy.

Murray Walker was following me.

I quickly looked in front of me, and without really even taking the time to think about it, I took the path up the cobbled streets of Royal Terrace instead of London Road. It ran adjacent to London Road on higher ground, but I knew there was a path by the church that would take me into Royal Terrace Gardens. I raced into the entrance, and the climb burned in my muscles, but I pushed on, taking the wide path that veered steeply up along the outskirts of Calton Hill. The precipitous pathway would eventually slope downward and bring me out onto Waterloo Place, and from there I'd go west back onto Princes Street. Then it was north to Dublin Street.

All that really mattered was misdirecting Murray.

He couldn't know where we lived.

I was so panicked at the thought of him finding the flat that I didn't think clearly and I didn't see the error in my plan.

Me. Alone. On a dark, rough, muddy pathway. At night.

The adrenaline was pumping through me as I marched upward. I attempted to listen for the sound of footsteps behind me, but my heart was racing so hard it was pulsing blood in rushing waves into my ears. The palms of my hands and my underarms were damp with cold sweat, and I couldn't breathe properly, my chest rising and falling in ragged breaths. I felt sick with fear.

When I finally heard the heavy footsteps behind me I glanced back and saw my dad's face under the wash of moonlight. He was pissed off.

All the determination I'd had earlier to stand and face him and show him he didn't scare me just disappeared. I couldn't let go of that little girl who was terrified of him.

And so, like her, I tried to run.

My feet slapped against the steps as I ran upward as hard and fast as I could, wishing I could conjure up people, witnesses. But no one was there.

I was alone.

Except for the pounding of heavy boots behind me.

At the hard, warm grip of his hand around my arm, I made a noise of loud distress that was quickly muffled by his other hand clamping down over my mouth. The smell of sweat and cigarette smoke flooded my nostrils as I fought him, my nails biting into his arm, my legs trying to kick out as I was dragged off the path. I lost my grip on my bag with my pepper spray as I fought him.

I wasn't strong enough, and now I was unarmed.

Murray slammed me back against the rocky, grass-covered slope of the hillside and pain shot through my skull before shooting all the way down to the tip of my toes. Tears leaked from my eyes as he held me there, his large hand around my throat.

I grunted against the other hand that was still clamped over my mouth.

He tightened his grip on my throat and I stopped squirming.

Despite the fact that his face was mostly cast in darkness, I could still make out the anger that stretched his features taut. "Trying to give me the runaround?" he hissed.

I didn't answer. I was too busy wondering morbidly what he was going to do to me. My body began to shake hard, and I lost complete control of my breathing. He felt the gulping breaths behind his palm and smirked.

"I won't hurt you, Jo. I just want to see my son."

Knowing it would bring me physical pain, I still shook my head "no."

Murray's smirk grew into a smug smile, as though he'd won something. "I suppose we better come to an arrangement then. I'm going to take my hand off your mouth and you're not going to scream. If you do, I won't hesitate to hurt you."

I nodded, wanting at least one of his disgusting paws off of me. As I stared up into his face, I saw not for the first time how there was nothing behind his eyes. I didn't think I had ever met anyone in my entire life who was as callously selfish as this man. Was he really my father? There had been no connection between us other than that of abuser and victim. To me he'd been the reason for the knot in my stomach when I heard his rattling old banger of a car pull up to the house. The affection I'd felt for Mick, the eagerness to see him, the warm contentment of safety he gave me, was exactly what I should have felt for this man. But a man was all he'd ever been to me. A man with mean eyes and even meaner fists. For the longest time I'd despaired that he didn't love me as a father should. I'd questioned whether there was something wrong with *me*. Looking at him now, I wondered how I could ever have questioned myself. I wasn't the problem. He was. He was the shameful one, not I.

I sucked in a deep breath when he let go of my mouth, but he put more pressure on the hand around my throat as an extra warning to be quiet.

"Now." He leaned into me and I could smell the beer and cigarettes on him. He hadn't been in Club 39, but he'd obviously been in one of the bars near it, waiting on me. "I might just give up my right to see the wee man if your boyfriend made it worth my while. Say a hundred grand?"

I knew it. And straight to the point. He didn't even care. He was as soulless as he'd ever been. How could someone be that way? Was he born soulless, black to his rotten core? Or did life make you that way? How could you hurt your own children and not feel like a monster? Maybe a monster was too far gone to realize he'd become one . . .

"I stopped seeing Malcolm months ago. You're out of luck."

He squeezed my throat and panic suffused me. I automatically grabbed his hand, my nails biting into his skin. He didn't seem to notice.

"I'm sure you can persuade him somehow." He pushed his face into mine, his breath reeking of smoke and stale beer. "I had myself a bonnie bairn. She's fucking useless but bonnie. It's a commodity, Jo. Use it or I'll come for Cole." He let me go and I sucked in a breath, my fingers brushing my neck to reassure myself that his hand was definitely no longer there. "If I wanted to, I could become a right pest in your lives, lass."

Fury that he could do this to me, to Cole, after so long, after thinking we were free, took over and the fear was burnt to hell in a blaze of rage. "Commodity's a pretty big word for you, Murray. Looks like someone finally taught you to read." I rebelliously hoped my eyes conveyed my condescension clearly even in the shadows. "But reading does not a smart man make. I don't have money. You'll need to whore yourself out to an old prison buddy."

I barely even saw the blur of his fist coming toward my face.

My head flew back, the muscles in my neck screaming with the impact and the burning heat of his fist hitting my mouth spread into my lower cheek and jaw. Tears of pain fell from my eyes as I brought my head slowly back around to face him, my lip feeling a million times bigger than normal. The warm trickle of blood oozed from an already stinging cut in my lower lip where my teeth had snagged the skin.

There was nothing behind his eyes as his other fist flew low and hit me hard in the gut, bowing me over. All control fled me as I panicked, trying to draw in air. I hit the ground knees first and he kicked me in the side, sending unbelievable pain flaring through my ribs as I collapsed on the muddy footpath, loose stones and dirt biting into my skin.

My body couldn't decide whether it couldn't breathe or was going to be sick.

Hard fingers bit into my chin and I cried out, the air rushing into my lungs. Every muscle, every nerve, every piece of bone felt as if it was on fire. I clutched my ribs as Murray held my head up by my chin. "You get me that money, lass. I'm renting the flat above the Halfway House on Fleshmarket Close for a few days. You've got two days to bring the money to me there. Got it?"

The hurt in my ribs was unbelievable. I could barely concentrate on what he was saying.

"I said got it?"

I nodded feebly, sighing with relief when he abruptly let go of my chin.

And then he was gone.

The thick scent of beer and nicotine had disappeared. I was lying on the cold ground, my lip throbbing, my ribs aching, and my head screaming with fury. At him. At myself.

I should have taken Cam up on those self-defense lessons.

At the thought of Cam I began to cry, cradling my sore side as I pushed myself up onto quivering legs. I swayed against the hillside, feeling light-headed. My body began to shake uncontrollably.

I think I was going into shock.

I shook my head, trying to clear it. I didn't have time to go into shock. I had two days to get the money to Murray. A burst of pained energy propelled me forward.

Malcolm would give me the money. Malcolm would take one look at me in this state and give me the money, no problem. He was that good of a guy.

I stumbled back down the path I'd run up, picking up my fallen purse, desperation and adrenaline making my progress hurried despite the pain I was in. I could phone Malcolm, get him to come and get me.

His name whirled in my brain as I came out of the gardens and did a U-turn at Leopold Place at the top of London Road. I kept to the trees where I could and then in shadow as much as possible in case I met anyone on my way. I didn't want the police involved. If I got the police involved they might start looking into my whole family life and . . . I just couldn't risk it.

If Malcolm paid, this would all go away.

· · ·

Before I knew it I was standing outside the familiar building.

At the sight of it I began to cry harder, my breath hissing as my teeth caught my burst lip.

Malcolm wouldn't pay.

Malcolm wouldn't pay because I didn't want Malcolm to help me. I didn't want anybody but Cameron.

I let myself into our building and pulled myself up the stairs, determined to get to him and to throw my arms around him. I cried harder. I needed to feel safe and only Cam could give me that.

I lightly hammered on his door, and sucked in my breath as agony ripped through me. Lifting my arm was like ripping a stitch across my ribs. My body moved forward to lean on the frame and then the door was suddenly wrenched open. My heart was wrenched out of my body with it.

Blinking, I tried to compute the image in front of me. I shook my head to clear it, but it didn't go away.

Blair gasped at the sight of me bloodied and crying. "Jo? What happened?"

My eyes traveled down the length of her and back up again.

Her short hair was wet and curling around her jaw and she was wearing Cam's QOTSA T-shirt. She was so small it fell to just above her knees. Her bare knees. Her bare legs.

Blair was at Cam's with wet hair, wearing only his T-shirt at two thirty in the morning?

"Oh, my God." She reached for me and I wobbled back. "Cam's in the bathroom. I'll just get hi— Jo!"

I was already running, stumbling, falling, tripping my way back down the stairs. In that moment I couldn't be anywhere near that building. I couldn't go home to Cole like this, and Cam . . .

I threw up beside the rubbish bins.

Wiping my hand across my mouth, I glanced up the road.

I needed a taxi.

I needed my friend.

If Cam . . . I stifled a sob, hurrying around the corner and up London Road . . . If Cam wasn't . . . then I had to go someplace that was safe.

The only good thing to happen to me that night came in the shape of a taxi with its light on. I threw out my hand and the cabbie pulled over. Still cradling my rib, I shakily got in.

"Dublin Street," I told him, speaking awkwardly with my split lip.

He eyed me warily. "You all right? Do you need a hospital?"

"Dublin Street."

"You're in a bit of a state—"

"My people are on Dublin Street," I insisted, tears pricking my eyes. "They'll take me."

The taxi driver's moment of hesitation was long enough for Cam to come skidding around the corner in T-shirt and jeans, his frenzied eyes searching up and down the street before swinging to meet mine in the cab. Features pale and drawn, he moved toward me just as the cab pulled away, his muffled shout reaching my ears over the sound of the engine.

My phone rang seconds later. I picked it up but didn't say anything.

"Jo?" he yelled, the word coming out in a puff that told me he was out of breath, probably from running after me. "Where are you going? What happened? Blair says you've been attacked? What's going on?"

Hearing the fear in his voice did nothing to soothe my heartbreak or quell the bitterness I felt for him in that moment. "I guess that's no longer your concern," I answered numbly and hung up to the sound of his frantic shouting.

———————

CHAPTER 29

"I'm going to kill him," Braden threatened with such quiet veracity that a shiver rippled down my spine. An unyielding blaze of retribution burned in his eyes. Another shiver followed in the wake of the last just as Joss dabbed at my lip.

I hissed at the sting of TCP against my cut and threw Joss a wounded look.

She winced, pulling back the cotton wool. "Sorry."

Braden took a step toward me, all bristling angry male and even in a T-shirt and jogging pants he was intimidating. "Where is he?"

I shook my head.

"Tell me, Jo."

When I didn't, he took another step toward me and demanded coldly, "Tell me."

"You, back off!" Joss yelled up at him, her own eyes bright with anger and anxiety. "You're starting to scare Jo." Her voice quieted but didn't lose its authority. "And I think she's been through enough for one night, don't you?"

They stared each other down for a moment and then Braden muttered something under his breath and stepped back. Renewed respect for this woman took hold in me. She might be small but she was extremely fierce—the kind of friend everyone needed on their side.

When Joss had opened the door after I hammered on it for what felt like five minutes, she'd stared at me in shock for a second, standing there half asleep in pajamas with her hair a wild mess around her shoulders. When I tripped toward her, my expression pained, dried blood crusted on my face and shirt, it was the first time I had real evidence of how deeply she cared about me. She pulled me inside and I felt her body trembling with anger as she helped me to the living room, her hoarse voice shouting to Braden for help.

I collapsed on their couch, exhaustion leaching all strength out of me now that I'd gotten to them. While Joss tried to clean the cut on my lip, I explained to them what had happened. Then Braden's scary caveman threatening began.

"Is it really bad?" I asked Joss softly, my quaking fingers tentatively touching the area around my lip. It felt tender and swollen.

Joss scowled. "You're lucky he didn't knock out a tooth." She looked down at my left side. "You'll need to have your ribs looked at."

"I don't think they're broken."

"Oh, are you a doctor now?"

"Joss," I said with a sigh, "if you take me to the hospital there will be questions and police and I can't have the social services looking into our situation right now. Mum is worse than ever. They might take Cole away."

"Jo, your mum can't help her illness, and you're there looking after him," Braden spoke up, his voice reassuring.

With my eyes I told Joss I thought she was amazing. She'd kept my secret and she'd even kept it from Braden. I appreciated it hugely, but I was more than a little tired of having the secret in the first place. As if it was something *I* should be ashamed of. "Braden, my mum doesn't have Chronic Fatigue Syndrome. She's a bedridden drunk."

Other than the slight raising of his eyebrows Braden didn't really react to the news. We sat in silence for a moment and then he stepped forward and lowered himself to the coffee table so he was sitting directly in front of me. For a moment I got lost in those concerned pale blue eyes of his. "I'll have my family doctor look at you in the morning. He can be very discreet. Will you agree to see him?"

"Yes, she will," Joss answered for me belligerently.

I wasn't even looking at her and I could feel her eyes boring into me, daring me to defy her. I nodded at him and I felt the couch move as Joss slumped back with relief.

"Before I see a doctor I need a plan." I glanced from Braden to Joss, desperation and determination vying for a place in my eyes. "I can't let him near Cole."

"And he wants money from Malcolm?" Joss curled her lip in disgust.

"Yes."

"Why didn't you go to Malcolm, then?" she asked, more than a little curiosity in her voice. "He would give you it."

"He would," I agreed, my voice soft but laced with an edge. "But he's from a life I don't even recognize anymore, and I don't want to go back there. Facing him, ensuring his loyalty, it means becoming someone else again. I can't do that. I'm just 'Jo' now. And I know I can't do everything by myself anymore." I gave her a wobbly smile. "Good thing I finally realized I have friends I can trust."

Joss swallowed hard and reached for my hand, threading her fingers through mine. "You do." Her eyes turned ferocious as she looked over at Braden. "We'll get him off your back. We'll pay the asshole to disappear."

As I turned my head I caught Braden's reluctant nod. Braden didn't want to pay him back in money. He wanted to pay him back in blood.

The ache in my side and my battered pride made me tend to agree with Braden. Would money really keep Murray away or would he eventually come back for more? He'd always been like that when we were younger. He'd take whatever extra cash Mum had lying around, disappear for days on end, and then return home when he'd run out. The only time he ever disappeared completely was when Uncle Mick beat the crap out of him and started playing bodyguard aro—

"Uncle Mick!" I breathed the words in excited, sudden realization, my hand gripping Joss's so hard it was probably painful.

"Mick?" Braden's eyebrows knitted together in confusion.

I nodded. "Mick. I'm not letting you guys pay Murray. He'll see that as weakness and he'll come back for more. No." I looked at them, unable to smile in triumph because of the cut. "There's only one person Murray Walker has ever been afraid of and he thinks that person is in the States."

Braden smirked. "Mick."

"Mick."

Turning to Joss, Braden nodded toward the door. "Come on, we're getting dressed. We're taking Jo to Mick and then Mick and I are paying Mr. Walker a wee visit."

"No, Braden, I don't want you—"

He held up a hand to quiet me. "I'm not going to fight him." His eyes darkened. "Mick and I will just have . . . a *word* with him."

"Shouldn't we call Cam?" Joss asked as she and Braden stood up.

Mention of his name shot pain far more excruciating than my physical wounds through my entire body. I felt my cheeks burn as I admitted softly, "I went to him first. He was a little preoccupied with Blair."

They were both silent for a moment as my meaning registered with them, and then Braden bit out a curse. He grazed past Joss, squeezing her shoulder as he flashed her a wolfish grin that didn't quite reach his eyes. "Better wrap my hand up. Looks like my fist will be meeting more than one face tonight." And with that pronouncement he strode out of the room, presumably to get changed.

I stared after him, wondering if he'd meant what I thought he'd meant.

Joss smiled weakly. "He's kidding. Braden doesn't fight. Well . . . normally . . ." She raised an eyebrow in thought. "He is a little overprotective, though. And he definitely doesn't like men who beat women and he doesn't like cheaters . . . but he's kidding . . ." She turned her head to look at the door. "I think."

The Caledonian was a Waldorf Astoria Hotel, so it was a *nice* place. To assure uninterrupted passage through it, Joss and Braden dressed well, and I huddled behind Joss for the entire walk across the quiet reception area. It was now four thirty in the morning. Braden gave the night receptionist a brisk, no-nonsense nod, and that together with his appearance—he was wearing a black Armani trench coat over his dress trousers and shirt—seemed to assure the receptionist that we belonged there.

Butterflies were in full riot in my stomach as we rode the lift up to the fourth floor. I felt guilty for dragging Joss, Braden, and Mick into this mess, but I wasn't doing it for me. I was doing it for Cole, and I had a proven track record of acting selfishly when it came to protecting Cole. Lucky for me, Joss, Braden, and Mick actually cared, and I knew that they would be doing this even if I hadn't asked it of them.

As we stopped outside Mick's hotel door, Braden knocked on it loudly and Joss put an arm around my shoulder and pulled me to her. It put pressure against my side and I winced, immediately rewarded with a rambling apology from Joss. It would have been funny how many times she called herself a dick if I hadn't been trying to catch my breath.

The hotel door swung open and I was surprised to find Uncle Mick fully dressed and alert. His eyes narrowed in on me and I saw the muscles in his jaw working against his fury. "I've been trying to call you," he said tersely.

Confused, I blinked rapidly. "Um . . . my phone's switched off." I'd turned it off when Cam had tried to call me again.

Mick nodded and then stepped back so we could enter his room. Braden led us in and stopped quite abruptly at the threshold. I knew why when I sidled up next to him with Joss.

Olivia and Cam were there.

Braden looked down at me, drawing my gaze. "I can hit him now if you want?"

I'm not going to lie—I seriously pondered the suggestion before finally saying with a sigh, "Not worth it."

"Jo?" Cam asked hoarsely.

I looked at him and felt Joss's hold on me tighten. Cam's blue eyes searched my face and just like Mick's had, his expression clouded over, undiluted rage sparking to life in his eyes. "Who the fuck did it?" he asked between gritted teeth.

I didn't answer his question. Having him here was incredibly painful. The anger he felt over my attack seemed fake in light of the fact that he'd cheated on me with Blair. "I want you to leave."

Cam closed his eyes as if he was in pain. "Jo, please, what you saw . . ."

"Just leave."

"Jo." Olivia stepped forward. "Give him a chance to explain."

"Later," Mick snapped, his gold eyes fixated on my wounded mouth. "I want a name. Now."

I gulped, feeling the threat of violence rise in the room. Not just from Mick—his anger was infecting Cam and Braden. "Murray."

Mick's nostrils flared at the name.

"Dad did it," I clarified.

"What?" he yelled, his question muffled by Cam's explosion of expletives.

Olivia strode between them, trying to calm them. "We'll get thrown out of the hotel," she warned them. She turned to me. "Explain what happened."

For the second time that night I related my tale, and when I was done the air was thick with testosterone. Cam finally couldn't take it anymore and he crossed the room, his shaking hand reaching to cup my chin. At the brush of his skin against mine, I tugged my head away, then grimaced at the sharp sting of pain in my neck from where I'd suffered whiplash from Murray's attack.

"Jo, I didn't do what you think I did," he insisted.

I couldn't look at him. All I could picture was his face above mine as he made love to me, his eyes telling me he cared, and then the image tearing down the center to reveal him and Blair writhing naked together on his bed. My stomach turned at the thought and the pain in my chest was indescribable. So this was what it was like to be heartbroken? "Why did you even come here?"

"I came here because I thought this was where you'd go if you were in trouble."

His response startled me. My eyes betrayed me and sought out his. He'd thought I would come here? "Not Malcolm's?"

He shook his head, his expression desperate.

That disconcerted me. I didn't like it. I dropped my gaze, my confused thoughts giving me a headache. Cam had trusted me not to turn to Malcolm after all. He did see me.

He saw *me*.

I scoffed at the hope bubbling up inside of me.

He'd also screwed Blair.

Deflated, I felt my shoulders slump.

"Where is he?" Mick demanded. "I'm going to sort that fucker out once and for all."

I wasn't big on violence. Anyone who really knew me knew that. But as I looked up into my uncle's distressed and bloodthirsty gaze, I couldn't find the willpower to lie to him. I wanted to believe fighting violence with violence was never the answer. I wanted to believe that there was a better way. And maybe for other people there was. Unfortunately, fear was the only thing Murray Walker understood. He was a schoolyard bully, and bullies really were cowards at heart. Murray definitely was . . . but only when it came to Mick.

One day I'd have to ask Mick why that was.

Not tonight, though.

"The flat above the Halfway House on Fleshmarket Close."

Mick grabbed his phone from the bedside table and stuffed it into his pocket. He turned to Olivia. "Take Jo home. I'll call you when we're done." He nodded at Cam and Braden. "You two are with me."

My eyes disobeyed me again, finding Cam's. The emotion roiling in those blue eyes of his was like an electrified net that caught me. Holding my gaze, he stepped toward me and cradled my face gently in his hands, then pressed his forehead against mine without a word. The familiar scent of him, the heat, the feel of his skin, all made me shudder with a rush of anguished longing.

"You know I didn't sleep with her, Jo," he whispered against my mouth, and everyone else just seemed to disappear. I wanted to believe him so badly.

Pulling back to gaze into my eyes, he refused to let go of me. We had a silent conversation.

You have to trust me.

I saw her there. In your T-shirt. What else am I supposed to think?

That I would never hurt you like that.

A deluge of images flashed in flutters and whispers of color and feeling. The tenderness in his eyes, the honesty I'd known from him, our laughter, searching hands that couldn't seem to get through a day without feeling my body beneath them . . .

Blair coming back into Cam's life was a problem for me. However, it had never been because I was worried he would do something so callous as cheat on me with her. Yes, I had worried that he'd leave me for her, but I never believed he would cut me like that. I'd *trusted* that he would never cut me like that. Did that trust still exist? I searched his face for the answer.

No. Cam would never cut me like that.

Something in his gaze shifted as he recognized my realization and he sighed.

There she is.

I pinned him with a look that told him he wasn't off the hook just yet. "We still need to talk."

He nodded, his gaze flickering to my mouth. His own lips thinned, a hard glitter entering his expression at the sight of my bruised and swollen lip.

"Does anyone else know what just happened here?" Mick asked impatiently.

Joss grunted. "I think Jo just said she believes Cam didn't sleep with this Blair chick."

Braden grumbled, "If only you were that intuitive about our relationship."

She glowered at him. "If I wasn't so damn worried about you going off to face this guy, I might just dump your ass."

I raised an eyebrow, looking over my shoulder at her fiancé. Braden narrowed his eyes and I watched another silent conversation unfold. Whatever he said in it made her squirm.

"Och, enough of this," Mick groused cantankerously as he wrenched open the hotel door and stormed out, followed by Braden. Cam gave me one more meaningful, soulful look before he disappeared behind them.

My stomach flipped as I thought about what they were going to do.

Another cab ride took Joss, Olivia, and me back to the flat. Although I was exhausted, I was awake enough to shoot the door to Cam's flat a glare so ferocious it was a wonder flames didn't erupt from the doorstep and devour it with the heat of my anger.

"He explained everything to me and Dad," Olivia suddenly said, obviously catching my look. "You need to talk to him."

"She doesn't need to do anything but rest right now," Joss insisted softly, taking my keys out of my purse as we climbed the steps to my flat.

"It's okay," I muttered. "I believe him. Seeing *her* was a shock, I didn't think clearly . . . but Cam wouldn't do that to me. Still doesn't mean he isn't *thinking* about doing it, though."

"He's not," Olivia assured me, but I was too weary to listen.

We tried to be quiet as I settled on the couch with Olivia while Joss made us all a cup of tea, but I heard Cole's door open nevertheless. I closed my eyes, drawing in a deep breath.

"What's going on?" I heard him ask, obviously talking to Joss.

She whispered something to him and the next thing I heard was his light footsteps across the hardwood floor.

"What the hell?"

My eyes flew open to find Cole standing over me in his pajamas. His eyes were wide and frightened as they took in my face, and just like that he was a wee boy again. "I'm okay." I attempted to reassure him, stifling a flinch of pain as I reached for his hand and dragged him down beside me.

The fear began to melt out of his eyes, to be replaced by something that was all too familiar tonight: the promise of male retribution.

"Who did it?"

Despite all the crap that had happened in the last twenty-four hours I was starting to feel rather loved, given all this anger and bristling on my behalf. "Dad," I answered honestly, having already decided I wasn't keeping this from him.

I told him everything. And not just about tonight. Bracing myself, I confessed to all three of them of my dad's abuse when I was young.

The last word had spilled from my mouth minutes before and still no one had said anything. We sat in the living room in a heavy silence. My stomach churned as I awaited my brother's response.

Joss was the first to speak up. "Well, now I hope Mick kills the swine."

"You don't mean that," I muttered.

"Doesn't she?" Olivia asked, surprising me with her anger. She was always so laid-back. "People can be . . . well, they can be wonderful. And sometimes, unfortunately, they can be monsters we hide from inside our homes. We worry that those monsters will find their way inside. We're not supposed to fear that they already *are* inside. Your mom and dad are supposed to protect you from that. They're not supposed to be the monster."

"She's right." Cole leaned forward, his elbows braced on his knees, his head bent low as he stared at the floor. "Mick needs to teach him another lesson. One that'll stick this time."

Hating to see him distressed, I put my hand on his back and began to rub soothing circles between his shoulder blades.

He looked back at me. "That's why you fly off the handle when Mum says I'm like him."

My mouth flattened. "You're nothing—"

"Like him," Cole finished. "Aye. I get that now."

We were silent again for a moment and then my wee brother looked over at me. "You have to stop trying to protect me from everything, Jo. I'm not a kid anymore. You handle everything by yourself and it's not fair on you. So stop. We're a team."

Pride and gratitude bundled together to create a lump in the back of my throat, so I nodded, brushing my hand affectionately through his hair. His eyes closed at the caress and to the surprise of everyone, he tucked himself into the side of me that wasn't sore and hugged me close. We sat there so long that I drifted asleep . . .

CHAPTER 30

The whispering of hushed but agitated voices seeped into my consciousness, thankfully pulling me out of a murky dreamscape of wet leaves, blood, and pounding footsteps. My sore eyes fluttered open, the blur of color focusing quickly to reveal that I had a busy sitting room.

Olivia and Cole still sat beside me, Joss was on the armchair, and Braden was perched on the arm of it, his fingers massaging the nape of her neck. Cam and Mick stood by the fireplace with an older man I didn't recognize, and Mum was seated on the other armchair.

They were all staring at me.

I was staring at Mick.

The air around him crackled, and although I could tell he had calmed somewhat, he had the aura of a man back from battle. There was a lot of pent-up energy around him.

My eyes traveled down his arm to his hand.

Bruised knuckles.

I swallowed hard.

"He won't be bothering you again, baby girl."

Our eyes caught and I felt my fear disintegrate. "He wasn't expecting you."

The corner of Mick's mouth quirked up. "No. That he was not. I had . . . *words* with him." He glanced quickly out of the corner of his eyes at the man I didn't recognize. "He's gone back to Glasgow and he knows if he comes back I'll forcefully remove him."

"What do you have over him, Mick?" I asked curiously, my voice raspy from sleep deprivation and pain.

He sighed, his eyes darkening. "It's not what I have over him. It's what I know about him. I know which buttons to push."

I shook my head, confused.

"Let's just say his dad was quick to violence as well."

That information froze me in place for a second.

Murray Walker had been abused? Now, didn't that make a whole lot of sense? A cycle of abuse. Of course.

I turned to Cole and brushed his hair back off his face. I may not have saved him from Mum's quick hands, but I'd saved him from Dad's brutality. It was a small kind of consolation.

At the thought of Mum, I focused on her. "We woke you up?" I asked blandly, not really giving a crap if we had or not. My father's attack had brought back my initial feelings of betrayal and anger when I first discovered she'd hit Cole.

Fiona's anxious eyes searched my face. Let's not forget this was also a woman who had known that Dad beat me as a child and had let it happen for far longer than she should have.

I stiffened.

Was that what I was doing with Cole? I knew Mum hadn't hit him since I confronted her in the kitchen, but did that really matter? He still had to live in an environment where I was nervous about leaving him alone in the flat with her. Was it selfish of me to keep him here because I feared losing him? If only she hadn't threatened to go to the authorities if I took him . . .

Resolve forced its way into my bones and my eyes narrowed on her. I was a little tired of threats.

"I wanted to make sure you were okay," she muttered before her eyes flickered over everyone. Her hand instinctively went to her un-washed hair. It was a rare moment of self-consciousness, and she fol-lowed it by pulling her robe more tightly around her frail body. "Now I know you're okay, I think I'll go back to bed."

I watched her silently shuffle away, a difficult decision weighing on me despite everything.

"Jo, this is Dr. Henderson," Braden informed me quietly, dragging my thoughts from Mum to the distinguished-looking older man in the room, who now took a step toward me. I was acutely aware of Cam standing beside him, but I still hadn't acknowledged his presence. There was too much going on and I was really too tired to think clearly on that subject. "He's going to examine you."

I smiled wanly at the doctor. "Thank you."

His kind eyes dropped to my lip. "Where would you like to do this, Jo? Somewhere private?"

"My room will be fine."

Dr. Henderson followed me silently down the hall to my small bedroom, and there he checked my cut, which Joss had already pro-tected against infection, and then inspected my stomach and ribs. There was slight bruising around my ribs that made him purse his lips.

"It seemed he wanted to frighten rather than maim entirely, Miss Walker," Dr. Henderson murmured with a hint of anger. I was guess-ing it was directed at my dad. "He could have caused some internal injuries if he'd kicked you any harder. As it is, I think your ribs are just bruised, although it's possible there could be a hairline fracture or two. You're going to feel some discomfort over the next few weeks. There's nothing I can do except advise you to take ibuprofen to reduce the in-flammation and to ice the injured area as well. I'll also write you a line for work. It would be best if you take at least a week off. You don't smoke, do you?"

I shook my head. "I quit a few months ago."

"Good. That's good. If you feel any shortness of breath, or the pain worsens, or you feel any pain in your abdomen, contact me." He held a business card out to me and I took it gratefully.

"Thank you."

"Now, I'm going to leave you to rest. Get some sleep."

Persuasion was not necessary, and I crawled into bed carefully, closing my eyes to the sound of my bedroom door shutting. I wriggled out of my jeans, hissing at the pain in my ribs. With a kick, my jeans fell out of my bed onto the floor and I pulled my duvet tighter around me.

For the first time in a very long time I felt absolutely safe. How could I not when I had a small army out there in my living room, willing to defend me until the last breath? I'd been so frightened last night, so panicked, but they had taken most of that away—Joss, Braden, Uncle Mick, Olivia, Cam, and Cole.

My family.

Tired muscles melted into my comfy mattress, and my eyelids drifted closed. Deep sleep claimed me for the first time in days.

It was the heat that woke me up.

Agitated, I threw off my covers and my eyes shot open with the pain as I let out a garbled cry.

"Johanna." Cam's voice was suddenly there.

My blinking, bleary eyes met his. He was sitting on the floor of my bedroom, his back against the wall, his knees drawn up, his hands dangling listlessly over them. Dark circles plagued his eyes, eyes that were lidded but still brimming with concern.

I rolled onto my elbow, clutching my ribs. It was light outside. "What time is it?" I asked, my voice cracking on the words. I felt icky and warm and my mouth was dry.

"It's eight o' clock in the morning. Sunday."

Oh, God. I'd slept for an entire day. With effort I processed Cam's ragged appearance. "Baby, have you not slept?"

Something sparked in his eyes at my question. "I've drifted in and out. I didn't want to leave you. Look what happened last night."

"Not your fault." My lips thinned and then I hissed at the sting. I'd forgotten about my lip.

"I want to hit him again."

My eyebrows shot skyward, his words waking me up. "You hit Murray, too?"

"I would have killed him, but Mick thought that might be a bad idea."

"Ah, Uncle Mick. A man of rationality. He's such a buzz kill."

Cam's lips twitched. "Glad to see your sense of humor is still intact."

I grimaced at the waking aches and pains. "It's about the only thing that is."

He leaned forward. "Can I get you anything?"

"Glass of water." Nodding, Cam got to his feet. "Where's Cole?"

"In his bed. Joss and Braden offered to come by and take him to the Nicholses' for lunch later."

"Good." I closed my eyes again.

A minute or so later, Cam was shaking me gently awake. "You need to drink something."

Reluctantly, I let him help me sit up, and I had to stop myself from leaning in and pressing my face against his neck. We still had way too much to discuss before we could even think about cuddling.

I took a big gulp of the ice-cold water he'd brought me and thanked him. And then before I could say anything, he gently nudged me over and got into the bed beside me, his arm coming around my shoulder to draw me against his chest. "What are you doing?" I mumbled, but I didn't really protest.

Cam sighed heavily, his fingers brushing through my hair. "I've been through hell and back in the last few days, Jo. Just let me hold you."

Tears pricked my eyes. "I know you didn't sleep with her."

"It looked bad, though, and you weren't in any state to think anything else but the obvious."

My fist clenched, curling into a tight ball. I hadn't even realized I'd done it until Cam pushed his fingers against mine, forcing me to relax my hand. His thumb rubbed soothingly over my palm where my nails had bitten into the skin. "I'm almost afraid to ask this, but . . . why was she there?"

I felt his hesitation and my heart automatically lodged a complaint with a *bang, bang, bang* against my chest. "Cam?"

He turned his head and pressed his mouth against my forehead, breathing me in. When he pulled back, he replied softly, "She turned up late at the flat, distraught and a bit drunk. I let her in. She threw herself at me."

It was decided. I hated her.

"I pushed her off, told her nothing could happen between us and I thought it was best she leave, but she broke down crying and I felt like a bastard. I couldn't just throw her out."

I swallowed past the lump in my throat. "She's still in love with you?"

"She doesn't know me," he answered, sounding irritated.

"I'll take that as a yes."

"We sat talking for ages, going around in circles until she started to sober up. She asked to use my shower and crash for the night. By then we were on the same page and I felt bad for her, so I said yes."

It took me a moment but I asked, "Same page?"

Cam shifted away from me tentatively, and only so he could look me in the eye. His haggard face was the most beautiful thing I'd ever seen and the ache in my chest intensified for him. I lifted my gaze from the soft, sexy curl of his upper lip to his eyes and my breath caught at his expression.

It was vulnerable and raw and open . . .

He was naked and bleeding for me.

"I told her something I should have told you ages ago." He cupped a large hand around my neck, drawing me closer. "I've never met anyone as quietly brave and strong as you. I've never met a woman so unassuming, so kind, and so selfless. You are a complex lady." His mouth curled up at the corners. "And you are smart, and passionate, and funny, and exciting, and you blow me fucking away. When I first saw you, I wanted you like I'd never wanted anyone. When you first tore me a new one, I wanted to know you. And when I got to know you, when I stood across a kitchen and you told me not to kill a spider because it didn't say much for us as a species if we killed something because we feared it, I knew. I knew that I would never meet anyone as beautiful or as compassionate or as determined. I've known for a while that I was in love with you, Jo. I've known and I should have told you."

Tears streamed down my cheeks and Cam's thumb did its best to catch them all. My chin trembled as I asked, "Why didn't you?"

He quirked an eyebrow at me. "Maybe for the same reason you didn't tell me." He leaned in to place a very careful but sweet kiss on my mouth. When he pulled back he continued. "Last week, the Saturday we met Blair and I went quiet on you?"

"Yeah?"

"It wasn't about Blair, baby. It was about you. About us."

"I don't understand."

Cam's hand slipped down my arm, his knuckles caressing my skin in soothing strokes. "When we bumped into Blair, it was a shock and it was strange. When she and I dated I thought I was in love with her. We were together three years and I didn't take it well when it ended. But standing there, looking at her, I didn't feel anything but a distant familiarity. There was no hurt or love or anything but a friendly gladness to see her." His eyes darkened. "As we were standing there I got stuck in this thought . . . the thought of me walking down Princes Street ten years in the future with some faceless woman on my arm, and bumping into you when you weren't mine anymore. Because everyone leaves eventually, I thought." He huffed in what seemed like pain and his grip on me tightened. "It winded me. No, it floored me. I think I've been in love with you since that moment in the kitchen, but last Saturday was the first time I realized how crazy I was about you. What I feel for you . . ." Cam sucked in a breath and I found myself reaching a hand up to his face, my heart pounding as I watched this man—this strong, irreverent man—overcome with emotion . . . emotion for me. "It's all-consuming," he breathed, leaning his forehead against mine again. "It's almost debilitating. It's too much. It's . . . I can't even describe it, but being with you is . . . There's this intensity inside me all the time, this . . . constant pull, desperation . . . it's like you're branded on me or something. And it bloody well burns."

"I know," I whispered soothingly, my tears falling faster. "I know. I feel it, too."

"You never told me that, though," he answered a little harshly. "You always kept something of yourself hidden from me, and I didn't know. I couldn't tell if you felt the same way. That's why I got drunk on Saturday night. That's why Nate came around the next morning to talk to me. He convinced me you felt the same way."

"How did he do that?"

"I asked for his opinion about you and he said, 'You've nothing to worry about, mate. That girl thinks you're "it" and I wouldn't say it if I didn't think it.'"

I suddenly remembered Cam's attitude once Nate had left. It was like someone had flipped a switch inside him. Gone was the quiet, subdued, moody man from the night before. In his place had been a seducer. The rough sex against his desk . . . I remember thinking at the time that it had felt like a claiming. Now I didn't think I'd been too far off the mark.

Relief, intense relief, washed through me and I rested my head against his warm chest "You told Blair this?" I murmured against his skin.

"I told her I was in love with you and that I didn't think it was a good idea to renew our friendship."

Another tear fell, splashing his skin.

"I hope those are happy tears."

I sobbed now, the well of emotion inside me too much to contain after everything I'd been through. "I love you," I cried, holding him tighter. "So much I want to kill you sometimes." I hiccupped attractively.

Cam laughed softly. "The feeling is definitely mutual, baby."

"So what now?" I sniffled.

"Now? I endure the agonizing wait for those ribs to heal up so I can have my wicked way with you and show you just how much I fucking love you."

I grinned through my tears. "I feel your pain."

Cam grunted in response.

We lay there in silence for a moment and then I pulled back to look up into his gorgeous face. "I think I have to leave Mum, Cam. I don't know how I'm going to bring myself to do it."

Another soft kiss grazed my lips and I tugged him back to me, ignoring the pain so I could kiss him, long, hard, and deep. We finally broke apart, panting.

God damn these stupid ribs.

"We'll worry about all that later," Cam said. "For now, let's just get you on the mend."

"Can I tell you I love you again?"

He nodded slowly, his expression earnest. "I'll never get tired of hearing it."

CHAPTER 31

"So any word from the mysterious Marco?" I asked Hannah, leaning against her bedroom wall, watching as she taped a poster of the lead singer of one of the biggest indie rock bands in the world to her wall. My girl had good taste.

Hannah blew air out between her lips, stepping back from the wall to analyze the poster. "I'm helping him with a paper for school, so I've seen him quite a bit."

"I detect from the tone that nothing of import has happened?"

She looked at me over her shoulder. "I think there might be some sexual tension between us."

The matter-of-fact reply caused no small amount of snort choking on my part. "Sexual tension?"

Turning fully toward me now, Hannah stared at me with the non-plussed expression of an academic facing a theory she found baffling. "Well, I fancy him, so I don't know if it's me projecting those feelings into the situation or if the tension between us is due to the fact that the feelings are mutual."

I thought of the tension between me and Cam before we started dating and then studied Hannah. The girl was stunning and way too built for a fifteen-year-old. A teenage boy's Kryptonite. I smirked. "He's feeling it back."

Her eyes brightened with hope. "You think?"

"Definitely."

Pleased, she began to hang up another poster, grinning like an idiot. "So how's your ribs?"

"Unfortunately still sore." It had been a week since the attack, and after spending seven days of bed rest in the flat, I'd begged Cam to let me attend Sunday dinner. Seeing my desperation, he'd agreed it was time I got out of the flat. Considering I had to go back to work tomorrow, I was counting it as a practice run. Leaving the flat with Cam and Cole in tow, I was surprised to find that I was still a little nervous and jittery being out and about. As we got on the bus, I found myself glancing back onto the street to make sure Murray Walker's face wasn't in the crowd.

Cam caught me and deduced what I was doing. The clouds that gathered in his eyes made me feel loved, but it upset me that part of the blackness in their depths originated from his feelings of helplessness over the whole situation. Basically, he felt guilty that he hadn't been there to stop it, which was sweet but silly and irrational. As it turned out, we both needed comforting about the whole ordeal. I'd taken his hand to let him know I understood, and he had kept me close beside him to let me know he understood.

Our relationship had changed in the last week. Our confessions of love had brought us both the security we needed. I didn't think it would cure either one of us of our possessiveness, or the flare of jealousy we felt when an ex-partner was mentioned, but knowing that we trusted each other had made us stronger.

It had also made me horny as hell, and not being able to do much about it was killing me.

Assuaging my frustration was the knowledge that it was killing Cam, too.

"Done." Hannah stepped back and we gazed around her newly poster-decorated bedroom. "What do you think?"

"I think Elodie's going to kill you."

"She said I could."

"She said 'a poster.' "

"Well, I just heard the permission part."

"Come on, you." I grinned, gesturing to the door. "Let's go enjoy dinner before Elodie discovers your bedroom's been transformed into a groupie's paradise."

Before I could exit Hannah asked quietly, "Are you really okay, Jo?"

Looking back at her over my shoulder, I was warmed by the concern on her face. "Baby girl, I'm fine. In fact, you know what? I'm more than fine. I'm great."

"But your dad . . ."

Needing to vent, Joss had told Ellie what had happened to me, and Ellie had told Elodie and Elodie had told Clark and apparently Hannah overheard the conversation between her mum and dad. I reached out for Hannah's hand, giving it a squeeze. "I know it must be difficult for you to understand because you've got such an amazing dad. I could let the fact that my dad doesn't care who he hurts, including his own children, get to me. Or I could find what he can't give me somewhere else. I have Uncle Mick. And I have family in all you guys. It doesn't change what my dad did, but you know, it goes a long way to helping me get over it." I smiled reassuringly at her. "Some people are born with family, and others have to make family." I shrugged. "I can live with that if it means I get to spend time with you sarcastic buggers."

Hannah laughed, the sadness fading from her eyes. She squeezed my hand back, and I led her to the dining room, where our family was waiting:

Cam, Cole, Uncle Mick, Olivia, Joss, Ellie, Braden, Adam, Elodie, Clark, and Declan.

What a beautiful sight for sore eyes. I smiled at Cam across the room as he pulled out a chair for me.

Once we were all settled around the table and the others were chatting loudly, Cam leaned over me. "How are the ribs holding up?"

I looked into his concerned eyes as I held a roast potato to my mouth. "Just as they were when you asked me that question twenty minutes ago."

"Well, excuse me for being a concerned boyfriend."

I made a face at him, and we shared another silent conversation.

You just want to know if we can have sex yet.

Cam's lips twitched around his mouthful of food.

Damn right.

Amused and turned on in equal measure, I searched for distraction from Ellie, who was talking about the bridesmaids' dresses for Joss and Braden's wedding.

"I saw these beautiful fuchsia gowns on this Spanish wedding designs Web site. I was thinking—"

"That I'm out of my mind if I think Joss will have the color fuchsia in her wedding," Joss finished for her drily.

Braden and Adam immediately began working diligently on their meal and I wondered just how many times they'd been pulled into a disagreement about the wedding between the bride and the maid of honor.

"Why don't we go more muted on the bridesmaids' dresses?" I suggested, throwing Ellie a pleading look.

Ellie looked so adorably disheartened I wanted to hug her. "But fuchsia is such a romantic color."

Clark's eyebrows dipped together. "What color is fuchsia again?"

"Pink," Joss bit out.

Braden snorted, and apparently unable to help himself, he gave his wee sister an incredulous look. "You're really trying to get pink into our wedding? *My* wedding . . . to *Joss?*"

"It's not just *pink*," Ellie argued as if they were idiots. "It's a luxurious pinkish purple magenta color."

Joss raised an eyebrow. "It's pink."

Ellie pouted. "You've not taken on any of my suggestions for the wedding."

"Ellie, I love you dearly, I do, but you are all sweetness and rainbows and I am everything that is not that."

I ventured forth with another idea. "What if we go for something in a metallic for our dresses?"

Ellie stewed over that for a moment and then her face brightened. "We would all look good in champagne. I think even Rhian would wear champagne."

Rhian was Joss's best friend from university and the two didn't get to see each other as much as they used to because Rhian lived in London. They kept in contact all the time, though, and they were to be in each other's upcoming weddings.

"Hmm." Joss swallowed a piece of chicken and shrugged. "I could work with that."

Everyone stopped eating to look at her. She glanced up, her eyes round at all the attention. She grimaced and shot Braden a dirty look. "What? I can compromise."

He laughed. "It's just the first time I've heard you actually agree about something to do with the wedding."

"That's because our wedding planner sucks. No offense, Els."

Ellie rolled her eyes. "Well, you could plan it yourself, you know."

"I only agreed to marry him under the condition that I didn't have to do that."

Cam swallowed a chuckle beside me.

Braden narrowed his eyes on his fiancée. "Why don't I plan the wedding, then?"

All of our eyebrows rose at that suggestion.

"You?" Joss gaped.

"Me." He shrugged and took a sip of water before adding, "We have the same taste, so you know you'll probably like what I decide. And I think I can get it done faster than you two squabbling mares."

"But you're so busy as it is—I can't ask you to do that."

He shrugged again and gave her a "So?" smile.

"Then I'll help," Joss announced determinedly. "We'll do it together."

"Really?"

"Really."

"But—" Ellie's crestfallen opposition to being ousted from the plans was cut off by Adam as he pressed a quick kiss to her lips. He pulled back and they had one of those silent conversations that seemed to be all the rage these days. Whatever passed between them, Ellie's shoulders slumped and she nodded, giving in.

"I'm glad that's sorted." Elodie beamed at us all. "If I'd had to deal with one more phone call asking me to referee, I was going to scream."

"Hear, hear," I murmured, ignoring Ellie's look of betrayal.

"So, Mick, Olivia"—Braden sharply changed the subject—"Jo tells us you both found flats."

Olivia nodded. "On Jamaica Lane. And Dad's just around the corner. We move in soon. It'll be nice to get out of that hotel. Oh, and Dad's got his first job lined up, thanks to you, Braden."

That was the first I'd heard of it. "Really, Uncle Mick? Where?"

Mick appeared more than a little pleased as he replied, "Doing a couple of show homes for a new development in Newhaven. Starts in two months. Gives me time to get a team together." He eyed me down the length of the table. "How about it, Jo? Do you feel like packing it in at the bar and the estate agency to become an apprentice?"

My fork clattered to my plate in shock. Was he . . . did he . . . was Uncle Mick really asking me to work for him? "Eh?" I answered intelligently.

"I asked if you wanted to work for me. It's a risk for us both, what with it being a new business, but I have every faith I can do this. I've done it twice before. So will you trust me? Will you come and work with me?"

"As a painter and decorator? With you?" Oh, my God, Uncle Mick thought I was good enough to work for him?

I know it may not sound glamorous to some—an apprenticeship to become a painter and decorator. But it took skill, and patience, and it was something I genuinely enjoyed doing. It would be an actual career, something I'd never thought I would have.

Because I didn't think I was good enough at anything to have one.

My old insecurities whispered and cursed in my ears, causing a flight of nervous butterflies in my stomach. Those insecurities wanted me to say no, so sure that it would only end in failure.

And it might. Not just because of me, but because, as Mick said, it was a new business. I could give up two secure jobs for this one and then have everything fall apart. Could I really be that selfish? Cole needed me to think logically about these things—

I felt Cam's hand slip into mine under the table and when I looked at him his eyes told me everything I needed to know. I shoved back the insecurities, the second-guessing.

The butterflies were a little harder to get rid of, but despite them, I nodded at Uncle Mick, a wondrous smile forming on my lips. "I'd love that."

A few hours later I was still stunned by Uncle Mick's offer. Sitting at Cam's desk in his living room, listening to Cole laugh at Olivia as she trash-talked Nate over a video game, I was still half in that moment back at Elodie and Clark's.

Cam, Cole, Olivia, and I had come back to Cam's to meet up with Nate and Peetie, who'd stopped by with beer, takeout, and the latest fighting video game.

Olivia had quickly fallen into a surprising camaraderie with Nate and the two of them were now throwing PG-13-rated (I was still aware enough to give them hell if they swore in front of Cole) comments at each other as they beat the crap out of each other's virtual counterparts.

"Dude, you suck!" Olivia grinned as the annoying commentator bellowed, "Knockout!"

Nate threw her a look of mock offense. "Give me a chance, Yank. I haven't played this game before."

"Neither have I."

"Aye, but you have smaller fingers. They're faster and more agile across the buttons."

Olivia burst out laughing. "Even your excuses suck."

"Dude," Cole agreed, shaking his head in disappointment.

"Och, now." Nate gestured to him in dejection. "Don't you be 'dude-ing' me." He narrowed his eyes on Olivia. "You've been here ten minutes and you've already managed to undo months of hero worship."

"Oh, come on," Olivia answered cheerily. "I did the kid a favor. He would have found out the truth eventually."

Lips twitching, Nate turned back to the television. "Right, Liv. Prepare to die."

"You're on."

I wondered when the grown-ups were finally going to allow Cole to play. Eyes on my wee brother, though, I could see he was enjoying himself just hanging out with the guys and listening to Olivia's banter with Nate. I actually suspected Cole might have a small crush on Olivia, but I would never embarrass him by asking.

As they laughed with one another, I stood up and quietly left the room, heading to Cam's bedroom for a moment of peace so I could wrap my head around the fact that in a few months' time I would be starting a new career.

A *career.*

Shaking my head in wonder, I closed Cam's door and then crept across the room to carefully lie on his bed. Getting comfortable, I kicked off my shoes, my mind whirring with new plans as I lay there.

My eyes snapped down from the ceiling at the sound of the door opening, and I wasn't surprised to see Cam slip inside the room, shutting the door behind him. He smiled at me as he came over and settled beside me.

"You all right?"

I nodded, reaching up to stroke his cheek. "Just needed a moment to process."

He cozied up to me and I rolled into him, enjoying the feel of his arms around me. I breathed in the smell of his aftershave and rubbed my forehead against the bristly line of his jaw.

"Today's a good day," I murmured, content.

"Well, I don't know if I'm about to make it better or worse."

Remembering the last time he'd said that, I tensed in expectation. It had been just before I discovered Uncle Mick and Olivia in his sitting room. Hopefully, whatever he was about to say would be as nice a surprise as that one. Fingers crossed. "Okay," I answered warily.

Cam took a measured breath. "You said last week you thought you needed to leave your mum and you didn't know what to do."

"Aye." My good mood fled at the thought of it.

"I think I have a solution, but I don't know how you're going to react to it."

I waited.

Cam's hand cupped my hip and he murmured above my head. "Move in with me. You and Cole."

At the life-altering suggestion, I jolted back and instantly flinched at the sharp pain in my side. Clearing my expression so he didn't think I was wincing at the thought of living with him, I gazed up into Cam's suddenly uncertain face. "You're asking us to move in with you?"

"Yeah." He gestured to the room. "There's plenty of space. It means you'll not have to worry about Cole being left in the flat with your mum, but it also means that you can check on your mum anytime you want to."

"But Mum's rent . . . her disability won't cover it."

"Keep paying it. We can use the place as extra storage as well."

"I can't afford to pay two rentals."

"You won't have to. I pay rent on this place anyway. I'll keep paying it. We'll just have to chip in on food and utilities together."

My heart was pounding hard at the offer, my emotions (and my body) screaming "Yes!" at the thought of getting to wake up next to him every morning, but my mind was playing it *way* more safe. "We can't intrude in your life like that, Cam. You're not just asking your girlfriend to move in with you. You're taking on a teenage boy as well."

My caution caused a smile to form on his perfect mouth. "Baby, I already have taken on a teenage boy. I spend just as much time with the kid as I spend with you. He's a good lad. I love him. I love you both. So will you move in with me?"

Tears started to fill my eyes as my chest compressed with too much feeling. "You love him?"

He shook his head at my tears. "Christ almighty, I've set you off."

I slapped at him halfheartedly. "Don't ruin the unbelievable ro-manticism of the moment."

"Was that a yes?"

Moving in with Cameron was a huge step for the three of us, but after all our ups and downs we'd come out stronger than ever. I believed we could do this, that I was ready, and that for now it was the best solu-tion to our problem with Mum.

I snuggled deeper into Cam's chest and closed my eyes as his arms automatically tightened around me. "That was a big, fat yes." As Cam relaxed beneath me, I realized how tense he'd been about asking, and an overwhelming rush of love for him washed over me. That love quickly turned into lusty tingles in all my lusty places as I felt the heat of his skin through his T-shirt. "God damn these ribs," I muttered, my voice now hoarse with sexual frustration.

Understanding, Cam groaned. "Baby, don't. I'm struggling as it is without hearing that you're struggling too."

"I know," I murmured plaintively, my wicked thoughts pouring into my hand as it slid slowly down Cam's stomach and over his jeans. He hissed, inhaling sharply as I rubbed my hand hard over his growing erection.

"Are you trying to torture me?"

I shook my head. "If you're up for nice and slow"—my fingers fumbled as I undid the button on his jeans and then slipped the zip down— "I can ease some of the pain."

"Jo, you don't have to," he argued, but it was a halfhearted protest, and I could feel his chest rising and falling in excited breaths.

"I want to."

That was all it took to convince him and he helped me release him from the confines of his jeans and underwear. Days of pent-up sexual frustration now faced me in one throbbing, thick, veiny cock, straining toward Cam's stomach. When I wrapped my cool hand around it, he tried to stifle another groan, his head falling back with the feeling.

My grip tight but slow, I began to stroke him. I couldn't move any faster for fear of pulling on my ribs, and the torturous momentum had a sexy effect on Cam. Instead of watching my hand, I studied his face. He'd closed his eyes, his eyelashes resting against his cheeks, his cheeks now flushed at the crests. His lips were slightly parted in pleasure.

God, he was hot.

I squeezed my legs together, feeling my sex throb and grow wet with need.

"Baby, I'm—" He sucked in a loud, harsh gasp for breath and I was suddenly glad that the volume on the television in the living room was up high. "Going to come—" His jaw clenched and he made this guttural noise as he came all over my hand and his T-shirt.

After a few seconds of listening to him pant, I bit my lip and mused aloud, indicating his T-shirt, "I hope that wasn't new."

His body started to shake with rueful laughter. He ran slightly shaking fingers through his hair, his eyes bright on me. "I just came like a callow youth."

"Magic hands," I teased.

Cam shook his head. "Jo hands," he corrected, then pressed a sweet kiss to my mouth.

After he'd cleaned up my hand and himself and changed into a fresh T-shirt, he got back on the bed, but this time he straddled me.

"What are you doing?" I breathed, excited but also still in pain. "We can't do anything."

He shook his head, his full of heat. "You don't have to do anything but stay as still as possible." And without another word he went to work on my jeans, carefully pulling them off, along with my underwear.

He pushed my thighs apart and crawled up the bed until his head was between my legs. Gently, he eased two fingers inside me and grunted. "Fuck, you're soaked."

"I enjoyed getting you off," I whispered, trying not to writhe at the delicious sensation of him inside me.

"I can feel that." Cam took a shuddering breath. "This is torture."

"Do you know what torture really is? Having your tongue so near and yet so far."

He threw me a wicked smile and then promptly put that tongue of his to better use.

The peace it brought me to look back and no longer see that wall Cam had helped me scale so long ago was indescribable. I would never be back behind that wall again, or have my colors muted and my personality trapped in the stranglehold of my insecurities. This was me. Life from now on would consist of being real, which was somehow scary and freeing all at the same time.

It helped that the pieces of my life were falling nicely into place for once.

Cole pretended to be indifferent to the news that we were moving into Cam's flat, but I could tell by the way he'd been enthusiastically packing, and slowly moving something new into the flat every day, that he was happy about the new arrangement.

As for Mum . . . well . . . first she'd gone off about how we were abandoning her, and how she wouldn't let me do this to her, and I couldn't take Cole, and I was a selfish little whore, and blah, blah, blah . . .

Allowing her to exhaust herself in a tirade seemed like the best way to cope with her. That way she tired herself out and had no energy to fight me as I calmly told her that if she didn't let me move Cole downstairs, if she even dared to call the authorities, I'd leave her ass in the dust and never look back. I assured her that this way I would check in with her, and if she needed me I was only a staircase away. Her silence was a bittersweet relief and it informed me in its heavy weightlessness that I'd won this particular argument.

She hadn't spoken to us for three weeks.

Wiping sweat off my forehead, I blew air out between my now completely healed lips and gazed around Cam's sitting room. Boxes surrounded me on every side. Cole and I were supposed to be officially moving into Cam's the next day—a Saturday—so that Cam and the guys could help us with all the boxes. Feeling a little overexcited about the whole thing, and restlessly wandering around the flat, I'd decided to take one of the lighter boxes downstairs to his (our) flat while he was at work. It was now late afternoon, my side was hurting a little, and I'd moved most of the boxes into their new home.

Cam would return from work in an hour or so and a few hours after that I had to be at the bar for one of my last shifts ever at Club 39. I was going to miss everyone at the bar. I'd still see Joss, of course, but that place had been a home away from home for the longest time, and I had spent time there with two of the most important people in my life. It was the end of an era.

However, something new and exciting awaited me. Uncle Mick had already given me two work T-shirts with his company name on them:. M HOLLOWAY'S PAINTER & DECORATOR. I loved them. They looked great with the new overalls Cam had bought me.

Humming to myself, I pulled out my iPod and stuck it in Cam's stereo dock, turning the volume up as I began unpacking. Time passed quickly as I sang along, dancing, and shaking my ass as I found places for all my stuff, attempting not to overwhelm Cam's space with my things.

Just as I was breaking up the empty boxes, a pair of strong arms slid around my waist and scared the bejesus out of me. I yelped and spun around to find a bemused Cameron smiling at me. He gestured silently to the room and all of the new objects.

"I got a little carried away," I explained, speaking loudly to be heard over the music.

He nodded, his gaze drifting over the mantel, where a photograph of me, him, and Cole now sat next to his own pictures. The stylish mantel clock from upstairs now dominated the center, the photographs dispersed evenly on either side of it. "I can see that."

"It saved us doing most of it tomorrow."

Blue eyes dropped to my side and his hand came up, his palm pressing gently against my ribs. At the proximity of his touch to my chest, I felt my nipples peak against my sweat-dampened tank top. We hadn't had sex since before the attack. Fooling around while we waited for my ribs to heal had been fun, but my hormones were becoming a tad impatient for the play that succeeded the fore.

"You didn't hurt yourself, did you?" Cam asked, his brows knitting together in concern.

Lying to him a little, I shook my head in response.

As if he knew, he scowled at me.

"Okay, I got a bit overeager. It's just because I'm excited to move in with you, baby." I tried to charm my way out of the coming admonishment.

It worked. With a roll of his eyes, he whipped his other arm out and pulled me against him. I wrapped my arms around his neck as he held me, resting my chin on his shoulder. Breathing Cam in, feeling the strength of him against me, and knowing that I could reach out and have this with him anytime I wanted made me sink deeper into him. Those lean, muscular arms of his tightened around me, not only comforting me but awakening another set of frustrated, neglected hormones.

Without really meaning to, we began to sway to the music, and Rihanna's mournful voice sang "Stay" at us. Goose bumps woke up all over my arms and I held on tighter to him, turning my head so our cheeks brushed. The song filled the room with such meaning it took my breath away, and as it hit the chorus Cameron whispered the lyrics in my ear, ". . . I can't live without you . . ."

With my heart pounding with the profundity of what he'd confessed so romantically, I pulled slowly away from him so I could look into his face, and his eyes seared into mine. He meant that. He meant every word.

I was too full. Too full of emotion. Too full of love. There was no room for words. Instead I kissed him, throwing every feeling I had for him into it, my mouth savoring his in wet, hard desperation. Cam started moving us backward as we kissed, his hands reaching out behind him as he led us out of the sitting room. He turned to guide us toward the bedroom, but I broke the kiss with a shake of my head, tugging on his hand.

Stumbling back against the wall in the hallway, I yanked him toward me. My skin flushed under his gaze as I whipped my T-shirt off and then pushed my leggings down. "Here," I told him, my voice shaking with anticipation. "Where it all started."

Realization dawned with the light of absolute adoration in Cam's eyes, an adoration I would never get tired of witnessing. He moved toward me, watching me as I stripped before him. "What about your side?" he murmured. "I don't want to hurt you."

I slid my hands up under his T-shirt, forcing it up and off him, my ravenous gaze eating up the sight of his roped, naked torso. "It'll be worth the pain." I reached back to unclip my bra and as it fluttered to the floor, Cam shot into action.

He kicked off his boots, fumbling with his jeans. He shoved his underwear and jeans down, not waiting another second before lifting me up by the ass. My legs wrapped around his hard hips and my hands gripped to his shoulders as he pushed us back against the wall.

I suddenly laughed, halting him. Cam's brow furrowed in perplexity. "Rihanna?" I giggled as I explained. "You know the lyrics to Rihanna?"

Cam's mouth curled sexily, arrogantly. He was not at all abashed at knowing Rihanna lyrics. "*You* know the lyrics to Rihanna. I just pay attention."

"Always got an answer for everything, you cocky bugger."

He laughed against my mouth. "I think you like my answers." Unable it seemed to wait another minute, Cam thrust up into me. I cried out at the thick invasion, my inner muscles clinging greedily to his cock as he pulled out almost completely and then roughly slammed back in.

"I missed you, baby," he groaned, using one hand to brace against the wall as the other hand clutched my butt cheek in its bruising grip.

"I missed you, too." I moaned as he thrust back into me, my nails digging into the muscles in his back. "Harder," I begged, sensing that he was holding back because of my injury.

"Jo—" He shook his head.

"Please," I pleaded into his ear in a purr. I nipped his lobe and felt his control snap.

Afterward, he carried me to our bedroom, put me down on the bed, and began to kiss his way up my body. With my assurance that Cole was enjoying the first days of his summer holidays at Jamie's house, Cam decided he had all the time in the world. He kissed, and licked, and sucked until I was almost wrung dry. After what felt like hours of foreplay, he wrapped my legs around his waist and braced himself over me as he kissed me.

His kisses were deep and slow. He brushed his mouth over mine in butterfly kisses one second, and then closed it over mine the next. His kisses never sped up, never hardened . . . Instead he reveled in the erotic building of anticipation as our tongues met in a breathless, wet waltz. When he eventually sucked hard on my tongue, setting off little jerks of reaction in my lower belly, I pushed for more. It seemed impossible, but I was ready for another orgasm. We made out, naked on his bed, for who knew how long, his hard-on rubbing over my sex, teasing my clit, as his body moved with his kisses. He squeezed my breast, his thumb rubbing over the sensitive nipple he'd sucked earlier—sucked and licked it so diligently that he'd only had to whisper his thumb over my clit to bring me to climax.

As he tormented me with the tantalizing nearness of his erection, I whined against his mouth and his answering smile was smug. He pulled back and brushed his fingers along my cheekbone, his eyes never leaving mine as he slowly pushed his cock inside me. He shifted, bracing his hands on either side of my head, and then began to move. His thrusts were gentle this time, languid, and the tension coiled to an excruciating level.

"I love you," he breathed harshly

I pulled my knees up more, to allow him in deeper, as I cupped his face in my hands. "I love you, too."

I gasped as he rotated his hips, starting to lose focus as the sensations of our lovemaking gained dominance.

"I love to fuck you," he whispered in my ear, his voice gravelly with emotion. "But I love to love you, too."

I nodded, understanding completely.

Cam kissed me deeply again, his thrusts growing more frantic as the tension increased inside us. Our skin was clammy with sweat as we slid against each other, our panting breathing mingling as our lips brushed back and forth with the movement of his body over mine.

Chasing climax, I tilted my hips up with force, meeting Cam's next plunge with a slam that snapped the coil. Sparks flew apart in the wake of its destruction and I cried out his name as I came, my sex pulsing around him, my lower body shaking from the climax.

Cam suddenly arranged my hands above my head on the bed, pumping into me harder as he held me down. He came with a guttural shout of my name, his hips jerking against mine as he flooded my womb with his release.

He collapsed on me and I felt a twinge of pain in my ribs. Almost as if he felt it too, Cam rolled onto his side, still in me, and pulled me against him, hooking my leg over his hip.

I felt another spark of pleasure between my legs as his cock twitched inside me.

"Well worth the wait," he sighed happily.

I nodded against his chest, thinking about all the wrong guys I'd dated before him. "Definitely."

Two weeks later
Cam and Jo's flat

Sweaty, tired, and covered in tiny flecks of paint from the gentle spray of the roller, I let myself into our flat and leaned back against the door with a contented sigh.

Uncle Mick had just dropped me off at home after our first day on the job together. We were decorating one of the show homes in the new development Mick had been contracted for. Today we'd painted all of the ceilings. Tomorrow and the next day would be more painting and then we'd get on with the wallpaper the designer had chosen.

"I'm home," I called, kicking off my work boots and unsnapping the straps on my overalls so they hung on me like baggy jeans.

"In here," Cam answered from the bedroom.

I strolled along the hallway, pulling the bandanna off my head and thinking how nice it was to feel this exhausted. It was an accomplished kind of exhausted and I loved it. I stopped in the doorway of the bedroom to find Cam sitting on the end of the bed with his hands behind his back.

Our room was now a weird mishmash of my stuff and his, but I didn't care. I just loved that when I woke up in the morning it was to a warm arm wrapped around my waist and usually a welcome morning erection nudging me in the ass.

I wouldn't swap it for anything.

The move had gone well for the most part. We were both pretty laid-back about the small things, so sharing space wasn't really an issue for me and Cam, and Cole had re-created his bedroom from upstairs in Cam's guest bedroom in record-breaking time. He seemed to be perfectly happy with his new home, and glad that our room was on the other side of the flat from his.

I was glad for that too.

Mum, on the other hand, was still pulling the silent treatment, refusing to talk to me whenever I popped upstairs to bring her groceries and clean the place.

Guilt would not find me. Not because of her.

Admittedly, though, some days were easier than others.

However, everything else had gone smoothly. Everyone was happy for us. Well, except Blair, I imagine, but since Cam had been as good as his word about breaking contact with her, I didn't know that for sure. The only argument we'd had so far was about a week ago when we'd been watching a movie and Malcolm had called me. I took the call. Malcolm had just wanted to chat, a chat in which I told him I'd moved in with Cam. Silence had fallen on the other side of the line and when Malcolm finally spoke, offering me congratulations, it was with such false cheer that I knew I'd hurt him. Again. Before I could respond—not that I knew what to say—he had made his excuses and hung up.

When I returned from the kitchen, I was promptly manhandled by Cameron into the bedroom, where he tried to calmly (and was unsuccessful in that endeavor) ask me what Malcolm wanted. It ended in an argument. Cam argued that since he stopped talking to Blair I should stop talking to Malcolm. I argued it wasn't the same thing since Blair was in love with him. Cam argued that Malcolm was in love with me. And since I thought he might be right, I let him win the argument, assuring him I wouldn't speak to Malcolm anymore. I didn't think that would be a problem. I had a feeling that was the last call I would ever receive from Malcolm.

As fiery as the disagreement had been, once it was done, it was done. We settled into our routines quickly, and so far, I would say the moving-in thing was an absolute success. The following Saturday we were having a little flat-warming party so all our friends could visit and make sarcastic comments about how sickeningly in love we were.

I couldn't wait!

Eyeing Cam suspiciously, thinking his behavior very odd as he sat there on the end of the bed, I asked, "What are you doing? Where's Cole?"

"At McDonald's with his friends. I said he could."

"That's fine. Maybe we should order in food instead of cooking, then."

"Sounds good."

He seemed off. "You okay?"

"How was the first day?" he countered, suddenly grinning at the state of me.

"Brilliant. I mean, my neck and back hurt and I have paint on my eyelashes, but it was brilliant." I sidled into the room and slumped down beside him, pressing a soft kiss to his mouth.

When I pulled back, Cam gave me a half smile. I studied him, definitely getting the impression something wasn't quite right. Did he look nervous? "Seriously, what's going on?"

"I have a present for you." He pulled his hand out from behind his back and held the gift-wrapped rectangular package out to me.

I grinned at him. "What's this for?" I took the proffered gift and ran my fingers over it, wondering what it could be.

Cam's lips curled up at the corners at my excitement. "It's just something to commemorate your first day as one of M. Holloway's painters and decorators."

I laughed, giving him another quick kiss, before turning to my present. I slowly unwrapped it, tucking the paper behind me as I turned the gift over. It was a paintbrush—and not just any paintbrush. It was one of the best, most expensive, professional paintbrushes.

"Oh, Cam." I sighed at his thoughtfulness as I pried open the plastic to get to it. "You shouldn't—" The words abruptly stuck in my throat as the light caught a sparkle on the end of the brush. I shot him a disbelieving look before zeroing in on the handle. Gently I pulled the brush out of its plastic and my jaw dropped at the sight of the object that had been placed through the tip of the handle.

It was a diamond ring.

A white gold ring with a simple princess-cut diamond set in raised prongs in the middle of the band.

My heart racing like mad at the implication, I slowly turned my head to gaze at Cam in stupefied wonder. He casually took the brush from my hand and pulled the ring off the handle. He rose from the bed and went down on one knee in front of me.

"Oh, my God," I breathed, my right hand fluttering against my throat as my pulse throbbed at super speed.

Cam took my trembling left hand in his, his gaze sincere as he looked into my eyes. "Johanna Walker, love of my life, I never want to spend another day not waking up beside you." He held the ring up to my hand. "Will you spend the rest of your life me? Will you marry me?"

I realized now, after years of waiting for the men before Cameron to ask me that question, that saying yes to any of them would have been absolutely the worst decision I would have ever made. There was one certainty I'd learned in the last few months: When a man asked you that question, there was only one thing you had to ask yourself. *Could I live without him?*

If the answer was no, then the answer was yes.

I nodded, my mouth quivering as the tears started to fall. "Yes. I'll marry you."

With a groan of exultation, Cam pulled me toward him for a kiss so deep I was literally breathless when he let me go. I panted against his mouth, smiling crookedly. "You know what this means?"

Cam's eyes glittered, and I was overwhelmed by the happiness in them. "What does it mean?"

"We'll never be able to live with Joss after this. She'll think she's Mrs. Matchmaker."

"I'll have a word with Braden. He'll keep her in line." He grinned boyishly. "We're good at that."

"You two think you're in charge, don't you?"

He shrugged but his eyes said, *Yes—yes, we do.*

Cupping his face between my hands, I gave him a condescending yet sympathetic smile. "Oh, baby, your naïveté is so endearing."

Laughing, Cam wrapped his arms around my waist and as he stood up he lifted me and threw me onto the bed. "Tonight at least, I'm in charge." He began to undress slowly as I sat up, braced on my elbows, to watch him, my body already coming alive in anticipation. "Now tell me again that you love me, Mrs. Soon-to-Be-MacCabe."

I sighed happily at the simultaneous sound of my soon-to-be surname and the zip on his jeans tugging down. As I prepared to give him what he wanted, it amazed me how easily those words came after having taken me so long to find the courage to say them to him in the first place. Just like I did with Cole, I promised myself there and then that Cam wouldn't live a day of his life without knowing how I felt about him.

"I love you, Cameron MacCabe."

With a cocky grin, Cam dropped his jeans to the floor. "I love you, too, Miss Walker-Soon-to-Be-MacCabe." And I knew then as I was lying on our bed staring up into his familiar and handsome face that I had something I'd never had before. I had someone who wasn't going to let me spend a single day of my life without knowing how much *I* was loved.

I think one of my favorite parts of it all was the fact that finding what we had together hadn't cost either of us a single penny.

Well . . . with the exception of an engagement ring and a new paint palette for our flat.

ACKNOWLEDGMENTS

Writing *Down London Road* has been one of the best times I've ever had. The process of writing the book, and all the exciting things that were taking place in my life during it, made the entire experience wonderful and unforgettable.

Through it all my fantastic agent, Lauren Abramo, has helped me navigate these new waters. Thank you, Lauren, for your kindness, your sound advice, and for being absolutely brilliant at what you do.

Kerry Donovan: It's been a dream working with you. Your unbelievable enthusiasm, great insights, and support are so appreciated. You see into the souls of my characters, you understand my writing and where it comes from, and then you help make it better. Thank you.

I also want to say a massive thank-you to Claire Pelly. Claire, thank you for your support, for believing in this world I've created, and for braving the harsh Scottish weather for me. I know that couldn't have been easy!

Nina Wegscheider: Thank you for embracing Joss, Braden, Jo and Cam and for introducing them to my German readers.

A lot of hard work has gone into reaching new readers and delivering these characters and the streets of Edinburgh to them. For all the interviews, the Twitter and Facebook Chats, the articles and guest posts, I want to thank Erin Galloway at New American Library and Katie

Sheldrake and Kimberly Watkins at Michael Joseph. Ladies, you have been phenomenal, and I want you to know, despite my grumbling about getting my photo taken, I appreciate all the hard work.

An extra wee thank-you to Katie for also braving the cold weather in Scotland and enduring an almost fatal toe situation to be by my side and support me through the wonderful madness of introducing my characters to the UK.

The buzz around the series in Scotland has been crazy, surreal, and awesome, and I have the kind, enthusiastic, indefatigable Moira MacMillan to thank for much of it. Thank you, Moira. You've gone above and beyond, kept my nerves company, and been a very good friend to have through this transition. Anyone who can make me laugh when I'm nervous as hell is a keeper!

To the teams at New American Library and Michael Joseph: Thank you to every single person who has contributed to this series. You've helped make a dream a reality.

I've always had so much respect for book bloggers and how much time and creativity they put into the love of a book. I want to say a massive thank-you to the ladies at Heroes & Heartbreakers, Smexy Books Romance Reviews, the Christian Grey Fan Page, and the SubClubBooks for helping spread the word about these characters. You might just be better than chocolate!

There are also readers out there whose support blows my mind. I wish I could list them all, but if I did, we'd be here forever (and that in itself is an awesome thing that I am so grateful for), so I'd like to thank one in particular who has really touched me with her enthusiasm for my work. Trish Patel Brinkley: Lady, you freaking rock! Thank you for your kindness, generosity, and consideration. I love my Keep Calm and Kiss Braden mug and will cherish it always.

Life is hectic these days, and it's nice to be able to turn to people who understand. To my fellow authors Shelly Crane, Amy Bartol, Michelle Leighton, Georgia Cates, Quinn Loftis, Angeline Kace, and Rachel Higginson, thank you for your friendship, insights, advice, genuine support, love, and appreciation. To Tiffany King, you are awesome. Your tweets of support are a highlight of my week. And a huge thank-you to Tammy Blackwell. Tammy, it's brilliant to find someone who shares the same weird sense of humor and enjoyment of numerical lists, but rare to really "get" someone when all you have to rely on is words on a screen. Your friendship and support have meant a lot to me, and I can't wait to meet you so intonation can finally play a part in our exchanges.

Last but by no means least I want to thank my family and friends for having my back always.

Mum and Dad: Your unwavering belief in me astounds me. I feel lucky every day to call you my parents and two of my best friends. I love you lots.

David: I'm glad we made it through those argumentative child-hood years only to come out great friends at the end of it. When you tell me you're proud of me, I feel ten feet tall. I probably don't say it enough, but I love you, big bro.

Deeanne: Thank you for being a friend through all this craziness. I appreciate it more than you know.

Shanine: You, my oldest friend, are one of the most genuine people I have ever known. I'm *proud* to know you, and I can't tell you how much your love and unbending support have meant to me over the years.

Kate McJ: My beautiful, intelligent, and wonderfully mad friend. Thank you for being you and thank you for allowing me to be me. I'll be forever grateful to that Ong Bak poster we bonded over.

And to Ashleen: We tend to see the world the same way, you and I, and there's nothing more magical or reassuring than that. Moreover, I think you just might be the busiest person I know, and yet you some-how manage to make time to be there for me. Thank you, hon. It means the world.

To you, my reader: You've changed my world, and for that, I am eternally grateful to you. Thank you.

Now that you've met Nate and Olivia, don't miss their smoldering passion in Samantha Young's next contemporary romance!

On sale in January 2014,
wherever books and e-books are sold!

Moving into her own little piece of heaven on Jamaica Lane, Olivia Holloway embraces Edinburgh, her new friends, her new job at the university library, and her secret crush on that cute postgrad student she sees on a daily basis. Everything is great on the surface. Olivia is bubbly, outgoing, and happy-go-lucky. Underneath it all, however, is a lonely, socially awkward, somewhat insecure wallflower who hasn't had sex in seven years. That secret crush of hers is going to stay secret unless she brushes up on the art of seduction, and learning to flirt would be a good place to start, since that's one skill she's never quite mastered.

The one guy Olivia can be herself around is her new best friend, Nate Sawyer. As soon as they met, Olivia and Nate just clicked. To other women, Nate is the ultimate player. To his acquaintances, Nate is cocky, funny, and charming. To his friends and family, he's kind, loyal, and a good guy with a past that haunts him. It's a past that created a bond between him and Olivia, who suffered through her own heartbreak when she lost her mother to cancer.

But the bond between them is merely friendship—until one night when Olivia drunkenly confesses to Nate about her lack of sexual experience and her hopeless crush on Library Guy. What starts out as simple lessons in flirtation escalates into lessons in seduction, and the passion that ignites between them teaches them both a lesson about themselves. With her newfound confidence, Olivia tries to help Nate heal from old wounds, and it soon becomes clear to him that their lessons have progressed into something much more serious.

Photo by Mark Archibald

Samantha Young is a twenty-seven-year-old Scottish writer who graduated from the University of Edinburgh in 2009. She studied ancient and medieval history, which really just means she likes old stuff. Since February 2011, Samantha has been self-publishing her Amazon best-selling young adult novels. She's the author of four series—ten novels and one novella. *On Dublin Street* was her debut into adult fiction.